Agatha Christie is known throughout the world as the Queen of Crime. She is the most widely published author of all time and in any language, outsold only by the Bible and Shakespeare. She is the author of 80 crime novels and short story collections, 19 plays, and six novels written under the name of Mary Westmacott.

Agatha Christie's first novel, *The Mysterious Affair at Styles*, was written towards the end of the First World War, in which she served as a VAD. In it she created Hercule Poirot, the little Belgian detective who was destined to become the most popular detective in crime fiction since Sherlock Holmes.

Agatha Christie was made a Dame in 1971. She died in 1976.

CAT AMONG THE PIGEONS

Late one night, two teachers investigate a mysterious flashing light in the sports pavilion, whilst the rest of the school sleeps. There, among the lacrosse sticks, they stumble upon the body of the unpopular games mistress — shot through the heart from point-blank range. The school is thrown into chaos when the 'cat' strikes again. Unfortunately, schoolgirl Julia Upjohn knows too much. In particular, she knows that without Hercule Poirot's help, she will be the next victim . . .

Agatha Christie

AGATHA CHRISTIE

❖

CAT AMONG THE PIGEONS

Complete and Unabridged

ULVERSCROFT
Leicester

First published in Great Britain in 1959 by
Collins
London

First Large Print Edition
published 2011
by arrangement with
HarperCollins*Publishers* Limited
London

British Library CIP Data

Christie, Agatha, *1890 – 1976.*
    Cat among the pigeons.
    1. Poirot, Hercule (Fictitious character)- -Fiction.
    2. Private investigators- -Belgium- -Fiction.
    3. Detective and mystery stories. 4. Large type books.
    I. Title
    823.9'12–dc22

    ISBN 978–1–44480–272–6

Published by
F. A. Thorpe (Publishing)
Anstey, Leicestershire
Set by Words & Graphics Ltd.
Anstey, Leicestershire
Printed and bound in Great Britain by
T. J. International Ltd., Padstow, Cornwall

This book is printed on acid-free paper

For Stella and Larry Kirwan

Contents

Prologue

Summer Term

I

It was the opening day of the summer term at Meadowbank school. The late afternoon sun shone down on the broad gravel sweep in front of the house. The front door was flung hospitably wide, and just within it, admirably suited to its Georgian proportions, stood Miss Vansittart, every hair in place, wearing an impeccably cut coat and skirt.

Some parents who knew no better had taken her for the great Miss Bulstrode herself, not knowing that it was Miss Bulstrode's custom to retire to a kind of holy of holies to which only a selected and privileged few were taken.

To one side of Miss Vansittart, operating on a slightly different plane, was Miss Chadwick, comfortable, knowledgeable, and so much a part of Meadowbank that it would have been impossible to imagine Meadowbank without her. It had never been without her. Miss Bulstrode and Miss Chadwick had started

Meadowbank school together. Miss Chadwick wore pince-nez, stooped, was dowdily dressed, amiably vague in speech, and happened to be a brilliant mathematician.

Various welcoming words and phrases, uttered graciously by Miss Vansittart, floated through the house.

'How do you do, Mrs Arnold? Well, Lydia, did you enjoy your Hellenic cruise? What a wonderful opportunity! Did you get some good photographs?

'Yes, Lady Garnett, Miss Bulstrode had your letter about the Art Classes and everything's been arranged.

'How are you, Mrs Bird? . . . Well? I don't think Miss Bulstrode will have time *today* to discuss the point. Miss Rowan is somewhere about if you'd like to talk to her about it?

'We've moved your bedroom, Pamela. You're in the far wing by the apple tree . . .

'Yes, indeed, Lady Violet, the weather has been terrible so far this spring. Is this your youngest? What is your name? Hector? What a nice aeroplane you have, Hector.

'*Très heureuse de vous voir, Madame. Ah, je regrette, ce ne serait pas possible, cette après-midi. Mademoiselle Bulstrode est tellement occupée.*

'Good afternoon, Professor. Have you been digging up some more interesting things?'

II

In a small room on the first floor, Ann Shapland, Miss Bulstrode's secretary, was typing with speed and efficiency. Ann was a nice-looking young woman of thirty-five, with hair that fitted her like a black satin cap. She could be attractive when she wanted to be but life had taught her that efficiency and competence often paid better results and avoided painful complications. At the moment she was concentrating on being everything that a secretary to the headmistress of a famous girls' school should be.

From time to time, as she inserted a fresh sheet in her machine, she looked out of the window and registered interest in the arrivals.

'Goodness!' said Ann to herself, awed, 'I didn't know there were so many chauffeurs left in England!'

Then she smiled in spite of herself, as a majestic Rolls moved away and a very small Austin of battered age drove up. A harassed-looking father emerged from it with a daughter who looked far calmer than he did.

As he paused uncertainly, Miss Vansittart emerged from the house and took charge.

'Major Hargreaves? And this is Alison? Do come into the house. I'd like you to see Alison's room for yourself. I — '

3

Ann grinned and began to type again.

'Good old Vansittart, the glorified under-study,' she said to herself. 'She can copy all the Bulstrode's tricks. In fact she's word perfect!'

An enormous and almost incredibly opu-lent Cadillac, painted in two tones, raspberry fool and azure blue, swept (with difficulty owing to its length) into the drive and drew up behind Major the Hon. Alistair Hargreaves' ancient Austin.

The chauffeur sprang to open the door, an immense bearded, dark-skinned man, wearing a flowing aba, stepped out, a Parisian fashion plate followed and then a slim dark girl.

That's probably Princess Whatshername herself, thought Ann. Can't imagine her in school uniform, but I suppose the miracle will be apparent tomorrow . . .

Both Miss Vansittart and Miss Chadwick appeared on this occasion.

'They'll be taken to the Presence,' decided Ann.

Then she thought that, strangely enough, one didn't quite like making jokes about Miss Bulstrode. Miss Bulstrode was Someone.

'So you'd better mind your P.s and Q.s, my girl,' she said to herself, 'and finish these letters without making any mistakes.'

Not that Ann was in the habit of making mistakes. She could take her pick of secretarial posts. She had been P.A. to the chief executive of an oil company, private secretary to Sir Mervyn Todhunter, renowned alike for his erudition, his irritability and the illegibility of his handwriting. She numbered two Cabinet Ministers and an important Civil Servant among her employers. But on the whole, her work had always lain amongst men. She wondered how she was going to like being, as she put it herself, completely submerged in women. Well — it was all experience! And there was always Dennis! Faithful Dennis returning from Malaya, from Burma, from various parts of the world, always the same, devoted, asking her once again to marry him. Dear Dennis! But it would be very dull to be married to Dennis.

She would miss the company of men in the near future. All these schoolmistressy characters — not a man about the place, except a gardener of about eighty.

But here Ann got a surprise. Looking out of the window, she saw there was a man clipping the hedge just beyond the drive — clearly a gardener but a long way from eighty. Young, dark, good-looking. Ann wondered about him — there had been some talk of getting extra labour — but this was no yokel. Oh well, nowadays people did every kind of job. Some young man trying to get together some money for some project or other, or indeed just to keep body and soul together. But he was cutting the hedge in a very expert manner. Presumably he was a real gardener after all!

'He looks,' said Ann to herself, 'he looks as though he *might* be amusing . . . '

Only one more letter to do, she was pleased to note, and then she might stroll round the garden . . .

III

Upstairs, Miss Johnson, the matron, was busy allotting rooms, welcoming newcomers, and greeting old pupils.

She was pleased it was term time again. She never knew quite what to do with herself in the holidays. She had two married sisters with whom she stayed in turn, but they were naturally more interested in their own doings and families than in Meadowbank. Miss Johnson, though dutifully fond of her sisters, was really only interested in Meadowbank.

Yes, it was nice that term had started —

'Miss Johnson?'

'Yes, Pamela.'

'I say, Miss Johnson. I think something's broken in my case. It's oozed all over things. I *think* it's hair oil.'

'Chut, chut!' said Miss Johnson, hurrying to help.

IV

On the grass sweep of lawn beyond the gravelled drive, Mademoiselle Blanche, the new French mistress, was walking. She looked with appreciative eyes at the powerful young man clipping the hedge.

'*Assez bien*,' thought Mademoiselle Blanche.

Mademoiselle Blanche was slender and mouselike and not very noticeable, but she herself noticed everything.

Her eyes went to the procession of cars sweeping up to the front door. She assessed them in terms of money. This Meadowbank was certainly *formidable*! She summed up mentally the profits that Miss Bulstrode must be making.

Yes, indeed! *Formidable!*

V

Miss Rich, who taught English and Geography, advanced towards the house at a rapid pace, stumbling a little now and then because, as usual, she forgot to look where she was

7

going. Her hair, also as usual, had escaped from its bun. She had an eager ugly face.

She was saying to herself:

'To be back again! To be *here* . . . It seems years . . . ' She fell over a rake, and the young gardener put out an arm and said:

'Steady, miss.'

Eileen Rich said 'Thank you,' without looking at him.

VI

Miss Rowan and Miss Blake, the two junior mistresses, were strolling towards the Sports Pavilion. Miss Rowan was thin and dark and intense, Miss Blake was plump and fair. They were discussing with animation their recent adventures in Florence: the pictures they had seen, the sculpture, the fruit blossom, and the attentions (hoped to be dishonourable) of two young Italian gentlemen.

'Of course one knows,' said Miss Blake, 'how Italians go on.'

'Uninhibited,' said Miss Rowan, who had studied Psychology as well as Economics. 'Thoroughly healthy, one feels. No repressions.'

'But Guiseppe was quite impressed when he found I taught at Meadowbank,' said Miss Blake. 'He became much more respectful at

8

once. He has a cousin who wants to come here, but Miss Bulstrode was not sure she had a vacancy.'

'Meadowbank is a school that really counts,' said Miss Rowan, happily. 'Really, the new Sports Pavilion looks most impressive. I never thought it would be ready in time.'

'Miss Bulstrode said it had to be,' said Miss Blake in the tone of one who has said the last word.

'Oh,' she added in a startled kind of way.

The door of the Sports Pavilion had opened abruptly, and a bony young woman with ginger-coloured hair emerged. She gave them a sharp unfriendly stare and moved rapidly away.

'That must be the new Games Mistress,' said Miss Blake. 'How uncouth!'

'Not a very pleasant addition to the staff,' said Miss Rowan, 'Miss Jones was always so friendly and sociable.'

'She absolutely glared at us,' said Miss Blake resentfully.

They both felt quite ruffled.

VII

Miss Bulstrode's sitting-room had windows looking out in two directions, one over the drive and lawn beyond, and another towards a bank of rhododendrons behind the house. It was quite an impressive room, and Miss Bulstrode was rather more than quite an impressive woman. She was tall, and rather noble looking, with well-dressed grey hair, grey eyes with plenty of humour in them, and a firm mouth. The success of her school (and Meadowbank was one of the most successful schools in England) was entirely due to the personality of its Headmistress. It was a very expensive school, but that was not really the point. It could be put better by saying that though you paid through the nose, you got what you paid for.

Your daughter was educated in the way you wished, and also in the way Miss Bulstrode wished, and the result of the two together seemed to give satisfaction. Owing to the high fees, Miss Bulstrode was able to employ a full staff. There was nothing mass produced about the school, but if it was individualistic, it also had discipline. Discipline without regimentation, was Miss Bulstrode's motto. Discipline, she held, was reassuring to the young, it gave them a feeling of security; regimentation gave rise to irritation. Her pupils were a varied lot. They included several foreigners of good family, often foreign royalty. There were also English girls of good family or of wealth, who wanted a training in culture and the arts, with a general knowledge of life and social facility who would be turned out agreeable, well groomed and able to take part in intelligent discussion on any subject. There were girls who wanted to work hard and pass entrance examinations, and eventually take degrees and who, to do so, needed only good teaching and special attention. There were girls who had reacted unfavourably to school life of the conventional type. But Miss Bulstrode had her rules, she did not accept morons, or juvenile delinquents, and she preferred to accept girls whose parents she liked, and girls in whom she herself saw a prospect of development. The ages of her pupils varied within wide limits. There were girls who would have been labelled in the past as 'finished', and there were girls little more than children, some of them with parents abroad, and for whom Miss Bulstrode had a scheme of interesting holidays. The last and final court of appeal was Miss Bulstrode's own approval.

She was standing now by the chimneypiece listening to Mrs Gerald Hope's slightly whining voice. With great foresight, she had not suggested that Mrs Hope should sit down.

'Henrietta, you see, is very highly strung.

Very highly strung indeed. Our doctor says — '

Miss Bulstrode nodded, with gentle reassurance, refraining from the caustic phrase she sometimes was tempted to utter.

'Don't you know, you idiot, that that is what every fool of a woman says about her child?'

She spoke with firm sympathy.

'You need have no anxiety, Mrs Hope. Miss Rowan, a member of our staff, is a fully trained psychologist. You'll be surprised, I'm sure, at the change you'll find in Henrietta' (Who's a nice intelligent child, and far too good for you) 'after a term or two here.'

'Oh I know. You did wonders with the Lambeth child — absolutely wonders! So I am quite happy. And I — oh yes, I forgot. We're going to the South of France in six weeks' time. I thought I'd take Henrietta. It would make a little break for her.'

'I'm afraid that's quite impossible,' said Miss Bulstrode, briskly and with a charming smile, as though she were granting a request instead of refusing one.

'Oh! but — ' Mrs Hope's weak petulant face wavered, showed temper. 'Really, I must insist. After all, she's *my* child.'

'Exactly. But it's *my* school,' said Miss Bulstrode.

'Surely I can take the child away from a school any time I like?'

'Oh yes,' said Miss Bulstrode. 'You can. Of course you can. But then, *I* wouldn't have her back.'

Mrs Hope was in a real temper now.

'Considering the size of the fees I pay here — '

'Exactly,' said Miss Bulstrode. 'You wanted my school for your daughter, didn't you? But it's take it as it is, or leave it. Like that very charming Balenciaga model you are wearing. It is Balenciaga, isn't it? It is so delightful to meet a woman with real clothes sense.'

Her hand enveloped Mrs Hope's, shook it, and imperceptibly guided her towards the door.

'Don't worry at all. Ah, here is Henrietta waiting for you.' (She looked with approval at Henrietta, a nice well-balanced intelligent child if ever there was one, and who deserved a better mother.) 'Margaret, take Henrietta Hope to Miss Johnson.'

Miss Bulstrode retired into her sitting-room and a few moments later was talking French.

'But certainly, Excellence, your niece can study modern ballroom dancing. Most important socially. And languages, also, are most necessary.'

The next arrivals were prefaced by such a gust of expensive perfume as almost to knock Miss Bulstrode backwards.

'Must pour a whole bottle of the stuff over herself every day,' Miss Bulstrode noted mentally, as she greeted the exquisitely dressed dark-skinned woman.

'*Enchantée, Madame.*'

Madame giggled very prettily.

The big bearded man in Oriental dress took Miss Bulstrode's hand, bowed over it, and said in very good English, 'I have the honour to bring to you the Princess Shaista.'

Miss Bulstrode knew all about her new pupil who had just come from a school in Switzerland, but was a little hazy as to who it was escorting her. Not the Emir himself, she decided, probably the Minister, or Chargé d'Affaires. As usual when in doubt, she used that useful title *Excellence*, and assured him that Princess Shaista would have the best of care.

Shaista was smiling politely. She was also fashionably dressed and perfumed. Her age, Miss Bulstrode knew, was fifteen, but like many Eastern and Mediterranean girls, she looked older — quite mature. Miss Bulstrode spoke to her about her projected studies and was relieved to find that she answered promptly in excellent English and without

14

giggling. In fact, her manners compared favourably with the awkward ones of many English school girls of fifteen. Miss Bulstrode had often thought that it might be an excellent plan to send English girls abroad to the Near Eastern countries to learn courtesy and manners there. More compliments were uttered on both sides and then the room was empty again though still filled with such heavy perfume that Miss Bulstrode opened both windows to their full extent to let some of it out.

The next comers were Mrs Upjohn and her daughter Julia.

Mrs Upjohn was an agreeable young woman in the late thirties with sandy hair, freckles and an unbecoming hat which was clearly a concession to the seriousness of the occasion, since she was obviously the type of young woman who usually went hatless.

Julia was a plain freckled child, with an intelligent forehead, and an air of good humour.

The preliminaries were quickly gone through and Julia was despatched via Margaret to Miss Johnson, saying cheerfully as she went, 'So long, Mum. Do be careful lighting that gas heater now that I'm not there to do it.'

Miss Bulstrode turned smilingly to Mrs

Upjohn, but did not ask her to sit. It was possible that, despite Julia's appearance of cheerful common-sense, her mother, too, might want to explain that her daughter was highly strung.

'Is there anything special you want to tell me about Julia?' she asked.

Mrs Upjohn replied cheerfully:

'Oh no, I don't think so. Julia's a very ordinary sort of child. Quite healthy and all that. I think she's got reasonably good brains, too, but I daresay mothers usually think that about their children, don't they?'

'Mothers,' said Miss Bulstrode grimly, 'vary!'

'It's wonderful for her to be able to come here,' said Mrs Upjohn. 'My aunt's paying for it, really, or helping. I couldn't afford it myself. But I'm awfully pleased about it. And so is Julia.' She moved to the window as she said enviously, 'How lovely your garden is. And so tidy. You must have lots of real gardeners.'

'We had three,' said Miss Bulstrode, 'but just now we're short-handed except for local labour.'

'Of course the trouble nowadays,' said Mrs Upjohn, 'is that what one calls a gardener usually isn't a gardener, just a milkman who wants to do something in his spare time, or an old man of eighty. I sometimes think — Why!' exclaimed Mrs Upjohn, still gazing out of the window — 'how extraordinary!'

Miss Bulstrode paid less attention to this sudden exclamation than she should have done. For at that moment she herself had glanced casually out of the other window which gave on to the rhododendron shrubbery, and had perceived a highly unwelcome sight, none other than Lady Veronica Carlton-Sandways, weaving her way along the path, her large black velvet hat on one side, muttering to herself and clearly in a state of advanced intoxication.

Lady Veronica was not an unknown hazard. She was a charming woman, deeply attached to her twin daughters, and very delightful when she was, as they put it, *herself* — but unfortunately at unpredictable intervals, she was not herself. Her husband, Major Carlton-Sandways, coped fairly well. A cousin lived with them, who was usually at hand to keep an eye on Lady Veronica and head her off if necessary. On Sports Day, with both Major Carlton-Sandways and the cousin in close attendance, Lady Veronica arrived completely sober and beautifully dressed and was a pattern of what a mother should be.

But there were times when Lady Veronica gave her well-wishers the slip, tanked herself up and made a bee-line for her daughters to assure them of her maternal love. The twins had arrived by train carly today, but no one had expected Lady Veronica.

Mrs Upjohn was still talking. But Miss Bulstrode was not listening. She was reviewing various courses of action, for she recognized that Lady Veronica was fast approaching the truculent stage. But suddenly, an answer to prayer, Miss Chadwick appeared at a brisk trot, slightly out of breath. Faithful Chaddy, thought Miss Bulstrode. Always to be relied upon, whether it was a severed artery or an intoxicated parent.

'Disgraceful,' said Lady Veronica to her loudly. 'Tried to keep me away — didn't want me to come down here — I fooled Edith all right. Went to have my rest — got out car — gave silly old Edith slip . . . regular old maid . . . no man would ever look at her twice . . . Had a row with police on the way . . . said I was unfit to drive car . . . nonshense . . . Going to tell Miss Bulstrode I'm taking the girls home — want 'em home, mother love. Wonderful thing, mother love — '

'Splendid, Lady Veronica,' said Miss Chadwick. 'We're so pleased you've come. I particularly want you to see the new Sports Pavilion. You'll love it.'

18

Adroitly she turned Lady Veronica's unsteady footsteps in the opposite direction, leading her away from the house.

'I expect we'll find your girls there,' she said brightly. 'Such a nice Sports Pavilion, new lockers, and a drying room for the swim suits — ' Their voices trailed away.

Miss Bulstrode watched. Once Lady Veronica tried to break away and return to the house, but Miss Chadwick was a match for her. They disappeared round the corner of the rhododendrons, headed for the distant loneliness of the new Sports Pavilion.

Miss Bulstrode heaved a sigh of relief. Excellent Chaddy. So reliable! Not modern. Not brainy — apart from mathematics — but always a present help in time of trouble.

She turned with a sigh and a sense of guilt to Mrs Upjohn who had been talking happily for some time . . .

' . . . though, of course,' she was saying, 'never real cloak and dagger stuff. Not dropping by parachute, or sabotage, or being a courier. I shouldn't have been brave enough. It was mostly dull stuff. Office work. And plotting. Plotting things on a map, I mean — not the story telling kind of plotting. But of course it was exciting sometimes and it was often quite funny, as I just said — all the secret agents followed each other round and

19

round Geneva, all knowing each other by sight, and often ending up in the same bar. I wasn't married then, of course. It was all great fun.'

She stopped abruptly with an apologetic and friendly smile.

'I'm sorry I've been talking so much. Taking up your time. When you've got such lots of people to see.'

She held out a hand, said goodbye and departed.

Miss Bulstrode stood frowning for a moment. Some instinct warned her that she had missed something that might be important.

She brushed the feeling aside. This was the opening day of summer term, and she had many more parents to see. Never had her school been more popular, more assured of success. Meadowbank was at its zenith.

There was nothing to tell her that within a few weeks Meadowbank would be plunged into a sea of trouble; that disorder, confusion and murder would reign there, that already certain events had been set in motion . . .

1

Revolution in Ramat

About two months earlier than the first day of the summer term at Meadowbank, certain events had taken place which were to have unexpected repercussions in that celebrated girls' school.

In the Palace of Ramat, two young men sat smoking and considering the immediate future. One young man was dark, with a smooth olive face and large melancholy eyes. He was Prince Ali Yusuf, Hereditary Sheikh of Ramat, which, though small, was one of the richest states in the Middle East. The other young man was sandy haired and freckled and more or less penniless, except for the handsome salary he drew as private pilot to His Highness Prince Ali Yusuf. In spite of this difference in status, they were on terms of perfect equality. They had been at the same public school and had been friends then and ever since.

'They shot at us, Bob,' said Prince Ali

almost incredulously.

'They shot at us all right,' said Bob Rawlinson.

'And they meant it. They meant to bring us down.'

'The bastards meant it all right,' said Bob grimly.

Ali considered for a moment.

'It would hardly be worth while trying again?'

'We mightn't be so lucky this time. The truth is, Ali, we've left things too late. You should have got out two weeks ago. I told you so.'

'One doesn't like to run away,' said the ruler of Ramat.

'I see your point. But remember what Shakespeare or one of these poetical fellows said about those who run away living to fight another day.'

'To think,' said the young Prince with feeling, 'of the money that has gone into making this a Welfare State. Hospitals, schools, a Health Service — '

Bob Rawlinson interrupted the catalogue.

'Couldn't the Embassy do something?'

Ali Yusuf flushed angrily.

'Take refuge in your Embassy? That, never. The extremists would probably storm the place — they wouldn't respect diplomatic immunity. Besides, if I did that, it really would be the end! Already the chief accusation against me is of being pro-Western.' He sighed. 'It is so difficult to understand.' He sounded wistful, younger than his twenty-five years. 'My grandfather was a cruel man, a real tyrant. He had hundreds of slaves and treated them ruthlessly. In his tribal wars, he killed his enemies unmercifully and executed them horribly. The mere whisper of his name made everyone turn pale. And yet — *he* is a legend still! Admired! Respected! The great Achmed Abdullah! And I? What have I done? Built hospitals and schools, welfare, housing . . . all the things people are said to want. Don't they want them? Would they prefer a reign of terror like my grandfather's?'

'I expect so,' said Bob Rawlinson. 'Seems a bit unfair, but there it is.'

'But why, Bob? *Why?*'

Bob Rawlinson sighed, wriggled and endeavoured to explain what he felt. He had to struggle with his own inarticulateness.

'Well,' he said. 'He put up a show — I suppose that's it really. He was — sort of — dramatic, if you know what I mean.'

He looked at his friend who was definitely not dramatic. A nice quiet decent chap, sincere and perplexed, that was what Ali was,

23

and Bob liked him for it. He was neither picturesque nor violent, but whilst in England people who are picturesque and violent cause embarrassment and are not much liked, in the Middle East, Bob was fairly sure, it was different.

'But democracy — ' began Ali.

'Oh, democracy — ' Bob waved his pipe. 'That's a word that means different things everywhere. One thing's certain. It never means what the Greeks originally meant by it. I bet you anything you like that if they boot you out of here, some spouting hot air merchant will take over, yelling his own praises, building himself up into God Almighty, and stringing up, or cutting off the heads of anyone who dares to disagree with him in any way. And, mark you, he'll *say* it's a Democratic Government — of the people and for the people. I expect the people will like it too. Exciting for them. Lots of bloodshed.'

'But we are not savages! We are civilized nowadays.'

'There are different kinds of civilization . . . ' said Bob vaguely. 'Besides — I rather think we've all got a bit of savage in us — if we can think up a good excuse for letting it rip.'

'Perhaps you are right,' said Ali sombrely.

24

'The thing people don't seem to want anywhere, nowadays,' said Bob, 'is anyone who's got a bit of common sense. I've never been a brainy chap — well, you know that well enough, Ali — but I often think that that's what the world really needs — just a bit of common sense.' He laid aside his pipe and sat in his chair. 'But never mind all that. The thing is how we're going to get you out of here. Is there anybody in the Army you can really trust?'

Slowly, Prince Ali Yusuf shook his head.

'A fortnight ago, I should have said 'Yes.' But now, I do not know . . . cannot be *sure* — '

Bob nodded. 'That's the hell of it. As for this palace of yours, it gives me the creeps.'

Ali acquiesced without emotion.

'Yes, there are spies everywhere in palaces . . . They hear everything — they — know everything.'

'Even down in the hangars — ' Bob broke off. 'Old Achmed's all right. He's got a kind of sixth sense. Found one of the mechanics trying to tamper with the plane — one of the men we'd have sworn was absolutely trustworthy. Look here, Ali, if we're going to have a shot at getting you away, it will have to be soon.'

'I know — I know. I think — I am quite

certain now — that if I stay I shall be killed.'

He spoke without emotion, or any kind of panic: with a mild detached interest.

'We'll stand a good chance of being killed anyway,' Bob warned him. 'We'll have to fly out north, you know. They can't intercept us that way. But it means going over the mountains — and at this time of year — '

He shrugged his shoulders. 'You've got to understand. It's damned risky.'

Ali Yusuf looked distressed.

'If anything happened to you, Bob — '

'Don't worry about me, Ali. That's not what I meant. I'm not important. And anyway, I'm the sort of chap that's sure to get killed sooner or later. I'm always doing crazy things. No — it's you — I don't want to persuade you one way or the other. If a portion of the Army *is* loyal — '

'I don't like the idea of running away,' said Ali simply. 'But I do not in the least want to be a martyr, and be cut to pieces by a mob.'

He was silent for a moment or two.

'Very well then,' he said at least with a sigh. 'We will make the attempt. When?'

Bob shrugged his shoulders.

'Sooner the better. We've got to get you to the airstrip in some natural way . . . How about saying you're going to inspect the new road construction out at Al Jasar? Sudden whim. Go this afternoon. Then, as your car passes the airstrip, stop there — I'll have the bus all ready and tuned up. The idea will be to go up to inspect the road construction from the air, see? We take off and *go*! We can't take any baggage, of course. It's got to be all quite impromptu.'

'There is nothing I wish to take with me — except one thing — '

He smiled, and suddenly the smile altered his face and made a different person of him. He was no longer the modern conscientious Westernized young man — the smile held all the racial guile and craft which had enabled a long line of his ancestors to survive.

'You are my friend, Bob, you shall see.'

His hand went inside his shirt and fumbled. Then he held out a little chamois leather bag.

'This?' Bob frowned and looked puzzled.

Ali took it from him, untied the neck, and poured the contents on the table.

Bob held his breath for a moment and then expelled it in a soft whistle.

'Good lord. Are they *real*?'

Ali looked amused.

'Of course they are real. Most of them belonged to my father. He acquired new ones every year. I, too. They have come from many places, bought for our family by men we can trust — from London, from Calcutta, from South Africa. It is a tradition of our family. To have these in case of need.' He added in a matter of fact voice: 'They are worth, at today's prices, about three quarters of a million.'

'Three quarters of a million pounds.' Bob let out a whistle, picked up the stones, let them run through his fingers. 'It's fantastic. Like a fairy tale. It does things to you.'

'Yes.' The dark young man nodded. Again that age-long weary look was on his face. 'Men are not the same when it comes to jewels. There is always a trail of violence to follow such things. Deaths, bloodshed, murder. And women are the worst. For with women it will not only be the value. It is something to do with the jewels themselves. Beautiful jewels drive women mad. They want to own them. To wear them round their throats, on their bosoms. I would not trust any woman with these. But I shall trust you.'

'Me?' Bob stared.

'Yes. I do not want these stones to fall into the hands of my enemies. I do not know when the rising against me will take place. It may be planned for today. I may not live to reach the airstrip this afternoon. Take the stones and do the best you can.'

'But look here — I don't understand. What

am I to do with them?'

'Arrange somehow to get them out of the country.'

Ali stared placidly at his perturbed friend.

'You mean, you want *me* to carry them instead of you?'

'You can put it that way. But I think, really, you will be able to think of some better plan to get them to Europe.'

'But look here, Ali, I haven't the first idea how to set about such a thing.'

Ali leaned back in his chair. He was smiling in a quietly amused manner.

'You have common sense. And you are honest. And I remember, from the days when you were my fag, that you could always think up some ingenious idea . . . I will give you the name and address of a man who deals with such matters for me — that is — in case I should not survive. Do not look so worried, Bob. Do the best you can. That is all I ask. I shall not blame you if you fail. It is as Allah wills. For me, it is simple. I do not want those stones taken from my dead body. For the rest — ' he shrugged his shoulders. 'It is as I have said. All will go as Allah wills.'

'You're nuts!'

'No. I am a fatalist, that is all.'

'But look here, Ali. You said just now I was honest. But three quarters of a million . . .

Don't you think that might sap any man's honesty?'

Ali Yusuf looked at his friend with affection.

'Strangely enough,' he said, 'I have no doubt on that score.'

2

The Woman on the Balcony

I

As Bob Rawlinson walked along the echoing marble corridors of the Palace, he had never felt so unhappy in his life. The knowledge that he was carrying three quarters of a million pounds in his trousers pocket caused him acute misery. He felt as though every Palace official he encountered must know the fact. He felt even that the knowledge of his precious burden must show in his face. He would have been relieved to learn that his freckled countenance bore exactly its usual expression of cheerful good nature.

The sentries outside presented arms with a clash. Bob walked down the main crowded street of Ramat, his mind still dazed. Where was he going? What was he planning to do? He had no idea. And time was short.

The main street was like most main streets in the Middle East. It was a mixture of squalor and magnificence. Banks reared their vast newly built magnificence. Innumerable

31

small shops presented a collection of cheap plastic goods. Babies' bootees and cheap cigarette lighters were displayed in unlikely juxtaposition. There were sewing machines, and spare parts for cars. Pharmacies displayed flyblown proprietary medicines, and large notices of penicillin in every form and antibiotics galore. In very few of the shops was there anything that you could normally want to buy, except possibly the latest Swiss watches, hundreds of which were displayed crowded into a tiny window. The assortment was so great that even there one would have shrunk from purchase, dazzled by sheer mass.

Bob, still walking in a kind of stupor, jostled by figures in native or European dress, pulled himself together and asked himself again where the hell he was going?

He turned into a native café and ordered lemon tea. As he sipped it, he began, slowly, to come to. The atmosphere of the café was soothing. At a table opposite him an elderly Arab was peacefully clicking through a string of amber beads. Behind him two men played tric trac. It was a good place to sit and think.

And he'd got to think. Jewels worth three quarters of a million had been handed to him, and it was up to him to devise some plan of getting them out of the country. No time to lose either. At any minute the balloon might go up . . .

Ali was crazy, of course. Tossing three quarters of a million light-heartedly to a friend in that way. And then sitting back quietly himself and leaving everything to Allah. Bob had not got that recourse. Bob's God expected his servants to decide on and perform their own actions to the best of the ability their God had given them.

What the hell was he going to do with those damned stones?

He thought of the Embassy. No, he couldn't involve the Embassy. The Embassy would almost certainly refuse to be involved.

What he needed was some person, some perfectly ordinary person who was leaving the country in some perfectly ordinary way. A business man, or a tourist would be best. Someone with no political connections whose baggage would, at most, be subjected to a superficial search or more probably no search at all. There was, of course, the other end to be considered . . . Sensation at London Airport. Attempt to smuggle in jewels worth three quarters of a million. And so on and so on. One would have to risk that —

Somebody ordinary — a *bona fide* traveller. And suddenly Bob kicked himself for a fool. Joan, of course. His sister Joan

Sutcliffe. Joan had been out here for two months with her daughter Jennifer who after a bad bout of pneumonia had been ordered sunshine and a dry climate. They were going back by 'long sea' in four or five days' time.

Joan was the ideal person. What was it Ali had said about women and jewels? Bob smiled to himself. Good old Joan! *She* wouldn't lose her head over jewels. Trust her to keep her feet on the earth. Yes — he could trust Joan.

Wait a minute, though . . . could he trust Joan? Her honesty, yes. But her discretion? Regretfully Bob shook his head. Joan would talk, would not be able to help talking. Even worse. She would hint. 'I'm taking home something very important, I mustn't say a word to *anyone*. It's really rather exciting . . . '

Joan had never been able to keep a thing to herself though she was always very incensed if one told her so. Joan, then, mustn't know what she was taking. It would be safer for her that way. He'd make the stones up into a parcel, an innocent-looking parcel. Tell her some story. A present for someone? A commission? He'd think of something . . .

Bob glanced at his watch and rose to his feet. Time was getting on.

34

He strode along the street oblivious of the midday heat. Everything seemed so normal. There was nothing to show on the surface. Only in the Palace was one conscious of the banked-down fires, of the spying, the whispers. The Army — it all depended on the Army.

Who was loyal? Who was disloyal? A coup d'état would certainly be attempted. Would it succeed or fail?

Bob frowned as he turned into Ramat's leading hotel. It was modestly called the Ritz Savoy and had a grand modernistic façade. It had opened with a flourish three years ago with a Swiss manager, a Viennese chef, and an Italian *Maître d'hôtel*. Everything had been wonderful. The Viennese chef had gone first, then the Swiss manager. Now the Italian head waiter had gone too. The food was still ambitious, but bad, the service abominable, and a good deal of the expensive plumbing had gone wrong.

The clerk behind the desk knew Bob well and beamed at him.

'Good morning, Squadron Leader. You want your sister? She has gone on a picnic with the little girl — '

'A picnic?' Bob was taken aback — of all the silly times to go for a picnic.

'With Mr and Mrs Hurst from the Oil

35

Company,' said the clerk informatively. Everyone always knew everything. 'They have gone to the Kalat Diwa dam.'

Bob swore under his breath. Joan wouldn't be home for hours.

'I'll go up to her room,' he said and held out his hand for the key which the clerk gave him.

He unlocked the door and went in. The room, a large double-bedded one, was in its usual confusion.

Joan Sutcliffe was not a tidy woman. Golf clubs lay across a chair, tennis racquets had been flung on the bed. Clothing lay about, the table was littered with rolls of film, postcards, paper-backed books and an assortment of native curios from the South, mostly made in Birmingham and Japan.

Bob looked round him, at the suitcases and the zip bags. He was faced with a problem. He wouldn't be able to see Joan before flying Ali out. There wouldn't be time to get to the dam and back. He could parcel up the stuff and leave it with a note — but almost immediately he shook his head. He knew quite well that he was nearly always followed. He'd probably been followed from the Palace to the cafe and from the cafe here. He hadn't spotted anyone — but he knew that they were good at the job. There was nothing suspicious in his coming to the hotel to see his sister — but if he left a parcel and a note, the note would be read and the parcel opened.

Time . . . time . . . He'd no *time* . . .

Three quarters of a million in precious stones in his trousers pocket.

He looked round the room . . .

Then, with a grin, he fished out from his pocket the little tool kit he always carried. His niece Jennifer had some plasticine, he noted, that would help.

He worked quickly and skilfully. Once he looked up, suspicious, his eyes going to the open window. No, there was no balcony outside this room. It was just his nerves that made him feel that someone was watching him.

He finished his task and nodded in approval. Nobody would notice what he had done — he felt sure of that. Neither Joan nor anyone else. Certainly not Jennifer, a self-centred child, who never saw or noticed anything outside herself.

He swept up all evidences of his toil and put them into his pocket . . . Then he hesitated, looking round.

He drew Mrs Sutcliffe's writing pad towards him and sat frowning —

He must leave a note for Joan —

But what could he say? It must be

something that Joan would understand — but which would mean nothing to anyone who read the note.

And really that was impossible! In the kind of thriller that Bob liked reading to fill up his spare moments, you left a kind of cryptogram which was always successfully puzzled out by someone. But he couldn't even begin to think of a cryptogram — and in any case Joan was the sort of common-sense person who would need the i's dotted and the t's crossed before she noticed anything at all —

Then his brow cleared. There was another way of doing it — divert attention away from Joan — leave an ordinary everyday note. Then leave a message with someone else to be given to Joan in England. He wrote rapidly —

Dear Joan — Dropped in to ask if you'd care to play a round of golf this evening but if you've been up at the dam, you'll probably be dead to the world. What about tomorrow? Five o'clock at the Club.
Yours, Bob.

A casual sort of a message to leave for a sister that he might never see again — but in some ways the more casual the better. Joan mustn't be involved in any funny business, mustn't even know that there was any funny business. Joan could not dissimulate. Her protection would be the fact that she clearly knew nothing.

And the note would accomplish a dual purpose. It would seem that he, Bob, had no plan for departure himself.

He thought for a minute or two, then he crossed to the telephone and gave the number of the British Embassy. Presently he was connected with Edmundson, the third secretary, a friend of his.

'John? Bob Rawlinson here. Can you meet me somewhere when you get off? . . . Make it a bit earlier than that? . . . You've got to, old boy. It's important. Well, actually, it's a girl . . . ' He gave an embarrassed cough. 'She's wonderful, quite wonderful. Out of this world. Only it's a bit tricky.'

Edmundson's voice, sounding slightly stuffed-shirt and disapproving, said, 'Really, Bob, you and your girls. All right, 2 o'clock do you?' and rang off. Bob heard the little echoing click as whoever had been listening in, replaced the receiver.

Good old Edmundson. Since all the telephones in Ramat had been tapped, Bob and John Edmundson had worked out a little code of their own. A wonderful girl who was 'out of this world' meant something urgent and important.

Edmundson would pick him up in his car outside the new Merchants Bank at 2 o'clock and he'd tell Edmundson of the hiding place. Tell him that Joan didn't know about it but that, if anything happened to him, it was important. Going by the long sea route Joan and Jennifer wouldn't be back in England for six weeks. By that time the revolution would almost certainly have happened and either been successful or have been put down. Ali Yusuf might be in Europe, or he and Bob might both be dead. He would tell Edmundson enough, but not too much.

Bob took a last look around the room. It looked exactly the same, peaceful, untidy, domestic. The only thing added was his harmless note to Joan. He propped it up on the table and went out. There was no one in the long corridor.

II

The woman in the room next to that occupied by Joan Sutcliffe stepped back from the balcony. There was a mirror in her hand.

She had gone out on the balcony originally to examine more closely a single hair that had

had the audacity to spring up on her chin. She dealt with it with tweezers, then subjected her face to a minute scrutiny in the clear sunlight.

It was then, as she relaxed, that she saw something else. The angle at which she was holding her mirror was such that it reflected the mirror of the hanging wardrobe in the room next to hers and in that mirror she saw a man doing something very curious.

So curious and unexpected that she stood there motionless, watching. He could not see her from where he sat at the table, and she could only see him by means of the double reflection.

If he had turned his head behind him, he might have caught sight of her mirror in the wardrobe mirror, but he was too absorbed in what he was doing to look behind him . . .

Once, it was true, he did look up suddenly towards the window, but since there was nothing to see there, he lowered his head again.

The woman watched him while he finished what he was doing. After a moment's pause he wrote a note which he propped up on the table. Then he moved out of her line of vision but she could just hear enough to realize that he was making a telephone call. She couldn't catch what was said, but it sounded

41

light-hearted — casual. Then she heard the door close.

The woman waited a few minutes. Then she opened her door. At the far end of the passage an Arab was flicking idly with a feather duster. He turned the corner out of sight.

The woman slipped quickly to the door of the next room. It was locked, but she had expected that. The hairpin she had with her and the blade of a small knife did the job quickly and expertly.

She went in, pushing the door to behind her. She picked up the note. The flap had only been stuck down lightly and opened easily. She read the note, frowning. There was no explanation there.

She sealed it up, put it back, and walked across the room.

There, with her hand outstretched, she was disturbed by voices through the window from the terrace below.

One was a voice that she knew to be the occupier of the room in which she was standing. A decided didactic voice, fully assured of itself.

She darted to the window.

Below on the terrace, Joan Sutcliffe, accompanied by her daughter Jennifer, a pale solid child of fifteen, was telling the world

42

and a tall unhappy looking Englishman from the British Consulate just what she thought of the arrangements he had come to make.

'But it's absurd! I never *heard* such nonsense. Everything's perfectly quiet here and everyone quite pleasant. I think it's all a lot of panicky fuss.'

'We hope so, Mrs Sutcliffe, we certainly hope so. But H.E. feels that the responsibility is such — '

Mrs Sutcliffe cut him short. She did not propose to consider the responsibility of ambassadors.

'We've a lot of baggage, you know. We were going home by long sea — next Wednesday. The sea voyage will be good for Jennifer. The doctor said so. I really must absolutely decline to alter all my arrangements and be flown to England in this silly flurry.'

The unhappy looking man said encouragingly that Mrs Sutcliffe and her daughter could be flown, not to England, but to Aden and catch their boat there.

'With our baggage?'

'Yes, yes, that can be arranged. I've got a car waiting — a station wagon. We can load everything right away.'

'Oh well.' Mrs Sutcliffe capitulated. 'I suppose we'd better pack.'

'At once, if you don't mind.'

The woman in the bedroom drew back hurriedly. She took a quick glance at the address on a luggage label on one of the suitcases. Then she slipped quickly out of the room and back into her own just as Mrs Sutcliffe turned the corner of the corridor.

The clerk from the office was running after her.

'Your brother, the Squadron Leader, has been here, Mrs Sutcliffe. He went up to your room. But I think that he has left again. You must just have missed him.'

'How tiresome,' said Mrs Sutcliffe. 'Thank you,' she said to the clerk and went on to Jennifer, 'I suppose Bob's fussing too. I can't see any sign of disturbance *myself* in the streets. This door's unlocked. How careless these people are.'

'Perhaps it was Uncle Bob,' said Jennifer.

'I wish I hadn't missed him . . . Oh, there's a note.' She tore it open.

'At any rate *Bob* isn't fussing,' she said triumphantly. 'He obviously doesn't know a thing about all this. Diplomatic wind up, that's all it is. How I hate trying to pack in the heat of the day. This room's like an oven. Come on, Jennifer, get your things out of the chest of drawers and the wardrobe. We must just shove everything in anyhow. We can repack later.'

'I've never been in a revolution,' said Jennifer thoughtfully.

'I don't expect you'll be in one this time,' said her mother sharply. 'It will be just as I say. Nothing will happen.'

Jennifer looked disappointed.

3

Introducing Mr Robinson

I

It was some six weeks later that a young man tapped discreetly on the door of a room in Bloomsbury and was told to come in.

It was a small room. Behind a desk sat a fat middle-aged man slumped in a chair. He was wearing a crumpled suit, the front of which was smothered in cigar ash. The windows were closed and the atmosphere was almost unbearable.

'Well?' said the fat man testily, and speaking with half-closed eyes. 'What is it now, eh?'

It was said of Colonel Pikeaway that his eyes were always just closing in sleep, or just opening after sleep. It was also said that his name was not Pikeaway and that he was not a colonel. But some people will say anything!

'Edmundson, from the F.O., is here sir.'

'Oh,' said Colonel Pikeaway.

He blinked, appeared to be going to sleep again and muttered:

46

'Third secretary at our Embassy in Ramat at the time of the Revolution. Right?'

'That's right, sir.'

'I suppose, then, I'd better see him,' said Colonel Pikeaway without any marked relish. He pulled himself into a more upright position and brushed off a little of the ash from his paunch.

Mr Edmundson was a tall fair young man, very correctly dressed with manners to match, and a general air of quiet disapproval.

'Colonel Pikeaway? I'm John Edmundson. They said you — er — might want to see me.'

'Did they? Well, they should know,' said Colonel Pikeaway. 'Siddown,' he added.

His eyes began to close again, but before they did so, he spoke:

'You were in Ramat at the time of the Revolution?'

'Yes, I was. A nasty business.'

'I suppose it would be. You were a friend of Bob Rawlinson's, weren't you?'

'I know him fairly well, yes.'

'Wrong tense,' said Colonel Pikeaway. 'He's dead.'

'Yes, sir, I know. But I wasn't sure — ' he paused.

'You don't have to take pains to be discreet here,' said Colonel Pikeaway. 'We know everything here. Or if we don't, we pretend

47

we do. Rawlinson flew Ali Yusuf out of Ramat on the day of the Revolution. Plane hasn't been heard of since. Could have landed in some inaccessible place, or could have crashed. Wreckage of a plane has been found in the Arolez mountains. Two bodies. News will be released to the Press tomorrow. Right?'

Edmundson admitted that it was quite right.

'We know all about things here,' said Colonel Pikeaway. 'That's what we're for. Plane flew into the mountain. Could have been weather conditions. Some reason to believe it was sabotage. Delayed action bomb. We haven't got the full reports yet. The plane crashed in a pretty inaccessible place. There was a reward offered for finding it, but these things take a long time to filter through. Then we had to fly out experts to make an examination. All the red tape, of course. Applications to a foreign government, permission from ministers, palm greasing — to say nothing of the local peasantry appropriating anything that might come in useful.'

He paused and looked at Edmundson.

'Very sad, the whole thing,' said Edmundson. 'Prince Ali Yusuf would have made an enlightened ruler, with democratic principles.'

'That's what probably did the poor chap in,' said Colonel Pikeaway. 'But we can't waste time in telling sad stories of the deaths of kings. We've been asked to make certain — inquiries. By interested parties. Parties, that is, to whom Her Majesty's Government is well disposed.' He looked hard at the other. 'Know what I mean?'

'Well, I have heard something.' Edmundson spoke reluctantly.

'You've heard perhaps, that nothing of value was found on the bodies, or amongst the wreckage, or as far as is known, had been pinched by the locals. Though as to that, you can never tell with peasants. They can clam up as well as the Foreign Office itself. And what else have you heard?'

'Nothing else.'

'You haven't heard that perhaps something of value *ought* to have been found? What did they send you to me for?'

'They said you might want to ask me certain questions,' said Edmundson primly.

'If I ask you questions I shall expect answers,' Colonel Pikeaway pointed out.

'Naturally.'

'Doesn't seem natural to you, son. Did Bob Rawlinson say anything to you before he flew out of Ramat? He was in Ali's confidence if anyone was. Come now, let's have it. Did he say anything?'

'As to what, sir?'

Colonel Pikeaway stared hard at him and scratched his ear.

'Oh, all right,' he grumbled. 'Hush up this and don't say that. Overdo it in my opinion! If you don't know what I'm talking about, you don't know, and there it is.'

'I think there was something — ' Edmundson spoke cautiously and with reluctance. 'Something important that Bob might have wanted to tell me.'

'Ah,' said Colonel Pikeaway, with the air of a man who has at last pulled the cork out of a bottle. 'Interesting. Let's have what you know.'

'It's very little, sir. Bob and I had a kind of simple code. We'd cottoned on to the fact that all the telephones in Ramat were being tapped. Bob was in the way of hearing things at the Palace, and I sometimes had a bit of useful information to pass on to him. So if one of us rang the other up and mentioned a girl or girls, in a certain way, using the term 'out of this world' for her, it meant something was up!'

'Important information of some kind or other?'

'Yes. Bob rang me up using those terms the day the whole show started. I was to meet him at our usual rendezvous — outside one of the banks. But rioting broke out in that particular quarter and the police closed the road. I couldn't make contact with Bob or he

50

with me. He flew Ali out the same afternoon.'

'I see,' said Pikeaway. 'No idea where he was telephoning from?'

'No. It might have been anywhere.'

'Pity.' He paused and then threw out casually:

'Do you know Mrs Sutcliffe?'

'You mean Bob Rawlinson's sister? I met her out there, of course. She was there with a schoolgirl daughter. I don't know her well.'

'Were she and Bob Rawlinson very close?'

Edmundson considered.

'No, I shouldn't say so. She was a good deal older than he was, and rather much of the elder sister. And he didn't much like his brother-in-law — always referred to him as a pompous ass.'

'So he is! One of our prominent industrialists — and how pompous can they get! So you don't think it likely that Bob Rawlinson would have confided an important secret to his sister?'

'It's difficult to say — but no, I shouldn't think so.'

'I shouldn't either,' said Colonel Pikeaway.

He sighed. 'Well, there we are, Mrs Sutcliffe and her daughter are on their way home by the long sea route. Dock at Tilbury on the *Eastern Queen* tomorrow.'

He was silent for a moment or two, whilst

his eyes made a thoughtful survey of the young man opposite him. Then, as though having come to a decision, he held out his hand and spoke briskly.

'Very good of you to come.'

'I'm only sorry I've been of such little use. You're sure there's nothing I can do?'

'No. No. I'm afraid not.'

John Edmundson went out.

The discreet young man came back.

'Thought I might have sent him to Tilbury to break the news to the sister,' said Pikeaway. 'Friend of her brother's — all that. But I decided against it. Inelastic type. That's the F.O. training. Not an opportunist. I'll send round what's his name.'

'Derek?'

'That's right,' Colonel Pikeaway nodded approval. 'Getting to know what I mean quite well, ain't you?'

'I try my best, sir.'

'Trying's not enough. You have to succeed. Send me along Ronnie first. I've got an assignment for him.'

II

Colonel Pikeaway was apparently just going off to sleep again when the young man called

Ronnie entered the room. He was tall, dark, muscular, and had a gay and rather impertinent manner.

Colonel Pikeaway looked at him for a moment or two and then grinned.

'How'd you like to penetrate into a girls' school?' he asked.

'A girls' school?' The young man lifted his eyebrows. 'That will be something new! What are they up to? Making bombs in the chemistry class?'

'Nothing of that kind. Very superior high-class school. Meadowbank.'

'Meadowbank!' the young man whistled. 'I can't believe it!'

'Hold your impertinent tongue and listen to me. Princess Shaista, first cousin and only near relative of the late Prince Ali Yusuf of Ramat, goes there this next term. She's been at school in Switzerland up to now.'

'What do I do? Abduct her?'

'Certainly not. I think it possible she may become a focus of interest in the near future. I want you to keep an eye on developments. I'll have to leave it vague. I don't know what or who may turn up, but if any of our more unlikeable friends seem to be interested, report it . . . A watching brief, that's what you've got.'

The young man nodded.

53

'And how do I get in to watch? Shall I be the drawing master?'

'The visiting staff is all female.' Colonel Pikeaway looked at him in a considering manner. 'I think I'll have to make you a gardener.'

'A gardener?'

'Yes. I'm right in thinking you know something about gardening?'

'Yes, indeed. I ran a column on *Your Garden* in the *Sunday Mail* for a year in my younger days.'

'Tush!' said Colonel Pikeaway. 'That's nothing! I could do a column on gardening myself without knowing a thing about it — just crib from a few luridly illustrated Nurseryman's catalogues and a Gardening Encyclopedia. I know all the patter. '*Why not break away from tradition and sound a really tropical note in your border this year? Lovely Amabellis Gossiporia, and some of the wonderful new Chinese hybrids of Sinensis Maka foolia. Try the rich blushing beauty of a clump of Sinistra Hopaless, not very hardy but they should be all right against a west wall.*' He broke off and grinned. 'Nothing to it! The fools buy the things and early frost sets in and kills them and they wish they'd stuck to wallflowers and forget-me-nots! No, my boy, I mean the real stuff. Spit on your hands and use the spade, be well acquainted with the compost heap, mulch diligently, use the Dutch hoe and every other kind of hoe, trench really deep for your sweet peas — and all the rest of the beastly business. Can you do it?'

'All these things I have done from my youth upwards!'

'Of course you have. I know your mother. Well, that's settled.'

'Is there a job going as a gardener at Meadowbank?'

'Sure to be,' said Colonel Pikeaway. 'Every garden in England is short staffed. I'll write you some nice testimonials. You'll see, they'll simply jump at you. No time to waste, summer term begins on the 29th.'

'I garden and I keep my eyes open, is that right?'

'That's it, and if any oversexed teenagers make passes at you, Heaven help you if you respond. I don't want you thrown out on your ear too soon.'

He drew a sheet of paper towards him. 'What do you fancy as a name?'

'Adam would seem appropriate.'

'Last name?'

'How about Eden?'

'I'm not sure I like the way your mind is running. Adam Goodman will do very nicely.

Go and work out your past history with
Jenson and then get cracking.' He looked at
his watch. 'I've no more time for you. I don't
want to keep Mr Robinson waiting. He ought
to be here by now.'

Adam (to give him his new name) stopped
as he was moving to the door.

'Mr Robinson?' he asked curiously. 'Is *he*
coming?'

'I said so.' A buzzer went on the desk.
'There he is now. Always punctual, Mr
Robinson.'

'Tell me,' said Adam curiously. 'Who is he
really? What's his real name?'

'His name,' said Colonel Pikeaway, 'is Mr
Robinson. That's all I know, and that's all
anybody knows.'

III

The man who came into the room did not
look as though his name was, or could ever
have been, Robinson. It might have been
Demetrius, or Isaacstein, or Perenna —
though not one or the other in particular.
He was not definitely Jewish, nor definitely
Greek nor Portuguese nor Spanish, nor
South American. What did seem highly
unlikely was that he was an Englishman

56

called Robinson. He was fat and well dressed, with a yellow face, melancholy dark eyes, a broad forehead, and a generous mouth that displayed rather over-large very white teeth. His hands were well shaped and beautifully kept. His voice was English with no trace of accent.

He and Colonel Pikeaway greeted each other rather in the manner of two reigning monarchs. Politenesses were exchanged.

Then, as Mr Robinson accepted a cigar, Colonel Pikeaway said:

'It is very good of you to offer to help us.'

Mr Robinson lit his cigar, savoured it appreciatively, and finally spoke.

'My dear fellow. I just thought — I hear things, you know. I know a lot of people, and they tell me things. I don't know why.'

Colonel Pikeaway did not comment on the reason why.

He said:

'I gather you've heard that Prince Ali Yusuf's plane has been found?'

'Wednesday of last week,' said Mr Robinson. 'Young Rawlinson was the pilot. A tricky flight. But the crash wasn't due to an error on Rawlinson's part. The plane had been tampered with — by a certain Achmed — senior mechanic. Completely trustworthy — or so Rawlinson thought. But he wasn't. He's got a very lucrative job with the new *régime* now.'

'So it was sabotage! We didn't know that for sure. It's a sad story.'

'Yes. That poor young man — Ali Yusuf, I mean — was ill equipped to cope with corruption and treachery. His public school education was unwise — or at least that is my view. But we do not concern ourselves with him now, do we? He is yesterday's news. Nothing is so dead as a dead king. We are concerned, you in your way, I in mine, with what dead kings leave behind them.'

'Which is?'

Mr Robinson shrugged his shoulders.

'A substantial bank balance in Geneva, a modest balance in London, considerable assets in his own country now taken over by the glorious new *régime* (and a little bad feeling as to how the spoils have been divided, or so I hear!), and finally a small personal item.'

'Small?'

'These things are relative. Anyway, small in bulk. Handy to carry upon the person.'

'They weren't on Ali Yusuf's person, as far as we know.'

'No. Because he had handed them over to young Rawlinson.'

'Are you sure of that?' asked Pikeaway sharply.

'Well, one is never sure,' said Mr Robinson apologetically. 'In a palace there is so much gossip. It cannot *all* be true. But there was a very strong rumour to that effect.'

'They weren't on young Rawlinson's person, either — '

'In that case,' said Mr Robinson, 'it seems as though they must have been got out of the country by some other means.'

'What other means? Have you any idea?'

'Rawlinson went to a café in the town after he had received the jewels. He was not seen to speak to anyone or approach anyone whilst he was there. Then he went to the Ritz Savoy Hotel where his sister was staying. He went up to her room and was there for about 20 minutes. She herself was out. He then left the hotel and went to the Merchants Bank in Victory Square where he cashed a cheque. When he came out of the bank a disturbance was beginning. Students rioting about something. It was some time before the square was cleared. Rawlinson then went straight to the airstrip where, in company with Sergeant Achmed, he went over the plane.

'Ali Yusuf drove out to see the new road construction, stopped his car at the airstrip, joined Rawlinson and expressed a desire to take a short flight and see the dam and the new highway construction from the air. They took off and did not return.'

'And your deductions from that?'

'My dear fellow, the same as yours. Why did Bob Rawlinson spend twenty minutes in his sister's room when she was out and he had been told that she was not likely to return until evening? He left her a note that would have taken him at most three minutes to scribble. What did he do for the rest of the time?'

'You are suggesting that he concealed the jewels in some appropriate place amongst his sister's belongings?'

'It seems indicated, does it not? Mrs Sutcliffe was evacuated that same day with other British subjects. She was flown to Aden with her daughter. She arrives at Tilbury, I believe, tomorrow.'

Pikeaway nodded.

'Look after her,' said Mr Robinson.

'We're going to look after her,' said Pikeaway. 'That's all arranged.'

'If she has the jewels, she will be in danger.' He closed his eyes. 'I so much dislike violence.'

'You think there is likely to be violence?'

'There are people interested. Various undesirable people — if you understand me.'

'I understand you,' said Pikeaway grimly.

'And they will, of course, double cross each other.'

Mr Robinson shook his head. 'So confusing.'

Colonel Pikeaway asked delicately: 'Have you yourself any — er — special interest in the matter?'

'I represent a certain group of interests,' said Mr Robinson. His voice was faintly reproachful. 'Some of the stones in question were supplied by my syndicate to his late highness — at a very fair and reasonable price. The group of people I represent who were interested in the recovery of the stones, would, I may venture to say, have had the approval of the late owner. I shouldn't like to say more. These matters are so delicate.'

'But you are definitely on the side of the angels,' Colonel Pikeaway smiled.

'Ah, angels! Angels — yes.' He paused. 'Do you happen to know who occupied the rooms in the hotel on either side of the room occupied by Mrs Sutcliffe and her daughter?'

Colonel Pikeaway looked vague.

'Let me see now — I believe I do. On the left hand side was Señora Angelica de Toredo — a Spanish — er — dancer appearing at the local cabaret. Perhaps not strictly Spanish and perhaps not a very good dancer. But popular with the clientèle. On the other side

61

was one of a group of school-teachers, I understand — '

Mr Robinson beamed approvingly.

'You are always the same. I come to tell you things, but nearly always you know them already.'

'No no.' Colonel Pikeaway made a polite disclaimer.

'Between us,' said Mr Robinson, 'we know a good deal.'

Their eyes met.

'I hope,' Mr Robinson said rising, 'that we know enough — '

4

Return of a Traveller

I

'Really!' said Mrs Sutcliffe, in an annoyed voice, as she looked out of her hotel window, 'I don't see why it always has to rain when one comes back to England. It makes it all seem so depressing.'

'I think it's lovely to be back,' said Jennifer. 'Hearing everyone talk English in the streets! And we'll be able to have a really good tea presently. Bread and butter and jam and proper cakes.'

'I wish you weren't so insular, darling,' said Mrs Sutcliffe. 'What's the good of my taking you abroad all the way to the Persian Gulf if you're going to say you'd rather have stayed at home?'

'I don't mind going abroad for a month or two,' said Jennifer. 'All I said was I'm glad to be back.'

'Now do get out of the way, dear, and let me make sure that they've brought up all the luggage. Really, I do feel — I've felt ever

63

since the war that people have got very dishonest nowadays. I'm sure if I hadn't kept an eye on things that man would have gone off with my green zip bag at Tilbury. And there was another man hanging about near the luggage. I saw him afterwards on the train. I believe, you know, that these sneak thieves meet the boats and if the people are flustered or seasick they go off with some of the suitcases.'

'Oh, you're always thinking things like that, Mother,' said Jennifer. 'You think everybody you meet is dishonest.'

'Most of them are,' said Mrs Sutcliffe grimly.

'Not English people,' said the loyal Jennifer.

'That's worse,' said her mother. 'One doesn't expect anything else from Arabs and foreigners, but in England one's off guard and that makes it easier for dishonest people. Now do let me count. That's the big green suitcase and the black one, and the two small brown and the zip bag and the golf clubs and the racquets and the hold-all and the canvas suitcase — and where's the green bag? Oh, there it is. And that local tin we bought to put the extra things in — yes, one, two, three, four, five, six — yes, that's all right. All fourteen things are here.'

'Can't we have some tea now?' said Jennifer.

'Tea? It's only three o'clock.'

'I'm awfully hungry.'

'All right, all right. Can you go down by yourself and order it? I really feel I must have a rest, and then I'll just unpack the things we'll need for tonight. It's too bad your father couldn't have met us. Why he had to have an important directors' meeting in Newcastle-on-Tyne today I simply cannot imagine. You'd think his wife and daughter would come first. Especially as he hasn't seen us for three months. Are you sure you can manage by yourself?'

'Good gracious, Mummy,' said Jennifer, 'what age do you think I am? Can I have some money, please? I haven't got any English money.'

She accepted the ten shilling note her mother handed to her, and went out scornfully.

The telephone rang by the bed. Mrs Sutcliffe went to it and picked up the receiver.

'Hallo . . . Yes . . . Yes, Mrs Sutcliffe speaking . . . '

There was a knock at the door. Mrs Sutcliffe said, 'Just one moment' to the receiver, laid it down and went over to the door. A young man in dark blue overalls was standing there with a small kit of tools.

'Electrician,' he said briskly. 'The lights in this suite aren't satisfactory. I've been sent up to see to them.'

'Oh — all right . . . '

She drew back. The electrician entered.

'Bathroom?'

'Through there — beyond the other bedroom.'

She went back to the telephone.

'I'm so sorry . . . What were you saying?'

'My name is Derek O'Connor. Perhaps I might come up to your suite, Mrs Sutcliffe. It's about your brother.'

'Bob? Is there — news of him?'

'I'm afraid so — yes.'

'Oh . . . Oh, I see . . . Yes, come up. It's on the third floor, 310.'

She sat down on the bed. She already knew what the news must be.

Presently there was a knock on the door and she opened it to admit a young man who shook hands in a suitably subdued manner.

'Are you from the Foreign Office?'

'My name's Derek O'Connor. My chief sent me round as there didn't seem to be anybody else who could break it to you.'

'Please tell me,' said Mrs Sutcliffe. 'He's been killed. Is that it?'

'Yes, that's it, Mrs Sutcliffe. He was flying Prince Ali Yusuf out from Ramat and they crashed in the mountains.'

'Why haven't I heard — why didn't someone wireless it to the boat?'

'There was no definite news until a few days ago. It was known that the plane was missing, that was all. But under the circumstances there might still have been hope. But now the wreck of the plane has been found . . . I am sure you will be glad to know that death was instantaneous.'

'The Prince was killed as well?'

'Yes.'

'I'm not at all surprised,' said Mrs Sutcliffe. Her voice shook a little but she was in full command of herself. 'I knew Bob would die young. He was always reckless, you know — always flying new planes, trying new stunts. I've hardly seen anything of him for the last four years. Oh well, one can't change people, can one?'

'No,' said her visitor, 'I'm afraid not.'

'Henry always said he'd smash himself up sooner or later,' said Mrs Sutcliffe. She seemed to derive a kind of melancholy satisfaction from the accuracy of her husband's prophecy. A tear rolled down her cheek and she looked for her handkerchief. 'It's been a shock,' she said.

'I know — I'm awfully sorry.'

'Bob couldn't run away, of course,' said Mrs Sutcliffe. 'I mean, he'd taken on the job of being the Prince's pilot. I wouldn't have wanted him to throw in his hand. And he was a good flier too. I'm sure if he ran into a mountain it wasn't his fault.'

'No,' said O'Connor, 'it certainly wasn't his fault. The only hope of getting the Prince out was to fly in no matter what conditions. It was a dangerous flight to undertake and it went wrong.'

Mrs Sutcliffe nodded.

'I quite understand,' she said. 'Thank you for coming to tell me.'

'There's something more,' said O'Connor, 'something I've got to ask you. Did your brother entrust anything to you to take back to England?'

'Entrust something to me?' said Mrs Sutcliffe. 'What do you mean?'

'Did he give you any — package — any small parcel to bring back and deliver to anyone in England?'

She shook her head wonderingly. 'No. Why should you think he did?'

'There was a rather important package which we think your brother may have given to someone to bring home. He called on you at your hotel that day — the day of the

Revolution, I mean.'

'I know. He left a note. But there was nothing in that — just some silly thing about playing tennis or golf the next day. I suppose when he wrote that note, he couldn't have known that he'd have to fly the Prince out that very afternoon.'

'That was all it said?'

'The note? Yes.'

'Have you kept it, Mrs Sutcliffe?'

'Kept the note he left? No, of course I haven't. It was quite trivial. I tore it up and threw it away. Why should I keep it?'

'No reason,' said O'Connor. 'I just wondered.'

'Wondered what?' said Mrs Sutcliffe crossly.

'Whether there might have been some — other message concealed in it. After all — ' he smiled, ' — there is such a thing as invisible ink, you know.'

'Invisible ink!' said Mrs Sutcliffe, with a great deal of distaste, 'do you mean the sort of thing they use in spy stories?'

'Well, I'm afraid I do mean just that,' said O'Connor, rather apologetically.

'How idiotic,' said Mrs Sutcliffe. 'I'm sure Bob would never use anything like invisible ink. Why should he? He was a dear matter-of-fact sensible person.' A tear dripped down her cheek again. 'Oh dear, where *is* my bag? I must have a handkerchief. Perhaps I left it in the other room.'

'I'll get it for you,' said O'Connor.

He went through the communicating door and stopped as a young man in overalls who was bending over a suitcase straightened up to face him, looking rather startled.

'Electrician,' said the young man hurriedly. 'Something wrong with the lights here.'

O'Connor flicked a switch.

'They seem all right to me,' he said pleasantly.

'Must have given me the wrong room number,' said the electrician.

He gathered up his tool bag and slipped out quickly through the door to the corridor.

O'Connor frowned, picked up Mrs Sutcliffe's bag from the dressing-table and took it back to her.

'Excuse me,' he said, and picked up the telephone receiver. 'Room 310 here. Have you just sent up an electrician to see to the light in this suite? Yes . . . Yes, I'll hang on.'

He waited.

'No? No, I thought you hadn't. No, there's nothing wrong.'

He replaced the receiver and turned to Mrs Sutcliffe.

'There's nothing wrong with any of the

lights here,' he said. 'And the office didn't send up an electrician.'

'Then what was that man doing? Was he a thief?'

'He may have been.'

Mrs Sutcliffe looked hurriedly in her bag. 'He hasn't taken anything out of my bag. The money is all right.'

'Are you sure, Mrs Sutcliffe, absolutely *sure* that your brother didn't give you anything to take home, to pack among your belongings?'

'I'm absolutely sure,' said Mrs Sutcliffe.

'Or your daughter — you have a daughter, haven't you?'

'Yes. She's downstairs having tea.'

'Could your brother have given anything to her?'

'No, I'm sure he couldn't.'

'There's another possibility,' said O'Connor. 'He might have hidden something in your baggage among your belongings that day when he was waiting for you in your room.'

'But why should Bob do such a thing? It sounds absolutely absurd.'

'It's not quite so absurd as it sounds. It seems possible that Prince Ali Yusuf gave your brother something to keep for him and that your brother thought it would be safer among your possessions than if he kept it himself.'

'Sounds very unlikely to me,' said Mrs Sutcliffe.

'I wonder now, would you mind if we searched?'

'Searched through my luggage, do you mean? Unpack?' Mrs Sutcliffe's voice rose with a wail on that word.

'I know,' said O'Connor. 'It's a terrible thing to ask you. But it might be very important. I could help you, you know,' he said persuasively. 'I often used to pack for my mother. She said I was quite a good packer.'

He exerted all the charm which was one of his assets to Colonel Pikeaway.

'Oh well,' said Mrs Sutcliffe, yielding, 'I suppose — If you say so — if, I mean, it's really important — '

'It might be very important,' said Derek O'Connor. 'Well, now,' he smiled at her. 'Suppose we begin.'

II

Three quarters of an hour later Jennifer returned from her tea. She looked round the room and gave a gasp of surprise.

'Mummy, what *have* you been doing?'

'We've been unpacking,' said Mrs Sutcliffe crossly. 'Now we're packing things up again.

This is Mr O'Connor. My daughter Jennifer.'

'But why are you packing and unpacking?'

'Don't ask me why,' snapped her mother. 'There seems to be some idea that your Uncle Bob put something in my luggage to bring home. He didn't give you anything, I suppose, Jennifer?'

'Uncle Bob give me anything to bring back? No. Have you been unpacking my things too?'

'We've unpacked everything,' said Derek O'Connor cheerfully, 'and we haven't found a thing and now we're packing them up again. I think you ought to have a drink of tea or something, Mrs Sutcliffe. Can I order you something? A brandy and soda perhaps?' He went to the telephone.

'I wouldn't mind a good cup of tea,' said Mrs Sutcliffe.

'I had a smashing tea,' said Jennifer. 'Bread and butter and sandwiches and cake and then the waiter brought me more sandwiches because I asked him if he'd mind and he said he didn't. It was lovely.'

O'Connor ordered the tea, then he finished packing up Mrs Sutcliffe's belongings again with a neatness and a dexterity which forced her unwilling admiration.

'Your mother seems to have trained you to pack very well,' she said.

'Oh, I've all sorts of handy accomplishments,' said O'Connor smiling.

His mother was long since dead, and his skill in packing and unpacking had been acquired solely in the service of Colonel Pikeaway.

'There's just one thing more, Mrs Sutcliffe. I'd like you to be very careful of yourself.'

'Careful of myself? In what way?'

'Well,' O'Connor left it vague. 'Revolutions are tricky things. There are a lot of ramifications. Are you staying in London long?'

'We're going down to the country tomorrow. My husband will be driving us down.'

'That's all right then. But — don't take any chances. If anything in the least out of the ordinary happens, ring 999 straight away.'

'Ooh!' said Jennifer, in high delight. 'Dial 999. I've always wanted to.'

'Don't be silly, Jennifer,' said her mother.

III

Extract from account in a local paper.

A man appeared before the Magistrate's court yesterday charged with breaking into the residence of Mr Henry Sutcliffe

74

with intent to steal. Mrs Sutcliffe's bedroom was ransacked and left in wild confusion whilst the members of the family were at Church on Sunday morning. The kitchen staff who were preparing the mid-day meal, heard nothing. Police arrested the man as he was making his escape from the house. Something had evidently alarmed him and he had fled without taking anything.

Giving his name as Andrew Ball of no fixed abode, he pleaded guilty. He said he had been out of work and was looking for money. Mrs Sutcliffe's jewellery, apart from a few pieces which she was wearing, is kept at her bank.

'I told you to have the lock of that drawing-room french window seen to,' had been the comment of Mr Sutcliffe in the family circle.

'My dear Henry,' said Mrs Sutcliffe, 'you don't seem to realize that I have been abroad for the last three months. And anyway, I'm sure I've read somewhere that if burglars want to get in they always can.'

She added wistfully, as she glanced again at the local paper:

'How beautifully grand 'kitchen staff'

sounds. So different from what it really is, old Mrs Ellis who is quite deaf and can hardly stand up and that half-witted daughter of the Bardwells who comes in to help on Sunday mornings.'

'What I don't see,' said Jennifer, 'is how the police found out the house was being burgled and got here in time to catch him?'

'It seems extraordinary that he didn't take anything,' commented her mother.

'Are you quite sure about that, Joan?' demanded her husband. 'You were a little doubtful at first.'

Mrs Sutcliffe gave an exasperated sigh.

'It's impossible to tell about a thing like that straight away. The mess in my bedroom — things thrown about everywhere, drawers pulled out and overturned. I had to look through everything before I could be sure — though now I come to think of it, I don't remember seeing my best Jacqmar scarf.'

'I'm sorry, Mummy. That was me. It blew overboard in the Mediterranean. I'd borrowed it. I meant to tell you but I forgot.'

'Really, Jennifer, how often have I asked you not to borrow things without telling me first?'

'Can I have some more pudding?' said Jennifer, creating a diversion.

'I suppose so. Really, Mrs Ellis has a wonderfully light hand. It makes it worth while having to shout at her so much. I do hope, though, that they won't think you too greedy at school. Meadowbank isn't quite an ordinary school, remember.'

'I don't know that I really want to go to Meadowbank,' said Jennifer. 'I knew a girl whose cousin had been there, and she said it was awful. They spent all their time telling you how to get in and out of Rolls-Royces, and how to behave if you went to lunch with the Queen.'

'That will do, Jennifer,' said Mrs Sutcliffe. 'You don't appreciate how extremely fortunate you are in being admitted to Meadowbank. Miss Bulstrode doesn't take every girl, I can tell you. It's entirely owing to your father's important position and the influence of your Aunt Rosamond. You are exceedingly lucky. And if,' added Mrs Sutcliffe, 'you are ever asked to lunch with the Queen, it will be a good thing for you to know how to behave.'

'Oh well,' said Jennifer. 'I expect the Queen often has to have people to lunch who don't know how to behave — African chiefs and jockeys and sheikhs.'

'African chiefs have the most polished manners,' said her father, who had recently returned from a short business trip to Ghana.

'So do Arab sheikhs,' said Mrs Sutcliffe. 'Really courtly.'

'D'you remember that sheikh's feast we went to,' said Jennifer. 'And how he picked out the sheep's eye and gave it to you, and Uncle Bob nudged you not to make a fuss and to eat it? I mean, if a sheikh did that with roast lamb at Buckingham Palace, it would give the Queen a bit of a jolt, wouldn't it?'

'That will do, Jennifer,' said her mother and closed the subject.

IV

When Andrew Ball of no fixed abode had been sentenced to three months for breaking and entering, Derek O'Connor, who had been occupying a modest position at the back of the Magistrate's Court, put through a call to a Museum number.

'Not a thing on the fellow when we picked him up,' he said. 'We gave him plenty of time too.'

'Who was he? Anyone we know?'

'One of the Gecko lot, I think. Small time. They hire him out for this sort of thing. Not much brain but he's said to be thorough.'

'And he took his sentence like a lamb?' At the other end of the line Colonel Pikeaway grinned as he spoke.

'Yes. Perfect picture of a stupid fellow

78

lapsed from the straight and narrow path. You'd never connect him with any big time stuff. That's his value, of course.'

'And he didn't find anything,' mused Colonel Pikeaway. 'And *you* didn't find anything. It rather looks, doesn't it, as though there isn't anything to find? Our idea that Rawlinson planted these things on his sister seems to have been wrong.'

'Other people appear to have the same idea.'

'It's a bit obvious really . . . Maybe we are meant to take the bait.'

'Could be. Any other possibilities?'

'Plenty of them. The stuff may still be in Ramat. Hidden somewhere in the Ritz Savoy Hotel, maybe. Or Rawlinson passed it to someone on his way to the airstrip. Or there may be something in that hint of Mr Robinson's. A woman may have got hold of it. Or it could be that Mrs Sutcliffe had it all the time unbeknownst to herself, and flung it overboard in the Red Sea with something she had no further use for.

'And that,' he added thoughtfully, 'might be all for the best.'

'Oh, come now, it's worth a lot of money, sir.'

'Human life is worth a lot, too,' said Colonel Pikeaway.

5

Letters from Meadowbank School

Letter from Julia Upjohn to her mother:

Dear Mummy,
I've settled in now and am liking it very much. There's a girl who is new this term too called Jennifer and she and I rather do things together. We're both awfully keen on tennis. She's rather good. She has a really smashing serve when it comes off, but it doesn't usually. She says her racquet's got warped from being out in the Persian Gulf. It's very hot out there. She was in all that Revolution that happened. I said wasn't it very exciting, but she said no, they didn't see anything at all. They were taken away to the Embassy or something and missed it.
Miss Bulstrode is rather a lamb, but she's pretty frightening too — or can be. She goes easy on you when you're new. Behind her back everyone calls her The

Bull or Bully. We're taught English literature by Miss Rich, who's terrific. When she
gets in a real state her hair comes down.
She's got a queer but rather exciting face
and when she reads bits of Shakespeare it
all seems different and real. She went on at
us the other day about Iago, and what he
felt — and a lot about jealousy and how it
ate into you and you suffered until you
went quite mad wanting to hurt the person
you loved. It gave us all the shivers
— except Jennifer, because nothing upsets
her. Miss Rich teaches us Geography, too.
I always thought it was such a dull subject,
but it isn't with Miss Rich. This morning
she told us all about the spice trade and
why they had to have spices because of
things going bad so easily.

I'm starting Art with Miss Laurie. She
comes twice a week and takes us up to
London to see picture galleries as well.
We do French with Mademoiselle
Blanche. She doesn't keep order very well.
Jennifer says French people can't. She
doesn't get cross, though, only bored. She
says 'Enfin, vous m'ennuiez, mes enfants!'
Miss Springer is awful. She does gym and
P. T. She's got ginger hair and smells
when she's hot. Then there's Miss Chad-
wick (Chaddy) — she's been here since

81

the school started. She teaches mathematics and is rather fussy, but quite nice. And there's Miss Vansittart who teaches History and German. She's a sort of Miss Bulstrode with the pep left out.

There are a lot of foreign girls here, two Italians and some Germans, and a rather jolly Swede (she's a Princess or something) and a girl who's half Turkish and half Persian and who says she would have been married to Prince Ali Yusuf who got killed in that aeroplane crash, but Jennifer says that isn't true, that Shaista only says so because she was a kind of cousin, and you're supposed to marry a cousin. But Jennifer says he wasn't going to. He liked someone else. Jennifer knows a lot of things but she won't usually tell them.

I suppose you'll be starting on your trip soon. Don't leave your passport behind you like you did last time!!! And take your first aid kit in case you have an accident.

Love from Julia

Letter from Jennifer Sutcliffe to her mother:

Dear Mummy,

It really isn't bad here. I'm enjoying it more than I expected to do. The weather has been very fine. We had to write a composition yesterday on 'Can a good quality be carried to excess?' I couldn't think of anything to say. Next week it will be 'Contrast the characters of Juliet and Desdemona.' That seems silly too. Do you think I could have a new tennis racquet? I know you had mine restrung last Autumn — but it feels all wrong. Perhaps it's got warped. I'd rather like to learn Greek. Can I? I love languages. Some of us are going to London to see the ballet next week. It's Swan Lake. The food here is jolly good. Yesterday we had chicken for lunch, and we had lovely home made cakes for tea.

I can't think of any more news — have you had any more burglaries?

Your loving daughter,
Jennifer

Letter from Margaret Gore-West, Senior Prefect, to her mother:

Dear Mummy,
There is very little news. I am doing German with Miss Vansittart this term. There is a rumour that Miss Bulstrode is going to retire and that Miss Vansittart will succeed her but they've been saying that for over a year now, and I'm sure it isn't

true. I asked Miss Chadwick (of course I wouldn't dare ask Miss Bulstrode!) and she was quite sharp about it. Said certainly not and don't listen to gossip. We went to the ballet on Tuesday. Swan Lake. Too dreamy for words!

Princess Ingrid is rather fun. Very blue eyes, but she wears braces on her teeth. There are two new German girls. They speak English quite well.

Miss Rich is back and looking quite well. We did miss her last term. The new Games Mistress is called Miss Springer. She's terribly bossy and nobody likes her much. She coaches you in tennis very well, though. One of the new girls, Jennifer Sutcliffe, is going to be really good, I think. Her backhand's a bit weak. Her great friend is a girl called Julia. We call them the Jays!

You won't forget about taking me out on the 20th, will you? Sports Day is June 19th.

Your Loving
Margaret

Letter from Ann Shapland to Dennis Rathbone:

Dear Dennis,

84

I shan't get any time off until the third week of term. I should like to dine with you then very much. It would have to be Saturday or Sunday. I'll let you know.

I find it rather fun working in a school. But thank God I'm not a schoolmistress! I'd go raving mad.

Yours ever,
Ann

Letter from Miss Johnson to her sister:

Dear Edith,

Everything much the same as usual here. The summer term is always nice. The garden is looking beautiful and we've got a new gardener to help old Briggs — young and strong! Rather good looking, too, which is a pity. Girls are so silly.

Miss Bulstrode hasn't said anything more about retiring, so I hope she's got over the idea. Miss Vansittart wouldn't be at all the same thing. I really don't believe I would stay on.

Give my love to Dick and to the children, and remember me to Oliver and Kate when you see them.

Elspeth

Letter from Mademoiselle Angèle Blanche to

René Dupont, Post Restante, Bordeaux.

Dear René,
All is well here, though I cannot say
that I amuse myself. The girls are neither
respectful nor well behaved. I think it
better, however, not to complain to Miss
Bulstrode. One has to be on one's guard
when dealing with that one!
There is nothing interesting at present
to tell you.
Mouche

Letter from Miss Vansittart to a friend:

Dear Gloria,
The summer term has started smoothly.
A very satisfactory set of new girls. The
foreigners are settling down well. Our
little Princess (the Middle East one, not
the Scandinavian) is inclined to lack
application, but I suppose one has to
expect that. She has very charming
manners.
The new Games Mistress, Miss
Springer, is not a success. The girls dislike her and she is far too high-handed
with them. After all, this is not an ordinary school. We don't stand or fall by
P.T.! She is also very inquisitive, and asks

86

far too many personal questions. That sort of thing can be very trying, and is so ill bred. Mademoiselle Blanche, the new French Mistress, is quite amiable but not up to the standard of Mademoiselle Depuy.

We had a near escape on the first day of term. Lady Veronica Carlton-Sandways turned up completely intoxicated!! But for Miss Chadwick spotting it and heading her off, we might have had a most unpleasant incident. The twins are such nice girls, too.

Miss Bulstrode has not said anything definite yet about the future — but from her manner, I think her mind is definitely made up. Meadowbank is a really fine achievement, and I shall be proud to carry on its traditions.

Give my love to Marjorie when you see her.

Yours ever,
Eleanor

Letter to Colonel Pikeaway, sent through the usual channels:

Talk about sending a man into danger! I'm the only able-bodied male in an establishment of, roughly, some hundred and ninety females.

Her Highness arrived in style. Cadillac of squashed strawberry and pastel blue, with Wog Notable in native dress, fashion-plate-from-Paris wife, and junior edition of same (H.R.H.).

Hardly recognized her the next day in her school uniform. There will be no difficulty in establishing friendly relations with her. She has already seen to that. Was asking me the names of various flowers in a sweet innocent way, when a female Gorgon with freckles, red hair, and a voice like a corncrake bore down upon her and removed her from my vicinity. She didn't want to go. I'd always understood these Oriental girls were brought up modestly behind the veil. This one must have had a little worldly experience during her schooldays in Switzerland, I think.

The Gorgon, alias Miss Springer, the Games Mistress, came back to give me a raspberry. Garden staff were not to talk to the pupils, etc. My turn to express innocent surprise. 'Sorry, Miss. The young lady was asking what these here delphiniums was. Suppose they don't have them in the parts she comes from.' The Gorgon was easily pacified, in the end she almost simpered. Less success with Miss Bulstrode's secretary. One of these coat and skirt country girls. French mistress if more cooperative. Demure and mousy to look at, but not such a mouse really. Also have made friends with three pleasant gigglers, Christian names, Pamela, Lois and Mary, surnames unknown, but of aristocratic lineage. A sharp old war-horse called Miss Chadwick keeps a wary eye on me, so I'm careful not to blot my copybook.

My boss, old Briggs, is a crusty kind of character whose chief subject of conversation is what things used to be in the good old days, when he was, I suspect, the fourth of a staff of five. He grumbles about most things and people, but has a wholesome respect for Miss Bulstrode herself. So have I. She had a few words, very pleasant, with me, but I had a horrid feeling she was seeing right through me and knowing all about me.

No sign, so far, of anything sinister — but I live in hope.

6

Early Days

I

In the Mistresses' Common Room news was being exchanged. Foreign travel, plays seen, Art Exhibitions visited. Snapshots were handed round. The menace of coloured transparencies was in the offing. All the enthusiasts wanted to show their own pictures, but to get out of being forced to see other people's.

Presently conversation became less personal. The new Sports Pavilion was both criticized and admired. It was admitted to be a fine building, but naturally everybody would have liked to improve its design in one way or another.

The new girls were then briefly passed in review, and, on the whole, the verdict was favourable.

A little pleasant conversation was made to the two new members of the staff. Had Mademoiselle Blanche been in England before? What part of France did she come from?

90

Mademoiselle Blanche replied politely but with reserve.

Miss Springer was more forthcoming.

She spoke with emphasis and decision. It might almost have been said that she was giving a lecture. Subject: The excellence of Miss Springer. How much she had been appreciated as a colleague. How headmistresses had accepted her advice with gratitude and had re-organized their schedules accordingly.

Miss Springer was not sensitive. A restlessness in her audience was not noticed by her. It remained for Miss Johnson to ask in her mild tones:

'All the same, I expect your ideas haven't always been accepted in the way they — er — should have been.'

'One must be prepared for ingratitude,' said Miss Springer. Her voice, already loud, became louder. 'The trouble is, people are so cowardly — won't face facts. They often prefer not to see what's under their noses all the time. I'm not like that. I go straight to the point. More than once I've unearthed a nasty scandal — brought it into the open. I've a good nose — once I'm on the trail, I don't leave it — not till I've pinned down my quarry.' She gave a loud jolly laugh. 'In my opinion, no one should teach in a school whose life isn't an open book. If anyone's got anything to hide, one can soon tell. Oh! you'd be surprised if I told you some of the things I've found out about people. Things that nobody else had dreamed of.'

'You enjoyed that experience, yes?' said Mademoiselle Blanche.

'Of course not. Just doing my duty. But I wasn't backed up. Shameful laxness. So I resigned — as a protest.'

She looked round and gave her jolly sporting laugh again.

'Hope nobody here has anything to hide,' she said gaily.

Nobody was amused. But Miss Springer was not the kind of woman to notice that.

II

'Can I speak to you, Miss Bulstrode?'

Miss Bulstrode laid her pen aside and looked up into the flushed face of the matron, Miss Johnson.

'Yes, Miss Johnson.'

'It's that girl Shaista — the Egyptian girl or whatever she is.'

'Yes?'

'It's her — er — underclothing.'

Miss Bulstrode's eyebrows rose in patient surprise.

'Her — well — her bust bodice.'

'What is wrong with her brassière?'

'Well — it isn't an ordinary kind — I mean it doesn't hold her in, exactly. It — er — well it pushes her up — really quite unnecessarily.'

Miss Bulstrode bit her lip to keep back a smile, as so often when in colloquy with Miss Johnson.

'Perhaps I'd better come and look at it,' she said gravely.

A kind of inquest was then held with the offending contraption held up to display by Miss Johnson, whilst Shaista looked on with lively interest.

'It's this sort of wire and — er — boning arrangement,' said Miss Johnson with disapprobation.

Shaista burst into animated explanation.

'But you see my breasts they are not very big — not nearly big enough. I do not look enough like a woman. And it is very important for a girl — to show she is a woman and not a boy.'

'Plenty of time for that. You're only fifteen,' said Miss Johnson.

'Fifteen — that *is* a woman! And I look like a woman, do I not?'

She appealed to Miss Bulstrode who nodded gravely.

'Only my breasts, they are poor. So I want

to make them look not so poor. You understand?'

'I understand perfectly,' said Miss Bulstrode. 'And I quite see your point of view. But in this school, you see, you are amongst girls who are, for the most part, English, and English girls are not very often women at the age of fifteen. I like my girls to use make-up discreetly and to wear clothes suitable to their stage of growth. I suggest that you wear your brassière when you are dressed for a party or for going to London, but not every day here. We do a good deal of sports and games here and for that your body needs to be free to move easily.'

'It is too much — all this running and jumping,' said Shaista sulkily, 'and the P.T. I do not like Miss Springer — she always says, 'Faster, faster, do not slack.' I get tired.'

'That will do, Shaista,' said Miss Bulstrode, her voice becoming authoritative. 'Your family has sent you here to learn English ways. All this exercise will be very good for your complexion, *and* for developing your bust.'

Dismissing Shaista, she smiled at the agitated Miss Johnson.

'It's quite true,' she said. 'The girl is fully mature. She might easily be over twenty by the look of her. And that is what she feels like.

You can't expect her to feel the same age as Julia Upjohn, for instance. Intellectually Julia is far ahead of Shaista. Physically, she could quite well wear a liberty bodice still.'

'I wish they were all like Julia Upjohn,' said Miss Johnson.

'I don't,' said Miss Bulstrode briskly. 'A schoolful of girls all alike would be very dull.'

Dull, she thought, as she went back to her marking of Scripture essays. That word had been repeating itself in her brain for some time now. *Dull* . . .

If there was one thing her school was not, it was dull. During her career as its headmistress, she herself had never felt dull. There had been difficulties to combat, unforeseen crises, irritations with parents, with children: domestic upheavals. She had met and dealt with incipient disasters and turned them into triumphs. It had all been stimulating, exciting, supremely worth while. And even now, though she had made up her mind to it, she did not want to go.

She was physically in excellent health, almost as tough as when she and Chaddy (faithful Chaddy!) had started the great enterprise with a mere handful of children and backing from a banker of unusual foresight. Chaddy's academic distinctions had been better than hers, but it was she who had

had the vision to plan and make of the school a place of such distinction that it was known all over Europe. She had never been afraid to experiment, whereas Chaddy had been content to teach soundly but unexcitingly what she knew. Chaddy's supreme achievement had always been to be *there*, at hand, the faithful buffer, quick to render assistance when assistance was needed. As on the opening day of term with Lady Veronica. It was on her solidity, Miss Bulstrode reflected, that an exciting edifice had been built.

Well, from the material point of view, both women had done very well out of it. If they retired now, they would both have a good assured income for the rest of their lives. Miss Bulstrode wondered if Chaddy would want to retire when she herself did? Probably not. Probably, to her, the school was home. She would continue, faithful and reliable, to buttress up Miss Bulstrode's successor.

Because Miss Bulstrode had made up her mind — a successor there must be. Firstly associated with herself in joint rule and then to rule alone. To know when to go — that was one of the great necessities of life. To go before one's powers began to fail, one's sure grip to loosen, before one felt the faint staleness, the unwillingness to envisage continuing effort.

Miss Bulstrode finished marking the essays and noted that the Upjohn child had an original mind. Jennifer Sutcliffe had a complete lack of imagination, but showed an unusually sound grasp of facts. Mary Vyse, of course, was scholarship class — a wonderful retentive memory. But what a dull girl! Dull — that word again. Miss Bulstrode dismissed it from her mind and rang for her secretary.

She began to dictate letters.

Dear Lady Valence. Jane has had some trouble with her ears. I enclose the doctor's report — etc.

Dear Baron Von Eisenger. We can certainly arrange for Hedwig to go to the Opera on the occasion of Hellstern's taking the role of Isolda —

An hour passed swiftly. Miss Bulstrode seldom paused for a word. Ann Shapland's pencil raced over the pad.

A very good secretary, Miss Bulstrode thought to herself. Better than Vera Lorrimer. Tiresome girl, Vera. Throwing up her post so suddenly. A nervous breakdown, she had said. Something to do with a man, Miss Bulstrode thought resignedly. It was usually a man.

'That's the lot,' said Miss Bulstrode, as she dictated the last word. She heaved a sigh of relief.

'So many dull things to be done,' she

remarked. 'Writing letters to parents is like feeding dogs. Pop some soothing platitude into every waiting mouth.'

Ann laughed. Miss Bulstrode looked at her appraisingly.

'What made you take up secretarial work?'

'I don't quite know. I had no special bent for anything in particular, and it's the sort of thing almost everybody drifts into.'

'You don't find it monotonous?'

'I suppose I've been lucky. I've had a lot of different jobs. I was with Sir Mervyn Todhunter, the archaeologist, for a year, then I was with Sir Andrew Peters in Shell. I was secretary to Monica Lord, the actress, for a while — that really was hectic!' She smiled in remembrance.

'There's a lot of that nowadays amongst you girls,' said Miss Bulstrode. 'All this chopping and changing.' She sounded disapproving.

'Actually, I can't do anything for very long. I've got an invalid mother. She's rather — well — difficult from time to time. And then I have to go back home and take charge.'

'I see.'

'But all the same, I'm afraid I should chop and change anyway. I haven't got the gift for continuity. I find chopping and changing far less dull.'

'Dull . . . ' murmured Miss Bulstrode, struck again by the fatal word.

Ann looked at her in surprise.

'Don't mind me,' said Miss Bulstrode. 'It's just that sometimes one particular word seems to crop up all the time. How would you have liked to be a schoolmistress?' she asked, with some curiosity.

'I'm afraid I should hate it,' said Ann frankly.

'Why?'

'I'd find it terribly dull — Oh, I am sorry.' She stopped in dismay.

'Teaching isn't in the least dull,' said Miss Bulstrode with spirit. 'It can be the most exciting thing in the world. I shall miss it terribly when I retire.'

'But surely — ' Ann stared at her. 'Are you thinking of retiring?'

'It's decided — yes. Oh, I shan't go for another year — or even two years.'

'But — why?'

'Because I've given my best to the school — and had the best from it. I don't want second best.'

'The school will carry on?'

'Oh yes. I have a good successor.'

'Miss Vansittart, I suppose?'

'So you fix on her automatically?' Miss Bulstrode looked at her sharply. 'That's interesting — '

'I'm afraid I hadn't really thought about it. I've just overheard the staff talking. I should think she'll carry on very well — exactly in your tradition. And she's very striking looking, handsome and with quite a presence. I imagine that's important, isn't it?'

'Yes, it is. Yes, I'm sure Eleanor Vansittart is the right person.'

'She'll carry on where you leave off,' said Ann gathering up her things.

But do I want that? thought Miss Bulstrode to herself as Ann went out. Carry on where I leave off? That's just what Eleanor *will* do! No new experiments, nothing revolutionary. That wasn't the way I made Meadowbank what it is. I took chances. I upset lots of people. I bullied and cajoled, and refused to follow the pattern of other schools. Isn't that what I want to follow on here now? Someone to pour new life into the school. Some dynamic personality . . . like — yes — Eileen Rich.

But Eileen wasn't old enough, hadn't enough experience. She was stimulating, though, she could teach. She had ideas. She would never be dull — Nonsense, she must get that word out of her mind. Eleanor Vansittart was not dull . . .

She looked up as Miss Chadwick came in.

'Oh, Chaddy,' she said. 'I *am* pleased to see you!'

Miss Chadwick looked a little surprised.

'Why? Is anything the matter?'

'I'm the matter. I don't know my own mind.'

'That's very unlike you, Honoria.'

'Yes, isn't it? How's the term going, Chaddy?'

'Quite all right, I think.' Miss Chadwick sounded a little unsure.

Miss Bulstrode pounced.

'Now then. Don't hedge. What's wrong?'

'Nothing. Really, Honoria, nothing at all. It's just — ' Miss Chadwick wrinkled up her forehead and looked rather like a perplexed Boxer dog — 'Oh, a feeling. But really it's nothing that I can put a finger on. The new girls seem a pleasant lot. I don't care for Mademoiselle Blanche very much. But then I didn't like Geneviève Depuy, either. *Sly*.'

Miss Bulstrode did not pay very much attention to this criticism. Chaddy always accused the French mistresses of being sly.

'She's not a good teacher,' said Miss Bulstrode. 'Surprising really. Her testimonials were so good.'

'The French never can teach. No discipline,' said Miss Chadwick. 'And really Miss Springer is a little too much of a good thing! Leaps about so. Springer by nature as well as by name . . .'

101

'She's good at her job.'

'Oh yes, first class.'

'New staff is always upsetting,' said Miss Bulstrode.

'Yes,' agreed Miss Chadwick eagerly. 'I'm sure it's nothing more than that. By the way, that new gardener is quite young. So unusual nowadays. No gardeners seem to be young. A pity he's so good-looking. We shall have to keep a sharp eye open.'

The two ladies nodded their heads in agreement. They knew, none better, the havoc caused by a good-looking young man to the hearts of adolescent girls.

7

Straws in the Wind

I

'Not too bad, boy,' said old Briggs grudgingly, 'not too bad.'

He was expressing approval of his new assistant's performance in digging a strip of ground. It wouldn't do, thought Briggs, to let the young fellow get above himself.

'Mind you,' he went on, 'you don't want to rush at things. Take it steady, that's what I say. Steady is what does it.'

The young man understood that his performance had compared rather too favourably with Briggs's own tempo of work.

'Now, along this here,' continued Briggs, 'we'll put some nice asters out. *She* don't like asters — but I pay no attention. Females has their whims, but if you don't pay no attention, ten to one they never notice. Though I will say *She* is the noticing kind on the whole. You'd think she 'ad enough to bother her head about, running a place like this.'

Adam understood that 'She' who figured so largely in Briggs's conversation referred to Miss Bulstrode.

'And who was it I saw you talking to just now?' went on Briggs suspiciously, 'when you went along to the potting shed for them bamboos?'

'Oh, that was just one of the young ladies,' said Adam.

'Ah. One of them two Eye-ties, wasn't it? Now you be careful, my boy. Don't you get mixed up with no Eye-ties, I know what I'm talkin' about. I knew Eye-ties, I did, in the first war and if I'd known then what I know now I'd have been more careful. See?'

'Wasn't no harm in it,' said Adam, putting on a sulky manner. 'Just passed the time of day with me, she did, and asked the names of one or two things.'

'Ah,' said Briggs, 'but you be careful. It's not your place to talk to any of the young ladies. *She* wouldn't like it.'

'I wasn't doing no harm and I didn't say anything I shouldn't.'

'I don't say you did, boy. But I say a lot o' young females penned up together here with not so much as a drawing master to take their minds off things — well, you'd better be careful. That's all. Ah, here comes the Old

Bitch now. Wanting something difficult, I'll be bound.'

Miss Bulstrode was approaching with a rapid step. 'Good morning, Briggs,' she said. 'Good morning — er — '

'Adam, miss.'

'Ah yes, Adam. Well, you seem to have got that piece dug very satisfactorily. The wire netting's coming down by the far tennis court, Briggs. You'd better attend to that.'

'All right, ma'am, all right. It'll be seen to.'

'What are you putting in front here?'

'Well ma'am, I had thought — '

'*Not* asters,' said Miss Bulstrode, without giving him time to finish. 'Pom Pom dahlias,' and she departed briskly.

'Coming along — giving orders,' said Briggs. 'Not that she isn't a sharp one. She soon notices if you haven't done work properly. And remember what I've said and be careful, boy. About Eye-ties and the others.'

'If she's any fault to find with me, I'll soon know what I can do,' said Adam sulkily. 'Plenty o' jobs going.'

'Ah. That's like you young men all over nowadays. Won't take a word from anybody. All I say is, mind your step.'

Adam continued to look sulky, but bent to his work once more.

105

Miss Bulstrode walked back along the path towards the school. She was frowning a little.

Miss Vansittart was coming in the opposite direction.

'What a hot afternoon,' said Miss Vansittart.

'Yes, it's very sultry and oppressive.' Again Miss Bulstrode frowned. 'Have you noticed that young man — the young gardener?'

'No, not particularly.'

'He seems to me — well — an odd type,' said Miss Bulstrode thoughtfully. 'Not the usual kind around here.'

'Perhaps he's just come down from Oxford and wants to make a little money.'

'He's good-looking. The girls notice him.'

'The usual problem.'

Miss Bulstrode smiled. 'To combine freedom for the girls *and* strict supervision — is that what you mean, Eleanor?'

'Yes.'

'We manage,' said Miss Bulstrode.

'Yes, indeed. You've never had a scandal at Meadowbank, have you?'

'We've come near it once or twice,' said Miss Bulstrode. She laughed. 'Never a dull moment in running a school.' She went on, 'Do you ever find life dull here, Eleanor?'

'No indeed,' said Miss Vansittart. 'I find the work here most stimulating and satisfying.

106

You must feel very proud and happy, Honoria, at the great success you have achieved.'

'I think I made a good job of things,' said Miss Bulstrode thoughtfully. 'Nothing, of course, is ever quite as one first imagined it . . .

'Tell me, Eleanor,' she said suddenly, 'if you were running this place instead of me, what changes would you make? Don't mind saying. I shall be interested to hear.'

'I don't think I should want to make any changes,' said Eleanor Vansittart. 'It seems to me the spirit of the place and the whole organization is well-nigh perfect.'

'You'd carry on on the same lines, you mean?'

'Yes, indeed. I don't think they could be bettered.'

Miss Bulstrode was silent for a moment. She was thinking to herself: I wonder if she said that in order to please me. One never knows with people. However close to them you may have been for years. Surely, she can't really mean that. Anybody with any creative feeling at all *must* want to make changes. It's true, though, that it mightn't have seemed tactful to say so . . . And tact *is* very important. It's important with parents, it's important with the girls, it's important with

107

the staff. Eleanor certainly has tact.

Aloud, she said, 'There must always be adjustments, though, mustn't there? I mean with changing ideas and conditions of life generally.'

'Oh, that, yes,' said Miss Vansittart. 'One has, as they say, to go with the times. But it's *your* school, Honoria, you've made it what it is and your traditions are the essence of it. I think tradition is very important, don't you?'

Miss Bulstrode did not answer. She was hovering on the brink of irrevocable words. The offer of a partnership hung in the air. Miss Vansittart, though seeming unaware in her well-bred way, must be conscious of the fact that it was there. Miss Bulstrode did not know really what was holding her back. Why did she so dislike to commit herself? Probably, she admitted ruefully, because she hated the idea of giving up control. Secretly, of course, she wanted to stay, she wanted to go on running her school. But surely nobody could be a worthier successor than Eleanor? So dependable, so reliable. Of course, as far as that went, so was dear Chaddy — reliable as they came. And yet you could never envisage Chaddy as headmistress of an outstanding school.

'What *do* I want?' said Miss Bulstrode to herself. 'How tiresome I am being! Really, indecision has never been one of my faults up to now.'

A bell sounded in the distance.

'My German class,' said Miss Vansittart. 'I must go in.' She moved at a rapid but dignified step towards the school buildings. Following her more slowly, Miss Bulstrode almost collided with Eileen Rich, hurrying from a side path.

'Oh, I'm so sorry, Miss Bulstrode. I didn't see you.' Her hair, as usual, was escaping from its untidy bun. Miss Bulstrode noted anew the ugly but interesting bones of her face, a strange, eager, compelling young woman.

'You've got a class?'

'Yes. English — '

'You enjoy teaching, don't you?' said Miss Bulstrode.

'I love it. It's the most fascinating thing in the world.'

'Why?'

Eileen Rich stopped dead. She ran a hand through her hair. She frowned with the effort of thought.

'How interesting. I don't know that I've really *thought* about it. Why *does* one like teaching? Is it because it makes one feel grand and important? No, no . . . it's not as bad as that. No, it's more like fishing, I think.

You don't know what catch you're going to get, what you're going to drag up from the sea. It's the quality of the *response*. It's so exciting when it comes. It doesn't very often, of course.'

Miss Bulstrode nodded in agreement. She had been right! This girl had something!

'I expect you'll run a school of your own some day,' she said.

'Oh, I hope so,' said Eileen Rich. 'I do hope so. That's what I'd like above anything.'

'You've got ideas already, haven't you, as to how a school should be run?'

'Everyone has ideas, I suppose,' said Eileen Rich. 'I daresay a great many of them are fantastic and they'd go utterly wrong. That would be a risk, of course. But one would have to try them out. I would have to learn by experience . . . The awful thing is that one can't go by other people's experience, can one?'

'Not really,' said Miss Bulstrode. 'In life one has to make one's own mistakes.'

'That's all right in life,' said Eileen Rich. 'In life you can pick yourself up and start again.' Her hands, hanging at her sides, clenched themselves into fists. Her expression was grim. Then suddenly it relaxed into humour. 'But if a school's gone to pieces, you can't very well pick that up and start again, can you?'

'If *you* ran a school like Meadowbank,' said Miss Bulstrode, 'would you make changes — experiment?'

Eileen Rich looked embarrassed. 'That's — that's an awfully hard thing to say,' she said.

'You mean you would,' said Miss Bulstrode. 'Don't mind speaking your mind, child.'

'One would always want, I suppose, to use one's own ideas,' said Eileen Rich. 'I don't say they'd work. They mightn't.'

'But it would be worth taking a risk?'

'It's always worth taking a risk, isn't it?' said Eileen Rich. 'I mean if you feel strongly enough about anything.'

'You don't object to leading a dangerous life. I see . . . ' said Miss Bulstrode.

'I think I've always led a dangerous life.' A shadow passed over the girl's face. 'I must go. They'll be waiting.' She hurried off.

Miss Bulstrode stood looking after her. She was still standing there lost in thought when Miss Chadwick came hurrying to find her.

'Oh! there you are. We've been looking everywhere for you. Professor Anderson has just rung up. He wants to know if he can take Meroe this next weekend. He knows it's against the rules so soon but he's going off quite suddenly to — somewhere that sounds like Azure Basin.'

111

'Azerbaijan,' said Miss Bulstrode automatically, her mind still on her own thoughts.

'Not enough experience,' she murmured to herself. 'That's the risk. What did you say, Chaddy?'

Miss Chadwick repeated the message.

'I told Miss Shapland to say that we'd ring him back, and sent her to find you.'

'Say it will be quite all right,' said Miss Bulstrode. 'I recognize that this is an exceptional occasion.'

Miss Chadwick looked at her keenly.

'You're worrying, Honoria.'

'Yes, I am. I don't really know my own mind. That's unusual for me — and it upsets me . . . I know what I'd like to do — but I feel that to hand over to someone without the necessary experience wouldn't be fair to the school.'

'I wish you'd give up this idea of retirement. You belong here. Meadowbank needs you.'

'Meadowbank means a lot to you, Chaddy, doesn't it?'

'There's no school like it anywhere in England,' said Miss Chadwick. 'We can be proud of ourselves, you and I, for having started it.'

Miss Bulstrode put an affectionate arm round her shoulders. 'We can indeed,

112

Chaddy. As for you, you're the comfort of my life. There's nothing about Meadowbank you don't know. You care for it as much as I do. And that's saying a lot, my dear.'

Miss Chadwick flushed with pleasure. It was so seldom that Honoria Bulstrode broke through her reserve.

II

'I simply can't play with the beastly thing. It's no good.'

Jennifer flung her racquet down in despair.

'Oh, Jennifer, what a fuss you make.'

'It's the balance,' Jennifer picked it up again and waggled it experimentally. 'It doesn't balance right.'

'It's much better than my old thing,' Julia compared her racquet. 'Mine's like a sponge. Listen to the sound of it.' She twanged. 'We meant to have it restrung, but Mummy forgot.'

'I'd rather have it than mine, all the same.' Jennifer took it and tried a swish or two with it.

'Well, I'd rather have *yours*. I could really hit something then. I'll swap, if you will.'

'All right then, swap.'

The two girls peeled off the small pieces of

adhesive plaster on which their names were written, and re-affixed them, each to the other's racquet.

'I'm not going to swap back again,' said Julia warningly. 'So it's no use saying you don't like my old sponge.'

III

Adam whistled cheerfully as he tacked up the wire netting round the tennis court. The door of the Sports Pavilion opened and Mademoiselle Blanche, the little mousy French Mistress, looked out. She seemed startled at the sight of Adam. She hesitated for a moment and then went back inside.

'Wonder what she's been up to,' said Adam to himself. It would not have occurred to him that Mademoiselle Blanche had been up to anything, if it had not been for her manner. She had a guilty look which immediately roused surmise in his mind. Presently she came out again, closing the door behind her, and paused to speak as she passed him.

'Ah, you repair the netting, I see.'

'Yes, miss.'

'They are very fine courts here, and the swimming pool and the pavilion too. Oh! *le*

114

sport! You think a lot in England of *le sport*, do you not?'

'Well, I suppose we do, miss.'

'Do you play tennis yourself?' Her eyes appraised him in a definitely feminine way and with a faint invitation in her glance. Adam wondered once more about her. It struck him that Mademoiselle Blanche was a somewhat unsuitable French Mistress for Meadowbank.

'No,' he said untruthfully, 'I don't play tennis. Haven't got the time.'

'You play cricket, then?'

'Oh well, I played cricket as a boy. Most chaps do.'

'I have not had much time to look around,' said Angèle Blanche. 'Not until today and it was so fine I thought I would like to examine the Sports Pavilion. I wish to write home to my friends in France who keep a school.'

Again Adam wondered a little. It seemed a lot of unnecessary explanation. It was almost as though Mademoiselle Blanche wished to excuse her presence out here at the Sports Pavilion. But why should she? She had a perfect right to go anywhere in the school grounds that she pleased. There was certainly no need to apologize for it to a gardener's assistant. It raised queries again in his mind. What had this young woman been doing in

115

the Sports Pavilion?

He looked thoughtfully at Mademoiselle Blanche. It would be a good thing perhaps to know a little more about her. Subtly, deliberately, his manner changed. It was still respectful but not quite so respectful. He permitted his eyes to tell her that she was an attractive-looking young woman.

'You must find it a bit dull sometimes working in a girls' school, miss,' he said.

'It does not amuse me very much, no.'

'Still,' said Adam, 'I suppose you get your times off, don't you?'

There was a slight pause. It was as though she were debating with herself. Then, he felt it was with slight regret, the distance between them was deliberately widened.

'Oh yes,' she said, 'I have adequate time off. The conditions of employment here are excellent.' She gave him a little nod of the head. 'Good morning.' She walked off towards the house.

'You've been up to something,' said Adam to himself, 'in the Sports Pavilion.'

He waited till she was out of sight, then he left his work, went across to the Sports Pavilion and looked inside. But nothing that he could see was out of place. 'All the same,' he said to himself, 'she was up to something.'

As he came out again, he was confronted

unexpectedly by Ann Shapland.

'Do you know where Miss Bulstrode is?' she asked.

'I think she's gone back to the house, miss. She was talking to Briggs just now.'

Ann was frowning.

'What are you doing in the Sports Pavilion?'

Adam was slightly taken aback. Nasty suspicious mind *she's* got, he thought. He said, with a faint insolence in his voice:

'Thought I'd like to take a look at it. No harm in looking, is there?'

'Oughtn't you to be getting on with your work?'

'I've just about finished nailing the wire round the tennis court.' He turned, looking up at the building behind him. 'This is new, isn't it? Must have cost a packet. The best of everything the young ladies here get, don't they?'

'They pay for it,' said Ann dryly.

'Pay through the nose, so I've heard,' agreed Adam.

He felt a desire he hardly understood himself, to wound or annoy this girl. She was so cool always, so self-sufficient. He would really enjoy seeing her angry.

But Ann did not give him that satisfaction. She merely said:

'You'd better finish tacking up the netting,' and went back towards the house. Half-way there, she slackened speed and looked back. Adam was busy at the tennis wire. She looked from him to the Sports Pavilion in a puzzled manner.

8

Murder

I

On night duty in Hurst St Cyprian Police Station, Sergeant Green yawned. The telephone rang and he picked up the receiver. A moment later his manner had changed completely. He began scribbling rapidly on a pad.

'Yes? Meadowbank? Yes — and the name? Spell it, please. S-P-R-I-N-G-for greengage?-E-R. Springer. Yes. Yes, please see that nothing is disturbed. Someone'll be with you very shortly.'

Rapidly and methodically he then proceeded to put into motion the various procedures indicated.

'Meadowbank?' said Detective Inspector Kelsey when his turn came. 'That's the girls' school, isn't it? Who is it who's been murdered?'

'Death of a Games Mistress,' said Kelsey, thoughtfully. 'Sounds like the title of a thriller on a railway bookstall.'

119

'Who's likely to have done her in, d'you think?' said the Sergeant. 'Seems unnatural.'

'Even Games Mistresses may have their love lives,' said Detective Inspector Kelsey. 'Where did they say the body was found?'

'In the Sports Pavilion. I suppose that's a fancy name for the gymnasium.'

'Could be,' said Kelsey. 'Death of a Games Mistress in the Gymnasium. Sounds a highly athletic crime, doesn't it? Did you say she was shot?'

'Yes.'

'They find the pistol?'

'No.'

'Interesting,' said Detective Inspector Kelsey, and having assembled his retinue, he departed to carry out his duties.

II

The front door at Meadowbank was open, with light streaming from it, and here Inspector Kelsey was received by Miss Bulstrode herself. He knew her by sight, as indeed most people in the neighbourhood did. Even in this moment of confusion and uncertainty, Miss Bulstrode remained eminently herself, in command of the situation and in command of her subordinates.

120

'Detective Inspector Kelsey, madam,' said the Inspector.

'What would you like to do first, Inspector Kelsey? Do you wish to go out to the Sports Pavilion or do you want to hear full details?'

'The doctor is with me,' said Kelsey. 'If you will show him and two of my men to where the body is, I should like a few words with you.'

'Certainly. Come into my sitting-room. Miss Rowan, will you show the doctor and the others the way?' She added, 'One of my staff is out there seeing that nothing is disturbed.'

'Thank you, madam.'

Kelsey followed Miss Bulstrode into her sitting-room. 'Who found the body?'

'The matron, Miss Johnson. One of the girls had earache and Miss Johnson was up attending to her. As she did so, she noticed the curtains were not pulled properly and going to pull them she observed that there was a light on in the Sports Pavilion which there should not have been at 1 a.m.,' finished Miss Bulstrode dryly.

'Quite so,' said Kelsey. 'Where is Miss Johnson now?'

'She is here if you want to see her?'

'Presently. Will you go on, madam.'

'Miss Johnson went and woke up another

member of my staff, Miss Chadwick. They decided to go out and investigate. As they were leaving by the side door they heard the sound of a shot, whereupon they ran as quickly as they could towards the Sports Pavilion. On arrival there — '

The Inspector broke in. 'Thank you, Miss Bulstrode. If, as you say, Miss Johnson is available, I will hear the next part from her. But first, perhaps, you will tell me something about the murdered woman.'

'Her name is Grace Springer.'

'She has been with you long?'

'No. She came to me this term. My former Games Mistress left to take up a post in Australia.'

'And what did you know about this Miss Springer?'

'Her testimonials were excellent,' said Miss Bulstrode.

'You didn't know her personally before that?'

'No.'

'Have you any idea at all, even the vaguest, of what might have precipitated this tragedy? Was she unhappy? Any unfortunate entanglements?'

Miss Bulstrode shook her head. 'Nothing that I know of. I may say,' she went on, 'that it seems to me most unlikely. She was not that kind of a woman.'

'You'd be surprised,' said Inspector Kelsey darkly.

'Would you like me to fetch Miss Johnson now?'

'If you please. When I've heard her story I'll go out to the gym — or the — what d'you call it — Sports Pavilion?'

'It is a newly built addition to the school this year,' said Miss Bulstrode. 'It is built adjacent to the swimming pool and it comprises a squash court and other features. The racquets, lacrosse and hockey sticks are kept there, and there is a drying room for swim suits.'

'Was there any reason why Miss Springer should be in the Sports Pavilion at night?'

'None whatever,' said Miss Bulstrode unequivocally.

'Very well, Miss Bulstrode. I'll talk to Miss Johnson now.'

Miss Bulstrode left the room and returned bringing the matron with her. Miss Johnson had had a sizeable dollop of brandy administered to her to pull her together after her discovery of the body. The result was a slightly added loquacity.

'This is Detective Inspector Kelsey,' said Miss Bulstrode. 'Pull yourself together, Elspeth, and tell him exactly what happened.'

123

'It's dreadful,' said Miss Johnson, 'it's really dreadful. Such a thing has never happened before in all my experience. Never! I couldn't have believed it, I really couldn't've believed it. Miss Springer too!'

Inspector Kelsey was a perceptive man. He was always willing to deviate from the course of routine if a remark struck him as unusual or worth following up.

'It seems to you, does it,' he said, 'very strange that it was Miss Springer who was murdered?'

'Well yes, it does, Inspector. She was so — well, so tough, you know. So hearty. Like the sort of woman one could imagine taking on a burglar single-handed — or two burglars.'

'Burglars? H'm,' said Inspector Kelsey. 'Was there anything to steal in the Sports Pavilion?'

'Well, no, really I can't see what there can have been. Swim suits of course, sports paraphernalia.'

'The sort of thing a sneak-thief might have taken,' agreed Kelsey. 'Hardly worth breaking in for, I should have thought. Was it broken into, by the way?'

'Well, really, I never thought to look,' said Miss Johnson. 'I mean, the door was open when we got there and — '

'It had not been broken into,' said Miss Bulstrode.

'I see,' said Kelsey. 'A key was used.' He looked at Miss Johnson. 'Was Miss Springer well liked?' he asked.

'Well, really, I couldn't say. I mean, after all, she's dead.'

'So, you didn't like her,' said Kelsey perceptively, ignoring Miss Johnson's finer feelings.

'I don't think anyone could have liked her very much,' said Miss Johnson. 'She had a very positive manner, you know. Never minded contradicting people flatly. She was very efficient and took her work very seriously I should say, wouldn't you, Miss Bulstrode?'

'Certainly,' said Miss Bulstrode.

Kelsey returned from the by-path he had been pursuing. 'Now, Miss Johnson, let's hear just what happened.'

'Jane, one of our pupils, had earache. She woke up with a rather bad attack of it and came to me. I got some remedies and when I'd got her back to bed, I saw the window curtains were flapping and thought perhaps it would be better for once if her window was not opened at night as it was blowing rather in that direction. Of course the girls always sleep with their windows open. We have difficulties sometimes with the foreigners, but

I always insist that — '

'That really doesn't matter now,' said Miss Bulstrode. 'Our general rules of hygiene would not interest Inspector Kelsey.'

'No, no, of course not,' said Miss Johnson. 'Well, as I say I went to shut the window and what was my surprise to see a light in the Sports Pavilion. It was quite distinct, I couldn't mistake it. It seemed to be moving about.'

'You mean it was not the electric light turned on but the light of a torch or flashlight?'

'Yes, yes, that's what it must have been. I thought at once 'Dear me, what's anyone doing out there at this time of night?' Of course I didn't think of burglars. That would have been a very fanciful idea, as you said just now.'

'What did you think of?' asked Kelsey.

Miss Johnson shot a glance at Miss Bulstrode and back again.

'Well, really, I don't know that I had any ideas in particular. I mean, well — well really, I mean I couldn't think — '

Miss Bulstrode broke in. 'I should imagine that Miss Johnson had the idea that one of our pupils might have gone out there to keep an assignation with someone,' she said. 'Is that right, Elspeth?'

Miss Johnson gasped. 'Well, yes, the idea did come into my head just for the moment. One of our Italian girls, perhaps. Foreigners are so much more precocious than English girls.'

'Don't be so insular,' said Miss Bulstrode. 'We've had plenty of English girls trying to make unsuitable assignations. It was a very natural thought to have occurred to you and probably the one that would have occurred to me.'

'Go on,' said Inspector Kelsey.

'So I thought the best thing,' went on Miss Johnson, 'was to go to Miss Chadwick and ask her to come out with me and see what was going on.'

'Why Miss Chadwick?' asked Kelsey. 'Any particular reason for selecting that particular mistress?'

'Well, I didn't want to disturb Miss Bulstrode,' said Miss Johnson, 'and I'm afraid it's rather a habit of ours always to go to Miss Chadwick if we don't want to disturb Miss Bulstrode. You see, Miss Chadwick's been here a very long time and has had so much experience.'

'Anyway,' said Kelsey, 'you went to Miss Chadwick and woke her up. Is that right?'

'Yes. She agreed with me that we must go out there immediately. We didn't wait to dress or anything, just put on pullovers and coats and went out by the side door. And it was then, just as we were standing on the path, that we heard a shot from the Sports Pavilion. So we ran along the path as fast as we could. Rather stupidly we hadn't taken a torch with us and it was hard to see where we were going. We stumbled once or twice but we got there quite quickly. The door was open. We switched on the light and — '

Kelsey interrupted. 'There was no light then when you got there. Not a torch or any other light?'

'No. The place was in darkness. We switched on the light and there she was. She — '

'That's all right,' said Inspector Kelsey kindly, 'you needn't describe anything. I shall be going out there now and I shall see for myself. You didn't meet anyone on your way there?'

'No.'

'Or hear anybody running away?'

'No. We didn't hear anything.'

'Did anybody else hear the shot in the school building?' asked Kelsey looking at Miss Bulstrode.

She shook her head. 'No. Not that I know of. Nobody has said that they heard it. The Sports Pavilion is some distance away and I rather doubt if the shot would be noticeable.'

'Perhaps from one of the rooms on the side of the house giving on the Sports Pavilion?'

'Hardly, I think, unless one were listening for such a thing. I'm sure it wouldn't be loud enough to wake anybody up.'

'Well, thank you,' said Inspector Kelsey. 'I'll be going out to the Sports Pavilion now.'

'I will come with you,' said Miss Bulstrode.

'Do you want me to come too?' asked Miss Johnson. 'I will if you like. I mean it's no good shirking things, is it? I always feel that one must face whatever comes and — '

'Thank you,' said Inspector Kelsey, 'there's no need, Miss Johnson. I wouldn't think of putting you to any further strain.'

'So awful,' said Miss Johnson, 'it makes it worse to feel I didn't like her very much. In fact, we had a disagreement only last night in the Common Room. I stuck to it that too much P.T. was bad for some girls — the more delicate girls. Miss Springer said nonsense, that they were just the ones who needed it. Toned them up and made new women of them, she said. I said to her that really she didn't know everything though she might think she did. After all I have been professionally trained and I know a great deal more about delicacy and illness than Miss Springer does — did, though I've no doubt that Miss Springer knows everything about parallel bars and vaulting horses and coaching tennis. But, oh dear, now I think of what's happened, I wish I hadn't said quite what I did. I suppose one always feels like that afterwards when something dreadful has occurred. I really do blame myself.'

'Now sit down there, dear,' said Miss Bulstrode, settling her on the sofa. 'You just sit down and rest and pay no attention to any little disputes you may have had. Life would be very dull if we agreed with each other on every subject.'

Miss Johnson sat down shaking her head, then yawned. Miss Bulstrode followed Kelsey into the hall.

'I gave her rather a lot of brandy,' she said, apologetically. 'It's made her a little voluble. But not confused, do you think?'

'No,' said Kelsey. 'She gave quite a clear account of what happened.'

Miss Bulstrode led the way to the side door.

'Is this the way Miss Johnson and Miss Chadwick went out?'

'Yes. You see it leads straight on to the path through the rhododendrons there which comes out at the Sports Pavilion.'

The Inspector had a powerful torch and he and Miss Bulstrode soon reached the building where the lights were now glaring.

'Fine bit of building,' said Kelsey, looking at it.

'It cost us a pretty penny,' said Miss Bulstrode, 'but we can afford it,' she added serenely.

The open door led into a fair-sized room. There were lockers there with the names of the various girls on them. At the end of the room there was a stand for tennis racquets and one for lacrosse sticks. The door at the side led off to showers and changing cubicles. Kelsey paused before going in. Two of his men had been busy. A photographer had just finished his job and another man who was busy testing for fingerprints looked up and said,

'You can walk straight across the floor, sir. You'll be all right. We haven't finished down this end yet.'

Kelsey walked forward to where the police surgeon was kneeling by the body. The latter looked up as Kelsey approached.

'She was shot from about four feet away,' he said.

'Bullet penetrated the heart. Death must have been pretty well instantaneous.'

'Yes. How long ago?'

'Say an hour or thereabouts.'

Kelsey nodded. He strolled round to look

at the tall figure of Miss Chadwick where she stood grimly, like a watchdog, against one wall. About fifty-five, he judged, good forehead, obstinate mouth, untidy grey hair, no trace of hysteria. The kind of woman, he thought, who could be depended upon in a crisis though she might be overlooked in ordinary everyday life.

'Miss Chadwick?' he said.

'Yes.'

'You came out with Miss Johnson and discovered the body?'

'Yes. She was just as she is now. She was dead.'

'And the time?'

'I looked at my watch when Miss Johnson roused me. It was ten minutes to one.'

Kelsey nodded. That agreed with the time that Miss Johnson had given him. He looked down thoughtfully at the dead woman. Her bright red hair was cut short. She had a freckled face, with a chin which jutted out strongly, and a spare, athletic figure. She was wearing a tweed skirt and a heavy, dark pullover. She had brogues on her feet with no stockings.

'Any sign of the weapon?' asked Kelsey.

One of his men shook his head. 'No sign at all, sir.'

'What about the torch?'

'There's a torch there in the corner.'

'Any prints on it?'

'Yes. The dead woman's.'

'So she's the one who had the torch,' said Kelsey thoughtfully. 'She came out here with a torch — why?' He asked it partly of himself, partly of his men, partly of Miss Bulstrode and Miss Chadwick. Finally he seemed to concentrate on the latter. 'Any ideas?'

Miss Chadwick shook her head. 'No idea at all. I suppose she might have left something here — forgotten it this afternoon or evening — and come out to fetch it. But it seems rather unlikely in the middle of the night.'

'It must have been something very important if she did,' said Kelsey.

He looked round him. Nothing seemed disturbed except the stand of racquets at the end. That seemed to have been pulled violently forward. Several of the racquets were lying about on the floor.

'Of course,' said Miss Chadwick, 'she could have seen a light here, like Miss Johnson did later, and have come out to investigate. That seems the most likely thing to me.'

'I think you're right,' said Kelsey. 'There's just one small matter. Would she have come out here alone?'

'Yes.' Miss Chadwick answered without hesitation.

'Miss Johnson,' Kelsey reminded her, 'came and woke you up.'

'I know,' said Miss Chadwick, 'and that's what I should have done if I'd seen the light. I would have woken up Miss Bulstrode or Miss Vansittart or somebody. But Miss Springer wouldn't. She would have been quite confident — indeed would have preferred to tackle an intruder on her own.'

'Another point,' said the Inspector. 'You came out through the side door with Miss Johnson. Was the side door unlocked?'

'Yes, it was.'

'Presumably left unlocked by Miss Springer?'

'That seems the natural conclusion,' said Miss Chadwick.

'So we assume,' said Kelsey, 'that Miss Springer saw a light out here in the gymnasium — Sports Pavilion — whatever you call it — that she came out to investigate and that whoever was here shot her.' He wheeled round on Miss Bulstrode as she stood motionless in the doorway. 'Does that seem right to you?' he asked.

'It doesn't seem right at all,' said Miss Bulstrode. 'I grant you the first part. We'll say Miss Springer saw a light out here and that she went out to investigate by herself. That's perfectly probable. But that the person she disturbed here should shoot her — that seems

134

to me all wrong. If anyone was here who had no business to be here they would be more likely to run away, or to try to run away. Why should someone come to this place at this hour of night with a pistol? It's ridiculous, that's what it is. Ridiculous! There's nothing here worth stealing, certainly nothing for which it would be worth while doing murder.'

'You think it more likely that Miss Springer disturbed a rendezvous of some kind?'

'That's the natural and most probable explanation,' said Miss Bulstrode. 'But it doesn't explain the fact of murder, does it? Girls in my school don't carry pistols about with them and any young man they might be meeting seems very unlikely to have a pistol either.'

Kelsey agreed. 'He'd have had a flick knife at most,' he said. 'There's an alternative,' he went on. 'Say Miss Springer came out here to meet a man — '

Miss Chadwick giggled suddenly. 'Oh no,' she said, 'not Miss Springer.'

'I do not mean necessarily an amorous assignment,' said the Inspector dryly. 'I'm suggesting that the murder was deliberate, that someone intended to murder Miss Springer, that they arranged to meet her here and shot her.'

9

Cat Among the Pigeons

I

Letter from Jennifer Sutcliffe to her mother:

Dear Mummy,
We had a murder last night. Miss
Springer, the gym mistress. It happened
in the middle of the night and the police
came and this morning they're asking
everybody questions.
Miss Chadwick told us not to talk to
anybody about it but I thought you'd like
to know.
With love,
Jennifer

II

Meadowbank was an establishment of sufficient importance to merit the personal
attention of the Chief Constable. While
routine investigation was going on Miss

136

Bulstrode had not been inactive. She rang up a Press magnate and the Home Secretary, both personal friends of hers. As a result of those manoeuvres, very little had appeared about the event in the papers. A games mistress had been found dead in the school gymnasium. She had been shot, whether by accident or not was as yet not determined. Most of the notices of the event had an almost apologetic note in them, as though it were thoroughly tactless of any games mistress to get herself shot in such circumstances.

Ann Shapland had a busy day taking down letters to parents. Miss Bulstrode did not waste time in telling her pupils to keep quiet about the event. She knew that it would be a waste of time. More or less lurid reports would be sure to be penned to anxious parents and guardians. She intended her own balanced and reasonable account of the tragedy to reach them at the same time.

Later that afternoon she sat in conclave with Mr Stone, the Chief Constable, and Inspector Kelsey. The police were perfectly amenable to having the Press play the thing down as much as possible. It enabled them to pursue their inquiries quietly and without interference.

'I'm very sorry about this, Miss Bulstrode,

very sorry indeed,' said the Chief Constable. 'I suppose it's — well — a bad thing for you.'

'Murder's a bad thing for any school, yes,' said Miss Bulstrode. 'It's no good dwelling on that now, though. We shall weather it, no doubt, as we have weathered other storms. All I do hope is that the matter will be cleared up *quickly*.'

'Don't see why it shouldn't, eh?' said Stone. He looked at Kelsey.

Kelsey said, 'It may help when we get her background.'

'D'you really think so?' asked Miss Bulstrode dryly.

'Somebody may have had it in for her,' Kelsey suggested.

Miss Bulstrode did not reply.

'You think it's tied up with this place?' asked the Chief Constable.

'Inspector Kelsey does really,' said Miss Bulstrode. 'He's only trying to save my feelings, I think.'

'I think it does tie up with Meadowbank,' said the Inspector slowly. 'After all, Miss Springer had her times off like all the other members of the staff. She could have arranged a meeting with anyone if she had wanted to do so at any spot she chose. Why choose the gymnasium here in the middle of the night?'

'You have no objection to a search being made of the school premises, Miss Bulstrode?' asked the Chief Constable.

'None at all. You're looking for the pistol or revolver or whatever it is, I suppose?'

'Yes. It was a small pistol of foreign make.'

'Foreign,' said Miss Bulstrode thoughtfully.

'To your knowledge, do any of your staff or any of the pupils have such a thing as a pistol in their possession?'

'Certainly not to my knowledge,' said Miss Bulstrode. 'I am fairly certain that none of the pupils have. Their possessions are unpacked for them when they arrive and such a thing would have been seen and noted, and would, I may say, have aroused considerable comment. But please, Inspector Kelsey, do exactly as you like in that respect. I see your men have been searching the grounds today.'

The Inspector nodded. 'Yes.'

He went on: 'I should also like interviews with the other members of your staff. One or other of them may have heard some remark made by Miss Springer that will give us a clue. Or may have observed some oddity of behaviour on her part.'

He paused, then went on, 'The same thing might apply to the pupils.'

Miss Bulstrode said: 'I had formed the plan of making a short address to the girls this evening after prayers. I would ask that if any of them has any knowledge that might possibly bear upon Miss Springer's death that they should come and tell me of it.'

'Very sound idea,' said the Chief Constable.

'But you must remember this,' said Miss Bulstrode, 'one or other of the girls may wish to make herself important by exaggerating some incident or even by inventing one. Girls do very odd things: but I expect you are used to dealing with that form of exhibitionism.'

'I've come across it,' said Inspector Kelsey. 'Now,' he added, 'please give me a list of your staff, also the servants.'

III

'I've looked through all the lockers in the Pavilion, sir.'

'And you didn't find anything?' said Kelsey.

'No, sir, nothing of importance. Funny things in some of them, but nothing in our line.'

'None of them were locked, were they?'

'No, sir, they can lock. There were keys in them, but none of them were locked.'

Kelsey looked round the bare floor thoughtfully. The tennis and lacrosse sticks had been replaced tidily on their stands.

'Oh well,' he said, 'I'm going up to the house now to have a talk with the staff.'

'You don't think it was an inside job, sir?'

'It could have been,' said Kelsey. 'Nobody's got an alibi except those two mistresses, Chadwick and Johnson and the child Jane that had the earache. Theoretically, everyone else was in bed and asleep, but there's no one to vouch for that. The girls all have separate rooms and naturally the staff do. Any one of them, including Miss Bulstrode herself, could have come out and met Springer here, or could have followed her here. Then, after she'd been shot, whoever it was could dodge back quietly through the bushes to the side door, and be nicely back in bed again when the alarm was given. It's motive that's difficult. Yes,' said Kelsey, 'it's motive. Unless there's something going on here that we don't know anything about, there doesn't seem to be any motive.'

He stepped out of the Pavilion and made his way slowly back to the house. Although it was past working hours, old Briggs, the gardener, was putting in a little work on a flower bed and he straightened up as the Inspector passed.

'You work late hours,' said Kelsey, smiling.

'Ah,' said Briggs. 'Young 'uns don't know what gardening is. Come on at eight and knock off at five — that's what they think it is. You've got to study your weather, some days you might as well not be out in the garden at all, and there's other days as you can work from seven in the morning until eight at night. That is if you love the place and have pride in the look of it.'

'You ought to be proud of this one,' said Kelsey. 'I've never seen any place better kept these days.'

'These days is right,' said Briggs. 'But I'm lucky I am. I've got a strong young fellow to work for me. A couple of boys, too, but they're not much good. Most of these boys and young men won't come and do this sort of work. All for going into factories, they are, or white collars and working in an office. Don't like to get their hands soiled with a bit of honest earth. But I'm lucky, as I say. I've got a good man working for me as come and offered himself.'

'Recently?' said Inspector Kelsey.

'Beginning of the term,' said Briggs. 'Adam, his name is. Adam Goodman.'

'I don't think I've seen him about,' said Kelsey.

'Asked for the day off today, he did,' said Briggs. 'I give it him. Didn't seem to be much doing today with you people tramping all over the place.'

'Somebody should have told me about him,' said Kelsey sharply.

'What do you mean, told you about him?'

'He's not on my list,' said the Inspector. 'Of people employed here, I mean.'

'Oh, well, you can see him tomorrow, mister,' said Briggs. 'Not that he can tell you anything, I don't suppose.'

'You never know,' said the Inspector.

A strong young man who had offered himself at the beginning of the term? It seemed to Kelsey that here was the first thing that he had come across which might be a little out of the ordinary.

IV

The girls filed into the hall for prayers that evening as usual, and afterwards Miss Bulstrode arrested their departure by raising her hand.

'I have something to say to you all. Miss Springer, as you know, was shot last night in the Sports Pavilion. If any of you has heard or seen anything in the past week — anything that has puzzled you relating to Miss Springer, anything Miss Springer may have said or someone else may have said of her that strikes you as at all significant, I should like to know it. You can come to me in my sitting-room any time this evening.'

'Oh,' Julia Upjohn sighed, as the girls filed out, 'how I wish we *did* know something! But we don't, do we, Jennifer?'

'No,' said Jennifer, 'of course we don't.'

'Miss Springer always seemed so very ordinary,' said Julia sadly, 'much too ordinary to get killed in a mysterious way.'

'I don't suppose it was so mysterious,' said Jennifer. 'Just a burglar.'

'Stealing our tennis racquets, I suppose,' said Julia with sarcasm.

'Perhaps someone was blackmailing her,' suggested one of the other girls hopefully.

'What about?' said Jennifer.

But nobody could think of any reason for blackmailing Miss Springer.

V

Inspector Kelsey started his interviewing of the staff with Miss Vansittart. A handsome woman, he thought, summing her up. Possibly forty or a little over; tall, well-built, grey hair tastefully arranged. She had dignity and composure, with a certain sense, he thought, of her own importance. She reminded him a little of Miss Bulstrode herself: she was the schoolmistress type all right. All the same, he reflected, Miss Bulstrode had something that Miss Vansittart had not. Miss Bulstrode had a quality of unexpectedness. He did not feel that Miss Vansittart would ever be unexpected.

Question and answer followed routine. In effect, Miss Vansittart had seen nothing, had noticed nothing, had heard nothing. Miss Springer had been excellent at her job. Yes, her manner had perhaps been a trifle brusque, but not, she thought, unduly so. She had not perhaps had a very attractive personality but that was really not a necessity in a Games Mistress. It was better, in fact, *not* to have mistresses who had attractive personalities. It did not do to let the girls get emotional about the mistresses. Miss Vansittart, having contributed nothing of value, made her exit.

'See no evil, hear no evil, think no evil. Same like the monkeys,' observed Sergeant Percy Bond, who was assisting Inspector Kelsey in his task.

Kelsey grinned. 'That's about right, Percy,' he said.

'There's something about schoolmistresses that gives me the hump,' said Sergeant Bond.

145

'Had a terror of them ever since I was a kid. Knew one that was a holy terror. So upstage and la-di-da you never knew what she was trying to teach you.'

The next mistress to appear was Eileen Rich. Ugly as sin was Inspector Kelsey's first reaction. Then he qualified it; she had a certain attraction. He started his routine questions, but the answers were not quite so routine as he had expected. After saying No, she had not heard or noticed anything special that anyone else had said about Miss Springer or that Miss Springer herself had said, Eileen Rich's next answer was not what he anticipated. He had asked:

'There was no one as far as you know who had a personal grudge against her?'

'Oh no,' said Eileen Rich quickly. 'One couldn't have. I think that was her tragedy, you know. That she wasn't a person one could ever hate.'

'Now just what do you mean by that, Miss Rich?'

'I mean she wasn't a person one could ever have wanted to destroy. Everything she did and was, was on the surface. She annoyed people. They often had sharp words with her, but it didn't mean anything. Not anything deep. I'm sure she wasn't killed for *herself*, if you know what I mean.'

146

'I'm not quite sure that I do, Miss Rich.'

'I mean if you had something like a bank robbery, she might quite easily be the cashier that gets shot, but it would be as a cashier, not as Grace Springer. Nobody would love her or hate her enough to want to do away with her. I think she probably felt that without thinking about it, and that's what made her so officious. About finding fault, you know, and enforcing rules and finding out what people were doing that they shouldn't be doing, and showing them up.'

'Snooping?' asked Kelsey.

'No, not exactly snooping.' Eileen Rich considered. 'She wouldn't tiptoe round on sneakers or anything of that kind. But if she found something going on that she didn't understand she'd be quite determined to get to the bottom of it. And she *would* get to the bottom of it.'

'I see.' He paused a moment. 'You didn't like her yourself much, did you, Miss Rich?'

'I don't think I ever thought about her. She was just the Games Mistress. Oh! What a horrible thing that is to say about anybody! Just this — just that! But that's how *she* felt about her job. It was a job that she took pride in doing well. She didn't find it fun. She wasn't keen when she found a girl who might be really good at tennis, or really fine at some

147

form of athletics. She didn't rejoice in it or triumph.'

Kelsey looked at her curiously. An odd young woman, this, he thought.

'You seem to have your ideas on most things, Miss Rich,' he said.

'Yes. Yes, I suppose I do.'

'How long have you been at Meadowbank?'

'Just over a year and a half.'

'There's never been any trouble before?'

'At Meadowbank?' She sounded startled.

'Yes.'

'Oh no. Everything's been quite all right until this term.'

Kelsey pounced.

'What's been wrong this term? You don't mean the murder, do you? You mean something else — '

'I don't — ' she stopped — 'Yes, perhaps I do — but it's all very nebulous.'

'Go on.'

'Miss Bulstrode's not been happy lately,' said Eileen slowly. 'That's one thing. You wouldn't know it. I don't think anybody else has even noticed it. But I have. And she's not the only one who's unhappy. But that isn't what you mean, is it? That's just people's feelings. The kind of things you get when you're cooped up together and think about one thing too much. You meant, was there

148

anything that didn't seem right just this term. That's it, isn't it?'

'Yes,' said Kelsey, looking at her curiously, 'yes, that's it. Well, what about it?'

'I think there *is* something wrong here,' said Eileen Rich slowly. 'It's as though there were someone among us who didn't belong.' She looked at him, smiled, almost laughed and said, 'Cat among the pigeons, that's the sort of feeling. We're the pigeons, all of us, and the cat's amongst us. But we can't *see* the cat.'

'That's very vague, Miss Rich.'

'Yes, isn't it? It sounds quite idiotic. I can hear that myself. What I really mean, I suppose, is that there has been something, some little thing that I've noticed but I don't know what I've noticed.'

'About anyone in particular?'

'No, I told you, that's just it. I don't know who it is. The only way I can sum it up is to say that there's *someone* here, who's — somehow — wrong! There's someone here — I don't know who — who makes me uncomfortable. Not when I'm looking at her but when she's looking at me because it's when she's looking at me that it shows, whatever it is. Oh, I'm getting more incoherent than ever. And anyway, it's only a feeling. It's not what you want. It isn't evidence.'

'No,' said Kelsey, 'it isn't evidence. Not yet. But it's interesting, and if your feeling gets any more definite, Miss Rich, I'd be glad to hear about it.'

She nodded. 'Yes,' she said, 'because it's serious, isn't it? I mean, someone's been killed — we don't know why — and the killer may be miles away, or, on the other hand, the killer may be here in the school. And if so that pistol or revolver or whatever it is, must be here too. That's not a very nice thought, is it?'

She went out with a slight nod. Sergeant Bond said,

'Crackers — or don't you think so?'

'No,' said Kelsey, 'I don't think she's crackers. I think she's what's called a sensitive. You know, like the people who know when there's a cat in the room long before they see it. If she'd been born in an African tribe she might have been a witch doctor.'

'They go round smelling out evil, don't they?' said Sergeant Bond.

'That's right, Percy,' said Kelsey. 'And that's exactly what I'm trying to do myself. Nobody's come across with any concrete facts so I've got to go about smelling out things. We'll have the French woman next.'

10

Fantastic Story

Mademoiselle Angèle Blanche was thirty-five at a guess. No make-up, dark brown hair arranged neatly but unbecomingly. A severe coat and skirt.

It was Mademoiselle Blanche's first term at Meadowbank, she explained. She was not sure that she wished to remain for a further term.

'It is not nice to be in a school where murders take place,' she said disapprovingly.

Also, there did not seem to be burglar alarms anywhere in the house — that was dangerous.

'There's nothing of any great value, Mademoiselle Blanche, to attract burglars.'

Mademoiselle Blanche shrugged her shoulders.

'How does one know? These girls who come here, some of them have very rich fathers. They may have something with them of great value. A burglar knows about that, perhaps, and he comes here because he thinks this is an easy place to steal it.'

'If a girl had something of value with her it wouldn't be in the gymnasium.'

'How do you know?' said Mademoiselle. 'They have lockers there, do they not, the girls?'

'Only to keep their sports kit in, and things of that kind.'

'Ah yes, that is what is supposed. But a girl could hide anything in the toe of a gym shoe, or wrapped up in an old pullover or in a scarf.'

'What sort of thing, Mademoiselle Blanche?'

But Mademoiselle Blanche had no idea what sort of thing.

'Even the most indulgent fathers don't give their daughters diamond necklaces to take to school,' the Inspector said.

Again Mademoiselle Blanche shrugged her shoulders.

'Perhaps it is something of a different kind of value — a scarab, say, or something that a collector would give a lot of money for. One of the girls has a father who is an archaeologist.'

Kelsey smiled. 'I don't really think that's likely, you know, Mademoiselle Blanche.'

She shrugged her shoulders. 'Oh well, I only make the suggestion.'

'Have you taught in any other English schools, Mademoiselle Blanche?'

'One in the north of England some time ago. Mostly I have taught in Switzerland and in France. Also in Germany. I think I will come to England to improve my English. I have a friend here. She went sick and she told me I could take her position here as Miss Bulstrode would be glad to find somebody quickly. So I came. But I do not like it very much. As I tell you, I do not think I shall stay.'

'Why don't you like it?' Kelsey persisted.

'I do not like places where there are shootings,' said Mademoiselle Blanche. 'And the children, they are not respectful.'

'They are not quite children, are they?'

'Some of them behave like babies, some of them might be twenty-five. There are all kinds here. They have much freedom. I prefer an establishment with more routine.'

'Did you know Miss Springer well?'

'I knew her practically not at all. She had bad manners and I conversed with her as little as possible. She was all bones and freckles and a loud ugly voice. She was like caricatures of Englishwomen. She was rude to me often and I did not like it.'

'What was she rude to you about?'

'She did not like me coming to her Sports

Pavilion. That seems to be how she feels about it — or felt about it, I mean — that it was *her* Sports Pavilion! I go there one day because I am interested. I have not been in it before and it is a new building. It is very well arranged and planned and I am just looking round. Then Miss Springer she comes and says 'What are you doing here? This is no business of yours to be in here.' She says that to me — *me*, a mistress in the school! What does she think I am, a pupil?'

'Yes, yes, very irritating, I'm sure,' said Kelsey, soothingly.

'The manners of a pig, that is what she had. And then she calls out 'Do not go away with the key in your hand.' She upset me. When I pull the door open the key fell out and I pick it up. I forget to put it back, because she has offended me. And then she shouts after me as though she thinks I was meaning to steal it. *Her* key, I suppose, as well as *her* Sports Pavilion.'

'That seems a little odd, doesn't it?' said Kelsey. 'That she should feel like that about the gymnasium, I mean. As though it were her private property, as though she were afraid of people finding something she had hidden there.' He made the faint feeler tentatively, but Angèle Blanche merely laughed.

154

'Hide something there — what could you hide in a place like that? Do you think she hides her love letters there? I am sure she has never had a love letter written to her! The other mistresses, they are at least polite. Miss Chadwick, she is old-fashioned and she fusses. Miss Vansittart, she is very nice, *grande dame*, sympathetic. Miss Rich, she is a little crazy I think, but friendly. And the younger mistresses are quite pleasant.'

Angèle Blanche was dismissed after a few more unimportant questions.

'Touchy,' said Bond. 'All the French are touchy.'

'All the same, it's interesting,' said Kelsey. 'Miss Springer didn't like people prowling about *her* gymnasium — Sports Pavilion — I don't know what to call the thing. Now *why*?'

'Perhaps she thought the Frenchwoman was spying on her,' suggested Bond.

'Well, but *why* should she think so? I mean, ought it to have mattered to her that Angèle Blanche should spy on her unless there was something she was afraid of Angèle Blanche finding out?

'Who have we got left?' he added.

'The two junior mistresses, Miss Blake and Miss Rowan, and Miss Bulstrode's secretary.'

Miss Blake was young and earnest with a round good-natured face. She taught Botany and Physics. She had nothing much to say that could help. She had seen very little of Miss Springer and had no idea of what could have led to her death.

Miss Rowan, as befitted one who held a degree in psychology, had views to express. It was highly probable, she said, that Miss Springer had committed suicide.

Inspector Kelsey raised his eyebrows.

'Why should she? Was she unhappy in any way?'

'She was aggressive,' said Miss Rowan, leaning forward and peering eagerly through her thick lenses. 'Very aggressive. I consider that significant. It was a defence mechanism, to conceal a feeling of inferiority.'

'Everything I've heard so far,' said Inspector Kelsey, 'points to her being very sure of herself.'

'*Too* sure of herself,' said Miss Rowan darkly. 'And several of the things she said bear out my assumption.'

'Such as?'

'She hinted at people being 'not what they seemed'. She mentioned that at the last school where she was employed, she had 'unmasked' someone. The Headmistress, however, had been prejudiced, and refused to listen to what she had found out. Several of the other mistresses, too, had been what she called 'against her'.

'You see what that means, Inspector?' Miss Rowan nearly fell off her chair as she leaned forward excitedly. Strands of lank dark hair fell forward across her face. 'The beginnings of a persecution complex.'

Inspector Kelsey said politely that Miss Rowan might be correct in her assumptions, but that he couldn't accept the theory of suicide, unless Miss Rowan could explain how Miss Springer had managed to shoot herself from a distance of at least four feet away, and had also been able to make the pistol disappear into thin air afterwards.

Miss Rowan retorted acidly that the police were well known to be prejudiced against psychology.

She then gave place to Ann Shapland.

'Well, Miss Shapland,' said Inspector Kelsey, eyeing her neat and businesslike appearance with favour, 'what light can you throw upon this matter?'

'Absolutely none, I'm afraid. I've got my own sitting-room, and I don't see much of the staff. The whole thing's unbelievable.'

'In what way unbelievable?'

'Well, first that Miss Springer should get shot at all. Say somebody broke into the gymnasium and she went out to see who it was. That's all right, I suppose, but who'd

157

want to break into the gymnasium?'

'Boys, perhaps, some young locals who wanted to help themselves to equipment of some kind or another, or who did it for a lark.'

'If that's so, I can't help feeling that what Miss Springer would have said was: 'Now then, what are you doing here? Be off with you,' and they'd have gone off.'

'Did it ever seem to you that Miss Springer adopted any particular attitude about the Sports Pavilion?'

Ann Shapland looked puzzled. 'Attitude?'

'I mean did she regard it as her special province and dislike other people going there?'

'Not that I know of. Why should she? It was just part of the school buildings.'

'You didn't notice anything yourself? You didn't find that if you went there she resented your presence — anything of that kind?'

Ann Shapland shook her head. 'I haven't been out there myself more than a couple of times. I haven't the time. I've gone out there once or twice with a message for one of the girls from Miss Bulstrode. That's all.'

'You didn't know that Miss Springer had objected to Mademoiselle Blanche being out there?'

'No, I didn't hear anything about that. Oh

yes, I believe I did. Mademoiselle Blanche was rather cross about something one day, but then she is a little bit touchy, you know. There was something about her going into the drawing class one day and resenting something the drawing mistress said to her. Of course she hasn't really very much to do — Mademoiselle Blanche, I mean. She only teaches one subject — French, and she has a lot of time on her hands. I think — ' she hesitated, 'I think she is perhaps rather an inquisitive person.'

'Do you think it likely that when she went into the Sports Pavilion she was poking about in any of the lockers?'

'The girls' lockers? Well, I wouldn't put it past her. She might amuse herself that way.'

'Does Miss Springer herself have a locker out there?'

'Yes, of course.'

'If Mademoiselle Blanche was caught poking about in Miss Springer's locker, then I can imagine that Miss Springer *would* be annoyed?'

'She certainly would!'

'You don't know anything about Miss Springer's private life?'

'I don't think anyone did,' said Ann. 'Did she have one, I wonder?'

'And there's nothing else — nothing

connected with the Sports Pavilion, for instance, that you haven't told me?'

'Well — ' Ann hesitated.

'Yes, Miss Shapland, let's have it.'

'It's nothing really,' said Ann slowly. 'But one of the gardeners — not Briggs, the young one. I saw him come out of the Sports Pavilion one day, and he had no business to be in there at all. Of course it was probably just curiosity on his part — or perhaps an excuse to slack off a bit from work — he was supposed to be nailing down the wire on the tennis court. I don't suppose really there's anything in it.'

'Still, you remembered it,' Kelsey pointed out. 'Now why?'

'I think — ' she frowned. 'Yes, because his manner was a little odd. Defiant. And — he sneered at all the money that was spent here on the girls.'

'That sort of attitude . . . I see.'

'I don't suppose there's really anything in it.'

'Probably not — but I'll make a note of it, all the same.'

'Round and round the mulberry bush,' said Bond when Ann Shapland had gone. 'Same thing over and over again! For goodness' sake let's hope we get something out of the servants.'

But they got very little out of the servants. 'It's no use asking me anything, young man,' said Mrs Gibbons, the cook. 'For one thing I can't hear what you say, and for another I don't know a thing. I went to sleep last night and I slept unusually heavy. Never heard anything of all the excitement there was. Nobody woke me up and told me anything about it.' She sounded injured. 'It wasn't until this morning I heard.'

Kelsey shouted a few questions and got a few answers that told him nothing.

Miss Springer had come new this term, and she wasn't as much liked as Miss Jones who'd held the post before her. Miss Shapland was new, too, but she was a nice young lady, Mademoiselle Blanche was like all the Frenchies — thought the other mistresses were against her and let the young ladies treat her something shocking in class. 'Not a one for crying, though,' Mrs Gibbons admitted. 'Some schools I've been in the French mistresses used to cry something awful!'

Most of the domestic staff were dailies. There was only one other maid who slept in the house, and she proved equally uninformative, though able to hear what was said to her. She couldn't say, she was sure. She didn't know nothing. Miss Springer was a bit sharp

161

in her manner. She didn't know nothing about the Sports Pavilion nor what was kept there, and she'd never seen nothing like a pistol nowhere.

This negative spate of information was interrupted by Miss Bulstrode. 'One of the girls would like to speak to you, Inspector Kelsey,' she said.

Kelsey looked up sharply. 'Indeed? She knows something?'

'As to that I'm rather doubtful,' said Miss Bulstrode, 'but you had better talk to her yourself. She is one of our foreign girls. Princess Shaista — niece of the Emir Ibrahim. She is inclined to think, perhaps, that she is of rather more importance than she is. You understand?'

Kelsey nodded comprehendingly. Then Miss Bulstrode went out and a slight dark girl of middle height came in.

She looked at them, almond eyed and demure.

'You are the police?'

'Yes,' said Kelsey smiling, 'we are the police. Will you sit down and tell me what you know about Miss Springer?'

'Yes, I will tell you.'

She sat down, leaned forward, and lowered her voice dramatically.

'There have been people watching this

162

place. Oh, they do not show themselves clearly, but they are there!'

She nodded her head significantly.

Inspector Kelsey thought that he understood what Miss Bulstrode had meant. This girl was dramatizing herself — and enjoying it.

'And why should they be watching the school?'

'Because of *me*! They want to kidnap me.'

Whatever Kelsey had expected, it was not this. His eyebrows rose.

'Why should they want to kidnap you?'

'To hold me to ransom, of course. Then they would make my relations pay much money.'

'Er — well — perhaps,' said Kelsey dubiously. 'But — er — supposing this is so, what has it got to do with the death of Miss Springer?'

'She must have found out about them,' said Shaista. 'Perhaps she told them she had found out something. Perhaps she threatened them. Then perhaps they promised to pay her money if she would say nothing. And she believed them. So she goes out to the Sports Pavilion where they say they will pay her the money, and then they shoot her.'

'But surely Miss Springer would never have accepted blackmail money?'

163

'Do you think it is such fun to be a school teacher — to be a teacher of gymnastics?' Shaista was scornful. 'Do you not think it would be nice instead to have money, to travel, to do what you want? Especially someone like Miss Springer who is not beautiful, at whom men do not even look! Do you not think that money would attract her more than it would attract other people?'

'Well — er — ' said Inspector Kelsey, 'I don't know quite what to say.' He had not had this point of view presented to him before.

'This is just — er — your own idea?' he said. 'Miss Springer never said anything to you?'

'Miss Springer never said anything except 'Stretch and bend', and 'Faster', and 'Don't slack',' said Shaista with resentment.

'Yes — quite so. Well, don't you think you may have imagined all this about kidnapping?'

Shaista was immediately much annoyed.

'You do not understand *at all*! My cousin was Prince Ali Yusuf of Ramat. He was killed in a revolution, or at least in fleeing from a revolution. It was understood that when I grew up I should marry him. So you see I am an important person. It may be perhaps the Communists who come here. Perhaps it is

164

not to kidnap. Perhaps they intend to assassinate me.'

Inspector Kelsey looked still more incredulous.

'That's rather far fetched, isn't it?'

'You think such things could not happen? I say they can. They are very wicked, the Communists! Everybody knows that.'

As he still looked dubious, she went on:

'Perhaps they think I know where the jewels are!'

'What jewels?'

'My cousin had jewels. So had his father. My family always has a hoard of jewels. For emergencies, you comprehend.'

She made it sound very matter of fact.

Kelsey stared at her.

'But what has all this got to do with you — or with Miss Springer?'

'But I already tell you! They think, perhaps, I know where the jewels are. So they will take me prisoner and force me to speak.'

'*Do* you know where the jewels are?'

'No, of course I do not know. They disappeared in the Revolution. Perhaps the wicked Communists take them. But again, perhaps not.'

'Who do they belong to?'

'Now my cousin is dead, they belong to me. No men in his family any more. His aunt,

165

my mother, is dead. He would want them to belong to me. If he were not dead, I marry him.'

'That was the arrangement?'

'I have to marry him. He is my cousin, you see.'

'And you would have got the jewels when you married him?'

'No, I would have had new jewels. From Cartier in Paris. These others would still be kept for emergencies.'

Inspector Kelsey blinked, letting this Oriental insurance scheme for emergencies sink into his consciousness.

Shaista was racing on with great animation.

'I think that is what happens. Somebody gets the jewels out of Ramat. Perhaps good person, perhaps bad. Good person would bring them to me, would say: 'These are yours,' and I should reward him.'

She nodded her head regally, playing the part.

Quite a little actress, thought the Inspector.

'But if it was a bad person, he would keep the jewels and sell them. Or he would come to me and say: 'What will you give me as a reward if I bring them to you?' And if it worth while, he brings — but if not, then not!'

'But in actual fact, nobody has said anything at all to you?'

'No,' admitted Shaista.

Inspector Kelsey made up his mind.

'I think, you know,' he said pleasantly, 'that you're really talking a lot of nonsense.'

Shaista flashed a furious glance at him.

'I tell you what I know, that is all,' she said sulkily.

'Yes — well, it's very kind of you, and I'll bear it in mind.'

He got up and opened the door for her to go out.

'The Arabian Nights aren't in it,' he said, as he returned to the table. 'Kidnapping and fabulous jewels! What next?'

11

Conference

When Inspector Kelsey returned to the station, the sergeant on duty said:

'We've got Adam Goodman here, waiting, sir.'

'Adam Goodman? Oh yes. The gardener.'

A young man had risen respectfully to his feet. He was tall, dark and good-looking. He wore stained corduroy trousers loosely held up by an aged belt, and an open-necked shirt of very bright blue.

'You wanted to see me, I hear.'

His voice was rough, and as that of so many young men of today, slightly truculent.

Kelsey said merely:

'Yes, come into my room.'

'I don't know anything about the murder,' said Adam Goodman sulkily. 'It's nothing to do with me. I was at home and in bed last night.'

Kelsey merely nodded noncommittally.

He sat down at his desk, and motioned to

the young man to take the chair opposite. A young policeman in plain clothes had followed the two men in unobtrusively and sat down a little distance away.

'Now then,' said Kelsey. 'You're Goodman — ' he looked at a note on his desk — 'Adam Goodman.'

'That's right, sir. But first, I'd like to show you this.'

Adam's manner had changed. There was no truculence or sulkiness in it now. It was quiet and deferential. He took something from his pocket and passed it across the desk. Inspector Kelsey's eyebrows rose very slightly as he studied it. Then he raised his head.

'I shan't need you, Barbar,' he said.

The discreet young policeman got up and went out. He managed not to look surprised, but he was.

'Ah,' said Kelsey. He looked across at Adam with speculative interest. 'So that's who you are? And what the hell, I'd like to know, are you — '

'Doing in a girls' school?' the young man finished for him. His voice was still deferential, but he grinned in spite of himself. 'It's certainly the first time I've had an assignment of that kind. Don't I look like a gardener?'

'Not around these parts. Gardeners are

169

usually rather ancient. Do you know anything about gardening?'

'Quite a lot. I've got one of these gardening mothers. England's speciality. She's seen to it that I'm a worthy assistant to her.'

'And what exactly is going on at Meadowbank — to bring you on the scene?'

'We don't know, actually, that there's anything going on at Meadowbank. My assignment is in the nature of a watching brief. Or was — until last night. Murder of a Games Mistress. Not quite in the school's curriculum.'

'It could happen,' said Inspector Kelsey. He sighed. 'Anything could happen — anywhere. I've learnt that. But I'll admit that it's a little off the beaten track. What's behind all this?'

Adam told him. Kelsey listened with interest.

'I did that girl an injustice,' he remarked — 'But you'll admit it sounds too fantastic to be true. Jewels worth between half a million and a million pounds? Who do you say they belong to?'

'That's a very pretty question. To answer it, you'd have to have a gaggle of international lawyers on the job — and they'd probably disagree. You could argue the case a lot of ways. They belonged, three months ago, to His Highness Prince Ali Yusuf of Ramat. But now? If they'd turned up in Ramat they'd have been the property of the present Government, they'd have made sure of that. Ali Yusuf may have willed them to someone. A lot would then depend on where the will was executed and whether it could be proved. They may belong to his family. But the real essence of the matter is, that if you or I happened to pick them up in the street and put them in our pockets, they would for all practical purposes belong to us. That is, I doubt if any legal machine exists that could get them away from us. They could try, of course, but the intricacies of international law are quite incredible . . . '

'You mean that, practically speaking, it's findings are keepings?' asked Inspector Kelsey. He shook his head disapprovingly. 'That's not very nice,' he said primly.

'No,' said Adam firmly. 'It's not very nice. There's more than one lot after them, too. None of them scrupulous. Word's got around, you see. It may be a rumour, it may be true, but the story is that they were got out of Ramat just before the bust up. There are a dozen different tales of *how.*'

'But why Meadowbank? Because of little Princess Butter-won't-melt-in-my-mouth?'

'Princess Shaista, first cousin of Ali Yusuf. Yes. Someone may try and deliver the goods

171

to her or communicate with her. There are some questionable characters from our point of view hanging about the neighbourhood. A Mrs Kolinsky, for instance, staying at the Grand Hotel. Quite a prominent member of what one might describe as International Riff Raff Ltd. Nothing in *your* line, always strictly within the law, all perfectly respectable, but a grand picker-up of useful information. Then there's a woman who was out in Ramat dancing in cabaret there. She's reported to have been working for a certain foreign government. Where she is now we don't know, we don't even know what she looks like, but there's a rumour that she *might* be in this part of the world. Looks, doesn't it, as though it were all centring round Meadowbank? And last night, Miss Springer gets herself killed.'

Kelsey nodded thoughtfully.

'Proper mix up,' he observed. He struggled a moment with his feelings. 'You see this sort of thing on the telly . . . far fetched — that's what you think . . . can't really happen. And it doesn't — not in the normal course of events.'

'Secret agents, robbery, violence, murder, double crossing,' agreed Adam. 'All preposterous — but that side of life exists.'

'But not at Meadowbank!'

172

The words were wrung from Inspector Kelsey.

'I perceive your point,' said Adam. 'Lese-majesty.'

There was a silence, and then Inspector Kelsey asked:

'What do *you* think happened last night?'

Adam took his time, then he said slowly:

'Springer was in the Sports Pavilion — in the middle of the night. Why? We've got to start there. It's no good asking ourselves who killed her until we've made up our minds why she was there, in the Sports Pavilion at that time of night. We can say that in spite of her blameless and athletic life she wasn't sleeping well, and got up and looked out of her window and saw a light in the Sports Pavilion — her window does look out that way?'

Kelsey nodded.

'Being a tough and fearless young woman, she went out to investigate. She disturbed someone there who was — doing what? We don't know. But it was someone desperate enough to shoot her dead.'

Again Kelsey nodded.

'That's the way we've been looking at it,' he said. 'But your last point had me worried all along. You don't shoot to kill — and come prepared to do so, unless — '

'Unless you're after something big? Agreed!

Well, that's the case of what we might call Innocent Springer — shot down in the performance of duty. But there's another possibility. Springer, as a result of private information, gets a job at Meadowbank or is detailed for it by her bosses — because of her qualification — She waits until a suitable night, then slips out to the Sports Pavilion (again our stumbling-block of a question — *why?*) — Somebody is following her — or waiting for her — someone who carries a pistol and is prepared to use it . . . But again — why? What for? In fact, what the devil is there about the Sports Pavilion? It's not the sort of place that one can imagine hiding anything.'

'There wasn't anything hidden there, I can tell you that. We went through it with a tooth comb — the girls' lockers, Miss Springer's ditto. Sports equipment of various kinds, all normal and accounted for. *And* a brand new building! There wasn't anything there in the nature of jewellery.'

'Whatever it was it could have been removed, of course. By the murderer,' said Adam. 'The other possibility is that the Sports Pavilion was simply used as a rendezvous — by Miss Springer or by someone else. It's quite a handy place for that. A reasonable distance from the house.

174

Not too far. And if anyone was noticed going out there, a simple answer would be that whoever it was thought they had seen a light, etc., etc. Let's say that Miss Springer went out to meet someone — there was a disagreement and she got shot. Or, a variation, Miss Springer noticed someone leaving the house, followed that someone, intruded upon something she wasn't meant to see or hear.'

'I never met her alive,' said Kelsey, 'but from the way everyone speaks of her, I get the impression that she might have been a nosey woman.'

'I think that's really the most probable explanation,' agreed Adam. 'Curiosity killed the cat. Yes, I think that's the way the Sports Pavilion comes into it.'

'But if it was a rendezvous, then — ' Kelsey paused.

Adam nodded vigorously.

'Yes. It looks as though there is someone in the school who merits our very close attention. Cat among the pigeons, in fact.'

'Cat among the pigeons,' said Kelsey, struck by the phrase. 'Miss Rich, one of the mistresses, said something like that today.'

He reflected a moment or two.

'There were three newcomers to the staff this term,' he said. 'Shapland, the secretary.

Blanche, the French Mistress, and, of course, Miss Springer herself. She's dead and out of it. If there is a cat among the pigeons, it would seem that one of the other two would be the most likely bet.' He looked towards Adam. 'Any ideas, as between the two of them?'

Adam considered.

'I caught Mademoiselle Blanche coming out of the Sports Pavilion one day. She had a guilty look. As though she'd been doing something she ought not to have done. All the same, on the whole — I think I'd plump for the other. For Shapland. She's a cool customer and she's got brains. I'd go into her antecedents rather carefully if I were you. What the devil are you laughing for?'

Kelsey was grinning.

'*She* was suspicious of *you*,' he said. 'Caught *you* coming out of the Sports Pavilion — and thought there was something odd about your manner!'

'Well, I'm damned!' Adam was indignant. 'The cheek of her!'

Inspector Kelsey resumed his authoritative manner.

'The point is,' he said, 'that we think a lot of Meadowbank round these parts. It's a fine school. And Miss Bulstrode's a fine woman. The sooner we can get to the bottom of all this, the better for the school. We want to clear things up and give Meadowbank a clean bill of health.'

He paused, looking thoughtfully at Adam.

'I think,' he said, 'we'll have to tell Miss Bulstrode who you are. She'll keep her mouth shut — don't fear for that.'

Adam considered for a moment. Then he nodded his head.

'Yes,' he said. 'Under the circumstances, I think it's more or less inevitable.'

12

New Lamps for Old

I

Miss Bulstrode had another faculty which demonstrated her superiority over most other women. She could listen.

She listened in silence to both Inspector Kelsey and Adam. She did not so much as raise an eyebrow. Then she uttered one word.

'Remarkable.'

It's you who are remarkable, thought Adam, but he did not say so aloud.

'Well,' said Miss Bulstrode, coming as was habitual to her straight to the point. 'What do you want me to do?'

Inspector Kelsey cleared his throat.

'It's like this,' he said. 'We felt that you ought to be fully informed — for the sake of the school.'

Miss Bulstrode nodded.

'Naturally,' she said, 'the school is my first concern. It has to be. I am responsible for the care and safety of my pupils — and in a lesser degree for that of my staff. And I would like to add now that if there can be as little publicity as possible about Miss Springer's death — the better it will be for me. This is a purely selfish point of view — though I think my school is important in itself — not only to me. And I quite realize that if full publicity is necessary for you, then you will have to go ahead. But is it?'

'No,' said Inspector Kelsey. 'In this case I should say the less publicity the better. The inquest will be adjourned and we'll let it get about that we think it was a local affair. Young thugs — or juvenile delinquents, as we have to call them nowadays — out with guns amongst them, trigger happy. It's usually flick knives, but some of these boys do get hold of guns. Miss Springer surprised them. They shot her. That's what I should like to let it go at — then we can get to work quiet-like. Not more than can be helped in the Press. But of course, Meadowbank's famous. It's news. And murder at Meadowbank will be hot news.'

'I think I can help you there,' said Miss Bulstrode crisply, 'I am not without influence in high places.' She smiled and reeled off a few names. These included the Home Secretary, two Press barons, a bishop and the Minister of Education. 'I'll do what I can.' She looked at Adam. 'You agree?'

179

Adam spoke quickly.

'Yes, indeed. We always like things nice and quiet.'

'Are you continuing to be my gardener?' inquired Miss Bulstrode.

'If you don't object. It puts me right where I want to be. And I can keep an eye on things.'

This time Miss Bulstrode's eyebrows did rise.

'I hope you're not expecting any more murders?'

'No, no.'

'I'm glad of that. I doubt if any school could survive two murders in one term.'

She turned to Kelsey.

'Have you people finished with the Sports Pavilion? It's awkward if we can't use it.'

'We've finished with it. Clean as a whistle — from our point of view, I mean. For whatever reason the murder was committed — there's nothing there now to help us. It's just a Sports Pavilion with the usual equipment.'

'Nothing in the girls' lockers?'

Inspector Kelsey smiled.

'Well – this and that — copy of a book — French — called *Candide* — with — er — illustrations. Expensive book.'

'Ah,' said Miss Bulstrode. 'So that's where

she keeps it! Giselle d'Aubray, I suppose?'

Kelsey's respect for Miss Bulstrode rose.

'You don't miss much, M'am,' he said.

'She won't come to harm with *Candide*,' said Miss Bulstrode. 'It's a classic. Some forms of pornography I do confiscate. Now I come back to my first question. You have relieved my mind about the publicity connected with the school. Can the school help you in any way? Can *I* help you?'

'I don't think so, at the moment. The only thing I can ask is, has anything caused you uneasiness this term? Any incident? Or any person?'

Miss Bulstrode was silent for a moment or two. Then she said slowly:

'The answer, literally, is: I don't know.'

Adam said quickly:

'You've got a feeling that something's wrong?'

'Yes — just that. It's not definite. I can't put my finger on any person, or any incident — unless — '

She was silent for a moment, then she said:

'I feel — I felt at the time — that I'd missed something that I ought not to have missed. Let me explain.'

She recited briefly the little incident of Mrs Upjohn and the distressing and unexpected arrival of Lady Veronica.

Adam was interested.

'Let me get this clear, Miss Bulstrode. Mrs Upjohn, looking out of the window, this front window that gives on the drive, recognized someone. There's nothing in that. You have over a hundred pupils and nothing is more likely than for Mrs Upjohn to see some parent or relation that she knew. But you are definitely of the opinion that she was *astonished* to recognize that person — in fact, that it was someone whom she would *not* have expected to see at Meadowbank?'

'Yes, that was exactly the impression I got.'

'And then through the window looking in the opposite direction you saw one of the pupils' mothers, in a state of intoxication, and that completely distracted your mind from what Mrs Upjohn was saying?'

Miss Bulstrode nodded.

'She was talking for some minutes?'

'Yes.'

'And when your attention did return to her, she was speaking of espionage, of Intelligence work she had done in the war before she married?'

'Yes.'

'It might tie up,' said Adam thoughtfully. 'Someone she had known in her war days. A parent or relation of one of your pupils, or it

182

could have been a member of your teaching staff.'

'Hardly a member of my staff,' objected Miss Bulstrode.

'It's possible.'

'We'd better get in touch with Mrs Upjohn,' said Kelsey. 'As soon as possible. You have her address, Miss Bulstrode?'

'Of course. But I believe she is abroad at the moment. Wait — I will find out.'

She pressed her desk buzzer twice, then went impatiently to the door and called to a girl who was passing.

'Find Julia Upjohn for me, will you, Paula?'

'Yes, Miss Bulstrode.'

'I'd better go before the girl comes,' Adam said. 'It wouldn't be natural for me to assist in the inquiries the Inspector is making. Ostensibly he's called me in here to get the low down on me. Having satisfied himself that he's got nothing on me for the moment, he now tells me to take myself off.'

'Take yourself off and remember I've got my eye on you!' growled Kelsey with a grin.

'By the way,' said Adam, addressing Miss Bulstrode as he paused by the door, 'will it be all right with you if I slightly abuse my position here? If I get, shall we say, a little too friendly with some members of your staff?'

'With which members of my staff?'

'Well — Mademoiselle Blanche, for instance.'

'Mademoiselle Blanche? You think that she — ?'

'I think she's rather bored here.'

'Ah!' Miss Bulstrode looked rather grim. 'Perhaps you're right. Anyone else?'

'I shall have a good try all round,' said Adam cheerfully. 'If you should find that some of your girls are being rather silly, and slipping off to assignations in the garden, please believe that my intentions are strictly sleuthial — if there is such a word.'

'You think the girls are likely to know something?'

'Everybody always knows something,' said Adam, 'even if it's something they don't know they know.'

'You may be right.'

There was a knock on the door, and Miss Bulstrode called — 'Come in.'

Julia Upjohn appeared, very much out of breath.

'Come in, Julia.'

Inspector Kelsey growled.

'You can go now, Goodman. Take yourself off and get on with your work.'

'I've told you I don't know a thing about anything,' said Adam sulkily. He went out, muttering 'Blooming Gestapo.'

'I'm sorry I'm so out of breath, Miss

184

Bulstrode,' apologized Julia. 'I've run all the way from the tennis courts.'

'That's quite all right. I just wanted to ask you your mother's address — that is, where can I get in touch with her?'

'Oh! You'll have to write to Aunt Isabel. Mother's abroad.'

'I have your aunt's address. But I need to get in touch with your mother personally.'

'I don't see how you can,' said Julia, frowning. 'Mother's gone to Anatolia on a bus.'

'On a *bus?*' said Miss Bulstrode, taken aback.

Julia nodded vigorously.

'She likes that sort of thing,' she explained. 'And of course it's frightfully cheap. A bit uncomfortable, but Mummy doesn't mind that. Roughly, I should think she'd fetch up in Van in about three weeks or so.'

'I see — yes. Tell me, Julia, did your mother ever mention to you seeing someone here whom she'd known in her war service days?'

'No, Miss Bulstrode, I don't think so. No, I'm sure she didn't.'

'Your mother did Intelligence work, didn't she?'

'Oh, yes. Mummy seems to have loved it. Not that it sounds really exciting to me. She never blew up anything. Or got caught by the

185

Gestapo. Or had her toe nails pulled out. Or anything like that. She worked in Switzerland, I think — or was it Portugal?'

Julia added apologetically: 'One gets rather bored with all that old war stuff; and I'm afraid I don't always listen properly.'

'Well, thank you, Julia. That's all.'

'Really!' said Miss Bulstrode, when Julia had departed. 'Gone to Anatolia on a bus! The child said it exactly as though she were saying her mother had taken a 73 bus to Marshall and Snelgrove's.'

II

Jennifer walked away from the tennis courts rather moodily, swishing her racquet. The amount of double faults she had served this morning depressed her. Not, of course, that you could get a hard serve with this racquet, anyway. But she seemed to have lost control of her service lately. Her backhand, however, had definitely improved. Springer's coaching had been helpful. In many ways it was a pity that Springer was dead.

Jennifer took tennis very seriously. It was one of the things she thought about.

'Excuse me — '

Jennifer looked up, startled. A well-dressed

186

woman with golden hair, carrying a long flat parcel, was standing a few feet away from her on the path. Jennifer wondered why on earth she hadn't seen the woman coming along towards her before. It did not occur to her that the woman might have been hidden behind a tree or in the rhododendron bushes and just stepped out of them. Such an idea would not have occurred to Jennifer, since why should a woman hide behind rhododendron bushes and suddenly step out of them?

Speaking with a slightly American accent the woman said, 'I wonder if you could tell me where I could find a girl called' — she consulted a piece of paper — 'Jennifer Sutcliffe.'

Jennifer was surprised.

'I'm Jennifer Sutcliffe.'

'Why! How ridiculous! That *is* a coincidence. That in a big school like this I should be looking for one girl and I should happen upon the girl herself to ask. And they say things like that don't happen.'

'I suppose they do happen sometimes,' said Jennifer, uninterested.

'I was coming down to lunch today with some friends down here,' went on the woman, 'and at a cocktail party yesterday I happened to mention I was coming, and your aunt — or was it your godmother? — I've got such a terrible memory. She told me her name and I've forgotten that too. But anyway, she said could I possibly call here and leave a new tennis racquet for you. She said you had been asking for one.'

Jennifer's face lit up. It seemed like a miracle, nothing less.

'It must have been my godmother, Mrs Campbell. I call her Aunt Gina. It wouldn't have been Aunt Rosamond. She never gives me anything but a mingy ten shillings at Christmas.'

'Yes, I remember now. That *was* the name. Campbell.'

The parcel was held out. Jennifer took it eagerly. It was quite loosely wrapped. Jennifer uttered an exclamation of pleasure as the racquet emerged from its coverings.

'Oh, it's smashing!' she exclaimed. 'A really *good* one. I've been longing for a new racquet — you can't play decently if you haven't got a decent racquet.'

'Why I guess that's so.'

'Thank you very much for bringing it,' said Jennifer gratefully.

'It was really no trouble. Only I confess I felt a little shy. Schools always make me feel shy. So many girls. Oh, by the way, I was asked to bring back your old racquet with me.'

She picked up the racquet Jennifer had dropped.

'Your aunt — no — godmother — said she would have it restrung. It needs it badly, doesn't it?'

'I don't think that it's really worth while,' said Jennifer, but without paying much attention.

She was still experimenting with the swing and balance of her new treasure.

'But an extra racquet is always useful,' said her new friend. 'Oh dear,' she glanced at her watch. 'It is much later than I thought. I must run.'

'Have you — do you want a taxi? I could telephone — '

'No, thank you, dear. My car is right by the gate. I left it there so that I shouldn't have to turn in a narrow space. Goodbye. So pleased to have met you. I hope you enjoy the racquet.'

She literally ran along the path towards the gate. Jennifer called after her once more. 'Thank you *very* much.'

Then, gloating, she went in search of Julia. 'Look,' she flourished the racquet dramatically.

'I say! Where did you get that?'

'My godmother sent it to me. Aunt Gina. She's not my aunt, but I call her that. She's frightfully rich. I expect Mummy told her about me grumbling about my racquet. It *is* smashing, isn't it? I *must* remember to write and thank her.'

'I should hope so!' said Julia virtuously.

'Well, you know how one does forget things sometimes. Even things you really mean to do. Look, Shaista,' she added as the latter girl came towards them. 'I've got a new racquet. Isn't it a beauty?'

'It must have been very expensive,' said Shaista, scanning it respectfully. 'I wish I could play tennis well.'

'You always run into the ball.'

'I never seem to know where the ball is going to come,' said Shaista vaguely. 'Before I go home, I must have some really good shorts made in London. Or a tennis dress like the American champion Ruth Allen wears. I think that is very smart. Perhaps I will have both,' she smiled in pleasurable anticipation.

'Shaista never thinks of anything except things to wear,' said Julia scornfully as the two friends passed on. 'Do you think *we* shall ever be like that?'

'I suppose so,' said Jennifer gloomily. 'It will be an awful bore.'

They entered the Sports Pavilion, now officially vacated by the police, and Jennifer put her racquet carefully into her press.

'Isn't it lovely?' she said, stroking it affectionately.

'What have you done with the old one?'

'Oh, she took it.'

'Who?'

'The woman who brought this. She'd met Aunt Gina at a cocktail party, and Aunt Gina asked her to bring me this as she was coming down here today, and Aunt Gina said to bring up my old one and she'd have it restrung.'

'Oh, I see . . . ' But Julia was frowning.

'What did Bully want with you?' asked Jennifer.

'Bully? Oh, nothing really. Just Mummy's address. But she hasn't got one because she's on a bus. In Turkey somewhere. Jennifer — look here. Your racquet didn't *need* restringing.'

'Oh, it did, Julia. It was like a sponge.'

'I know. But it's *my* racquet really. I mean, we exchanged. It was *my* racquet that needed restringing. Yours, the one I've got now, *was* restrung. You said yourself your mother had had it restrung before you went abroad.'

'Yes, that's true.' Jennifer looked a little startled. 'Oh well, I suppose this woman — whoever she was — I ought to have asked her name, but I was so entranced — just saw that it needed restringing.'

'But you said that *she* said that it was your

191

Aunt Gina who had said it needed restringing. And your Aunt Gina couldn't have thought it needed restringing if it didn't.'

'Oh, well — ' Jennifer looked impatient. 'I suppose — I suppose — '

'You suppose what?'

'Perhaps Aunt Gina just thought that *if* I wanted a new racquet, it was because the old one wanted restringing. Anyway what does it matter?'

'I suppose it doesn't matter,' said Julia slowly. 'But I do think it's odd, Jennifer. It's like — like new lamps for old. Aladdin, you know.'

Jennifer giggled.

'Fancy rubbing my old racquet — your old racquet, I mean, and having a genie appear! If you rubbed a lamp and a genie did appear, what would you ask him for, Julia?'

'Lots of things,' breathed Julia ecstatically. 'A tape recorder, and an Alsatian — or perhaps a Great Dane, and a hundred thousand pounds, and a black satin party frock, and oh! lots of other things . . . What would you?'

'I don't really know,' said Jennifer. 'Now I've got this smashing new racquet, I don't really want anything else.'

13

Catastrophe

I

The third weekend after the opening of term followed the usual plan. It was the first weekend on which parents were allowed to take pupils out. As a result Meadowbank was left almost deserted.

On this particular Sunday there would only be twenty girls left at the school itself for the midday meal. Some of the staff had weekend leave, returning late Sunday night or early Monday morning. On this particular occasion Miss Bulstrode herself was proposing to be absent for the weekend. This was unusual since it was not her habit to leave the school during term time. But she had her reasons. She was going to stay with the Duchess of Welsham at Welsington Abbey. The duchess had made a special point of it and had added that Henry Banks would be there. Henry Banks was the Chairman of the Governors. He was an important industrialist and he had been one of the original backers of the school. The invitation was therefore almost in the nature of a command. Not that Miss Bulstrode would have allowed herself to be commanded if she had not wished to do so. But as it happened, she welcomed the invitation gladly. She was by no means indifferent to duchesses and the Duchess of Welsham was an influential duchess, whose own daughters had been sent to Meadow-bank. She was also particularly glad to have the opportunity of talking to Henry Banks on the subject of the school's future and also to put forward her own account of the recent tragic occurrence.

Owing to the influential connections at Meadowbank the murder of Miss Springer had been played down very tactfully in the Press. It had become a sad fatality rather than a mysterious murder. The impression was given, though not said, that possibly some young thugs had broken into the Sports Pavilion and that Miss Springer's death had been more accident than design. It was reported vaguely that several young men had been asked to come to the police station and 'assist the police'. Miss Bulstrode herself was anxious to mitigate any unpleasant impression that might have been given to these two influential patrons of the school. She knew that they wanted to discuss the veiled hint that she had thrown out of her coming retirement. Both the duchess and Henry Banks were anxious to persuade her to remain on. Now was the time, Miss Bulstrode felt, to push the claims of Eleanor Vansittart, to point out what a splendid person she was, and how well fitted to carry on the traditions of Meadowbank.

On Saturday morning Miss Bulstrode was just finishing off her correspondence with Ann Shapland when the telephone rang. Ann answered it.

'It's the Emir Ibrahim, Miss Bulstrode. He's arrived at Claridge's and would like to take Shaista out tomorrow.'

Miss Bulstrode took the receiver from her and had a brief conversation with the Emir's equerry. Shaista would be ready any time from eleven-thirty onwards on Sunday morning, she said. The girl must be back at the school by eight p.m.

She rang off and said:

'I wish Orientals sometimes gave you a little more warning. It has been arranged for Shaista to go out with Giselle d'Aubray tomorrow. Now that will have to be cancelled. Have we finished all the letters?'

'Yes, Miss Bulstrode.'

'Good, then I can go off with a clear conscience. Type them and send them off, and then you, too, are free for the weekend. I shan't want you until lunch time on Monday.'

'Thank you, Miss Bulstrode.'

'Enjoy yourself, my dear.'

'I'm going to,' said Ann.

'Young man?'

'Well — yes.' Ann coloured a little. 'Nothing serious, though.'

'Then there ought to be. If you're going to marry, don't leave it too late.'

'Oh this is only an old friend. Nothing exciting.'

'Excitement,' said Miss Bulstrode warningly, 'isn't always a good foundation for married life. Send Miss Chadwick to me, will you?'

Miss Chadwick bustled in.

'The Emir Ibrahim, Shaista's uncle, is taking her out tomorrow Chaddy. If he comes himself, tell him she is making good progress.'

'She's not very bright,' said Miss Chadwick.

'She's immature intellectually,' agreed Miss Bulstrode. 'But she has a remarkably mature mind in other ways. Sometimes, when you talk to her, she might be a woman of twenty-five. I suppose it's because of the sophisticated life she's led. Paris, Teheran, Cairo, Istanbul and all the rest of it. In this

196

country we're inclined to keep our children too young. We account it a merit when we say: 'She's still quite a child.' It isn't a merit. It's a grave handicap in life.'

'I don't know that I quite agree with you there, dear,' said Miss Chadwick. 'I'll go now and tell Shaista about her uncle. You go away for your weekend and don't worry about anything.'

'Oh! I shan't,' said Miss Bulstrode. 'It's a good opportunity, really, for leaving Eleanor Vansittart in charge and seeing how she shapes. With you and her in charge nothing's likely to go wrong.'

'I hope not, indeed. I'll go and find Shaista.'

Shaista looked surprised and not at all pleased to hear that her uncle had arrived in London.

'He wants to take me out tomorrow?' she grumbled. 'But Miss Chadwick, it is all arranged that I go out with Giselle d'Aubray and her mother.'

'I'm afraid you'll have to do that another time.'

'But I would much rather go out with Giselle,' said Shaista crossly. 'My uncle is not at all amusing. He eats and then he grunts and it is all very dull.'

'You mustn't talk like that. It is impolite,'

197

said Miss Chadwick. 'Your uncle is only in England for a week, I understand, and naturally he wants to see you.'

'Perhaps he has arranged a new marriage for me,' said Shaista, her face brightening. 'If so, that would be fun.'

'If that is so, he will no doubt tell you so. But you are too young to get married yet awhile. You must first finish your education.'

'Education is very boring,' said Shaista.

II

Sunday morning dawned bright and serene — Miss Shapland had departed soon after Miss Bulstrode on Saturday. Miss Johnson, Miss Rich and Miss Blake left on Sunday morning.

Miss Vansittart, Miss Chadwick, Miss Rowan and Mademoiselle Blanche were left in charge.

'I hope all the girls won't talk too much,' said Miss Chadwick dubiously. 'About poor Miss Springer I mean.'

'Let us hope,' said Eleanor Vansittart, 'that the whole affair will soon be forgotten.' She added: 'If any parents talk to *me* about it, I shall discourage them. It will be best, I think, to take quite a firm line.'

The girls went to church at 10 o'clock accompanied by Miss Vansittart and Miss Chadwick. Four girls who were Roman Catholics were escorted by Angèle Blanche to a rival religious establishment. Then, about half past eleven, the cars began to roll into the drive. Miss Vansittart, graceful, poised and dignified, stood in the hall. She greeted mothers smilingly, produced their offspring and adroitly turned aside any unwanted references to the recent tragedy.

'Terrible,' she said, 'yes, quite terrible, but, you do understand, *we don't talk about it here*. All these young minds — such a pity for them to dwell on it.'

Chaddy was also on the spot greeting old friends among the parents, discussing plans for the holidays and speaking affectionately of the various daughters.

'I do think Aunt Isabel might have come and taken *me* out,' said Julia who with Jennifer was standing with her nose pressed against the window of one of the classrooms, watching the comings and goings on the drive outside.

'Mummy's going to take me out next weekend,' said Jennifer. 'Daddy's got some important people coming down this weekend so she couldn't come today.'

'There goes Shaista,' said Julia, 'all togged

up for London. Oo-ee! Just look at the heels on her shoes. I bet old Johnson doesn't like those shoes.'

A liveried chauffeur was opening the door of a large Cadillac. Shaista climbed in and was driven away.

'You can come out with me next weekend, if you like,' said Jennifer. 'I told Mummy I'd got a friend I wanted to bring.'

'I'd love to,' said Julia. 'Look at Vansittart doing her stuff.'

'Terribly gracious, isn't she?' said Jennifer.

'I don't know why,' said Julia, 'but somehow it makes me want to laugh. It's a sort of copy of Miss Bulstrode, isn't it? Quite a good copy, but it's rather like Joyce Grenfell or someone doing an imitation.'

'There's Pam's mother,' said Jennifer. 'She's brought the little boys. How they can all get into that tiny Morris Minor I don't know.'

'They're going to have a picnic,' said Julia. 'Look at all the baskets.'

'What are you going to do this afternoon?' asked Jennifer. 'I don't think I need write to Mummy this week, do you, if I'm going to see her next week?'

'You are slack about writing letters, Jennifer.'

'I never can think of anything to say,' said Jennifer.

'I can,' said Julia, 'I can think of lots to say.' She added mournfully, 'But there isn't really anyone much to write to at present.'

'What about your mother?'

'I told you she's gone to Anatolia in a bus. You can't write letters to people who go to Anatolia in buses. At least you can't write to them all the time.'

'Where do you write to when you do write?'

'Oh, consulates here and there. She left me a list. Stamboul is the first and then Ankara and then some funny name.' She added, 'I wonder why Bully wanted to get in touch with Mummy so badly? She seemed quite upset when I said where she'd gone.'

'It can't be about you,' said Jennifer. 'You haven't done anything awful, have you?'

'Not that I know of,' said Julia. 'Perhaps she wanted to tell her about Springer.'

'Why should she?' said Jennifer. 'I should think she'd be jolly glad that there's at least one mother who *doesn't* know about Springer.'

'You mean mothers might think that their daughters were going to get murdered too?'

'I don't think my mother's quite as bad as that,' said Jennifer. 'But she did get in quite a flap about it.'

'If you ask me,' said Julia, in a meditative

manner, 'I think there's a lot that they haven't told us about Springer.'

'What sort of things?'

'Well, funny things seem to be happening. Like your new tennis racquet.'

'Oh, I meant to tell you,' said Jennifer, 'I wrote and thanked Aunt Gina and this morning I got a letter from her saying she was very glad I'd got a new racquet but that she never sent it to me.'

'I told you that racquet business was peculiar,' said Julia triumphantly, 'and you had a burglary, too, at your home, didn't you?'

'Yes, but they didn't take anything.'

'That makes it even more interesting,' said Julia. 'I think,' she added thoughtfully, 'that we shall probably have a second murder soon.'

'Oh really, Julia, why should we have a second murder?'

'Well, there's usually a second murder in books,' said Julia. 'What I think is, Jennifer, that you'll have to be frightfully careful that it isn't *you* who gets murdered.'

'Me?' said Jennifer, surprised. 'Why should anyone murder me?'

'Because somehow you're mixed up in it all,' said Julia. She added thoughtfully, 'We must try and get a bit more out of your mother next week, Jennifer. Perhaps some-body gave her some secret papers out in Ramat.'

'What sort of secret papers?'

'Oh, how should I know,' said Julia. 'Plans or formulas for a new atomic bomb. That sort of thing.'

Jennifer looked unconvinced.

III

Miss Vansittart and Miss Chadwick were in the Common Room when Miss Rowan entered and said:

'Where is Shaista? I can't find her anywhere. The Emir's car has just arrived to call for her.'

'What?' Chaddy looked up surprised. 'There must be some mistake. The Emir's car came for her about three quarters of an hour ago. I saw her get into it and drive off myself. She was one of the first to go.'

Eleanor Vansittart shrugged her shoulders. 'I suppose a car must have been ordered twice over, or something,' she said.

She went out herself and spoke to the chauffeur. 'There must be some mistake,' she said. 'The young lady has already left for London three quarters of an hour ago.'

203

The chauffeur seemed surprised. 'I suppose there must be some mistake, if you say so, madam,' he said. 'I was definitely given instructions to call at Meadowbank for the young lady.'

'I suppose there's bound to be a muddle sometimes,' said Miss Vansittart.

The chauffeur seemed unperturbed and unsurprised. 'Happens all the time,' he said. 'Telephone messages taken, written down, forgotten. All that sort of thing. But we pride ourselves in our firm that we *don't* make mistakes. Of course, if I may say so, you never know with these Oriental gentlemen. They've sometimes got quite a big entourage with them, and orders get given twice and even three times over. I expect that's what must have happened in this instance.' He turned his large car with some adroitness and drove away.

Miss Vansittart looked a little doubtful for a moment or two, but she decided there was nothing to worry about and began to look forward with satisfaction to a peaceful afternoon.

After luncheon the few girls who remained wrote letters or wandered about the grounds. A certain amount of tennis was played and the swimming pool was well patronized. Miss Vansittart took her fountain pen and her writing pad to the shade of the cedar tree. When the telephone rang at half past four it was Miss Chadwick who answered it.

'Meadowbank School?' The voice of a well-bred young Englishman spoke. 'Oh, is Miss Bulstrode there?'

'Miss Bulstrode's not here today. This is Miss Chadwick speaking.'

'Oh, it's about one of your pupils. I am speaking from Claridge's, the Emir Ibrahim's suite.'

'Oh yes? You mean about Shaista?'

'Yes. The Emir is rather annoyed at not having got a message of any kind.'

'A message? Why should he get a message?'

'Well, to say that Shaista couldn't come, or wasn't coming.'

'Wasn't coming! Do you mean to say she hasn't arrived?'

'No, no, she's certainly not arrived. Did she leave Meadowbank then?'

'Yes. A car came for her this morning — oh, about half past eleven I should think, and she drove off.'

'That's extraordinary because there's no sign of her here . . . I'd better ring up the firm that supplies the Emir's cars.'

'Oh dear,' said Miss Chadwick, 'I do hope there hasn't been an accident.'

'Oh, don't let's assume the worst,' said the

young man cheerfully. 'I think you'd have heard, you know, if there'd been an accident. Or we would. I shouldn't worry if I were you.'

But Miss Chadwick did worry.

'It seems to me very odd,' she said.

'I suppose — ' the young man hesitated.

'Yes?' said Miss Chadwick.

'Well, it's not quite the sort of thing I want to suggest to the Emir, but just between you and me there's no — er — well, no boy friend hanging about, is there?'

'Certainly not,' said Miss Chadwick with dignity.

'No, no, well I didn't think there would be, but, well one never knows with girls, does one? You'd be surprised at some of the things I've run into.'

'I can assure you,' said Miss Chadwick with dignity, 'that anything of that kind is quite impossible.'

But was it impossible? Did one ever know with girls?

She replaced the receiver and rather unwillingly went in search of Miss Vansittart. There was no reason to believe that Miss Vansittart would be any better able to deal with the situation than she herself but she felt the need of consulting with someone. Miss Vansittart said at once,

'The second car?'

They looked at each other.

'Do you think,' said Chaddy slowly, 'that we ought to report this to the police?'

'Not to the *police*,' said Eleanor Vansittart in a shocked voice.

'She did say, you know,' said Chaddy, 'that somebody might try to kidnap her.'

'Kidnap her? Nonsense!' said Miss Vansittart sharply.

'You don't think — ' Miss Chadwick was persistent.

'Miss Bulstrode left me in charge here,' said Eleanor Vansittart, 'and I shall certainly not sanction anything of the kind. We don't want any more trouble here with the police.'

Miss Chadwick looked at her without affection. She thought Miss Vansittart was being short-sighted and foolish. She went back into the house and put through a call to the Duchess of Welsham's house. Unfortunately everyone was out.

14

Miss Chadwick Lies Awake

I

Miss Chadwick was restless. She turned to and fro in her bed counting sheep, and employing other time-honoured methods of invoking sleep. In vain.

At eight o'clock, when Shaista had not returned, and there had been no news of her, Miss Chadwick had taken matters into her own hands and rung up Inspector Kelsey. She was relieved to find that he did not take the matter too seriously. She could leave it all to him, he assured her. It would be an easy matter to check up on a possible accident. After that, he would get in touch with London. Everything would be done that was necessary. Perhaps the girl herself was playing truant. He advised Miss Chadwick to say as little as possible at the school. Let it be thought that Shaista was staying the night with her uncle at Claridge's.

'The last thing you want, or that Miss Bulstrode would want, is any more publicity,' said Kelsey. 'It's most unlikely that the girl has been kidnapped. So don't worry, Miss Chadwick. Leave it all to us.'

But Miss Chadwick did worry.

Lying in bed, sleepless, her mind went from possible kidnapping back to murder.

Murder at Meadowbank. It was terrible! Unbelievable! *Meadowbank.* Miss Chadwick loved Meadowbank. She loved it, perhaps, even more than Miss Bulstrode did, though in a somewhat different way. It had been such a risky, gallant enterprise. Following Miss Bulstrode faithfully into the hazardous undertaking, she had endured panic more than once. Supposing the whole thing should fail. They hadn't really had much capital. If they did not succeed — if their backing was withdrawn — Miss Chadwick had an anxious mind and could always tabulate innumerable ifs. Miss Bulstrode had enjoyed the adventure, the hazard of it all, but Chaddy had not. Sometimes, in an agony of apprehension, she had pleaded for Meadowbank to be run on more conventional lines. It would be *safer*, she urged. But Miss Bulstrode had been uninterested in safety. She had her vision of what a school should be and she had pursued it unafraid. And she had been justified in her audacity. But oh, the relief to Chaddy when success was a *fait accompli.* When Meadowbank was established, safely established, as a great English institution. It was then that her love for Meadowbank had flowed most fully. Doubts, fears, anxieties, all slipped from her. Peace and prosperity had come. She basked in the prosperity of Meadowbank like a purring tabby cat.

She had been quite upset when Miss Bulstrode had first begun to talk of retirement. Retire *now* — when everything was set fair? What madness! Miss Bulstrode talked of travel, of all the things in the world to see. Chaddy was unimpressed. Nothing, anywhere, could be half as good as Meadowbank! It had seemed to her that nothing could affect the well-being of Meadowbank — But now — Murder!

Such an ugly violent word — coming in from the outside world like an ill-mannered storm wind. Murder — a word associated by Miss Chadwick only with delinquent boys with flick knives, or evil-minded doctors poisoning their wives. But murder here — at a school — and not any school — at Meadowbank. Incredible.

Really, Miss Springer — poor Miss Springer, naturally it wasn't her *fault* — but, illogically, Chaddy felt that it must have been her fault in some way. She didn't know the traditions of Meadowbank. A tactless woman. She must in some way have invited murder. Miss Chadwick rolled over, turned her pillow, said 'I mustn't go on thinking of it all. Perhaps I had better get up and take some aspirin. I'll just try counting to fifty . . . '

Before she had got to fifty, her mind was off again on the same track. Worrying. Would all this — and perhaps kidnapping too — get into the papers? Would parents, reading, hasten to take their daughters away . . .

Oh dear, she *must* calm down and go to sleep. What time was it? She switched on her light and looked at her watch — Just after a quarter to one. Just about the time that poor Miss Springer . . . No, she would *not* think of it any more. And, how stupid of Miss Springer to have gone off by herself like that without waking up somebody else.

'Oh dear,' said Miss Chadwick. 'I'll have to take some aspirin.'

She got out of bed and went over to the washstand. She took two aspirins with a drink of water. On her way back, she pulled aside the curtain of the window and peered out. She did so to reassure herself more than for any other reason. She wanted to feel that of course there would never again be a light in the Sports Pavilion in the middle of the night.

But there was.

In a minute Chaddy had leapt to action. She thrust her feet into stout shoes, pulled on a thick coat, picked up her electric torch and rushed out of her room and down the stairs. She had blamed Miss Springer for not obtaining support before going out to investigate, but it never occurred to her to do so. She was only eager to get out to the Pavilion and find out who the intruder was. She did pause to pick up a weapon — not perhaps a very good one, but a weapon of kinds, and then she was out of the side door and following quickly along the path through the shrubbery. She was out of breath, but completely resolute. Only when she got at last to the door, did she slacken up and take care to move softly. The door was slightly ajar. She pushed it further open and looked in . . .

II

At about the time when Miss Chadwick was rising from bed in search of aspirin, Ann Shapland, looking very attractive in a black dance frock, was sitting at a table in Le Nid Sauvage eating Supreme of Chicken and smiling at the young man opposite her. Dear Dennis, thought Ann to herself, always so exactly the same. It is what I simply couldn't bear if I married him. He *is* rather a pet, all the same. Aloud she remarked:

'What fun this is, Dennis. Such a glorious *change.*'

'How is the new job?' said Dennis.

'Well, actually, I'm rather enjoying it.'

'Doesn't seem to me quite your sort of thing.'

Ann laughed. 'I'd be hard put to it to say what is my sort of thing. I like variety, Dennis.'

'I never can see why you gave up your job with old Sir Mervyn Todhunter.'

'Well, chiefly because of Sir Mervyn Todhunter. The attention he bestowed on me was beginning to annoy his wife. And it's part of my policy never to annoy wives. They can do you a lot of harm, you know.'

'Jealous cats,' said Dennis.

'Oh no, not really,' said Ann. 'I'm rather on the wives' side. Anyway I liked Lady Todhunter much better than old Mervyn. Why are you surprised at my present job?'

'Oh, a school. You're not scholastically minded at all, I should have said.'

'I'd hate to *teach* in a school. I'd hate to be penned up. Herded with a lot of women. But the work as the secretary of a school like Meadowbank is rather fun. It really is a unique place, you know. And Miss Bulstrode's unique. She's really something, I can

213

tell you. Her steel-grey eye goes through you and sees your innermost secrets. And she keeps you on your toes. I'd hate to make a mistake in any letters I'd taken down for her. Oh yes, she's certainly something.'

'I wish you'd get tired of all these jobs,' said Dennis. 'It's quite time, you know, Ann, that you stopped all this racketing about with jobs here and jobs there and — and settled down.'

'You are sweet, Dennis,' said Ann in a noncommittal manner.

'We could have quite fun, you know,' said Dennis.

'I daresay,' said Ann, 'but I'm not ready yet. And anyway, you know, there's my mamma.'

'Yes, I was — going to talk to you about that.'

'About my mamma? What were you going to say?'

'Well, Ann, you know I think you're wonderful. The way you get an interesting job and then you chuck it all up and go home to her.'

'Well, I have to now and again when she gets a really bad attack.'

'I know. As I say, I think it's wonderful of you. But all the same there are places, you know, very good places nowadays where — where people like your mother are well

214

looked after and all that sort of thing. Not really loony bins.'

'And which cost the earth,' said Ann.

'No, no, not necessarily. Why, even under the Health Scheme — '

A bitter note crept into Ann's voice. 'Yes, I daresay it will come to that one day. But in the meantime I've got a nice old pussy who lives with Mother and who can cope normally. Mother is quite reasonable most of the time — And when she — isn't, I come back and lend a hand.'

'She's — she isn't — she's never — ?'

'Are you going to say violent, Dennis? You've got an extraordinarily lurid imagination. No. My dear mamma is *never* violent. She just gets fuddled. She forgets where she is and who she is and wants to go for long walks, and then as like as not she'll jump into a train or a bus and take off somewhere and — well, it's all very difficult, you see. Sometimes it's too much for one person to cope with. But she's quite happy, even when she *is* fuddled. And sometimes quite funny about it. I remember her saying: 'Ann, darling, it really is very embarrassing. I knew I was going to Tibet and there I was sitting in that hotel in Dover with no idea how to get there. Then I thought why was I going to Tibet? And I thought I'd better come home.

215

Then I couldn't remember how long ago it was when I left home. It makes it very embarrassing, dear, when you can't quite remember things.' Mummy was really very funny over it all, you know. I mean she quite sees the humorous side herself.'

'I've never actually met her,' Dennis began.

'I don't encourage people to meet her,' said Ann. 'That's the one thing I think you *can* do for your people. Protect them from — well, curiosity and pity.'

'It's not curiosity, Ann.'

'No, I don't think it would be that with you. But it would be pity. I don't want that.'

'I can see what you mean.'

'But if you think I mind giving up jobs from time to time and going home for an indefinite period, I don't,' said Ann. 'I never meant to get embroiled in anything too deeply. Not even when I took my first post after my secretarial training. I thought the thing was to get really good at the job. Then if you're really good you can pick and choose your posts. You see different places and you see different kinds of life. At the moment I'm seeing school life. The best school in England seen from within! I shall stay there, I expect, about a year and a half.'

'You never really get caught up in things, do you, Ann?'

'No,' said Ann thoughtfully, 'I don't think I do. I think I'm one of those people who is a born observer. More like a commentator on the radio.'

'You're so detached,' said Dennis gloomily. 'You don't really care about anything or anyone.'

'I expect I shall some day,' said Ann encouragingly.

'I do understand more or less how you're thinking and feeling.'

'I doubt it,' said Ann.

'Anyway, I don't think you'll last a year. You'll get fed up with all those women,' said Dennis.

'There's a very good-looking gardener,' said Ann. She laughed when she saw Dennis's expression. 'Cheer up, I'm only trying to make you jealous.'

'What's this about one of the mistresses having been killed?'

'Oh, that.' Ann's face became serious and thoughtful.

'That's odd, Dennis. Very odd indeed. It was the Games Mistress. You know the type. I-am-a-plain-Games-Mistress. I think there's a lot more behind it than has come out yet.'

'Well, don't you get mixed up in anything unpleasant.'

'That's easy to say. I've never had any

217

chance at displaying my talents as a sleuth. I think I *might* be rather good at it.'

'Now, Ann.'

'Darling, I'm not going to trail dangerous criminals. I'm just going to — well, make a few logical deductions. Why and who. And what for? That sort of thing. I've come across one piece of information that's rather interesting.'

'Ann!'

'Don't look so agonized. Only it doesn't seem to link up with anything,' said Ann thoughtfully. 'Up to a point it all fits in very well. And then, suddenly, it doesn't.' She added cheerfully, 'Perhaps there'll be a second murder, and that will clarify things a little.'

It was at exactly that moment that Miss Chadwick pushed open the Sports Pavilion door.

15

Murder Repeats Itself

'Come along,' said Inspector Kelsey, entering the room with a grim face. 'There's been another.'

'Another what?' Adam looked up sharply.

'Another murder,' said Inspector Kelsey. He led the way out of the room and Adam followed him. They had been sitting in the latter's room drinking beer and discussing various probabilities when Kelsey had been summoned to the telephone.

'Who is it?' demanded Adam, as he followed Inspector Kelsey down the stairs.

'Another mistress — Miss Vansittart.'

'Where?'

'In the Sports Pavilion.'

'The Sports Pavilion again,' said Adam. 'What is there about this Sports Pavilion?'

'*You'd* better give it the once-over this time,' said Inspector Kelsey. 'Perhaps your technique of searching may be more successful than ours has been. There must be *something* about that Sports Pavilion or why should everyone get killed there?'

He and Adam got into his car. 'I expect the doctor will be there ahead of us. He hasn't so far to go.'

It was, Kelsey thought, like a bad dream repeating itself as he entered the brilliantly lighted Sports Pavilion. There, once again, was a body with the doctor kneeling beside it. Once again the doctor rose from his knees and got up.

'Killed about half an hour ago,' he said. 'Forty minutes at most.'

'Who found her?' said Kelsey.

One of his men spoke up. 'Miss Chadwick.'

'That's the old one, isn't it?'

'Yes. She saw a light, came out here, and found her dead. She stumbled back to the house and more or less went into hysterics. It was the matron who telephoned, Miss Johnson.'

'Right,' said Kelsey. 'How was she killed? Shot again?'

The doctor shook his head. 'No. Slugged on the back of the head, this time. Might have been a cosh or a sandbag. Something of that kind.'

A golf club with a steel head was lying near the door. It was the only thing that looked remotely disorderly in the place.

'What about that?' said Kelsey, pointing. 'Could she have been hit with that?'

The doctor shook his head. 'Impossible. There's no mark on her. No, it was definitely a heavy rubber cosh or a sandbag, something of that sort.'

'Something — professional?'

'Probably, yes. Whoever it was, didn't mean to make any noise this time. Came up behind her and slugged her on the back of the head. She fell forward and probably never knew what hit her.'

'What was she doing?'

'She was probably kneeling down,' said the doctor. 'Kneeling in front of this locker.'

The Inspector went up to the locker and looked at it. 'That's the girl's name on it, I presume,' he said. 'Shaista — let me see, that's the — that's the Egyptian girl, isn't it? Her Highness Princess Shaista.' He turned to Adam. 'It seems to tie in, doesn't it? Wait a minute — that's the girl they reported this evening as missing?'

'That's right, sir,' said the Sergeant. 'A car called for her here, supposed to have been sent by her uncle who's staying at Claridge's in London. She got into it and drove off.'

'No reports come in?'

'Not as yet, sir. Got a network out. And the Yard is on it.'

'A nice simple way of kidnapping anyone,' said Adam. 'No struggle, no cries. All you've got to know is that the girl's expecting a car to fetch her and all you've got to do is to look like a high-class chauffeur and arrive there before the other car does. The girl will step in without a second thought and you can drive off without her suspecting in the least what's happening to her.'

'No abandoned car found anywhere?' asked Kelsey.

'We've had no news of one,' said the Sergeant. 'The Yard's on it now as I said,' he added, 'and the Special Branch.'

'May mean a bit of a political schemozzle,' said the Inspector. 'I don't suppose for a minute they'll be able to take her out of the country.'

'What do they want to kidnap her for anyway?' asked the doctor.

'Goodness knows,' said Kelsey gloomily. 'She told me she was afraid of being kidnapped and I'm ashamed to say I thought she was just showing off.'

'I thought so, too, when you told me about it,' said Adam.

'The trouble is we don't know enough,' said Kelsey. 'There are far too many loose ends.' He looked around. 'Well, there doesn't seem to be anything more that I can do here.

Get on with the usual stuff — photographs, fingerprints, etc. I'd better go along to the house.'

At the house he was received by Miss Johnson. She was shaken but preserved her self-control.

'It's terrible, Inspector,' she said. 'Two of our mistresses killed. Poor Miss Chadwick's in a dreadful state.'

'I'd like to see her as soon as I can.'

'The doctor gave her something and she's much calmer now. Shall I take you to her?'

'Yes, in a minute or two. First of all, just tell me what you can about the last time you saw Miss Vansittart.'

'I haven't seen her at all today,' said Miss Johnson. 'I've been away all day. I arrived back here just before eleven and went straight up to my room. I went to bed.'

'You didn't happen to look out of your window towards the Sports Pavilion?'

'No. No, I never thought of it. I'd spent the day with my sister whom I hadn't seen for some time and my mind was full of home news. I took a bath and went to bed and read a book, and I turned off the light and went to sleep. The next thing I knew was when Miss Chadwick burst in, looking as white as a sheet and shaking all over.'

'Was Miss Vansittart absent today?'

'No, she was here. She was in charge. Miss Bulstrode's away.'

'Who else was here, of the mistresses, I mean?'

Miss Johnson considered a moment. 'Miss Vansittart, Miss Chadwick, the French mistress, Mademoiselle Blanche, Miss Rowan.'

'I see. Well, I think you'd better take me to Miss Chadwick now.'

Miss Chadwick was sitting in a chair in her room. Although the night was a warm one the electric fire had been turned on and a rug was wrapped round her knees. She turned a ghastly face towards Inspector Kelsey.

'She's dead — she *is* dead? There's no chance that — that she might come round?'

Kelsey shook his head slowly.

'It's so awful,' said Miss Chadwick, 'with Miss Bulstrode away.' She burst into tears. 'This will ruin the school,' she said. 'This will ruin Meadowbank. I can't bear it — I really can't bear it.'

Kelsey sat down beside her. 'I know,' he said sympathetically, 'I know. It's been a terrible shock to you, but I want you to be brave, Miss Chadwick, and tell me all you know. The sooner we can find out who did it, the less trouble and publicity there will be.'

'Yes, yes, I can see that. You see, I — I went to bed early because I thought it would be nice for once to have a nice long night. But I couldn't go to sleep. I was worrying.'

'Worrying about the school?'

'Yes. And about Shaista being missing. And then I began thinking of Miss Springer and whether — whether her murder would affect the parents, and whether perhaps they wouldn't send their girls back here next term. I was so terribly upset for Miss Bulstrode. I mean, she's *made* this place. It's been such a fine achievement.'

'I know. Now go on telling me — you were worried, and you couldn't sleep?'

'No, I counted sheep and everything. And then I got up and took some aspirin and when I'd taken it I just happened to draw back the curtains from the window. I don't quite know why. I suppose because I'd been thinking about Miss Springer. Then you see, I saw . . . I saw a light there.'

'What kind of a light?'

'Well, a sort of dancing light. I mean — I think it must have been a torch. It was just like the light that Miss Johnson and I saw before.'

'It was just the same, was it?'

'Yes. Yes, I think so. Perhaps a little feebler, but I don't know.'

'Yes. And then?'

'And then,' said Miss Chadwick, her voice

suddenly becoming more resonant, 'I was determined that *this* time I would see who it was out there and what they were doing. So I got up and pulled on my coat and my shoes, and I rushed out of the house.'

'You didn't think of calling anyone else?'

'No. No, I didn't. You see I was in such a hurry to get there, I was so afraid the person — whoever it was — would go away.'

'Yes. Go on, Miss Chadwick.'

'So I went as fast as I could. I went up to the door and just before I got there I went on tiptoe so that — so that I should be able to look in and nobody would hear me coming. I got there. The door was not shut — just ajar and I pushed it very slightly open. I looked round it and — and there she was. Fallen forward on her face, *dead . . .* '

She began to shake all over.

'Yes, yes, Miss Chadwick, it's all right. By the way, there was a golf club out there. Did you take it out? Or did Miss Vansittart?'

'A golf club?' said Miss Chadwick vaguely. 'I can't remember — Oh, yes, I think I picked it up in the hall. I took it out with me in case — well, in case I should have to use it. When I saw Eleanor I suppose I just dropped it. Then I got back to the house somehow and I found Miss Johnson — Oh! I can't bear it. I can't bear it — this will be the end of Meadowbank — '

Miss Chadwick's voice rose hysterically. Miss Johnson came forward.

'To discover two murders is too much of a strain for anyone,' said Miss Johnson. 'Certainly for anyone her age. You don't want to ask her any more, do you?'

Inspector Kelsey shook his head.

As he was going downstairs, he noticed a pile of old-fashioned sandbags with buckets in an alcove. Dating from the war, perhaps, but the uneasy thought occurred to him that it needn't have been a professional with a cosh who had slugged Miss Vansittart. Someone in the building, someone who hadn't wished to risk the sound of a shot a second time, and who, very likely, had disposed of the incriminating pistol after the last murder, could have helped themselves to an innocent-looking but lethal weapon — and possibly even replaced it tidily afterwards!

16

Riddle of the Sports Pavilion

I

'*My head is bloody but unbowed*,' said Adam to himself.

He was looking at Miss Bulstrode. He had never, he thought, admired a woman more. She sat, cool and unmoved, with her lifework falling in ruins about her.

From time to time telephone calls came through announcing that yet another pupil was being removed.

Finally Miss Bulstrode had taken her decision. Excusing herself to the police officers, she summoned Ann Shapland, and dictated a brief statement. The school would be closed until the end of term. Parents who found it inconvenient to have their children home, were welcome to leave them in her care and their education would be continued.

'You've got the list of parents' names and addresses? And their telephone numbers?'

'Yes, Miss Bulstrode.'

'Then start on the telephone. After that see

228

a typed notice goes to everyone.'

'Yes, Miss Bulstrode.'

On her way out, Ann Shapland paused near the door.

She flushed and her words came with a rush.

'Excuse me, Miss Bulstrode. It's not my business — but isn't it a pity to — to be premature? I mean — after the first panic, when people have had time to think — surely they won't want to take the girls away. They'll be sensible and think better of it.'

Miss Bulstrode looked at her keenly.

'You think I'm accepting defeat too easily?'

Ann flushed.

'I know — you think it's cheek. But — but, well then, yes, I do.'

'You're a fighter, child, I'm glad to see. But you're quite wrong. I'm not accepting defeat. I'm going on my knowledge of human nature. Urge people to take their children away, force it on them — and they won't want to nearly so much. They'll think up reasons for letting them remain. Or at the worst they'll decide to let them come back next term — if there is a next term,' she added grimly.

She looked at Inspector Kelsey.

'That's up to you,' she said. 'Clear these murders up — catch whoever is responsible for them — and we'll be all right.'

Inspector Kelsey looked unhappy. He said: 'We're doing our best.'

Ann Shapland went out.

'Competent girl,' said Miss Bulstrode. 'And loyal.'

This was in the nature of a parenthesis. She pressed her attack.

'Have you absolutely *no* idea of who killed two of my mistresses in the Sports Pavilion? You ought to, by this time. And this kidnapping on top of everything else. I blame myself there. The girl talked about someone wanting to kidnap her. I thought, God forgive me, she was making herself important. I see now that there must have been something behind it. Someone must have hinted, or warned — one doesn't know which — ' She broke off, resuming: 'You've no news of any kind?'

'Not yet. But I don't think you need worry too much about that. It's been passed to the C.I.D. The Special Branch is on to it, too. They ought to find her within twenty-four hours, thirty-six at most. There are advantages in this being an island. All the ports, airports, etc., are alerted. And the police in every district are keeping a lookout. It's actually easy enough to kidnap anyone — it's keeping them hidden that's the problem. Oh, we'll find her.'

'I hope you'll find her alive,' said Miss Bulstrode grimly. 'We seem to be up against someone who isn't too scrupulous about human life.'

'They wouldn't have troubled to kidnap her if they'd meant to do away with her,' said Adam. 'They could have done that here easily enough.'

He felt that the last words were unfortunate. Miss Bulstrode gave him a look.

'So it seems,' she said dryly.

The telephone rang. Miss Bulstrode took up the receiver.

'Yes?'

She motioned to Inspector Kelsey.

'It's for you.'

Adam and Miss Bulstrode watched him as he took the call. He grunted, jotted down a note or two, said finally: 'I see. Alderton Priors. That's Wallshire. Yes, we'll cooperate. Yes, Super. I'll carry on here, then.'

He put down the receiver and stayed a moment lost in thought. Then he looked up.

'His Excellency got a ransom note this morning. Typed on a new Corona. Postmark Portsmouth. Bet that's a blind.'

'Where and how?' asked Adam.

'Crossroads two miles north of Alderton Priors. That's a bit of bare moorland. Envelope containing money to be put under stone behind A.A. box there at 2 a.m. tomorrow morning.'

'How much?'

'Twenty thousand.' He shook his head. 'Sounds amateurish to me.'

'What are you going to do?' asked Miss Bulstrode.

Inspector Kelsey looked at her. He was a different man. Official reticence hung about him like a cloak.

'The responsibility isn't mine, madam,' he said. 'We have our methods.'

'I hope they're successful,' said Miss Bulstrode.

'Ought to be easy,' said Adam.

'Amateurish?' said Miss Bulstrode, catching at a word they had used. 'I wonder . . . '

Then she said sharply:

'What about my staff? What remains of it, that is to say? Do I trust them, or don't I?'

As Inspector Kelsey hesitated, she said,

'You're afraid that if you tell me who is *not* cleared, I should show it in my manner to them. You're wrong. I shouldn't.'

'I don't think you would,' said Kelsey. 'But I can't afford to take any chances. It doesn't look, on the face of it, as though any of your staff *can* be the person we're looking for. That is, not so far as we've been able to checkup on them. We've paid special attention to those who are new this term — that is Mademoiselle Blanche, Miss Springer and your secretary, Miss Shapland. Miss Shapland's past is completely corroborated. She's the daughter of a retired general, she has held the posts she says she did and her former employers vouch for her. In addition she has an alibi for last night. When Miss Vansittart was killed, Miss Shapland was with a Mr Dennis Rathbone at a night club. They're both well known there, and Mr Rathbone has an excellent character. Mademoiselle Blanche's antecedents have also been checked. She has taught at a school in the north of England and at two schools in Germany, and has been given an excellent character. She is said to be a first-class teacher.'

'Not by our standards,' sniffed Miss Bulstrode.

'Her French background has also been checked. As regards Miss Springer, things are not quite so conclusive. She did her training where she says, but there have been gaps since in her periods of employment which are not fully accounted for.

'Since, however, she was killed,' added the Inspector, 'that seems to exonerate her.'

'I agree,' said Miss Bulstrode dryly, 'that both Miss Springer and Miss Vansittart are *hors de combat* as suspects. Let us talk sense. Is Mademoiselle Blanche, in spite of her blameless background, still a suspect merely because she is still alive?'

'She *could* have done both murders. She was here, in the building, last night,' said Kelsey. 'She *says* she went to bed early and slept and heard nothing until the alarm was given. There's no evidence to the contrary. We've got nothing against her. But Miss Chadwick says definitely that she's sly.'

Miss Bulstrode waved that aside impatiently.

'Miss Chadwick always finds the French Mistresses sly. She's got a thing about them.' She looked at Adam. 'What do *you* think?'

'I think she pries,' said Adam slowly. 'It may be just natural inquisitiveness. It may be something more. I can't make up my mind. She doesn't *look* to me like a killer, but how does one know?'

'That's just it,' said Kelsey. 'There *is* a killer here, a ruthless killer who has killed twice — but it's very hard to believe that it's one of the staff. Miss Johnson was with her sister last night at Limeston on Sea, and anyway she's been with you seven years. Miss Chadwick's been with you since you started. Both of them, anyway, are clear of Miss Springer's death. Miss Rich has been with you over a year and was staying last night at the Alton Grange Hotel, twenty miles away, Miss Blake was with friends at Littleport, Miss Rowan has been with you for a year and has a good background. As for your servants, frankly I can't see any of them as murderers. They're all local, too . . . '

Miss Bulstrode nodded pleasantly.

'I quite agree with your reasoning. It doesn't leave much, does it? So — ' She paused and fixed an accusing eye on Adam. 'It looks really — as though it must be *you*.'

His mouth opened in astonishment.

'On the spot,' she mused. 'Free to come and go . . . Good story to account for your presence here. Background OK but you *could* be a double crosser, you know.'

Adam recovered himself.

'Really, Miss Bulstrode,' he said admiringly, 'I take off my hat to you. You think of *everything*!'

II

'Good gracious!' cried Mrs Sutcliffe at the breakfast table. 'Henry!'

She had just unfolded her newspaper.

The width of the table was between her and her husband since her weekend guests had not yet put in an appearance for the meal.

Mr Sutcliffe, who had opened his paper to the financial page, and was absorbed in the unforeseen movements of certain shares, did not reply.

'*Henry!*'

The clarion call reached him. He raised a startled face.

'What's the matter, Joan?'

'The matter? Another murder! At Meadowbank! At Jennifer's school.'

'What? Here, let *me* see!'

Disregarding his wife's remark that it would be in his paper, too, Mr Sutcliffe leant across the table and snatched the sheet from his wife's grasp.

'Miss Eleanor Vansittart . . . Sports Pavilion . . . same spot where Miss Springer, the Games Mistress . . . hm . . . hm . . . '

'I can't believe it!' Mrs Sutcliffe was wailing. 'Meadowbank. Such an exclusive school. Royalty there and everything . . . '

Mr Sutcliffe crumpled up the paper and threw it down on the table.

'Only one thing to be done,' he said. 'You get over there right away and take Jennifer out of it.'

'You mean take her away — altogether?'

'That's what I mean.'

'You don't think that would be a little too drastic? After Rosamond being so good about it and managing to get her in?'

'You won't be the only one taking your daughter away! Plenty of vacancies soon at your precious Meadowbank.'

'Oh, Henry, do you think so?'

'Yes, I do. Something badly wrong there. Take Jennifer away today.'

'Yes — of course — I suppose you're right. What shall we do with her?'

'Send her to a secondary modern somewhere handy. They don't have murders there.'

'Oh, Henry, but they *do*. Don't you remember? There was a boy who shot the science master at one. It was in last week's *News of the World*.'

'I don't know what England's coming to,' said Mr Sutcliffe.

Disgusted, he threw his napkin on the table and strode from the room.

III

Adam was alone in the Sports Pavilion . . . His deft fingers were turning over the contents of the lockers. It was unlikely that he would find anything where the police had failed but after all, one could never be sure.

As Kelsey had said every department's technique varied a little.

What was there that linked this expensive modern building with sudden and violent death? The idea of a rendezvous was out. No one would choose to keep a rendezvous a second time in the same place where murder had occurred. It came back to it, then, that there was something here that someone was looking for. Hardly a *cache* of jewels. That seemed ruled out. There could be no secret hiding place, false drawers, spring catches, etc. And the contents of the lockers were pitifully simple. They had their secrets, but they were the secrets of school life. Photographs of pin up heroes, packets of cigarettes, an occasional unsuitable cheap paperback. Especially he returned to Shaista's locker. It was while bending over that that Miss Vansittart had been killed. What had Miss Vansittart expected to find there? Had she found it? Had her killer taken it from her dead hand and then slipped out of the building in the nick of time to miss being discovered by Miss Chadwick?

In that case it was no good looking. Whatever it was, was gone.

The sound of footsteps outside aroused him from his thoughts. He was on his feet and lighting a cigarette in the middle of the floor when Julia Upjohn appeared in the doorway, hesitating a little.

'Anything you want, miss?' asked Adam.

'I wondered if I could have my tennis racquet.'

'Don't see why not,' said Adam. 'Police constable left me here,' he explained mendaciously. 'Had to drop back to the station for something. Told me to stop here while he was away.'

'To see if he came back, I suppose,' said Julia.

'The police constable?'

'No. I mean, the murderer. They do, don't they? Come back to the scene of the crime. They have to! It's a compulsion.'

'You may be right,' said Adam. He looked up at the serried rows of racquets in their presses. 'Whereabouts is yours?'

'Under U,' said Julia. 'Right at the far end. We have our names on them,' she explained, pointing out the adhesive tape as he handed the racquet to her.

'Seen some service,' said Adam. 'But been a good racquet once.'

'Can I have Jennifer Sutcliffe's too?' asked Julia.

'New,' said Adam appreciatively, as he handed it to her.

'Brand new,' said Julia. 'Her aunt sent it to her only the other day.'

'Lucky girl.'

'She ought to have a good racquet. She's very good at tennis. Her backhand's come on like anything this term.' She looked round. 'Don't you think he *will* come back?'

Adam was a moment or two getting it.

'Oh. The murderer? No, I don't think it's really likely. Bit risky, wouldn't it be?'

'You don't think murderers feel they *have* to?'

'Not unless they've left something behind.'

'You mean a clue? I'd like to find a clue. Have the police found one?'

'They wouldn't tell me.'

'No. I suppose they wouldn't . . . Are you interested in crime?'

She looked at him inquiringly. He returned her glance. There was, as yet, nothing of the woman in her. She must be of much the same age as Shaista, but her eyes held nothing but interested inquiry.

'Well — I suppose — up to a point — we all are.'

Julia nodded in agreement.

'Yes. I think so, too . . . I can think of all sorts of solutions — but most of them are very far fetched. It's rather fun, though.'

'You weren't fond of Miss Vansittart?'

240

'I never really thought about her. She was all right. A bit like the Bull — Miss Bulstrode — but not really like her. More like an understudy in a theatre. I didn't mean it was fun she was dead. I'm sorry about that.'

She walked out holding the two racquets.

Adam remained looking round the Pavilion.

'What the hell could there ever have been here?' he muttered to himself.

IV

'Good lord,' said Jennifer, allowing Julia's forehand drive to pass her. 'There's Mummy.'

The two girls turned to stare at the agitated figure of Mrs Sutcliffe, shepherded by Miss Rich, rapidly arriving and gesticulating as she did so.

'More fuss, I suppose,' said Jennifer resignedly. 'It's the murder. You *are* lucky, Julia, that your mother's safely on a bus in the Caucasus.'

'There's still Aunt Isabel.'

'Aunts don't mind in the same way.'

'Hallo, Mummy,' she added, as Mrs Sutcliffe arrived.

'You must come and pack your things, Jennifer. I'm taking you back with me.'

'Back home?'

'Yes.'

'But — you don't mean altogether? Not for good?'

'Yes. I do.'

'But you can't — really. My tennis has come on like anything. I've got a very good chance of winning the singles and Julia and I *might* win the doubles, though I don't think it's very likely.'

'You're coming home with me today.'

'Why?'

'Don't ask questions.'

'I suppose it's because of Miss Springer and Miss Vansittart being murdered. But no one's murdered any of the girls. I'm sure they wouldn't want to. And Sports Day is in three weeks' time. I *think* I shall win the Long Jump and I've a good chance for the Hurdling.'

'Don't argue with me, Jennifer. You're coming back with me today. Your father insists.'

'But, Mummy — '

Arguing persistently Jennifer moved towards the house by her mother's side.

Suddenly she broke away and ran back to the tennis court.

'Goodbye, Julia. Mummy seems to have got the wind up thoroughly. Daddy, too, apparently. Sickening, isn't it? Goodbye, I'll write to you.'

'I'll write to you, too, and tell you all that happens.'

'I hope they don't kill Chaddy next. I'd rather it was Mademoiselle Blanche, wouldn't you?'

'Yes. She's the one we could spare best. I say, did you notice how black Miss Rich was looking?'

'She hasn't said a word. She's furious at Mummy coming and taking me away.'

'Perhaps she'll stop her. She's very forceful, isn't she? Not like anyone else.'

'She reminds me of someone,' said Jennifer.

'I don't think she's a bit like anybody. She always seems to be quite different.'

'Oh yes. She is different. I meant in appearance. But the person I knew was quite fat.'

'I can't imagine Miss Rich being fat.'

'Jennifer . . . ' called Mrs Sutcliffe.

'I do think parents are trying,' said Jennifer crossly. 'Fuss, fuss, fuss. They never stop. I do think you're lucky to — '

'I know. You said that before. But just at the moment, let me tell you, I wish Mummy were a good deal nearer, and *not* on a bus in Anatolia.'

'Jennifer . . . '

'Coming . . . '

Julia walked slowly in the direction of the Sports Pavilion. Her steps grew slower and slower and finally she stopped altogether. She stood, frowning, lost in thought.

The luncheon bell sounded, but she hardly heard it. She stared down at the racquet she was holding, moved a step or two along the path, then wheeled round and marched determinedly towards the house. She went in by the front door, which was not allowed, and thereby avoided meeting any of the other girls. The hall was empty. She ran up the stairs to her small bedroom, looked round her hurriedly, then lifting the mattress on her bed, shoved the racquet flat beneath it. Then, rapidly smoothing her hair, she walked demurely downstairs to the dining-room.

17

Aladdin's Cave

I

The girls went up to bed that night more quietly than usual. For one thing their numbers were much depleted. At least thirty of them had gone home. The others reacted according to their several dispositions. Excitement, trepidation, a certain amount of giggling that was purely nervous in origin and there were some again who were merely quiet and thoughtful.

Julia Upjohn went up quietly amongst the first wave. She went into her room and closed the door. She stood there listening to the whispers, giggles, footsteps and goodnights. Then silence closed down — or a near silence. Faint voices echoed in the distance, and footsteps went to and fro to the bathroom.

There was no lock on the door. Julia pulled a chair against it, with the top of the chair wedged under the handle. That would give her warning if anyone should come in. But no one was likely to come in. It was strictly forbidden for the girls to go into each other's rooms, and the only mistress who did so was Miss Johnson, if one of the girls was ill or out of sorts.

Julia went to her bed, lifted up the mattress and groped under it. She brought out the tennis racquet and stood a moment holding it. She had decided to examine it now, and not later. A light in her room showing under the door might attract attention when all lights were supposed to be off. Now was the time when a light was normal for undressing and for reading in bed until half past ten if you wanted to do so.

She stood staring down at the racquet. How could there be anything hidden in a tennis racquet?

'But there must be,' said Julia to herself. 'There *must*. The burglary at Jennifer's home, the woman who came with that silly story about a new racquet . . . '

Only Jennifer would have believed that, thought Julia scornfully.

No, it was 'new lamps for old' and that meant, like in Aladdin, that there was *something* about this particular tennis racquet. Jennifer and Julia had never mentioned to anyone that they had swopped racquets — or at least, she herself never had.

So really then, *this* was the racquet that everyone was looking for in the Sports Pavilion. And it was up to her to find out *why!* She examined it carefully. There was nothing unusual about it to look at. It was a good quality racquet, somewhat the worse for wear, but restrung and eminently usable. Jennifer had complained of the balance.

The only place you could possibly conceal anything in a tennis racquet was in the handle. You could, she supposed, hollow out the handle to make a hiding place. It sounded a little far fetched but it was possible. And if the handle had been tampered with, that probably *would* upset the balance.

There was a round of leather with lettering on it, the lettering almost worn away. That of course was only stuck on. If one removed that? Julia sat down at her dressing table and attacked it with a penknife and presently managed to pull the leather off. Inside was a round of thin wood. It didn't look quite right. There was a join all round it. Julia dug in her penknife. The blade snapped. Nail scissors were more effective. She succeeded at last in prising it out. A mottled red and blue substance now showed. Julia poked it and enlightenment came to her. *Plasticine!* But surely handles of tennis racquets didn't normally contain plasticine? She grasped the nail scissors firmly and began to dig out lumps of plasticine. The stuff was encasing something. Something that felt like buttons or pebbles.

She attacked the plasticine vigorously.

Something rolled out on the table — then another something. Presently there was quite a heap.

Julia leaned back and gasped.

She stared and stared and stared . . .

Liquid fire, red and green and deep blue and dazzling white . . .

In that moment, Julia grew up. She was no longer a child. She became a woman. A woman looking at jewels . . .

All sorts of fantastic snatches of thought raced through her brain. Aladdin's cave . . . Marguerite and her casket of jewels . . . (They had been taken to Covent Garden to hear Faust last week) . . . Fatal stones . . . the Hope diamond . . . Romance . . . herself in a black velvet gown with a flashing necklace round her throat . . .

She sat and gloated and dreamed . . . She held the stones in her fingers and let them fall through in a rivulet of fire, a flashing stream of wonder and delight.

And then something, some slight sound perhaps, recalled her to herself.

She sat thinking, trying to use her common

sense, deciding what she ought to do. That faint sound had alarmed her. She swept up the stones, took them to the washstand and thrust them into her sponge bag and rammed her sponge and nail brush down on top of them. Then she went back to the tennis racquet, forced the plasticine back inside it, replaced the wooden top and tried to gum down the leather on top again. It curled upwards, but she managed to deal with that by applying adhesive plaster the wrong way up in thin strips and then pressing the leather on to it.

It was done. The racquet looked and felt just as before, its weight hardly altered in feel. She looked at it and then cast it down carelessly on a chair.

She looked at her bed, neatly turned down and waiting. But she did not undress. Instead she sat listening. Was that a footstep outside?

Suddenly and unexpectedly she knew fear. Two people had been killed. If anyone knew what she had found, *she* would be killed.

There was a fairly heavy oak chest of drawers in the room. She managed to drag it in front of the door, wishing that it was the custom at Meadowbank to have keys in the locks. She went to the window, pulled up the top sash and bolted it. There was no tree growing near the window and no creepers.

249

She doubted if it was possible for anyone to come in that way but she was not going to take any chances.

She looked at her small clock. Half past ten. She drew a deep breath and turned out the light. No one must notice anything unusual. She pulled back the curtain a little from the window. There was a full moon and she could see the door clearly. Then she sat down on the edge of the bed. In her hand she held the stoutest shoe she possessed.

'If anyone tries to come in,' Julia said to herself, 'I'll rap on the wall here as hard as I can. Mary King is next door and that will wake her up. *And* I'll scream — at the top of my voice. And then, if lots of people come, I'll say I had a nightmare. Anyone might have a nightmare after all the things that have been going on here.'

She sat there and time passed. Then she heard it — a soft step along the passage. She heard it stop outside her door. A long pause and then she saw the handle slowly turning.

Should she scream? Not yet.

The door was pushed — just a crack, but the chest of drawers held it. That must have puzzled the person outside.

Another pause, and then there was a knock, a very gentle little knock, on the door. Julia held her breath. A pause, and then the knock came again — but still soft and muted.

'I'm asleep,' said Julia to herself. 'I don't hear *anything*.'

Who would come and knock on her door in the middle of the night? If it was someone who had a right to knock, they'd call out, rattle the handle, make a noise. But this person couldn't afford to make a noise . . .

For a long time Julia sat there. The knock was not repeated, the handle stayed immovable. But Julia sat tense and alert.

She sat like that for a long time. She never knew herself how long it was before sleep overcame her. The school bell finally awoke her, lying in a cramped and uncomfortable heap on the edge of the bed.

II

After breakfast, the girls went upstairs and made their beds, then went down to prayers in the big hall and finally dispersed to various classrooms.

It was during that last exercise, when girls were hurrying in different directions, that Julia went into one classroom, out by a further door, joined a group hurrying round the house, dived behind a rhododendron, made a series of further strategic dives and arrived finally near the wall of the grounds where a lime tree had thick growth almost down to the ground. Julia climbed the tree with ease, she had climbed trees all her life. Completely hidden in the leafy branches, she sat, glancing from time to time at her watch. She was fairly sure she would not be missed for some time. Things were disorganized, two teachers were missing, and more than half the girls had gone home. That meant that all classes would have been reorganized, so nobody would be likely to observe the absence of Julia Upjohn until lunch time and by then —

Julia looked at her watch again, scrambled easily down the tree to the level of the wall, straddled it and dropped neatly on the other side. A hundred yards away was a bus stop where a bus ought to arrive in a few minutes. It duly did so, and Julia hailed and boarded it, having by now abstracted a felt hat from inside her cotton frock and clapped it on her slightly dishevelled hair. She got out at the station and took a train to London.

In her room, propped up on the washstand, she had left a note addressed to Miss Bulstrode.

Dear Miss Bulstrode,
I have not been kidnapped or run away,

*so don't worry. I will come back as soon
as I can.*
Yours very sincerely,
Julia Upjohn

III

At 228 Whitehouse Mansions, George, Hercule Poirot's immaculate valet and manservant, opened the door and contemplated with some surprise a schoolgirl with a rather dirty face.

'Can I see M. Hercule Poirot, please?'

George took just a shade longer than usual to reply. He found the caller unexpected.

'Mr Poirot does not see anyone without an appointment,' he said.

'I'm afraid I haven't time to wait for that. I really must see him now. It is very urgent. It's about some murders and a robbery and things like that.'

'I will ascertain,' said George, 'if Mr Poirot will see you.'

He left her in the hall and withdrew to consult his master.

'A young lady, sir, who wishes to see you urgently.'

'I daresay,' said Hercule Poirot. 'But things do not arrange themselves as easily as that.'

253

'That is what I told her, sir.'

'What kind of a young lady?'

'Well, sir, she's more of a little girl.'

'A little girl? A young lady? Which do you mean, Georges? They are really not the same.'

'I'm afraid you did not quite get my meaning sir. She is, I should say, a little girl — of school age, that is to say. But though her frock is dirty and indeed torn, she is essentially a young lady.'

'A social term. I see.'

'And she wishes to see you about some murders and a robbery.'

Poirot's eyebrows went up.

'*Some* murders, and *a robbery*. Original. Show the little girl — the young lady — in.'

Julia came into the room with only the slightest trace of diffidence. She spoke politely and quite naturally.

'How do you do, M. Poirot. I am Julia Upjohn. I think you know a great friend of Mummy's. Mrs Summerhayes. We stayed with her last summer and she talked about you a lot.'

'Mrs Summerhayes . . . ' Poirot's mind went back to a village that climbed a hill and to a house on top of that hill. He recalled a charming freckled face, a sofa with broken springs, a large quantity of dogs, and other things both agreeable and disagreeable.

'Maureen Summerhayes,' he said. 'Ah yes.'

'I call her Aunt Maureen, but she isn't really an aunt at all. She told us how wonderful you'd been and saved a man who was in prison for murder, and when I couldn't think of what to do and who to go to, I thought of you.'

'I am honoured,' said Poirot gravely.

He brought forward a chair for her.

'Now tell me,' he said. 'Georges, my servant, told me you wanted to consult me about a robbery and some murders — more than one murder, then?'

'Yes,' said Julia. 'Miss Springer and Miss Vansittart. And of course there's the kidnapping, too — but I don't think that's really my business.'

'You bewilder me,' said Poirot. 'Where have all these exciting happenings taken place?'

'At my school — Meadowbank.'

'Meadowbank,' exclaimed Poirot. 'Ah.' He stretched out his hand to where the newspapers lay neatly folded beside him. He unfolded one and glanced over the front page, nodding his head.

'I begin to comprehend,' he said. 'Now tell me, Julia, tell me everything from the beginning.'

Julia told him. It was quite a long story and a comprehensive one — but she told it clearly

— with an occasional break as she went back over something she had forgotten.

She brought her story up to the moment when she had examined the tennis racquet in her bedroom last night.

'You see, I thought it was just like Aladdin — new lamps for old — and there must be something about that tennis racquet.'

'And there was?'

'Yes.'

Without any false modesty, Julia pulled up her skirt, rolled up her knicker leg nearly to her thigh and exposed what looked like a grey poultice attached by adhesive plaster to the upper part of her leg.

She tore off the strips of plaster, uttering an anguished 'Ouch' as she did so, and freed the poultice which Poirot now perceived to be a packet enclosed in a portion of grey plastic sponge bag. Julia unwrapped it and without warning poured a heap of glittering stones on the table.

'*Nom d'un nom d'un nom!*' ejaculated Poirot in an awe-inspired whisper.

He picked them up, letting them run through his fingers.

'*Nom d'un nom d'un nom!* But they are *real*. Genuine.'

Julia nodded.

'I think they must be. People wouldn't kill

other people for them otherwise, would they? But I can understand people killing for *these*!'

And suddenly, as had happened last night, a woman looked out of the child's eyes.

Poirot looked keenly at her and nodded.

'Yes — you understand — you feel the spell. They cannot be to you just pretty coloured playthings — more is the pity.'

'They're *jewels*!' said Julia, in tones of ecstasy.

'And you found them, you say, in this tennis racquet?'

Julia finished her recital.

'And you have now told me everything?'

'I think so. I may, perhaps, have exaggerated a little here and there. I do exaggerate sometimes. Now Jennifer, my great friend, she's the other way round. She can make the most exciting things sound dull.' She looked again at the shining heap. 'M. Poirot, who do they really belong to?'

'It is probably very difficult to say. But they do not belong to either you or to me. We have to decide now what to do next.'

Julia looked at him in an expectant fashion.

'You leave yourself in my hands? Good.'

Hercule Poirot closed his eyes.

Suddenly he opened them and became brisk.

'It seems that this is an occasion when I cannot, as I prefer, remain in my chair. There must be order and method, but in what you tell me, there is no order and method. That is because we have here many threads. But they all converge and meet at one place, Meadowbank. Different people, with different aims, and representing different interests — all converge at Meadowbank. So, I, too, go to Meadowbank. And as for you — where is your mother?'

'Mummy's gone in a bus to Anatolia.'

'Ah, your mother has gone in a bus to Anatolia. *Il ne manquait que ça!* I perceive well that she might be a friend of Mrs Summerhayes! Tell me, did you enjoy your visit with Mrs Summerhayes?'

'Oh yes, it was great fun. She's got some lovely dogs.'

'The dogs, yes, I well remember.'

'They come in and out through all the windows — like in a pantomime.'

'You are so right! And the food? Did you enjoy the food?'

'Well, it was a bit peculiar sometimes,' Julia admitted.

'Peculiar, yes, indeed.'

'But Aunt Maureen makes smashing omelettes.'

'She makes smashing omelettes.' Poirot's

voice was happy. He sighed.

'Then Hercule Poirot has not lived in vain,' he said. 'It was *I* who taught your Aunt Maureen to make an omelette.' He picked up the telephone receiver.

'We will now reassure your good schoolmistress as to your safety and announce my arrival with you at Meadowbank.'

'She knows I'm all right. I left a note saying I hadn't been kidnapped.'

'Nevertheless, she will welcome further reassurance.'

In due course he was connected, and was informed that Miss Bulstrode was on the line.

'Ah, Miss Bulstrode? My name is Hercule Poirot. I have with me here your pupil Julia Upjohn. I propose to motor down with her immediately, and for the information of the police officer in charge of the case, a certain packet of some value has been safely deposited in the bank.'

He rang off and looked at Julia.

'You would like a *sirop*?' he suggested.

'Golden syrup?' Julia looked doubtful.

'No, a syrup of fruit juice. Blackcurrant, raspberry, *groseille* — that is, red currant?'

Julia settled for red currant.

'But the jewels aren't in the bank,' she pointed out.

'They will be in a very short time,' said

Poirot. 'But for the benefit of anyone who listens in at Meadowbank, or who overhears, or who is told, it is as well to think they are already there and no longer in your possession. To obtain jewels from a bank requires time and organization. And I should very much dislike anything to happen to you, my child. I will admit that I have formed a high opinion of your courage and your resource.'

Julia looked pleased but embarrassed.

18

Consultation

I

Hercule Poirot had prepared himself to beat down an insular prejudice that a headmistress might have against aged foreigners with pointed patent leather shoes and large moustaches. But he was agreeably surprised. Miss Bulstrode greeted him with cosmopolitan aplomb. She also, to his gratification, knew all about him.

'It was kind of you, M. Poirot,' she said, 'to ring up so promptly and allay our anxiety. All the more so because that anxiety had hardly begun. You weren't missed at lunch, Julia, you know,' she added, turning to the girl. 'So many girls were fetched away this morning, and there were so many gaps at table, that half the school could have been missing, I think, without any apprehension being aroused. These are unusual circumstances,' she said, turning back to Poirot. 'I assure you we would not be so slack normally. When I received your telephone call,' she went on, 'I went to Julia's room and found the note she had left.'

'I didn't want you to think I'd been kidnapped, Miss Bulstrode,' said Julia.

'I appreciate that, but I think, Julia, that you might have told me what you were planning to do.'

'I thought I'd better not,' said Julia, and added unexpectedly, '*Les oreilles ennemies nous écoutent.*'

'Mademoiselle Blanche doesn't seem to have done much to improve your accent yet,' said Miss Bulstrode, briskly. 'But I'm not scolding you, Julia.' She looked from Julia to Poirot. 'Now, if you please, I want to hear exactly what has happened.'

'You permit?' said Hercule Poirot. He stepped across the room, opened the door and looked out. He made an exaggerated gesture of shutting it. He returned beaming.

'We are alone,' he said mysteriously. 'We can proceed.'

Miss Bulstrode looked at him, then she looked at the door, then she looked at Poirot again. Her eyebrows rose. He returned her gaze steadily. Very slowly Miss Bulstrode inclined her head. Then, resuming her brisk manner, she said, 'Now then, Julia, let's hear all about this.'

Julia plunged into her recital. The exchange

262

of tennis racquets, the mysterious woman. And finally her discovery of what the racquet contained. Miss Bulstrode turned to Poirot. He nodded his head gently.

'Mademoiselle Julia has stated everything correctly,' he said. 'I took charge of what she brought me. It is safely lodged in a bank. I think therefore that you need anticipate no further developments of an unpleasant nature here.'

'I see,' said Miss Bulstrode. 'Yes, I see . . . ' She was quiet for a moment or two and then she said, 'You think it wise for Julia to remain here? Or would it be better for her to go to her aunt in London?'

'Oh please,' said Julia, 'do let me stay here.'

'You're happy here then?' said Miss Bulstrode.

'I love it,' said Julia. 'And besides, there have been such exciting things going on.'

'That is *not* a normal feature of Meadow-bank,' said Miss Bulstrode, dryly.

'I think that Julia will be in no danger here now,' said Hercule Poirot. He looked again towards the door.

'I think I understand,' said Miss Bulstrode.

'But for all that,' said Poirot, 'there should be discretion. Do you understand discretion, I wonder?' he added, looking at Julia.

'M. Poirot means,' said Miss Bulstrode,

'that he would like you to hold your tongue about what you found. Not talk about it to the other girls. Can you hold your tongue?'

'Yes,' said Julia.

'It is a very good story to tell to your friends,' said Poirot. 'Of what you found in a tennis racquet in the dead of night. But there are important reasons why it would be advisable that that story should not be told.'

'I understand,' said Julia.

'Can I trust you, Julia?' said Miss Bulstrode.

'You can trust me,' said Julia. 'Cross my heart.'

Miss Bulstrode smiled. 'I hope your mother will be home before long,' she said.

'Mummy? Oh, I do hope so.'

'I understand from Inspector Kelsey,' said Miss Bulstrode, 'that every effort is being made to get in touch with her. Unfortunately,' she added, 'Anatolian buses are liable to unexpected delays and do not always run to schedule.'

'I can tell Mummy, can't I?' said Julia.

'Of course. Well, Julia, that's all settled. You'd better run along now.'

Julia departed. She closed the door after her. Miss Bulstrode looked very hard at Poirot.

'I have understood you correctly, I think,'

she said. 'Just now, you made a great parade of closing that door. Actually — you deliberately left it slightly open.'

Poirot nodded.

'So that what we said could be overheard?'

'Yes — if there was anyone who wanted to overhear. It was a precaution of safety for the child — the news must get round that what she found is safely in a bank, and not in her possession.'

Miss Bulstrode looked at him for a moment — then she pursed her lips grimly together.

'There's got to be an end to all this,' she said.

II

'The idea is,' said the Chief Constable, 'that we try to pool our ideas and information. We are very glad to have you with us, M. Poirot,' he added. 'Inspector Kelsey remembers you well.'

'It's a great many years ago,' said Inspector Kelsey. 'Chief Inspector Warrender was in charge of the case. I was a fairly raw sergeant, knowing my place.'

'The gentleman called, for convenience's sake by us — Mr Adam Goodman, is not known to you, M. Poirot, but I believe you do know his — his — er — chief. Special Branch,' he added.

'Colonel Pikeaway?' said Hercule Poirot thoughtfully.

'Ah, yes it is some time since I have seen him. Is he still as sleepy as ever?' he asked Adam.

Adam laughed. 'I see you know him all right, M. Poirot. I've never seen him wide awake. When I do, I'll know that for once he isn't paying attention to what goes on.'

'You have something there, my friend. It is well observed.'

'Now,' said the Chief Constable, 'let's get down to things. I shan't push myself forward or urge my own opinions. I'm here to listen to what the men who are actually working on the case know and think. There are a great many sides to all this, and one thing perhaps I ought to mention first of all. I'm saying this as a result of representations that have been made to me from — er — various quarters high up.' He looked at Poirot. 'Let's say,' he said, 'that a little girl — a schoolgirl — came to you with a pretty tale of something she'd found in the hollowed-out handle of a tennis racquet. Very exciting for her. A collection, shall we say, of coloured stones, paste, good imitation — something of that kind — or even semi-precious stones which often look as attractive as the other kind. Anyway let's say something that a child would be excited to find. She might even have exaggerated ideas of its value. That's quite possible, don't you think?' He looked very hard at Hercule Poirot.

'It seems to me eminently possible,' said Hercule Poirot.

'Good,' said the Chief Constable. 'Since the person who brought these — er — coloured stones into the country did so quite unknowingly and innocently, we don't want any question of illicit smuggling to arise.

'Then there is the question of our foreign policy,' he went on. 'Things, I am led to understand, are rather — delicate just at present. When it comes to large interests in oil, mineral deposits, all that sort of thing, we have to deal with whatever government's in power. We don't want any awkward questions to arise. You can't keep murder out of the Press, and murder hasn't been kept out of the Press. But there's been no mention of anything like jewels in connection with it. For the present, at any rate, there needn't be.'

'I agree,' said Poirot. 'One must always consider international complications.'

'Exactly,' said the Chief Constable. 'I think I'm right in saying that the late ruler of

Ramat was regarded as a friend of this country, and that the powers that be would like his wishes in respect of any property of his that *might* be in this country to be carried out. What that amounts to, I gather, nobody knows at present. If the new Government of Ramat is claiming certain property which they allege belongs to them, it will be much better if we know nothing about such property being in this country. A plain refusal would be tactless.'

'One does not give plain refusals in diplomacy,' said Hercule Poirot. 'One says instead that such a matter shall receive the utmost attention but that at the moment nothing definite is known about any little — nest egg, say — that the late ruler of Ramat may have possessed. It may be still in Ramat, it may be in the keeping of a faithful friend of the late Prince Ali Yusuf, it may have been taken out of the country by half a dozen people, it may be hidden somewhere in the city of Ramat itself.' He shrugged his shoulders. 'One simply does not know.'

The Chief Constable heaved a sigh. 'Thank you,' he said. 'That's just what I mean.' He went on, 'M. Poirot, you have friends in very high quarters in this country. They put much trust in you. Unofficially they would like to leave a certain article in your hands if you do not object.'

'I do not object,' said Poirot. 'Let us leave it at that. We have more serious things to consider, have we not?' He looked round at them. 'Or perhaps you do not think so? But after all, what is three quarters of a million or some such sum in comparison with human life?'

'You're right, M. Poirot,' said the Chief Constable.

'You're right every time,' said Inspector Kelsey. 'What we want is a murderer. We shall be glad to have your opinion, M. Poirot,' he added, 'because it's largely a question of guess and guess again and your guess is as good as the next man's and sometimes better. The whole thing's like a snarl of tangled wool.'

'That is excellently put,' said Poirot, 'one has to take up that snarl of wool and pull out the one colour that we seek, the colour of a murderer. Is that right?'

'That's right.'

'Then tell me, if it is not too tedious for you to indulge in repetition, all that is known so far.'

He settled down to listen.

He listened to Inspector Kelsey, and he listened to Adam Goodman. He listened to the brief summing up of the Chief Constable. Then he leaned back, closed his eyes, and slowly nodded his head.

'Two murders,' he said, 'committed in the same place and roughly under the same conditions. One kidnapping. The kidnapping of a girl who might be the central figure of the plot. Let us ascertain first *why* she was kidnapped.'

'I can tell you what she said herself,' said Kelsey.

He did so, and Poirot listened.

'It does not make sense,' he complained.

'That's what I thought at the time. As a matter of fact I thought she was just making herself important . . . '

'But the fact remains that she *was* kidnapped. Why?'

'There have been ransom demands,' said Kelsey slowly, 'but — ' he paused.

'But they have been, you think, phoney? They have been sent merely to bolster up the kidnapping theory?'

'That's right. The appointments made weren't kept.'

'Shaista, then, was kidnapped for some other reason. What reason?'

'So that she could be made to tell where the — er — valuables were hidden?' suggested Adam doubtfully.

Poirot shook his head.

'She did not know where they were hidden,' he pointed out. 'That at least, is clear. No, there must be something . . . '

His voice tailed off. He was silent, frowning, for a moment or two. Then he sat up, and asked a question.

'Her knees,' he said. 'Did you ever notice her knees?'

Adam stared at him in astonishment.

'No,' he said. 'Why should I?'

'There are many reasons why a man notices a girl's knees,' said Poirot severely. 'Unfortunately, you did not.'

'Was there something odd about her knees? A scar? Something of that kind? I wouldn't know. They all wear stockings most of the time, and their skirts are just below knee length.'

'In the swimming pool, perhaps?' suggested Poirot hopefully.

'Never saw her go in,' said Adam. 'Too chilly for her, I expect. She was used to a warm climate. What are you getting at? A scar? Something of that kind?'

'No, no, that is not it at all. Ah well, a pity.'

He turned to the Chief Constable.

'With your permission, I will communicate with my old friend, the Préfet, at Geneva. I think he may be able to help us.'

'About something that happened when she was at school there?'

'It is possible, yes. You do permit? Good. It is just a little idea of mine.' He paused and went on: 'By the way, there has been nothing in the papers about the kidnapping?'

'The Emir Ibrahim was most insistent.'

'But I did notice a little remark in a gossip column. About a certain foreign young lady who had departed from school very suddenly. A budding romance, the columnist suggested? To be nipped in the bud if possible!'

'That was my idea,' said Adam. 'It seemed a good line to take.'

'Admirable. So now we pass from kidnapping to something more serious. Murder. Two murders at Meadowbank.'

19

Consultation Continued

I

'Two murders at Meadowbank,' repeated Poirot thoughtfully.

'We've given you the facts,' said Kelsey. 'If you've any ideas — '

'Why the Sports Pavilion?' said Poirot. 'That was your question, wasn't it?' he said to Adam. 'Well, now we have the answer. Because in the Sports Pavilion there was a tennis racquet containing a fortune in jewels. Someone knew about that racquet. Who was it? It could have been Miss Springer herself. She was, so you all say, rather peculiar about that Sports Pavilion. Disliked people coming there — unauthorized people, that is to say. She seemed to be suspicious of their motives. Particularly was that so in the case of Mademoiselle Blanche.'

'Mademoiselle Blanche,' said Kelsey thoughtfully.

Hercule Poirot again spoke to Adam.

'You yourself considered Mademoiselle

273

Blanche's manner odd where it concerned the Sports Pavilion?'

'She explained,' said Adam. 'She explained too much. I should never have questioned her right to be there if she had not taken so much trouble to explain it away.'

Poirot nodded.

'Exactly. That certainly gives one to think. But all we *know* is that Miss Springer was killed in the Sports Pavilion at one o'clock in the morning when she had no business to be there.'

He turned to Kelsey.

'Where was Miss Springer before she came to Meadowbank?'

'We don't know,' said the Inspector. 'She left her last place of employment,' he mentioned a famous school, 'last summer. Where she has been since we do not know.' He added dryly: 'There was no occasion to ask the question until she was dead. She has no near relatives, nor, apparently, any close friends.'

'She *could* have been in Ramat, then,' said Poirot thoughtfully.

'I believe there was a party of school teachers out there at the time of the trouble,' said Adam.

'Let us say, then, that she was there, that in some way she learned about the tennis racquet. Let us assume that after waiting a short time to familiarize herself with the routine at Meadowbank she went out one night to the Sports Pavilion. She got hold of the racquet and was about to remove the jewels from their hiding place when — ' he paused — 'when someone interrupted her. Someone who had been watching her? Following her that evening? Whoever it was had a pistol — and shot her — but had no time to prise out the jewels, or to take the racquet away, because people were approaching the Sports Pavilion who had heard the shot.'

He stopped.

'You think that's what happened?' asked the Chief Constable.

'I do not know,' said Poirot. 'It is one possibility. The other is that that person with the pistol was there first, and was surprised by Miss Springer. Someone whom Miss Springer was already suspicious of. She was, you have told me, that kind of woman. A noser out of secrets.'

'And the other woman?' asked Adam.

Poirot looked at him. Then, slowly, he shifted his gaze to the other two men.

'You do not know,' he said. 'And I do not know. It could have been someone from outside — ?'

His voice half asked a question.

Kelsey shook his head.

'I think not. We have sifted the neighbourhood very carefully. Especially, of course, in the case of strangers. There was a Madam Kolinsky staying nearby — known to Adam here. But she could not have been concerned in either murder.'

'Then it comes back to Meadowbank. And there is only one method to arrive at the truth — elimination.'

Kelsey sighed.

'Yes,' he said. 'That's what it amounts to. For the first murder, it's a fairly open field. Almost anybody could have killed Miss Springer. The exceptions are Miss Johnson and Miss Chadwick — and a child who had the earache. But the second murder narrows things down. Miss Rich, Miss Blake and Miss Shapland are out of it. Miss Rich was staying at the Alton Grange Hotel, twenty miles away, Miss Blake was at Littleport on Sea, Miss Shapland was in London at a night club, the Nid Sauvage, with Mr Dennis Rathbone.'

'And Miss Bulstrode was also away, I understand?'

Adam grinned. The Inspector and the Chief Constable looked shocked.

'Miss Bulstrode,' said the Inspector severely,

'was staying with the Duchess of Welsham.'

'That eliminates Miss Bulstrode then,' said Poirot gravely. 'And leaves us — what?'

'Two members of the domestic staff who sleep in, Mrs Gibbons and a girl called Doris Hogg. I can't consider either of them seriously. That leaves Miss Rowan and Mademoiselle Blanche.'

'And the pupils, of course.'

Kelsey looked startled.

'Surely you don't suspect them?'

'Frankly, no. But one must be exact.'

Kelsey paid no attention to exactitude. He plodded on.

'Miss Rowan has been here over a year. She has a good record. We know nothing against her.'

'So we come, then, to Mademoiselle Blanche. It is there that the journey ends.'

There was a silence.

'There's no evidence,' said Kelsey. 'Her credentials seem genuine enough.'

'They would have to be,' said Poirot.

'She snooped,' said Adam. 'But snooping isn't evidence of murder.'

'Wait a minute,' said Kelsey, 'there was something about a key. In our first interview with her — I'll look it up — something about the key of the Pavilion falling out of the door and she picked it up and forgot to replace it

277

— walked out with it and Springer bawled her out.'

'Whoever wanted to go out there at night and look for the racquet would have had to have a key to get in with,' said Poirot. 'For that, it would have been necessary to take an impression of the key.'

'Surely,' said Adam, 'in that case she would never have mentioned the key incident to you.'

'That doesn't follow,' said Kelsey. 'Springer might have talked about the key incident. If so, she might think it better to mention it in a casual fashion.'

'It is a point to be remembered,' said Poirot.

'It doesn't take us very far,' said Kelsey.

He looked gloomily at Poirot.

'There would seem,' said Poirot, '(that is, if I have been informed correctly), one possibility. Julia Upjohn's mother, I understand, recognized someone here on the first day of term. Someone whom she was surprised to see. From the context, it would seem likely that that someone was connected with foreign espionage. If Mrs Upjohn definitely points out Mademoiselle as the person she recognized, then I think we could proceed with some assurance.'

'Easier said than done,' said Kelsey. 'We've

been trying to get in contact with Mrs Upjohn, but the whole thing's a headache! When the child said a bus, I thought she meant a proper coach tour, running to schedule, and a party all booked together. But that's not it at all. Seems she's just taking local buses to any place she happens to fancy! She's not done it through Cook's or a recognized travel agency. She's all on her own, wandering about. What can you do with a woman like that? She might be anywhere. There's a lot of Anatolia!'

'It makes it difficult, yes,' said Poirot.

'Plenty of nice coach tours,' said the Inspector in an injured voice. 'All made easy for you — where you stop and what you see, and all-in fares so that you know exactly where you are.'

'But clearly, that kind of travel does not appeal to Mrs Upjohn.'

'And in the meantime, here we are,' went on Kelsey. 'Stuck! That Frenchwoman can walk out any moment she chooses. We've nothing on which we could hold her.'

Poirot shook his head.

'She will not do that.'

'You can't be sure.'

'I am sure. If you have committed murder, you do not want to do anything out of character, that may draw attention to you.

Mademoiselle Blanche will remain here quietly until the end of the term.'

'I hope you're right.'

'I am sure I am right. And remember, the person whom Mrs Upjohn saw, *does not know that Mrs Upjohn saw her.* The surprise when it comes will be complete.'

Kelsey sighed.

'If that's all we've got to go on — '

'There are other things. Conversation, for instance.'

'Conversation?'

'It is very valuable, conversation. Sooner or later, if one has something to hide, one says too much.'

'Gives oneself away?' The Chief Constable sounded sceptical.

'It is not quite so simple as that. One is guarded about the thing one is trying to hide. But often one says too much about other things. And there are other uses for conversation. There are the innocent people who know things, but are unaware of the importance of what they know. And that reminds me — '

He rose to his feet.

'Excuse me, I pray. I must go and demand of Miss Bulstrode if there is someone here who can draw.'

'Draw?'

'Draw.'

'Well,' said Adam, as Poirot went out. 'First girls' knees, and now draughtsmanship! What next, I wonder?'

II

Miss Bulstrode answered Poirot's questions without evincing any surprise.

'Miss Laurie is our visiting Drawing Mistress,' she said briskly. 'But she isn't here today. What do you want her to draw for you?' she added in a kindly manner as though to a child.

'Faces,' said Poirot.

'Miss Rich is good at sketching people. She's clever at getting a likeness.'

'That is exactly what I need.'

Miss Bulstrode, he noted with approval, asked him no questions as to his reasons. She merely left the room and returned with Miss Rich.

After introductions, Poirot said: 'You can sketch people? Quickly? With a pencil?'

Eileen Rich nodded.

'I often do. For amusement.'

'Good. Please, then, sketch for me the late Miss Springer.'

'That's difficult. I knew her for such a

short time. I'll try.' She screwed up her eyes, then began to draw rapidly.

'*Bien*,' said Poirot, taking it from her. 'And now, if you please, Miss Bulstrode, Miss Rowan, Mademoiselle Blanche and — yes — the gardener Adam.'

Eileen Rich looked at him doubtfully, then set to work. He looked at the result, and nodded appreciatively.

'You are good — you are very good. So few strokes — and yet the likeness is there. Now I will ask you to do something more difficult. Give, for example, to Miss Bulstrode a different hair arrangement. Change the shape of her eyebrows.'

Eileen stared at him as though she thought he was mad.

'No,' said Poirot. 'I am not mad. I make an experiment, that is all. Please do as I ask.'

In a moment or two she said: 'Here you are.'

'Excellent. Now do the same for Mademoiselle Blanche and Miss Rowan.'

When she had finished he lined up the three sketches.

'Now I will show you something,' he said. 'Miss Bulstrode, in spite of the changes you have made is still unmistakably Miss Bulstrode. But look at the other two. Because their features are negative, and since they have not Miss Bulstrode's personality, they appear almost different people, do they not?'

'I see what you mean,' said Eileen Rich.

She looked at him as he carefully folded the sketches away.

'What are you going to do with them?' she asked.

'Use them,' said Poirot.

20

Conversation

'Well — I don't know what to say,' said Mrs Sutcliffe. 'Really I don't know what to say — '

She looked with definite distaste at Hercule Poirot.

'Henry, of course,' she said, 'is not at home.'

The meaning of this pronouncement was slightly obscure, but Hercule Poirot thought that he knew what was in her mind. Henry, she was feeling, would be able to deal with this sort of thing. Henry had so many international dealings. He was always flying to the Middle East and to Ghana and to South America and to Geneva, and even occasionally, but not so often, to Paris.

'The whole thing,' said Mrs Sutcliffe, 'has been *most* distressing. I was so glad to have Jennifer safely at home with me. Though, I must say,' she added, with a trace of vexation, 'Jennifer has really been most tiresome. After having made a great fuss about going to

Meadowbank and being quite sure she wouldn't like it there, and saying it was a snobby kind of school and not the kind she wanted to go to, *now* she sulks all day long because I've taken her away. It's really too bad.'

'It is undeniably a very good school,' said Hercule Poirot. 'Many people say the best school in England.'

'It *was*, I daresay,' said Mrs Sutcliffe.

'And will be again,' said Hercule Poirot.

'You think so?' Mrs Sutcliffe looked at him doubtfully. His sympathetic manner was gradually piercing her defences. There is nothing that eases the burden of a mother's life more than to be permitted to unburden herself of the difficulties, rebuffs and frustrations which she has in dealing with her offspring. Loyalty so often compels silent endurance. But to a foreigner like Hercule Poirot Mrs Sutcliffe felt that this loyalty was not applicable. It was not like talking to the mother of another daughter.

'Meadowbank,' said Hercule Poirot, 'is just passing through an unfortunate phase.'

It was the best thing he could think of to say at the moment. He felt its inadequacy and Mrs Sutcliffe pounced upon the inadequacy immediately.

'Rather more than unfortunate!' she said.

'Two murders! And a girl kidnapped. You can't send your daughter to a school where the mistresses are being murdered all the time.'

It seemed a highly reasonable point of view.

'If the murders,' said Poirot, 'turn out to be the work of one person and that person is apprehended, that makes a difference, does it not?'

'Well — I suppose so. Yes,' said Mrs Sutcliffe doubtfully. 'I mean — you mean — oh, I see, you mean like Jack the Ripper or that other man — who was it? Something to do with Devonshire. Cream? Neil Cream. Who went about killing an unfortunate type of woman. I suppose this murderer just goes about killing schoolmistresses! If once you've got him safely in prison, and hanged too, I hope, because you're only allowed one murder, aren't you? — like a dog with a bite — what was I saying? Oh yes, if he's safely caught, well, then I suppose it *would* be different. Of course there can't be many people like that, can there?'

'One certainly hopes not,' said Hercule Poirot.

'But then there's this kidnapping too,' pointed out Mrs Sutcliffe. 'You don't want to send your daughter to a school where she may be kidnapped, either, do you?'

'Assuredly not, madame. I see how clearly you have thought out the whole thing. You are so right in all you say.'

Mrs Sutcliffe looked faintly pleased. Nobody had said anything like that to her for some time. Henry had merely said things like 'What did you want to send her to Meadowbank for anyway?' and Jennifer had sulked and refused to answer.

'I *have* thought about it,' she said. 'A great deal.'

'Then I should not let kidnapping worry you, madame. *Entre nous*, if I may speak in confidence, about Princess Shaista — It is not exactly a kidnapping — one suspects a romance — '

'You mean the naughty girl just ran away to marry somebody?'

'My lips are sealed,' said Hercule Poirot. 'You comprehend it is not desired that there should be any scandal. This is in confidence *entre nous*. I know you will say nothing.'

'Of course not,' said Mrs Sutcliffe virtuously. She looked down at the letter that Poirot had brought with him from the Chief Constable. 'I don't quite understand who you are, M. — er — Poirot. Are you what they call in books — a private eye?'

'I am a consultant,' said Hercule Poirot loftily.

This flavour of Harley Street encouraged Mrs Sutcliffe a great deal.

'What do you want to talk to Jennifer about?' she demanded.

'Just to get her impressions of things,' said Poirot. 'She is observant — yes?'

'I'm afraid I wouldn't say that,' said Mrs Sutcliffe. 'She's not what I call a noticing kind of child at all. I mean, she is always so matter of fact.'

'It is better than making up things that have never happened at all,' said Poirot.

'Oh, Jennifer wouldn't do *that* sort of thing,' said Mrs Sutcliffe, with certainty. She got up, went to the window and called 'Jennifer.'

'I wish,' she said, to Poirot, as she came back again, 'that you'd try and get it into Jennifer's head that her father and I are only doing our best for her.'

Jennifer came into the room with a sulky face and looked with deep suspicion at Hercule Poirot.

'How do you do?' said Poirot. 'I am a very old friend of Julia Upjohn. She came to London to find me.'

'Julia went to London?' said Jennifer, slightly surprised. 'Why?'

'To ask my advice,' said Hercule Poirot.

Jennifer looked unbelieving.

'I was able to give it to her,' said Poirot.

'She is now back at Meadowbank,' he added.

'So her Aunt Isabel didn't *take* her away,' said Jennifer, shooting an irritated look at her mother.

Poirot looked at Mrs Sutcliffe and for some reason, perhaps because she had been in the middle of counting the laundry when Poirot arrived and perhaps because of some unexplained compulsion, she got up and left the room.

'It's a bit hard,' said Jennifer, 'to be out of all that's going on there. All this fuss! I told Mummy it was silly. After all, none of the *pupils* have been killed.'

'Have you any ideas of your own about the murders?' asked Poirot.

Jennifer shook her head. 'Someone who's batty?' she offered. She added thoughtfully, 'I suppose Miss Bulstrode will have to get some new mistresses now.'

'It seems possible, yes,' said Poirot. He went on, 'I am interested, Mademoiselle Jennifer, in the woman who came and offered you a new racquet for your old one. Do you remember?'

'I should think I do remember,' said Jennifer. 'I've never found out to this day who really sent it. It wasn't Aunt Gina at all.'

'What did this woman look like?' said Poirot.

'The one who brought the racquet?' Jennifer half closed her eyes as though thinking. 'Well, I don't know. She had on a sort of fussy dress with a little cape, I think. Blue, and a floppy sort of hat.'

'Yes?' said Poirot. 'I meant perhaps not so much her clothes as her face.'

'A good deal of make-up, I think,' said Jennifer vaguely. 'A bit too much for the country, I mean, and fair hair. I think she was an American.'

'Had you ever seen her before?' asked Poirot.

'Oh no,' said Jennifer. 'I don't think she lived down there. She said she'd come down for a luncheon party or a cocktail party or something.'

Poirot looked at her thoughtfully. He was interested in Jennifer's complete acceptance of everything that was said to her. He said gently,

'But she might not have been speaking the truth?'

'Oh,' said Jennifer. 'No, I suppose not.'

'You're quite sure you hadn't seen her before? She could not have been, for instance, one of the girls dressed up? Or one of the mistresses?'

'Dressed up?' Jennifer looked puzzled.

Poirot laid before her the sketch Eileen

Rich had done for him of Mademoiselle Blanche.

'This was not the woman, was it?'

Jennifer looked at it doubtfully.

'It's a little like her — but I don't think it's her.'

Poirot nodded thoughtfully.

There was no sign that Jennifer recognized that this was actually a sketch of Mademoiselle Blanche.

'You see,' said Jennifer, 'I didn't really look at her much. She was an American and a stranger, and then she told me about the racquet — '

After that, it was clear, Jennifer would have had eyes for nothing but her new possession.

'I see,' said Poirot. He went on, 'Did you ever see at Meadowbank anyone that you'd seen out in Ramat?'

'In Ramat?' Jennifer thought. 'Oh no — at least — I don't think so.'

Poirot pounced on the slight expression of doubt. 'But you are not *sure*, Mademoiselle Jennifer.'

'Well,' Jennifer scratched her forehead with a worried expression, 'I mean, you're always seeing people who look like somebody else. You can't quite remember who it is they look like. Sometimes you see people that you *have* met but you don't remember who they are.

And they say to you 'You don't remember me,' and then that's awfully awkward because really you don't. I mean, you sort of know their face but you can't remember their names or where you saw them.'

'That is very true,' said Poirot. 'Yes, that is very true. One often has that experience.' He paused a moment then he went on, prodding gently, 'Princess Shaista, for instance, you probably recognized *her* when you saw her because you must have seen her in Ramat.'

'Oh, was she in Ramat?'

'Very likely,' said Poirot. 'After all she is a relation of the ruling house. You might have seen her there?'

'I don't think I did,' said Jennifer frowning. 'Anyway, she wouldn't go about with her face showing there, would she? I mean, they all wear veils and things like that. Though they take them off in Paris and Cairo, I believe. And in London, of course,' she added.

'Anyway, you had no feeling of having seen anyone at Meadowbank whom you had seen before?'

'No, I'm sure I hadn't. Of course most people do look rather alike and you might have seen them anywhere. It's only when somebody's got an odd sort of face like Miss Rich, that you notice it.'

'Did you think you'd seen Miss Rich

somewhere before?'

'I hadn't really. It must have been someone like her. But it was someone much fatter than she was.'

'Someone much fatter,' said Poirot thoughtfully.

'You couldn't imagine Miss Rich being fat,' said Jennifer with a giggle. 'She's so frightfully thin and nobbly. And anyway Miss Rich couldn't have been in Ramat because she was away ill last term.'

'And the other girls?' said Poirot, 'had you seen any of the girls before?'

'Only the ones I knew already,' said Jennifer. 'I did know one or two of them. After all, you know, I was only there three weeks and I really don't know half of the people there even by sight. I wouldn't know most of them if I met them tomorrow.'

'You should notice things more,' said Poirot severely.

'One can't notice everything,' protested Jennifer. She went on: 'If Meadowbank is carrying on I would like to go back. See if you can do anything with Mummy. Though really,' she added, 'I think it's Daddy who's the stumbling-block. It's awful here in the country. I get *no* opportunity to improve my tennis.'

'I assure you I will do what I can,' said Poirot.

21

Gathering Threads

I

'I want to talk to you, Eileen,' said Miss Bulstrode.

Eileen Rich followed Miss Bulstrode into the latter's sitting-room. Meadowbank was strangely quiet. About twenty-five pupils were still there. Pupils whose parents had found it either difficult or unwelcome to fetch them. The panic-stricken rush had, as Miss Bulstrode had hoped, been checked by her own tactics. There was a general feeling that by next term everything would have been cleared up. It was much wiser of Miss Bulstrode, they felt, to close the school.

None of the staff had left. Miss Johnson fretted with too much time on her hands. A day in which there was too little to do did not in the least suit her. Miss Chadwick, looking old and miserable, wandered round in a kind of coma of misery. She was far harder hit to all appearance than Miss

Bulstrode. Miss Bulstrode, indeed, managed apparently without difficulty to be completely herself, unperturbed, and with no sign of strain or collapse. The two younger mistresses were not averse to the extra leisure. They bathed in the swimming pool, wrote long letters to friends and relations and sent for cruise literature to study and compare. Ann Shapland had a good deal of time on her hands and did not appear to resent the fact. She spent a good deal of that time in the garden and devoted herself to gardening with quite unexpected efficiency. That she preferred to be instructed in the work by Adam rather than by old Briggs was perhaps a not unnatural phenomenon.

'Yes, Miss Bulstrode?' said Eileen Rich.

'I've been wanting to talk to you,' said Miss Bulstrode. 'Whether this school can continue or not I do not know. What people will feel is always fairly incalculable because they will all feel differently. But the result will be that whoever feels most strongly will end by converting all the rest. So either Meadowbank is finished — '

'No,' said Eileen Rich, interrupting, 'not finished.' She almost stamped her foot and her hair immediately began coming down. 'You mustn't let it be stopped,' she said. 'It would be a sin — a crime.'

'You speak very strongly,' said Miss Bulstrode.

'I feel strongly. There are so many things that really don't seem worth while a bit, but Meadowbank does seem worth while. It seemed worth while to me the first moment I came here.'

'You're a fighter,' said Miss Bulstrode. 'I like fighters, and I assure you that I don't intend to give in tamely. In a way I'm going to enjoy the fight. You know, when everything's too easy and things go too well one gets — I don't know the exact word I mean — complacent? Bored? A kind of hybrid of the two. But I'm not bored now and I'm not complacent and I'm going to fight with every ounce of strength I've got, and with every penny I've got, too. Now what I want to say to you is this: If Meadowbank continues, will you come in on a partnership basis?'

'Me?' Eileen Rich stared at her. 'Me?'

'Yes, my dear,' said Miss Bulstrode. 'You.'

'I couldn't,' said Eileen Rich. 'I don't know enough. I'm too young. Why, I haven't got the experience, the knowledge that you'd want.'

'You must leave it to me to know what I want,' said Miss Bulstrode. 'Mind you, this isn't, at the present moment of talking, a good offer. You'd probably do better for yourself elsewhere. But I want to tell you this, and you've got to believe me. I had already decided before Miss Vansittart's unfortunate death, that you were the person I wanted to carry on this school.'

'You thought so then?' Eileen Rich stared at her. 'But I thought — we all thought — that Miss Vansittart . . . '

'There was no arrangement made with Miss Vansittart,' said Miss Bulstrode. 'I had her in mind, I will confess. I've had her in mind for the last two years. But something's always held me back from saying anything definite to her about it. I daresay everyone assumed that she'd be my successor. She may have thought so herself. I myself thought so until very recently. And then I decided that she was not what I wanted.'

'But she was so suitable in every way,' said Eileen Rich. 'She would have carried out things in exactly your ways, in exactly your ideas.'

'Yes,' said Miss Bulstrode, 'and that's just what would have been wrong. You can't hold on to the past. A certain amount of tradition is good but never too much. A school is for the children of *today.* It's not for the children of fifty years ago or even of thirty years ago. There are some schools in which tradition is more important than others, but Meadowbank is not one of those. It's not a school with a long tradition behind it. It's a creation, if I may say it, of one woman. Myself. I've tried certain ideas and carried them out to the best of my ability, though occasionally I've had to modify them when they haven't produced the results I'd expected. It's not been a conventional school, but it has not prided itself on being an unconventional school either. It's a school that tries to make the best of both worlds: the past and the future, but the real stress is on the present. That's how it's going to go on, how it ought to go on. Run by someone with ideas — ideas of the present day. Keeping what is wise from the past, looking forward towards the future. You're very much the age I was when I started here but you've got what I no longer can have. You'll find it written in the Bible. *Their old men dream dreams and their young men have visions.* We don't need dreams here, we need vision. I believe you to have vision and that's why I decided that you were the person and not Eleanor Vansittart.'

'It would have been wonderful,' said Eileen Rich. 'Wonderful. The thing I should have liked above all.'

Miss Bulstrode was faintly surprised by the tense, although she did not show it. Instead she agreed promptly.

'Yes,' she said, 'it would have been wonderful. But it isn't wonderful now? Well, I suppose I understand that.'

'No, no, I don't mean that at all,' said Eileen Rich. 'Not at all. I — I can't go into details very well, but if you had — if you had asked me, spoken to me like this a week or a fortnight ago, I should have said at once that I couldn't, that it would have been quite impossible. The only reason why it — why it might be possible now is because — well, because it *is* a case of fighting — of taking on things. May I — may I think it over, Miss Bulstrode? I don't know what to say now.'

'Of course,' said Miss Bulstrode. She was still surprised. One never really knew, she thought, about anybody.

II

'There goes Rich with her hair coming down again,' said Ann Shapland as she straightened herself up from a flower bed. 'If she can't control it I can't think why she doesn't get it cut off. She's got a good-shaped head and she would look better.'

'You ought to tell her so,' said Adam.

'We're not on those terms,' said Ann Shapland. She went on, 'D'you think this place will be able to carry on?'

'That's a very doubtful question,' said

Adam, 'and who am I to judge?'

'You could tell as well as another I should think,' said Ann Shapland. 'It might, you know. The old Bull, as the girls call her, has got what it takes. A hypnotizing effect on parents to begin with. How long is it since the beginning of term — only a month? It seems like a year. I shall be glad when it comes to an end.'

'Will you come back if the school goes on?'

'No,' said Ann with emphasis, 'no indeed. I've had enough of schools to last me for a lifetime. I'm not cut out for being cooped up with a lot of women anyway. And, frankly, I don't like murder. It's the sort of thing that's fun to read about in the paper or to read yourself to sleep with in the way of a nice book. But the real thing isn't so good. I think,' added Ann thoughtfully, 'that when I leave here at the end of the term I shall marry Dennis and settle down.'

'Dennis?' said Adam. 'That's the one you mentioned to me, wasn't it? As far as I remember his work takes him to Burma and Malaya and Singapore and Japan and places like that. It won't be exactly settling down, will it, if you marry him?'

Ann laughed suddenly. 'No, no, I suppose it won't. Not in the physical, geographical sense.'

'I think you can do better than Dennis,' said Adam.

'Are you making me an offer?' said Ann.

'Certainly not,' said Adam. 'You're an ambitious girl, you wouldn't like to marry a humble jobbing gardener.'

'I was wondering about marrying into the C.I.D.,' said Ann.

'I'm not in the C.I.D.,' said Adam.

'No, no, of course not,' said Ann. 'Let's preserve the niceties of speech. You're not in the C.I.D., Shaista wasn't kidnapped, everything in the garden's lovely. It is rather,' she added, looking round. 'All the same,' she said after a moment or two, 'I don't understand in the least about Shaista turning up in Geneva or whatever the story is. How did she get there? All you people must be very slack to allow her to be taken out of this country.'

'My lips are sealed,' said Adam.

'I don't think you know the first thing about it,' said Ann.

'I will admit,' said Adam, 'that we have to thank Monsieur Hercule Poirot for having had a bright idea.'

'What, the funny little man who brought Julia back and came to see Miss Bulstrode?'

'Yes. He calls himself,' said Adam, 'a consultant detective.'

'I think he's pretty much of a has-been,' said Ann.

'I don't understand what he's up to at all,'

said Adam. 'He even went to see my mother — or some friend of his did.'

'Your mother?' said Ann. 'Why?'

'I've no idea. He seems to have a kind of morbid interest in mothers. He went to see Jennifer's mother too.'

'Did he go and see Miss Rich's mother, and Chaddy's?'

'I gather Miss Rich hasn't got a mother,' said Adam. 'Otherwise, no doubt, he would have gone to see her.'

'Miss Chadwick's got a mother in Cheltenham, she told me,' said Ann, 'but she's about eighty-odd, I believe. Poor Miss Chadwick, she looks about eighty herself. She's coming to talk to us now.'

Adam looked up. 'Yes,' he said, 'she's aged a lot in the last week.'

'Because she really loves the school,' said Ann. 'It's her whole life. She can't bear to see it go downhill.'

Miss Chadwick indeed looked ten years older than she had done on the day of the opening term. Her step had lost its brisk efficiency. She no longer trotted about, happy and bustling. She came up to them now, her steps dragging a little.

'Will you please come to Miss Bulstrode,' she said to Adam. 'She has some instruction about the garden.'

'I'll have to clean up a bit first,' said Adam. He laid down his tools and moved off in the direction of the potting shed.

Ann and Miss Chadwick walked together towards the house.

'It does seem quiet, doesn't it,' said Ann, looking round. 'Like an empty house at the theatre,' she added thoughtfully, 'with people spaced out by the box office as tactfully as possible to make them look like an audience.'

'It's dreadful,' said Miss Chadwick, 'dreadful! Dreadful to think that Meadowbank has come to *this*. I can't get over it. I can't sleep at night. Everything in ruins. All the years of work, of building up something really fine.'

'It may get all right again,' said Ann cheerfully. 'People have got very short memories, you know.'

'Not as short as all that,' said Miss Chadwick grimly.

Ann did not answer. In her heart she rather agreed with Miss Chadwick.

III

Mademoiselle Blanche came out of the classroom where she had been teaching French literature.

She glanced at her watch. Yes, there would

be plenty of time for what she intended to do. With so few pupils there was always plenty of time these days.

She went upstairs to her room and put on her hat. She was not one of those who went about hatless. She studied her appearance in the mirror with satisfaction. Not a personality to be noticed! Well, there could be advantages in that! She smiled to herself. It had made it easy for her to use her sister's testimonials. Even the passport photograph had gone unchallenged. It would have been a thousand pities to waste those excellent credentials when Angèle had died. Angèle had really enjoyed teaching. For herself, it was unutterable boredom. But the pay was excellent. Far above what she herself had ever been able to earn. And besides, things had turned out unbelievably well. The future was going to be very different. Oh yes, very different. The drab Mademoiselle Blanche would be transformed. She saw it all in her mind's eye. The Riviera. Herself smartly dressed, suitably made up. All one needed in this world was money. Oh yes, things were going to be very pleasant indeed. It was worth having come to this detestable English school.

She picked up her handbag, went out of her room and along the corridor. Her eyes dropped to the kneeling woman who was busy there. A new daily help. A police spy, of course. How simple they were — to think that one would not know!

A contemptuous smile on her lips, she went out of the house and down the drive to the front gate. The bus stop was almost opposite. She stood at it, waiting. The bus should be here in a moment or two.

There were very few people about in this quiet country road. A car, with a man bending over the open bonnet. A bicycle leaning against a hedge. A man also waiting for the bus.

One or other of the three would, no doubt, follow her. It would be skilfully done, not obviously. She was quite alive to the fact, and it did not worry her. Her 'shadow' was welcome to see where she went and what she did.

The bus came. She got in. A quarter of an hour later, she got out in the main square of the town. She did not trouble to look behind her. She crossed to where the shop windows of a fairly large departmental store showed their display of new model gowns. Poor stuff, for provincial tastes, she thought, with a curling lip. But she stood looking at them as though much attracted.

Presently she went inside, made one or two trivial purchases, then went up to the first floor and entered the Ladies Rest Room. There was a writing table there, some easy chairs, and a telephone box. She went into the box, put the necessary coins in, dialled the number she wanted, waiting to hear if the right voice answered.

She nodded in approval, pressed button A and spoke.

'This is the Maison Blanche. You understand me, the Maison *Blanche*? I have to speak of an account that is owed. You have until tomorrow evening. Tomorrow evening. To pay into the account of the Maison Blanche at the Credit Nationale in London, Ledbury St branch the sum that I tell you.'

She named the sum.

'If that money is not paid in, then it will be necessary for me to report in the proper quarters what I observed on the night of the 12th. The reference — pay — attention — is to Miss Springer. You have a little over twenty-four hours.'

She hung up and emerged into the rest room. A woman had just come in from outside. Another customer of the shop, perhaps, or again perhaps not. But if the latter, it was too late for anything to be overheard.

Mademoiselle Blanche freshened herself up in the adjoining cloak room, then she went and tried on a couple of blouses, but did not buy them; she went out into the street again, smiling to herself. She looked into a bookshop, and then caught a bus back to Meadowbank.

She was still smiling to herself as she walked up the drive. She had arranged matters very well. The sum she had demanded had not been too large — not impossible to raise at short notice. And it would do very well to go on with. Because, of course, in the future, there would be further demands . . .

Yes, a very pretty little source of income this was going to be. She had no qualms of conscience. She did not consider it in any way her duty to report what she knew and had seen to the police. That Springer had been a detestable woman, rude, *mal élevée*. Prying into what was no business of hers. Ah, well, she had got her deserts.

Mademoiselle Blanche stayed for a while by the swimming pool. She watched Eileen Rich diving. Then Ann Shapland, too, climbed up and dived — very well, too. There was laughing and squeals from the girls.

A bell rang, and Mademoiselle Blanche went in to take her junior class. They were inattentive and tiresome, but Mademoiselle Blanche hardly noticed. She would soon have done with teaching for ever.

She went up to her room to tidy herself for supper. Vaguely, without really noticing, she saw that, contrary to her usual practice, she had thrown her garden coat across a chair in the corner instead of hanging it up as usual.

She leaned forward, studying her face in the glass. She applied powder, lipstick —

The movement was so quick that it took her completely by surprise. Noiseless! Professional. The coat on the chair seemed to gather itself together, drop to the ground and in an instant behind Mademoiselle Blanche a hand with a sandbag rose and, as she opened her lips to scream, fell, dully, on the back of her neck.

22

Incident in Anatolia

Mrs Upjohn was sitting by the side of the road overlooking a deep ravine. She was talking partly in French and partly with gestures to a large and solid-looking Turkish woman who was telling her with as much detail as possible under these difficulties of communications all about her last miscarriage. Nine children she had had, she explained. Eight of them boys, and five miscarriages. She seemed as pleased at the miscarriages as she did at the births.

'And you?' she poked Mrs Upjohn amiably in the ribs. '*Combien?* — *garçons?* — *filles?* — *combien?*' She held up her hands ready to indicate on the fingers.

'*Une fille,*' said Mrs Upjohn.

'*Et garçons?*'

Seeing that she was about to fall in the Turkish woman's estimation, Mrs Upjohn in a surge of nationalism proceeded to perjure herself. She held up five fingers of her right hand.

'*Cinq*,' she said.

'*Cinq garçons? Très bien!*'

The Turkish woman nodded with approbation and respect. She added that if only her cousin who spoke French really fluently was here they could understand each other a great deal better. She then resumed the story of her last miscarriage.

The other passengers were sprawled about near them, eating odd bits of food from the baskets they carried with them. The bus, looking slightly the worse for wear, was drawn up against an overhanging rock, and the driver and another man were busy inside the bonnet. Mrs Upjohn had lost complete count of time. Floods had blocked two of the roads, *détours* had been necessary and they had once been stuck for seven hours until the river they were fording subsided. Ankara lay in the not impossible future and that was all she knew. She listened to her friend's eager and incoherent conversation, trying to gauge when to nod admiringly, when to shake her head in sympathy.

A voice cut into her thoughts, a voice highly incongruous with her present surroundings.

'Mrs Upjohn, I believe,' said the voice.

Mrs Upjohn looked up. A little way away a car had driven up. The man standing opposite her had undoubtedly alighted from it. His face was unmistakably British, as was his voice. He was impeccably dressed in a grey flannel suit.

'Good heavens,' said Mrs Upjohn. 'Dr Livingstone?'

'It must seem rather like that,' said the stranger pleasantly. 'My name's Atkinson. I'm from the Consulate in Ankara. We've been trying to get in touch with you for two or three days, but the roads have been cut.'

'You wanted to get in touch with me? Why?' Suddenly Mrs Upjohn rose to her feet. All traces of the gay traveller had disappeared. She was all mother, every inch of her. 'Julia?' she said sharply. 'Has something happened to Julia?'

'No, no,' Mr Atkinson reassured her. 'Julia's quite all right. It's not that at all. There's been a spot of trouble at Meadow-bank and we want to get you home there as soon as possible. I'll drive you back to Ankara, and you can get on a plane in about an hour's time.'

Mrs Upjohn opened her mouth and then shut it again. Then she rose and said, 'You'll have to get my bag off the top of that bus. It's the dark one.' She turned, shook hands with her Turkish companion, said: 'I'm sorry, I have to go home now,' waved to the rest of the bus load with the utmost friendliness, called out a Turkish farewell greeting which was part of her small stock of Turkish, and prepared to follow Mr Atkinson immediately without asking any further questions. It occurred to him as it had occurred to many other people that Mrs Upjohn was a very sensible woman.

23

Showdown

I

In one of the smaller classrooms Miss Bulstrode looked at the assembled people. All the members of her staff were there: Miss Chadwick, Miss Johnson, Miss Rich and the two younger mistresses. Ann Shapland sat with her pad and pencil in case Miss Bulstrode wanted her to take notes. Beside Miss Bulstrode sat Inspector Kelsey and beyond him, Hercule Poirot. Adam Goodman sat in a no-man's-land of his own halfway between the staff and what he called to himself the executive body. Miss Bulstrode rose and spoke in her practised, decisive voice.

'I feel it is due to you all,' she said, 'as members of my staff, and interested in the fortunes of the school, to know exactly to what point this inquiry has progressed. I have been informed by Inspector Kelsey of several facts. M. Hercule Poirot who has international connections, has obtained valuable assistance from Switzerland and will report himself on that particular matter. We have not yet come to the end of the inquiry, I am sorry to say, but certain minor matters have been cleared up and I thought it would be a relief to you all to know how matters stand at the present moment.' Miss Bulstrode looked towards Inspector Kelsey, and he rose.

'Officially,' he said, 'I am not in a position to disclose all that I know. I can only reassure you to the extent of saying that we are making progress and we are beginning to have a good idea who is responsible for the three crimes that have been committed on the premises. Beyond that I will not go. My friend, M. Hercule Poirot, who is not bound by official secrecy and is at perfect liberty to give you his own ideas, will disclose to you certain information which he himself has been influential in procuring. I am sure you are all loyal to Meadowbank and to Miss Bulstrode and will keep to yourselves various matters upon which M. Poirot is going to touch and which are not of any public interest. The less gossip or speculation about them the better, so I will ask you to keep the facts that you will learn here today to yourselves. Is that understood?'

'Of course,' said Miss Chadwick, speaking first and with emphasis. 'Of course we're all loyal to Meadowbank, I should hope.'

'Naturally,' said Miss Johnson.

'Oh yes,' said the two younger mistresses.

'I agree,' said Eileen Rich.

'Then perhaps, M. Poirot?'

Hercule Poirot rose to his feet, beamed on his audience and carefully twisted his moustaches. The two younger mistresses had a sudden desire to giggle, and looked away from each other pursing their lips together.

'It has been a difficult and anxious time for you all,' he said. 'I want you to know first that I do appreciate that. It has naturally been worst of all for Miss Bulstrode herself, but you have all suffered. You have suffered first the loss of three of your colleagues, one of whom has been here for a considerable period of time. I refer to Miss Vansittart. Miss Springer and Mademoiselle Blanche were, of course, newcomers, but I do not doubt that their deaths were a great shock to you and a distressing happening. You must also have suffered a good deal of apprehension yourselves, for it must have seemed as though there were a kind of vendetta aimed against the mistresses of Meadowbank school. That I can assure you, and Inspector Kelsey will assure you also, is not so. Meadowbank by a fortuitous series of chances became the centre for the attentions of various undesirable interests. There has been, shall we say, a cat among the pigeons. There have been three murders here and also a kidnapping. I will deal first with the kidnapping, for all through this business the difficulty has been to clear out of the way extraneous matters which, though criminal in themselves, obscure the most important thread — the thread of a ruthless and determined killer in your midst.'

He took from his pocket a photograph.

'First, I will pass round this photograph.'

Kelsey took it, handed it to Miss Bulstrode and she in turn handed it to the staff. It was returned to Poirot. He looked at their faces, which were quite blank.

'I ask you, all of you, do you recognize the girl in that photograph?'

One and all they shook their heads.

'You should do so,' said Poirot. 'Since that is a photograph obtained by me from Geneva of Princess Shaista.'

'But it's not Shaista at all,' cried Miss Chadwick.

'Exactly,' said Poirot. 'The threads of all this business start in Ramat where, as you know, a revolutionary *coup d'état* took place about three months ago. The ruler, Prince Ali Yusuf, managed to escape, flown out by his own private pilot. Their plane, however, crashed in the mountains north of Ramat and was not discovered until later in the year. A certain article of great value, which was always carried on Prince Ali's person, was missing. It was not found in the wreck and there were rumours that it had been brought to this country. Several groups of people were anxious to get hold of this very valuable article. One of their leads to it was Prince Ali Yusuf's only remaining relation, his first cousin, a girl who was then at a school in Switzerland. It seemed likely that if the precious article had been safely got out of Ramat it would be brought to Princess Shaista or to her relatives and guardians. Certain agents were detailed to keep an eye on her uncle, the Emir Ibrahim, and others to keep an eye on the Princess herself. It was known that she was due to come to this school, Meadowbank, this term. Therefore it would have been only natural that someone should be detailed to obtain employment here and to keep a close watch on anyone who approached the Princess, her letters, and any telephone messages. But an even simpler and more efficacious idea was evolved, that of kidnapping Shaista and sending one of their own number to the school as Princess Shaista herself. This could be done successfully since the Emir Ibrahim was in Egypt and did not propose to visit England until late summer. Miss Bulstrode herself had not seen the girl and all arrangements that she had made concerning her reception had been made with the Embassy in London.

'The plan was simple in the extreme. The real Shaista left Switzerland accompanied by a representative from the Embassy in London. Or so it was supposed. Actually, the Embassy in London was informed that a representative from the Swiss school would accompany the girl to London. The real Shaista was taken to a very pleasant chalet in Switzerland where she has been ever since, and an entirely different girl arrived in London, was met there by a representative of the Embassy and subsequently brought to this school. This substitute, of course, was necessarily much older than the real Shaista. But that would hardly attract attention since Eastern girls noticeably look much more mature than their age. A young French actress who specializes in playing schoolgirl parts was the agent chosen.

'I did ask,' said Hercule Poirot, in a thoughtful voice, 'as to whether anyone had noticed Shaista's knees. Knees are a very good indication of age. The knees of a woman of twenty-three or twenty-four can never really be mistaken for the knees of a girl of fourteen or fifteen. Nobody, alas, had noticed her knees.

'The plan was hardly as successful as had been hoped. Nobody attempted to get in touch with Shaista, no letters or telephone calls of significance arrived for her and as time went on an added anxiety arose. The Emir Ibrahim might arrive in England ahead of schedule. He was not a man who announced his plans ahead. He was in the habit, I understand, of saying one evening, 'Tomorrow I go to London' and thereupon to go.

'The false Shaista, then, was aware that at any moment someone who knew the real Shaista might arrive. Especially was this so after the murder and therefore she began to prepare the way for a kidnapping by talking about it to Inspector Kelsey. Of course, the actual kidnapping was nothing of the kind. As soon as she learned that her uncle was coming to take her out the following morning, she sent a brief message by telephone, and half an hour earlier than the genuine car, a showy car with false C.D. plates on it arrived and Shaista was officially 'kidnapped'. Actually, of course, she was set down by the car in the first large town where she at once resumed her own personality. An amateurish ransom note was sent just to keep up the fiction.'

Hercule Poirot paused, then said, 'It was, as you can see, merely the trick of the conjurer. Misdirection. You focus the eyes on the kidnapping *here* and it does not occur to anyone that the kidnapping *really* occurred three weeks earlier in Switzerland.'

What Poirot really meant, but was too polite to say, was that it had not occurred to anyone but himself!

'We pass now,' he said, 'to something far more serious than kidnapping — murder.

'The false Shaista could, of course, have killed Miss Springer but she could not have killed Miss Vansittart or Mademoiselle Blanche, and would have had no motive to kill anybody, nor was such a thing required of her. Her role was simply to receive a valuable packet if, as seemed likely, it should be brought to her: or, alternatively, to receive news of it.

'Let us go back now to Ramat where all this started. It was widely rumoured in Ramat that Prince Ali Yusuf had given this valuable packet to Bob Rawlinson, his private pilot, and that Bob Rawlinson had arranged for its despatch to England. On the day in question Rawlinson went to Ramat's principal hotel where his sister, Mrs Sutcliffe, and her daughter Jennifer were staying. Mrs Sutcliffe and Jennifer were out, but Bob Rawlinson went up to their room where he remained for at least twenty minutes. That is rather a long time under the circumstances. He might of course have been writing a long letter to his sister. But that was not so. He merely left a short note which he could have scribbled in a couple of minutes.

'It was a very fair inference then, inferred by several separate parties, that during his time in her room he had placed this object amongst his sister's effects and that she had brought it back to England. Now we come to what I may call the dividing of two separate threads. One set of interests — (or possibly more than one set) — assumed that Mrs Sutcliffe had brought this article back to England and in consequence her house in the country was ransacked and a thorough search made. This showed that whoever was searching *did not know where exactly the article was hidden*. Only that it was probably *somewhere* in Mrs Sutcliffe's possession.

'But somebody else knew very definitely exactly where that article was, and I think that by now it will do no harm for me to tell you where, in fact, Bob Rawlinson did conceal it. He concealed it in the handle of a tennis racquet, hollowing out the handle and afterwards piecing it together again so skilfully that it was difficult to see what had been done.

'The tennis racquet belonged, not to his sister, but to her daughter Jennifer. Someone who knew exactly where the cache was, went out to the Sports Pavilion one night, having previously taken an impression of the key and got a key cut. At that time of night everyone should have been in bed and asleep. But that was not so. Miss Springer saw the light of a torch in the Sports Pavilion from the house, and went out to investigate. She was a tough hefty young woman and had no doubts of her own ability to cope with anything she might find. The person in question was probably sorting through the tennis racquets to find the right one. Discovered and recognized by Miss Springer, there was no hesitation . . . The searcher was a killer, and shot Miss Springer dead. Afterwards, however, the killer had to act fast. The shot had been heard, people were approaching. At all costs the killer must get out of the Sports Pavilion unseen. The racquet must be left where it was for the moment . . .

'Within a few days another method was tried. A strange woman with a faked American accent waylaid Jennifer Sutcliffe as she was coming from the tennis courts, and told her a plausible story about a relative of hers having sent her down a new tennis racquet. Jennifer unsuspiciously accepted this story and gladly exchanged the racquet she was carrying for the new, expensive one the stranger had brought. But a circumstance had arisen which the woman with the American accent knew nothing about. That was that a few days previously Jennifer Sutcliffe and Julia Upjohn had exchanged racquets so that what the strange woman took away with her was in actual fact Julia Upjohn's old racquet, though the identifying tape on it bore Jennifer's name.

'We come now to the second tragedy. Miss Vansittart for some unknown reason, but possibly connected with the kidnapping of Shaista which had taken place that afternoon, took a torch and went out to the Sports Pavilion after everybody had gone to bed. Somebody who had followed her there struck her down with a cosh or a sandbag, as she was stooping down by Shaista's locker. Again the crime was discovered almost immediately. Miss Chadwick saw a light in the Sports Pavilion and hurried out there.

'The police once more took charge at the Sports Pavilion, and again the killer was debarred from searching and examining the tennis racquets there. But by now, Julia Upjohn, an intelligent child, had thought things over and had come to the logical conclusion that the racquet she possessed and which had originally belonged to Jennifer, was in some way important. She investigated on her own behalf, found that she was correct in her surmise, and brought the contents of the racquet to me.

'These are now,' said Hercule Poirot, 'in safe custody and need concern us here no longer.' He paused and then went on, 'It remains to consider the third tragedy.

'What Mademoiselle Blanche knew or suspected we shall never know. She may have seen someone leaving the house on the night of Miss Springer's murder. Whatever it was that she knew or suspected, she knew the identity of the murderer. And she kept that knowledge to herself. She planned to obtain money in return for her silence.

'There is nothing,' said Hercule Poirot, with feeling, 'more dangerous than levying blackmail on a person who has killed perhaps twice already. Mademoiselle Blanche may have taken her own precautions but whatever they were, they were inadequate. She made an appointment with the murderer and she was killed.'

He paused again.

'So there,' he said, looking round at them, 'you have the account of this whole affair.'

They were all staring at him. Their faces, which at first had reflected interest, surprise, excitement, seemed now frozen into a uniform calm. It was as though they were terrified to display any emotion. Hercule Poirot nodded at them.

'Yes,' he said, 'I know how you feel. It has come, has it not, very near home? That is why, you see, I and Inspector Kelsey and Mr Adam Goodman have been making the inquiries. We have to know, you see, if there is still a cat among the pigeons! You understand what I mean? Is there still someone here who is masquerading under false colours?'

There was a slight ripple passing through those who listened to him, a brief almost furtive sidelong glance as though they wished to look at each other, but did not dare do so.

'I am happy to reassure you,' said Poirot. 'All of you here at this moment *are exactly who you say you are*. Miss Chadwick, for instance, is Miss Chadwick — that is certainly not open to doubt, she has been here as long as Meadowbank itself! Miss Johnson, too, is unmistakably Miss Johnson. Miss Rich is Miss Rich. Miss Shapland is Miss Shapland. Miss Rowan and Miss Blake are Miss Rowan and Miss Blake. To go further,' said Poirot, turning his head, 'Adam Goodman who works here in the garden, is, if not precisely Adam Goodman, at any rate the person whose name is on his credentials. So then, where are we? We must seek not for someone masquerading as someone else, but for someone who is, in his or her proper identity, a murderer.'

The room was very still now. There was menace in the air.

Poirot went on.

'We want, primarily, *someone who was in Ramat three months ago*. Knowledge that the prize was concealed in the tennis racquet could only have been acquired in one way. Someone must have *seen* it put there by Bob Rawlinson. It is as simple as that. Who then, of all of you present here, was in Ramat three months ago? Miss Chadwick was here, Miss Johnson was here.' His eyes went on to the two junior Mistresses. 'Miss Rowan and Miss Blake were here.'

His finger went out pointing.

'But Miss Rich — Miss Rich was not here last term, was she?'

'I — no. I was ill.' She spoke hurriedly. 'I was away for a term.'

'That is the thing we did not know,' said Hercule Poirot, 'until a few days ago somebody mentioned it casually. When questioned by the police originally, you merely said that you had been at Meadowbank for a year and a

326

half. That in itself is true enough. But you were absent last term. You could have been in Ramat — I think you were in Ramat. Be careful. It can be verified, you know, from your passport.'

There was a moment's silence, then Eileen Rich looked up.

'Yes,' she said quietly. 'I was in Ramat. Why not?'

'Why did you go to Ramat, Miss Rich?'

'You already know. I had been ill. I was advised to take a rest — to go abroad. I wrote to Miss Bulstrode and explained that I must take a term off. She quite understood.'

'That is so,' said Miss Bulstrode. 'A doctor's certificate was enclosed which said that it would be unwise for Miss Rich to resume her duties until the following term.'

'So — you went to Ramat?' said Hercule Poirot.

'Why shouldn't I go to Ramat?' said Eileen Rich. Her voice trembled slightly. 'There are cheap fares offered to schoolteachers. I wanted a rest. I wanted sunshine. I went out to Ramat. I spent two months there. *Why not? Why not, I say?*'

'You have never mentioned that you were at Ramat at the time of the Revolution.'

'Why should I? What has it got to do with anyone here? I haven't killed anyone, I tell you. I haven't killed anyone.'

'You were recognized, you know,' said Hercule Poirot. 'Not recognized definitely, but indefinitely. The child Jennifer was very vague. She said she thought she'd seen you in Ramat but concluded it couldn't be you because, she said, the person she had seen was *fat*, not thin.' He leaned forward, his eyes boring into Eileen Rich's face.

'What have you to say, Miss Rich?'

She wheeled round. 'I know what you're trying to make out!' she cried. 'You're trying to make out that it wasn't a secret agent or anything of that kind who did these murders. That it was someone who just *happened* to be there, someone who *happened* to see this treasure hidden in a tennis racquet. Someone who realized that the child was coming to Meadowbank and that she'd have an opportunity to take for herself this hidden thing. But I tell you it isn't *true*!'

'I think that is what happened. Yes,' said Poirot. 'Someone saw the jewels being hidden and forgot all other duties or interests in the determination to possess them!'

'It isn't true, I tell you. I saw nothing — '

'Inspector Kelsey.' Poirot turned his head.

Inspector Kelsey nodded — went to the door, opened it, and Mrs Upjohn walked into the room.

'How do you do, Miss Bulstrode,' said Mrs Upjohn, looking rather embarrassed. 'I'm sorry I'm looking rather untidy, but I was somewhere near Ankara yesterday and I've just flown home. I'm in a terrible mess and I really haven't had time to clean myself up or do *anything*.'

'That does not matter,' said Hercule Poirot. 'We want to ask you something.'

'Mrs Upjohn,' said Kelsey, 'when you came here to bring your daughter to the school and you were in Miss Bulstrode's sitting-room, you looked out of the window — the window which gives on the front drive — and you uttered an exclamation as though you recognized someone you saw there. That is so, is it not?'

Mrs Upjohn stared at him. 'When I was in Miss Bulstrode's sitting-room? I looked — oh, yes, of *course*! Yes, I did see someone.'

'Someone you were surprised to see?'

'Well, I was rather . . . You see, it had all been such years ago.'

'You mean the days when you were working in Intelligence towards the end of the war?'

'Yes. It was about fifteen years ago. Of course, she looked much older, but I recognized her at once. And I wondered what on earth she could be doing *here*.'

'Mrs Upjohn, will you look round this room and tell me if you see that person here now?'

'Yes, of course,' said Mrs Upjohn. 'I saw her as soon as I came in. That's her.'

She stretched out a pointing finger. Inspector Kelsey was quick and so was Adam, but they were not quick enough. Ann Shapland had sprung to her feet. In her hand was a small wicked-looking automatic and it pointed straight at Mrs Upjohn. Miss Bulstrode, quicker than the two men, moved sharply forward, but swifter still was Miss Chadwick. It was not Mrs Upjohn that she was trying to shield, it was the woman who was standing between Ann Shapland and Mrs Upjohn.

'No, you shan't,' cried Chaddy, and flung herself on Miss Bulstrode just as the small automatic went off.

Miss Chadwick staggered, then slowly crumpled down. Miss Johnson ran to her. Adam and Kelsey had got hold of Ann Shapland now. She was struggling like a wild cat, but they wrested the small automatic from her.

Mrs Upjohn said breathlessly:

'They said then that she was a killer.

Although she was so young. One of the most dangerous agents they had. Angelica was her code name.'

'You lying bitch!' Ann Shapland fairly spat out the words.

Hercule Poirot said:

'She does not lie. You are dangerous. You have always led a dangerous life. Up to now, you have never been suspected in your own identity. All the jobs you have taken in your own name have been perfectly genuine jobs, efficiently performed — but they have all been jobs with a purpose, and that purpose has been the gaining of information. You have worked with an Oil Company, with an archaeologist whose work took him to a certain part of the globe, with an actress whose protector was an eminent politician. Ever since you were seventeen you have worked as an agent — though for many different masters. Your services have been for hire and have been highly paid. You have played a dual role. Most of your assignments have been carried out in your own name, but there were certain jobs for which you assumed different identities. Those were the times when ostensibly you had to go home and be with your mother.

'But I strongly suspect, Miss Shapland, that the elderly woman I visited who lives in a small village with a nurse-companion to look after her, an elderly woman who is genuinely a mental patient with a confused mind, is not your mother at all. She has been your excuse for retiring from employment and from the circle of your friends. The three months this winter that you spent with your 'mother' who had one of her 'bad turns' covers the time when you went out to Ramat. Not as Ann Shapland but as Angelica de Toredo, a Spanish, or near-Spanish cabaret dancer. You occupied the room in the hotel next to that of Mrs Sutcliffe and somehow you managed to see Bob Rawlinson conceal the jewels in the racquet. You had no opportunity of taking the racquet then for there was the sudden evacuation of all British people, but you had read the labels on their luggage and it was easy to find out something about them. To obtain a secretarial post here was not difficult. I have made some inquiries. You paid a substantial sum to Miss Bulstrode's former secretary to vacate her post on the plea of a 'breakdown'. And you had quite a plausible story. You had been commissioned to write a series of articles on a famous girls' school 'from within'.

'It all seemed quite easy, did it not? If a child's racquet was missing, what of it? Simpler still, you would go out at night to the

332

Sports Pavilion, and abstract the jewels. But you had not reckoned with Miss Springer. Perhaps she had already seen you examining the racquets. Perhaps she just happened to wake that night. She followed you out there and you shot her. Later, Mademoiselle Blanche tried to blackmail you, and you killed her. It comes natural to you, does it not, to kill?'

He stopped. In a monotonous official voice, Inspector Kelsey cautioned his prisoner.

She did not listen. Turning towards Hercule Poirot, she burst out in a low-pitched flood of invective that startled everyone in the room.

'Whew!' said Adam, as Kelsey took her away. 'And I thought she was a nice girl!'

Miss Johnson had been kneeling by Miss Chadwick.

'I'm afraid she's badly hurt,' she said. 'She'd better not be moved until the doctor comes.'

24

Poirot Explains

I

Mrs Upjohn, wandering through the corridors of Meadowbank School, forgot the exciting scene she had just been through. She was for the moment merely a mother seeking her young. She found her in a deserted classroom. Julia was bending over a desk, her tongue protruding slightly, absorbed in the agonies of composition.

She looked up and stared. Then flung herself across the room and hugged her mother.

'Mummy!'

Then, with the self-consciousness of her age, ashamed of her unrestrained emotion, she detached herself and spoke in a carefully casual tone — indeed almost accusingly.

'Aren't you back rather *soon*, Mummy?'

'I flew back,' said Mrs Upjohn, almost apologetically, 'from Ankara.'

'Oh,' said Julia. 'Well — I'm glad you're back.'

'Yes,' said Mrs Upjohn, 'I am very glad too.'

They looked at each other, embarrassed. 'What are you doing?' said Mrs Upjohn, advancing a little closer.

'I'm writing a composition for Miss Rich,' said Julia. 'She really does set the most exciting subjects.'

'What's this one?' said Mrs Upjohn. She bent over.

The subject was written at the top of the page. Some nine or ten lines of writing in Julia's uneven and sprawling hand-writing came below. 'Contrast the Attitudes of Macbeth and Lady Macbeth to Murder,' read Mrs Upjohn.

'Well,' she said doubtfully, 'you can't say that the subject isn't topical!'

She read the start of her daughter's essay. 'Macbeth,' Julia had written, 'liked the idea of murder and had been thinking of it a lot, but he needed a push to get him started. Once he'd got started he enjoyed murdering people and had no more qualms or fears. Lady Macbeth was just greedy and ambitious. She thought she didn't mind what she did to get what she wanted. But once she'd done it she found she didn't like it after all.'

'Your language isn't very elegant,' said Mrs Upjohn. 'I think you'll have to polish it up a bit, but you've certainly got something there.'

II

Inspector Kelsey was speaking in a slightly complaining tone.

'It's all very well for you, Poirot,' he said. 'You can say and do a lot of things we can't: and I'll admit the whole thing was well stage managed. Got her off her guard, made her think we were after Rich, and then, Mrs Upjohn's sudden appearance made her lose her head. Thank the lord she kept that automatic after shooting Springer. If the bullet corresponds — '

'It will, *mon ami*, it will,' said Poirot.

'Then we've got her cold for the murder of Springer. And I gather Miss Chadwick's in a bad way. But look here, Poirot, I still can't see how she can possibly have killed Miss Vansittart. It's physically impossible. She's got a cast iron alibi — unless young Rathbone and the whole staff of the Nid Sauvage are in it with her.'

Poirot shook his head. 'Oh, no,' he said. 'Her alibi is perfectly good. She killed Miss Springer and Mademoiselle Blanche. But Miss Vansittart — ' he hesitated for a moment, his eyes going to where Miss Bulstrode sat listening to them. 'Miss Vansittart was killed by Miss Chadwick.'

'Miss Chadwick?' exclaimed Miss Bulstrode and Kelsey together.

Poirot nodded. 'I am sure of it.'

'But — why?'

'I think,' said Poirot, 'Miss Chadwick loved Meadowbank too much . . . ' His eyes went across to Miss Bulstrode.

'I see . . . ' said Miss Bulstrode. 'Yes, yes, I see . . . I ought to have known.' She paused. 'You mean that she — ?'

'I mean,' said Poirot, 'that she started here with you, that all along she has regarded Meadowbank as a joint venture between you both.'

'Which in one sense it was,' said Miss Bulstrode.

'Quite so,' said Poirot. 'But that was merely the financial aspect. When you began to talk of retiring she regarded herself as the person who would take over.'

'But she's far too old,' objected Miss Bulstrode.

'Yes,' said Poirot, 'she is too old and she is not suited to be a headmistress. But she herself did not think so. She thought that when you went she would be headmistress of Meadowbank as a matter of course. And then she found that was not so. That you were considering someone else, that you had fastened upon Eleanor Vansittart. And she loved Meadowbank. She loved the school and she did not like Eleanor Vansittart. I think in the end she hated her.'

'She might have done,' said Miss Bulstrode. 'Yes, Eleanor Vansittart was — how shall I put it? — she was always very complacent, very superior about everything. That would be hard to bear if you were jealous. That's what you mean, isn't it? Chaddy was jealous.'

'Yes,' said Poirot. 'She was jealous of Meadowbank and jealous of Eleanor Vansittart. She couldn't bear the thought of the school and Miss Vansittart together. And then perhaps something in your manner led her to think that you were weakening?'

'I did weaken,' said Miss Bulstrode. 'But I didn't weaken in the way that perhaps Chaddy thought I would weaken. Actually I thought of someone younger still than Miss Vansittart — I thought it over and then I said No, she's too young . . . Chaddy was with me then, I remember.'

'And she thought,' said Poirot, 'that you were referring to Miss Vansittart. That you were saying Miss Vansittart was too young. She thoroughly agreed. She thought that experience and wisdom such as she had got were far more important things. But then, after all, you returned to your original decision. You chose Eleanor Vansittart as the right person and left her in charge of the school that weekend. This is what I think happened. On that Sunday night Miss Chadwick was restless, she got up and she saw the light in the squash court. She went out there exactly as she says she went. There is only one thing different in her story from what she said. It wasn't a golf club she took with her. She picked up one of the sandbags from the pile in the hall. She went out there all ready to deal with a burglar, with someone who for a second time had broken into the Sports Pavilion. She had the sandbag ready in her hand to defend herself if attacked. And what did she find? She found Eleanor Vansittart kneeling down looking in a locker, and she thought, it may be — (for I am good,' said Hercule Poirot in a parenthesis, ' — at putting myself into other people's minds —) she thought *if* I were a marauder, a burglar, I would come up behind her and strike her down. And as the thought came into her mind, only half conscious of what she was doing, she raised the sandbag and struck. And there was Eleanor Vansittart dead, out of her way. She was appalled then, I think, at what she had done. It has preyed on her ever since — for she is not a natural killer, Miss Chadwick. She was driven, as some are driven, by jealousy and by obsession. The obsession of love for Meadowbank. Now that

Eleanor Vansittart was dead she was quite sure that she would succeed you at Meadowbank. So she didn't confess. She told her story to the police exactly as it had occurred but for the one vital fact, that it was *she* who had struck the blow. But when she was asked about the golf club which presumably Miss Vansittart took with her being nervous after all that had occurred, Miss Chadwick said quickly that she had taken it out there. She didn't want you to think even for a moment that she had handled the sandbag.'

'Why did Ann Shapland also choose a sandbag to kill Mademoiselle Blanche?' asked Miss Bulstrode.

'For one thing, she could not risk a pistol shot in the school building, and for another she is a very clever young woman. She wanted to tie up this third murder with the second one, for which she had an alibi.'

'I don't really understand what Eleanor Vansittart was doing herself in the Sports Pavilion,' said Miss Bulstrode.

'I think one could make a guess. She was probably far more concerned over the disappearance of Shaista than she allowed to appear on the surface. She was as upset as Miss Chadwick was. In a way it was worse for her, because she had been left by you in charge — and the kidnapping had happened whilst she was responsible. Moreover she had pooh-poohed it as long as possible through an unwillingness to face unpleasant facts squarely.'

'So there was weakness behind the *façade*,' mused Miss Bulstrode. 'I sometimes suspected it.'

'She, too, I think, was unable to sleep. And I think she went out quietly to the Sports Pavilion to make an examination of Shaista's locker in case there might be some clue there to the girl's disappearance.'

'You seem to have explanations for everything, Mr Poirot.'

'That's his speciality,' said Inspector Kelsey with slight malice.

'And what was the point of getting Eileen Rich to sketch various members of my staff?'

'I wanted to test the child Jennifer's ability to recognize a face. I soon satisfied myself that Jennifer was so entirely preoccupied by her own affairs, that she gave outsiders at most a cursory glance, taking in only the external details of their appearance. She did not recognize a sketch of Mademoiselle Blanche with a different hairdo. Still less, then, would she have recognized Ann Shapland who, as your secretary, she seldom saw at close quarters.'

'You think that the woman with the racquet was Ann Shapland herself.'

'Yes. It has been a one woman job all through. You remember that day, you rang for her to take a message to Julia but in the end, as the buzzer went unanswered, sent a girl to find Julia. Ann was accustomed to quick disguise. A fair wig, differently pencilled eyebrows, a 'fussy' dress and hat. She need only be absent from her typewriter for about twenty minutes. I saw from Miss Rich's clever sketches how easy it is for a woman to alter her appearance by purely external matters.'

'Miss Rich — I wonder — ' Miss Bulstrode looked thoughtful.

Poirot gave Inspector Kelsey a look and the Inspector said he must be getting along.

'Miss Rich?' said Miss Bulstrode again.

'Send for her,' said Poirot. 'It is the best way.'

Eileen Rich appeared. She was white faced and slightly defiant.

'You want to know,' she said to Miss Bulstrode, 'what I was doing in Ramat?'

'I think I have an idea,' said Miss Bulstrode.

'Just so,' said Poirot. 'Children nowadays know all the facts of life — but their eyes often retain innocence.'

He added that he, too, must be getting

along, and slipped out.

'That was it, wasn't it?' said Miss Bulstrode. Her voice was brisk and business-like. 'Jennifer merely described it as fat. She didn't realize it was a pregnant woman she had seen.'

'Yes,' said Eileen Rich. 'That was it. I was going to have a child. I didn't want to give up my job here. I carried on all right through the autumn, but after that, it was beginning to show. I got a doctor's certificate that I wasn't fit to carry on, and I pleaded illness. I went abroad to a remote spot where I thought I wasn't likely to meet anyone who knew me. I came back to this country and the child was born — dead. I came back this term and I hoped that no one would ever know . . . But you understand now, don't you, why I said I should have had to refuse your offer of a partnership if you'd made it? Only now, with the school in such a disaster, I thought that, after all, I might be able to accept.'

She paused and said in a matter of fact voice,

'Would you like me to leave now? Or wait until the end of term?'

'You'll stay till the end of the term,' said Miss Bulstrode, 'and if there is a new term here, which I still hope, you'll come back.'

'Come back?' said Eileen Rich. 'Do you

mean you still want me?'

'Of course I want you,' said Miss Bulstrode. 'You haven't murdered anyone, have you? — not gone mad over jewels and planned to kill to get them? I'll tell you what you've done. You've probably denied your instincts too long. There was a man, you fell in love with him, you had a child. I suppose you couldn't marry.'

'There was never any question of marriage,' said Eileen Rich. 'I knew that. He isn't to blame.'

'Very well, then,' said Miss Bulstrode. 'You had a love affair and a child. You wanted to have that child?'

'Yes,' said Eileen Rich. 'Yes, I wanted to have it.'

'So that's that,' said Miss Bulstrode. 'Now I'm going to tell you something. I believe that in spite of this love affair, your real vocation in life is teaching. I think your profession means more to you than any normal woman's life with a husband and children would mean.'

'Oh yes,' said Eileen Rich. 'I'm sure of that. I've known that all along. That's what I really want to do — that's the real passion of my life.'

'Then don't be a fool,' said Miss Bulstrode. 'I'm making you a very good offer. If, that is, things come right. We'll spend two or three years together putting Meadowbank back on the map. You'll have different ideas as to how that should be done from the ideas that I have. I'll listen to your ideas. Maybe I'll even give in to some of them. You want things to be different, I suppose, at Meadowbank?'

'I do in some ways, yes,' said Eileen Rich. 'I won't pretend. I want more emphasis on getting girls that really matter.'

'Ah,' said Miss Bulstrode, 'I see. It's the snob element that you don't like, is that it?'

'Yes,' said Eileen, 'it seems to me to spoil things.'

'What you don't realize,' said Miss Bulstrode, 'is that to get the kind of girl you want you've *got* to have that snob element. It's quite a small element really, you know. A few foreign royalties, a few great names and everybody, all the silly parents all over this country and other countries want their girls to come to Meadowbank. Fall over themselves to get their girl admitted to Meadowbank. What's the result? An enormous waiting list, and I look at the girls and I see the girls and I choose! You get your pick, do you see? I choose my girls. I choose them very carefully, some for character, some for brains, some for pure academic intellect. Some because I think they haven't had a chance but are capable of being made something of that's worth while. You're young, Eileen. You're full of ideals — it's the teaching that matters to you and the ethical side of it. Your vision's quite right. It's the girls that matter, but if you want to make a success of anything, you know, you've got to be a good tradesman as well. Ideas are like everything else. They've got to be marketed. We'll have to do some pretty slick work in future to get Meadowbank going again. I'll have to get my hooks into a few people, former pupils, bully them, plead with them, get them to send their daughters here. And then the others will come. You let me be up to my tricks, and then you shall have your way. Meadowbank will go on and it'll be a fine school.'

'It'll be the finest school in England,' said Eileen Rich enthusiastically.

'Good,' said Miss Bulstrode, ' — and Eileen, I should go and get your hair properly cut and shaped. You don't seem able to manage that bun. And now,' she said, her voice changing, 'I must go to Chaddy.'

She went in and came up to the bed. Miss Chadwick was lying very still and white. The blood had all gone from her face and she looked drained of life. A policeman with a notebook sat nearby and Miss Johnson sat on the other side of the bed. She looked at Miss Bulstrode and shook her head gently.

'Hallo, Chaddy,' said Miss Bulstrode. She took up the limp hand in hers. Miss Chadwick's eyes opened.

'I want to tell you,' she said, 'Eleanor — it was — it was me.'

'Yes, dear, I know,' said Miss Bulstrode.

'Jealous,' said Chaddy. 'I wanted — '

'I know,' said Miss Bulstrode.

Tears rolled very slowly down Miss Chadwick's cheeks. 'It's so awful . . . I didn't mean — I don't know how I came to do such a thing!'

'Don't think about it any more,' said Miss Bulstrode.

'But I can't — you'll never — I'll never forgive myself — '

'Listen, dear,' she said. 'You saved my life, you know. My life and the life of that nice woman, Mrs Upjohn. That counts for something, doesn't it?'

'I only wish,' said Miss Chadwick, 'I could have given *my* life for you both. That would have made it all right . . . '

Miss Bulstrode looked at her with great pity. Miss Chadwick took a great breath, smiled, then, moving her head very slightly to one side, she died . . .

'You *did* give your life, my dear,' said Miss Bulstrode softly. 'I hope you realize that — now.'

25

Legacy

I

'A Mr Robinson has called to see you, sir.'

'Ah!' said Hercule Poirot. He stretched out his hand and picked up a letter from the desk in front of him. He looked down on it thoughtfully.

He said: 'Show him in, Georges.'

The letter was only a few lines,

Dear Poirot,

A Mr Robinson may call upon you in the near future. You may already know something about him. Quite a prominent figure in certain circles. There is a demand for such men in our modern world . . . I believe, if I may so put it, that he is, in this particular matter, on the side of the angels. This is just a recommendation, if you should be in doubt. Of course, and I underline this, we have no idea as to the matter on which he wishes to consult you . . .

Ha ha! and likewise ho ho!
Yours ever,
Ephraim Pikeaway

Poirot laid down the letter and rose as Mr Robinson came into the room. He bowed, shook hands, indicated a chair.

Mr Robinson sat, pulled out a handkerchief and wiped his large yellow face. He observed that it was a warm day.

'You have not, I hope, walked here in this heat?'

Poirot looked horrified at the idea. By a natural association of ideas, his fingers went to his moustache. He was reassured. There was no limpness.

Mr Robinson looked equally horrified.

'No, no, indeed. I came in my Rolls. But these traffic blocks . . . One sits for half an hour sometimes.'

Poirot nodded sympathetically.

There was a pause — the pause that ensues on part one of conversation before entering upon part two.

'I was interested to hear — of course one hears so many things — most of them quite untrue — that you had been concerning yourself with the affairs of a girls' school.'

'Ah,' said Poirot. 'That!'

He leaned back in his chair.

'Meadowbank,' said Mr Robinson thoughtfully. 'Quite one of the premier schools of England.'

'It is a fine school.'

'Is? Or was?'

'I hope the former.'

'I hope so, too,' said Mr Robinson. 'I fear it may be touch and go. Ah well, one must do what one can. A little financial backing to tide over a certain inevitable period of depression. A few carefully chosen new pupils. I am not without influence in European circles.'

'I, too, have applied persuasion in certain quarters. If, as you say, we can tide things over. Mercifully, memories are short.'

'That is what one hopes. But one must admit that events have taken place there that might well shake the nerves of fond mammas — and papas also. The Games Mistress, the French Mistress, and yet another mistress — all murdered.'

'As you say.'

'I hear,' said Mr Robinson, '(one hears so many things), that the unfortunate young woman responsible has suffered from a phobia about schoolmistresses since her youth. An unhappy childhood at school. Psychiatrists will make a good deal of this. They will try at least for a verdict of diminished responsibility, as they call it nowadays.'

'That line would seem to be the best choice,' said Poirot. 'You will pardon me for saying that I hope it will not succeed.'

'I agree with you entirely. A most cold-blooded killer. But they will make much of her excellent character, her work as secretary to various well-known people, her war record — quite distinguished, I believe — counter espionage — '

He let the last words out with a certain significance — a hint of a question in his voice.

'She was very good, I believe,' he said more briskly. 'So young — but quite brilliant, of great use — to both sides. That was her métier — she should have stuck to it. But I can understand the temptation — to play a lone hand, and gain a big prize.' He added softly, 'A very big prize.'

Poirot nodded.

Mr Robinson leaned forward.

'Where are they, M. Poirot?'

'I think you know where they are.'

'Well, frankly, yes. Banks are such useful institutions are they not?'

Poirot smiled.

'We needn't beat about the bush really, need we, my dear fellow? What are you going to do about them?'

'I have been waiting.'

'Waiting for what?'

'Shall we say — for suggestions?'

'Yes — I see.'

'You understand they do not belong to me. I would like to hand them over to the person they do belong to. But that, if I appraise the position correctly, is not so simple.'

'Governments are in such a difficult position,' said Mr Robinson. 'Vulnerable, so to speak. What with oil, and steel, and uranium, and cobalt and all the rest of it, foreign relations are a matter of the utmost delicacy. The great thing is to be able to say that Her Majesty's Government, etc., etc., has absolutely *no* information on the subject.'

'But I cannot keep this important deposit at my bank indefinitely.'

'Exactly. That is why I have come to propose that you should hand it over to me.'

'Ah,' said Poirot. 'Why?'

'I can give you some excellent reasons. These jewels — mercifully we are not official, we can call things by their right names — were unquestionably the personal property of the late Prince Ali Yusuf.'

'I understand that is so.'

'His Highness handed them over to Squadron Leader Robert Rawlinson with certain instructions. They were to be got out of Ramat, and they were to be delivered to *me*.'

'Have you proof of that?'

'Certainly.'

Mr Robinson drew a long envelope from his pocket. Out of it he took several papers. He laid them before Poirot on the desk.

Poirot bent over them and studied them carefully.

'It seems to be as you say.'

'Well, then?'

'Do you mind if I ask a question?'

'Not at all.'

'What do you, personally, get out of this?'

Mr Robinson looked surprised.

'My dear fellow. Money, of course. Quite a lot of money.'

Poirot looked at him thoughtfully.

'It is a very old trade,' said Mr Robinson. 'And a lucrative one. There are quite a lot of us, a network all over the globe. We are, how shall I put it, the Arrangers behind the scenes. For kings, for presidents, for politicians, for all those, in fact, upon whom the fierce light beats, as a poet has put it. We work in with one another and remember this: we keep faith. Our profits are large but we are honest. Our services are costly — but we do render service.'

'I see,' said Poirot. '*Eh bien!* I agree to what you ask.'

'I can assure you that that decision will

please everyone.' Mr Robinson's eyes just rested for a moment on Colonel Pikeaway's letter where it lay at Poirot's right hand.

'But just one little moment. I am human. I have curiosity. What are you going to do with these jewels?'

Mr Robinson looked at him. Then his large yellow face creased into a smile. He leaned forward.

'I shall tell you.'

He told him.

II

Children were playing up and down the street. Their raucous cries filled the air. Mr Robinson, alighting ponderously from his Rolls, was cannoned into by one of them.

Mr Robinson put the child aside with a not unkindly hand and peered up at the number on the house.

No. 15. This was right. He pushed open the gate and went up the three steps to the front door. Neat white curtains at the windows, he noted, and a well-polished brass knocker. An insignificant little house in an insignificant street in an insignificant part of London, but it was well kept. It had self-respect.

The door opened. A girl of about

twenty-five, pleasant looking, with a kind of fair, chocolate box prettiness, welcomed him with a smile.

'Mr Robinson? Come in.'

She took him into the small sitting-room. A television set, cretonnes of a Jacobean pattern, a cottage piano against the wall. She had on a dark skirt and a grey pullover.

'You'll have some tea? I've got the kettle on.'

'Thank you, but no. I never drink tea. And I can only stay a short time. I have only come to bring you what I wrote to you about.'

'From Ali?'

'Yes.'

'There isn't — there couldn't be — any hope? I mean — it's really true — that he was killed? There couldn't be any mistake?'

'I'm afraid there was no mistake,' said Mr Robinson gently.

'No — no, I suppose not. Anyway, I never expected — When he went back there I didn't think really I'd ever see him again. I don't mean I thought he was going to be killed or that there would be a Revolution. I just mean — well, you know — he'd have to carry on, do his stuff — what was expected of him. Marry one of his own people — all that.'

Mr Robinson drew out a package and laid it down on the table.

'Open it, please.'

Her fingers fumbled a little as she tore the wrappings off and then unfolded the final covering . . .

She drew her breath in sharply.

Red, blue, green, white, all sparkling with fire, with life, turning the dim little room into Aladdin's cave . . .

Mr Robinson watched her. He had seen so many women look at jewels . . .

She said at last in a breathless voice,

'Are they — they can't be — *real?*'

'They are real.'

'But they must be worth — they must be worth — '

Her imagination failed.

Mr Robinson nodded.

'If you wish to dispose of them, you can probably get at least half a million pounds for them.'

'No — no, it's not possible.'

Suddenly she scooped them up in her hands and re-wrapped them with shaking fingers.

'I'm scared,' she said. 'They frighten me. What am I to do with them?'

The door burst open. A small boy rushed in.

'Mum, I got a smashing tank off Billy. He — '

He stopped, staring at Mr Robinson.

An olive skinned, dark boy.

His mother said,

'Go in the kitchen, Allen, your tea's all ready. Milk and biscuits and there's a bit of gingerbread.'

'Oh good.' He departed noisily.

'You call him Allen?' said Mr Robinson.

She flushed.

'It was the nearest name to Ali. I couldn't call him Ali — too difficult for him and the neighbours and all.'

She went on, her face clouding over again.

'What am I to do?'

'First, have you got your marriage certificate? I have to be sure you're the person you say you are.'

She stared a moment, then went over to a small desk. From one of the drawers she brought out an envelope, extracted a paper from it and brought it to him.

'Hm . . . yes . . . Register of Edmonstow . . . Ali Yusuf, student . . . Alice Calder, spinster . . . Yes, all in order.'

'Oh it's legal all right — as far as it goes. And no one ever tumbled to who he was. There's so many of these foreign Moslem students, you see. We knew it didn't mean anything really. He was a Moslem and he could have more than one wife, and he knew

357

he'd have to go back and do just that. We talked about it. But Allen was on the way, you see, and he said this would make it all right for him — we were married all right in this country and Allen would be legitimate. It was the best he could do for me. He really did love me, you know. He really did.'

'Yes,' said Mr Robinson. 'I am sure he did.'

He went on briskly.

'Now, supposing that you put yourself in my hands. I will see to the selling of these stones. And I will give you the address of a lawyer, a really good and reliable solicitor. He will advise you, I expect, to put most of the money in a trust fund. And there will be other things, education for your son, and a new way of life for you. You'll want social education and guidance. You're going to be a very rich woman and all the sharks and the confidence tricksters and the rest of them will be after you. Your life's not going to be easy except in the purely material sense. Rich people don't have an easy time in life, I can tell you — I've seen too many of them to have that illusion. But you've got character. I think you'll come through. And that boy of yours may be a happier man than his father ever was.'

He paused. 'You agree?'

'Yes. Take them.' She pushed them towards him, then said suddenly: 'That schoolgirl

— the one who found them — I'd like her to have one of them — which — what colour do you think she'd like?'

Mr Robinson reflected. 'An emerald, I think — green for mystery. A good idea of yours. She will find that very thrilling.'

He rose to his feet.

'I shall charge you for my services, you know,' said Mr Robinson. 'And my charges are pretty high. But I shan't cheat you.'

She gave him a level glance.

'No, I don't think you will. And I need someone who knows about business, because I don't.'

'You seem a very sensible woman if I may say so. Now then, I'm to take these? You don't want to keep — just one — say?'

He watched her with curiosity, the sudden flicker of excitement, the hungry covetous eyes — and then the flicker died.

'No,' said Alice. 'I won't keep — even one.' She flushed. 'Oh I daresay that seems daft to you — not to keep just one big ruby or an emerald — just as a keepsake. But you see, he and I — he was a Moslem but he let me read bits now and again out of the Bible. And we read that bit — about a woman whose price was above rubies. And so — I won't have any jewels. I'd rather not . . . '

'A most unusual woman,' said Mr Robinson to himself as he walked down the path and into his waiting Rolls.

He repeated to himself,
'A most unusual woman . . . '

A MURDER IS ANNOUNCED
THEY DO IT WITH MIRRORS
A POCKET FULL OF RYE
4.50 FROM PADDINGTON
THE MIRROR CRACK'D
FROM SIDE TO SIDE
A CARIBBEAN MYSTERY
AT BERTRAM'S HOTEL
NEMESIS
SLEEPING MURDER
MISS MARPLE'S FINAL CASES

POIROT
THE MYSTERIOUS AFFAIR AT STYLES
THE MURDER ON THE LINKS
POIROT INVESTIGATES
THE MURDER OF ROGER ACKROYD
THE BIG FOUR
THE MYSTERY OF THE BLUE TRAIN
PERIL AT END HOUSE
LORD EDGWARE DIES
MURDER ON THE ORIENT EXPRESS
THREE ACT TRAGEDY
DEATH IN THE CLOUDS
THE ABC MURDERS
MURDER IN MESOPOTAMIA
CARDS ON THE TABLE
MURDER IN THE MEWS
DUMB WITNESS
DEATH ON THE NILE
APPOINTMENT WITH DEATH

HERCULE POIROT'S CHRISTMAS
SAD CYPRESS
ONE, TWO, BUCKLE MY SHOE
EVIL UNDER THE SUN
FIVE LITTLE PIGS
THE HOLLOW
THE LABOURS OF HERCULES
TAKEN AT THE FLOOD
MRS McGINTY'S DEAD
AFTER THE FUNERAL
HICKORY DICKORY DOCK
DEAD MAN'S FOLLY
CAT AMONG THE PIGEONS
THE ADVENTURE OF THE
CHRISTMAS PUDDING
THE CLOCKS
THIRD GIRL
HALLOWE'EN PARTY
ELEPHANTS CAN REMEMBER
POIROT'S EARLY CASES
CURTAIN: POIROT'S LAST CASE

TOMMY & TUPPENCE
THE SECRET ADVERSARY
PARTNERS IN CRIME
N OR M?
BY THE PRICKING OF MY THUMBS
POSTERN OF FATE

We do hope that you have enjoyed reading this large print book.

Did you know that all of our titles are available for purchase?

We publish a wide range of high quality large print books including:
Romances, Mysteries, Classics
General Fiction
Non Fiction and Westerns

Special interest titles available in large print are:
The Little Oxford Dictionary
Music Book
Song Book
Hymn Book
Service Book

Also available from us courtesy of Oxford University Press:
Young Readers' Dictionary
(large print edition)
Young Readers' Thesaurus
(large print edition)

For further information or a free brochure, please contact us at:
Ulverscroft Large Print Books Ltd.,
The Green, Bradgate Road, Anstey,
Leicester, LE7 7FU, England.
Tel: (00 44) **0116 236 4325**
Fax: (00 44) **0116 234 0205**

Stage One
Riding & Stable Management

by

Hazel Reed BHSAI

and

Jody Redhead BHSAI

Publications

Stage One - Riding & Stable Management

First published in Great Britain by Nova Publications, 1995.
Reprinted 1995
Reprinted 1996
Reprinted 1998
Second Edition 1999
Reprinted 2000

Nova Publications,
Olive House, 22, Frys Lane, Yateley, Hants. GU46 7TJ, United Kingdom.
Tel - (+44) 01252 874981

ISBN 0 9525859 5 2
British Library Cataloguing in Publication Data.
A Catalogue record for this book is available from the British Library.

Typeset in Yateley by Dreke.
Printed and bound by Intype, Input Typesetting Ltd., Wimbledon.

Illustrations by Hazel Reed and Tracey Humphreys.
Computer Graphics by Hazel Reed.

Contents

Foreword

This book deals systematically with the requirements for the BHS Stage One examination in a clear, comprehensive and practical way. It will prove a valuable reference book for all students.

It is often difficult to find all the relevant information for an examination in one book, but I feel the authors have achieved this. The information offered is further enhanced by the friendly manner in which it has been written.

This book will have a place for all students whether embarking on a career with horses or wishing purely to further their knowledge of horsemastership.

Valerie Lee.

Valerie Lee, BHSI
Chief Examiner.

Acknowledgements

We would like to thank all those persons who made this project possible; Caroline Lycett, BHSII.BHSSM (Registered), Jamie Whitehorn, Diane Salt BHSAI, Ian Spalding, Tracey Humphreys, Andrea Hinks, Bronia Hill, BHSII (Registered), Jackie Shaw, Jackie Penny, Rachel Mabere BHSAI, Gina and Bob Kendall. Thanks also to Derek Reed and Jamie Whitehorn for all their tremendous help as back up support on the Computer.

We would also like to express our gratitude to all those who gave *their* time so that we could spend *our* time writing, namely my husband Derek, my children Sophie, Martyn and Helena.

Thanks also to Mr. & Mrs. J Sayers at Perrybridge Farm, Sandhurst, Berks., for allowing us to photograph at their Livery Yard and to Mr. & Mrs. W. Hundley, Rycroft School of Equitation, Eversley, Hants.

A special thank you to Sharon Sayers who is an absolute angel.

We dedicate this book to some great equine characters, Sue, Autumn Beauty, Harry, Bella and Murphy.

Note: We do apologise to all fillies and mares for the use throughout of the male gender. We wanted to avoid using 'it', as this sounds impersonal. 'He or she' makes the text difficult to read. 'He', 'his' or 'him', with respect, refers to all horses and ponies everywhere.

Cover Photograph by David Hart. Taken at Rycroft School of Equitation, a BHS Examination Centre, with the kind permission of Mr. & Mrs. W. Hundley.

Introduction

There are many excellent books on riding and horse care but at the time of writing, no specific book that covers each British Horse Society Stage Examination. We wanted to create a series of books that exclusively and comprehensively cover the 'Stages'. This series starts with the 'Stage I' and is followed by 'The Riding and Road Safety Test & Stage II' and 'The Preliminary Teaching Test & Stage III'. These guides give all the information required for each particular exam, drastically reducing the need for a vast library of books.

Each guide in the series has a 'cut off point' giving sufficient information to take students up to the level required for that particular exam. It is often difficult for students to decide exactly how much to learn for each stage, particularly when most books delve deeply into specific aspects of horse care. These Guides provide information that will enable students and their lecturers to prepare for the exams with confidence.

Purpose of the Stage I Guide

The purpose of this Guide is to encourage all those who own, ride or work with horses, to enter and pass the BHS Stage One Examination. Anyone interested in horses and ponies can gain a personal achievement through their experience and study, whether it is for a career or just out of the pure love of equestrianism.

The Guide details the Stage I syllabus, describing the theoretical and practical knowledge the student will require to enter and pass the Examination. Included in the text are aids for learning and memorising relevant points as well as exam tips and information gained from personal experiences.

Whilst each subject is comprehensively covered, the text includes basic information. This is for two reasons. Firstly, experience has proved that in the assumption that students have a basic knowledge, it is the simplest facts that are often overlooked. Secondly, the more knowledgeable student can use these elementary sections as revision.

The riding section covers the technical knowledge needed for the Stage I examination. Examples of movements and figures are included and can be practised in a school under the auspices of a BHS instructor. Whilst there are many excellent instructors who are not BHS qualified, the importance of good training with a BHS instructor cannot be over emphasised.

As well as being instructive, we hope this guide will be enjoyable. There are times when humour can emphasise important points or facts, helping us to remember and understand their relevance. Working with and caring for horses is a dedicated profession and, whilst many aspects are serious especially with regard to safety, we believe that learning about horses should be enjoyed. By whichever means we increase our knowledge, this will eventually benefit horses and ponies improving their care and well being.

C H A P T E R   1
General Information

Passing the Stage I is, for those wishing to make a career with horses, the first step to gaining a British Horse Society qualification and a personal achievement for those who ride as a recreation. The training offers a structured approach to learning about horses both in riding and care, covering a wide variety of subjects. For all students the Stage I is a comprehensive introduction to the world of equestrianism.

Eligibility

All applicants for the Stage I must be:

* A member of the British Horse Society at the time of application and on the day of the examination.

* 16 years or over.

The Syllabus

The exam is divided into two main sections - Riding and Horse Knowledge/Care. The Horse Knowledge section is split into Theory, Practical and Practical Oral sessions.

Riding

For the Stage I the examiners are assessing the rider's knowledge and capability in the basic principles of equitation.

General   Assess the horse's tack for fitting and condition - check and tighten the girth from the ground - lead a fully tacked horse in hand at trot and walk - mount and dismount correctly from the ground and from a mounting block - help other riders to mount by assisting from a mounting block or by giving a leg up - check and alter stirrups - check and tighten the girth when mounted.

Equitation A correct, balanced position at walk, trot and canter - at rising and sitting trot - without stirrups at walk and trot. The correct basic techniques when performing simple school figures and when asking the horse for transitions from one pace to another - how to halt and keep the horse still in halt. The ability to ride the horse forwards in all paces - an elementary understanding of how the horse moves - knowledge of diagonals at trot and the ability to ride on the correct diagonal - the correct leading leg in canter and the ability to ask for the correct leading leg.

Shorten the stirrups and show work at rising/sitting trot and canter. Work in the light seat around the school as a ride and in open order over ground poles showing balance and harmony with the horse.

Safety Knowledge of school commands and etiquette - an awareness of other riders and the ability to maintain safe distances from other horses.

Horse Knowledge and Care

The assessment for this section is based on the practical experience and knowledge that the candidate shows.

General The correct method of approaching and handling horses - the principle of correction and reward for discipline - knowledge and practical experience of working under supervision with horses in the stable and at grass. Understanding the importance of physical fitness and the general principles of yard work - care and use of stable equipment - a sensible, caring attitude to horses and to fellow workers.

Psychology Knowledge and experience of the horse's characteristics and instincts - how the horse reacts in different environments - how to handle the horse safely and the need for calmness, competence and confidence in handling.

Anatomy The points of the horse - the main external areas - colours and markings.

Health Recognising and describing the signs of good or ill health for horses and ponies in the stable and at grass - why an immediate report is essential.

General Management
Basic daily routine and why this is essential. Knowledge and practical experience of fitting, putting on, and leading a horse in a headcollar - how and where to tie a horse up safely - how to stand a horse up correctly for inspection or shoeing. Grooming procedures, equipment and the importance of grooming. How to fill, weigh and tie up a haynet.

Bedding	Types of bedding, advantages and disadvantages - mucking out and bedding down - setting fair stable and yard. Care of muck heaps.
Watering	Rules and considerations of watering - methods of watering in the stable and the field.
Feeding	Aims, rules and considerations of feeding - types of feed and their basic values - cooked feed - amounts to feed horses and ponies in light work. Types of hay and their respective values.
Saddlery	The Snaffle Bridle - points of the bridle - fitting and condition - different types of snaffle bit - different nosebands. The General Purpose saddle - points of the saddle - fitting and condition. Numnahs and saddle cloths. Care, cleaning and storage of saddlery.
Clothing	Types of rugs and their uses - putting on, fitting and taking off rugs correctly. Care, cleaning and storage of rugs.
Shoeing	The horse's foot - importance of regular shoeing - recognising when the horse needs shoeing and signs of good shoeing.

Grassland Management

Field inspections and maintenance - recognising good and bad pasture - turning out and bringing in the horse correctly. Safety in the field.

General Knowledge

Safety precautions - in the stable - the yard - when riding in the countryside and on the public highway. Accident procedures. The aims of the British Horse Society.

BHS Examination Structure

The BHS Stage I is the first of a progressive series of examinations. Students who pass the Riding and Horse Knowledge sections in Stage I, II and III, the Riding and Road Safety Test, the Preliminary Teaching Test and teach for the appropriate number of hours will be awarded the Assistant Instructor's Certificate.

If the student has also obtained a First Aid certificate to Health and Safety at work standard, he or she will be eligible for inclusion into the British Horse Society's list of registered instructors. They will be entitled to put after their name, BHSAI (Reg'd).

The Riding and Horse Knowledge sections may be taken separately in all the stage examinations. Passing the Horse Knowledge and Care section up to Stage III will allow the successful student to gain the BHS Groom's Certificate.

There are further qualifications to be gained after the AI or the Grooms Certificate; the BHS Intermediate Instructor qualification, the full Instructor Certificate and the ultimate qualification; the Fellowship of the British Horse Society.

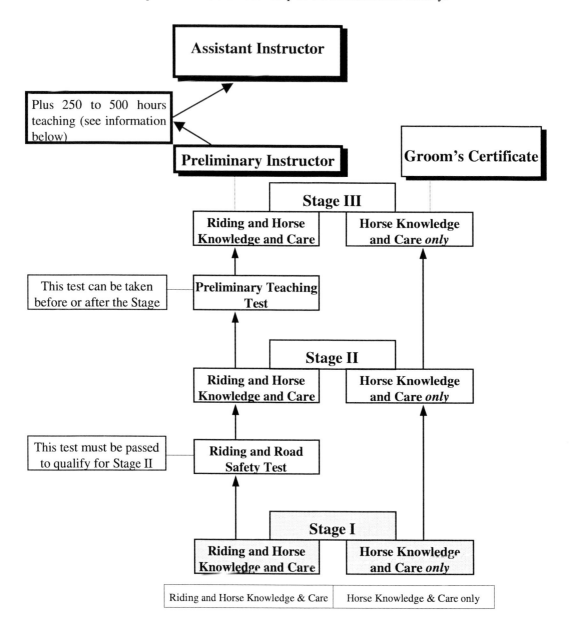

Figure 1: Table of BHS Qualifications up to Assistant Instructor level

New structure

From January 1st 1996 a new structure was introduced. All those passing the Stage exams, the Riding and Road Safety and the Preliminary Teaching tests, will be awarded the Preliminary Teacher's certificate.

To achieve an Assistant Instructors certificate, Preliminary Teachers must gain at least 250 hours teaching experience within a BHS 'Where to train' centre (listed in the 'Where to train' book). Those who teach at other establishments need 500 hours. Freelance instructors, teaching at various centres, will be able to count one hour as two when they teach at a 'Where to train' centre. Some of the hours required may be offset by attending teaching courses given by the British Horse Society.

The Escorts' Exam

Another examination that has been introduced is the Riding Escort Certificate. This tests candidates on their competency to take charge of a hack and is designed for those in charge of clients riding out in the countryside and on the road. It aims to promote a more efficient escort who is knowledgeable about safety precautions and first aid. Details for this may be obtained from the British Horse Society. *This examination does not constitute part of the requirements for the AI qualification.*

Where to train

The best place to train is at a BHS Approved riding school. Here working pupils will be given formal training and private students can choose to have riding and stable management lessons when available. Each BHS approved establishment is regularly inspected and assessed so that it can offer a level of teaching to a specified standard. The BHS book on Approved Establishments lists the schools and centres in the UK and describes the standard to which each school can train candidates.

There are also a number of colleges offering courses, which will take the student up to Assistant Instructor level and beyond. Most colleges offer comprehensive courses which, with equestrian studies, include training for business, secretarial and GCSE 'A' level qualifications. These advertise regularly in equestrian magazines and are usually excellent value.

Proficiency Tests

As an introduction to the BHS examination format there are the Proficiency tests. These are **not compulsory** for students of the Stage I and are aimed mostly at the recreational rider. They are an excellent preparation for the BHS stages especially for children or the less confident adult. These short tests, which subdivide the riding and horse care categories into smaller sections, are conducted and assessed internally by the Riding School at which they are held. Details of the Proficiency tests can be obtained from most BHS Approved Establishments.

Preparation for the Exam

Students should practise all the exercises expected in the riding section. Even the simple exercises such as mounting, checking and altering stirrups and girths need to be performed in a safe and correct way. This will create a confidence that will be of tremendous help during the examination.

Having lessons in a BHS approved Riding School, in an indoor school or menage with other riders and being instructed by a BHS qualified instructor is of paramount importance. A rider who is not used to school commands or rules and who is confused by riding school figures with others will find the exam difficult. This will be a pity, particularly if the rider has good riding ability.

For the Horse Knowledge, students need to study from relevant literature (this book!), to attend lectures at an Approved establishment and to gain personal experience in the practical aspects of stable management.

With good preparation, regular instruction, a reasonable physical fitness and a willingness to learn, the Stage I is well within the reach of all students.

Note: though correct at going to press, and whilst every effort is made to keep these books up to date, the contents of the syllabus can change at any time. Candidates are always advised to contact the British Horse Society or the Examination Centre prior to their Exam to discover if any alterations or additions have been made.

CHAPTER 2
Equitation

Training for the Stage I provides a solid basis on which to progress to more advanced riding. The rider is taught, and will learn to acquire, the suppleness and co-ordination needed to gain an effective, balanced position at the three basic paces of walk, trot and canter.

This chapter outlines the requirements needed for the rider at the Stage I level and describes the examination format; dealing with the school figures and exercises that the rider will need to know. Though the techniques of riding can only be taught in practical terms with a qualified instructor, some of the basic points are given here to help the student and to act as a revision prior to the exam.

General Preparation

The importance of good quality instruction from the very start is essential. This is particularly so with respect to riding. If the correct techniques are taught from the beginning they will last a lifetime and be a foundation on which to build and progress. Bad habits that are allowed to creep in during the basic stages will be incredibly difficult to overcome later. It is worth finding a good qualified instructor from the beginning.

Lessons on the lunge are excellent for teaching balance and for strengthening and deepening the seat. Some time spent riding without stirrups also teaches balance, supples the hip joint and stretches the muscles and tendons in the legs. This exercise should only be performed for short periods. If continued over long periods or until the rider becomes tired the value is lost as the rider tenses and grips.

Once the riding position has been established, (and most people deciding to take their Stage I have been riding for some time), the rider continues to learn by performing school figures and by improving the quality of the horse's paces and transitions.

The rider needs to learn to ride safely with others and to follow the commands given by the Instructor. This knowledge can only be gained from practical experience; taking lessons with other riders in a school or menage. The student for the Stage I should also ride a variety of horses. This will increase the awareness and adaptability of the rider. The owner/rider who only rides one horse will find it very difficult to cope with two or three 'school' horses on the exam day.

Basic Principles of Equitation

The Rider's Position

The rider sits in the deepest part of the saddle with an even weight on both seat bones. The thighs and knees lie softly against the saddle with the lower legs touching the horse's sides. The feet point forwards with the heel slightly lower than the toe. With the leg in position the stirrup leather should hang down vertically from the stirrup bar.

The back is straight, the ribcage lifted, the shoulders level and relaxed. The upper arms lie lightly by the rider's side with the elbows bent. The hands are held level and, together with the lower arms, form a straight line from the elbow to bit. The hands are positioned with the thumb on top and the fingers encircling the reins. The hand should not make a fist or clench the reins tightly.

The head faces forward and the rider looks towards the direction of travel. The head should not tilt to either side or be bowed with the rider looking at the ground.

The whole position, whilst held straight, should be one of controlled relaxation. The rider will then be capable of applying the aids correctly and effectively.

The Aids

The aids are the method by which the rider communicates with the horse; the language through which the rider asks the horse to act. There are two types of aid - the natural and the artificial. The natural aids are the *legs*, *seat and body*, *hands* and *voice*. The main artificial aids are the *whip* and *spurs*.

When referring to aids, the terms 'inside' and 'outside' are often used. The '**inside**' is the *side to which the horse is bent*. Though this usually means the inside of the school or a circle, because the horse is bending that way, in some more advanced movements the horse is bent away from the inside of the school. Similarly the '**outside**' is the side away from the bend of the horse.

The '**bend**' of a horse is the way in which his body is curved. On a circle to the right the horse will have a right 'bend', circling to the left he will have a left 'bend'.

The Natural Aids

The aids are used in conjunction with each other and by co-ordinating the leg and hand aids the rider asks for energy and maintains the desired pace. The aids should only be used when necessary; *at all other times the rider should sit as quietly as possible.*

The Legs

The legs ask for energy, bend and forward movement or, in more advanced riding, sideways movement. The leg aids are applied by increasing the pressure against the horse's side in a squeezing action either in the region of the girth or for some movements slightly behind the girth.

The Seat and Body

The seat and body aids are used more as the rider progresses into advanced riding. At this level the rider should sit in balance with the horse, learning to feel and be in 'tune' with his movements.

The Hands

The hands should always be used in conjunction with other aids; the legs or the seat and body. They control the direction and speed of the horse by a 'squeeze and relax' action on the reins.

The Voice

This aid is used mainly when training and lungeing horses. The use of the voice is not encouraged when performing flatwork and is penalised in dressage tests when the horse is expected to respond to the other aids. There are times though when the rider can use the voice to encourage, pacify, reprimand or praise the horse when necessary.

Artificial Aids

The Whip

The whip is used to discipline the horse if he does not respect the leg aid. If a horse constantly refuses to respond to the leg aids he must be reprimanded or he will continue to ignore the rider. This will result in a sluggish, unresponsive horse. If the horse does not respond to the leg, the aid is repeated and at the same time the whip is used behind that leg to reinforce the aid. With a short whip this does mean the rider has to take a hand off the reins.

When riding in a school or menage, the whip is normally carried in the inside hand to back up the leg asking for impulsion. The whip needs to be transferred to the new inside hand when changing the rein. The whip is passed from one hand to another *after* the new rein is established; this will prevent the horse shying away from the whip at a difficult moment.

The Spurs

This artificial aid is not permitted in the Stage I. When used for more advanced riding spurs are applied lightly for a more immediate response to a gentler aid. They should not be jabbed into the horse's side to strengthen the leg.

The Three Basic Paces

Each pace, walk, trot and canter, has its own beat or series of footfalls; the sequence in which the horse's feet touch the ground. The rhythm of each movement depends on the regularity of the beat.

The Walk

This has a four-time beat with each foot touching the ground at different times; left hind, left fore, right hind and right fore. The horse should walk actively as though he is marching, with a definite 1-2-3-4 rhythm.

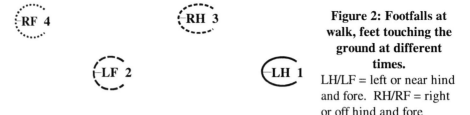

Figure 2: Footfalls at walk, feet touching the ground at different times.
LH/LF = left or near hind and fore. RH/RF = right or off hind and fore

The Trot

This is a two-time beat with the diagonal feet touching the ground in a 1-2, 1-2 rhythm; for instance, right fore and left hind then left fore and right hind.

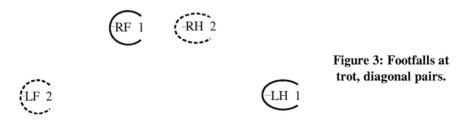

Figure 3: Footfalls at trot, diagonal pairs.

To help the horse move freely and balance himself the rider rises to the trot; sitting for one beat and rising for the alternate beat. In the school the horse's inside hind leg takes most of the weight of both horse and rider. The rider sits when the inside hind is on the ground and rises when it is lifted, to allow the forward movement. This is called being on the 'correct diagonal'.

When the rein is changed the diagonal is also changed by the rider sitting for two consecutive beats. When crossing the school or riding serpentines the rider changes the diagonal in the centre of the school or on the centre line. When riding a half circle and inclining back to the track, the diagonal is changed on reaching the track.

The Canter

This is a three-time beat with a hind leg pushing into canter, followed by a diagonal pair and then a fore. For instance when cantering to the left the right hind strikes off first, followed by the diagonal pair of left hind/right fore and lastly the left fore (the leading leg). For canter to the right - the left hind strikes off, followed by right hind/left fore and finally the right fore.

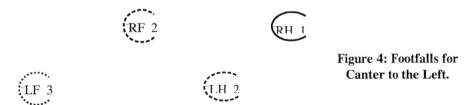

Figure 4: Footfalls for Canter to the Left.

Variations in pace

There are variations within each movement - walk may be collected, medium, extended and free; trot may be collected, working, medium and extended and canter can be collected, working, medium and extended. In addition to the three paces the horse's fourth natural gait is gallop. For the Stage I the rider is required to ride at medium walk, working trot and working canter.

Transitions

This is a change from one pace to another or from one variation of a pace to another, for example working trot to medium trot. An upward transition is from a slower to a faster pace and a downward transition from a faster to a slower pace. A transition made from one pace to the next is called progressive - walk to trot. A transition made from one pace to another out of sequence is called direct - walk to canter. (Riders will not be required to ride a direct transition in the Stage I.)

Good transitions are important to keep the horse and rider in balance and to ensure that the new pace is active and in rhythm. Transitions should be smooth with the horse going forwards (even in downward transitions).

The important point to remember with all transitions is the **preparation**. First the horse must be moving actively and going forward. Then, a few strides before the transition, the rider prepares the horse by slightly increasing the pressure of the legs whilst at the the same time, squeezing and relaxing the hand on the outside rein. This is the basic 'half-halt' which balances and prepares the horse in readiness for the change of pace. This preparation is especially vital for downward transitions to prevent the horse from suddenly dropping or falling into the slower pace.

The half-halt should be a subtle and almost invisible signal between rider and horse. It should be applied softly but effectively without restricting the horse's forward movement.

Upward transitions

For halt to walk and walk to trot, the rider increases the pressure of the legs equally and allows the forward movement with the hands. For the transition trot to canter, the trot must be active **but not fast**; springing rather than racing. The rider sits to the trot a few strides before the transition point. The inside hand squeezes the rein to indicate the direction of travel; the outside hand remains steady to keep the trot rhythm and tempo. The inside leg aid is applied on the girth and the outside leg aid slightly behind the girth.

Downward Transitions

The rider sits a little deeper into the saddle keeping the seat 'soft'. The outside hand aid is applied with a squeeze and relax action whilst the inside hand remains in contact and still. The legs are kept in contact with the horse's side to maintain the impulsion throughout the transition.

The Halt

The horse at halt should ideally stand evenly and squarely on all four legs. The rider achieves this during the transition from walk by maintaining impulsion with the legs evenly and by squeezing and relaxing both hands with equal pressure. The rider should then sit quietly and evenly in the saddle to maintain the halt.

Turns and Circles

These are used to change direction, to vary the movements within the school and to supple, stretch and build up the horse's muscles. To perform a correct turn or circle the horse must be balanced and 'straight'. It sounds a contradiction in terms to be 'straight on a circle' but this straightness refers to the 'line' through the horse's body from poll to tail. This should be a direct, constant line. When this is achieved the horse's hind feet will step on the same 'line' as the corresponding fore feet.

For the horse to achieve this the rider must sit centrally in the saddle, with the inside shoulder slightly behind the outside shoulder. Try walking a circle at home and look to see where the inside shoulder is in relation to the outside shoulder. Now try walking the circle with the inside shoulder in front of the outside shoulder; this is much more difficult.

To maintain the line on a turn or circle the rider increases the pressure of the inside leg on the girth encouraging bend. If the horse's outside shoulder starts to drift, the outside hand squeezes the rein to regain the curve.

The turn most frequently ridden badly is the turn at each corner of the school. The horse must be encouraged to bend himself into the corners by the use of the rider's inside leg, which sometimes needs applying quite firmly.

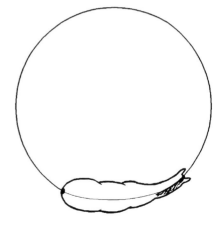

Figure 5: Horse on Turn.   Figure 6: Horse on Circle.

The Stage One Examination

This part of the chapter follows the exam format giving descriptions of exercises and figures required in the syllabus.

The candidates will be divided into groups and each group will be taken in turn to the school for the riding session. Once in the school each rider will be allocated a horse and asked to check the horse's tack for fitting and condition. (See the chapters dealing with Saddlery.)

The examiners will then request that the riders lead their horse in hand at walk and trot. Each rider should make sure that they take the horse out and allow themselves plenty of room for leading and for the turn at the end of the school.

Leading a saddled and bridled horse in hand

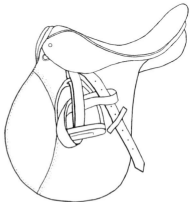

Check that the saddle is secure first, if necessary by tightening the girth. The stirrups are made safe.

For greater security the loop of the stirrup leather can be taken under the bottom of the iron and placed behind the leather in the centre.

The end of the leather is then passed through the loop and secured.

Figure 7: One method of securing the stirrups.

If there is no martingale attachment to the bridle, the reins are taken from the horse's neck, over his head and held near the horse's mouth with the right hand, if leading from the left. The reins are separated by the index finger. The buckle end, together with the whip, is held in the left hand and the horse led from the position of his shoulder. The rider should not exert any pressure on the horse's mouth through the bit.

For horses wearing a martingale, the reins remain on the neck. The reins are held in the right hand near the bit with the index finger separating them. The whip is held in the left hand.

Each rider must make sure that the horse is moving actively and is turned correctly with the rider on the outside. (See chapter on Headcollars for turning.) The examiners will be assessing the movement and action of the horse and the control the handler shows when leading.

Whilst the horse is normally led from the near or left side, there are circumstances when he must be led from the offside. For example, a handler leading a horse on the road does so on the offside, between the horse and the traffic. Here the reins are held in the left hand under the chin, the whip and buckle end of the reins in the right.

After the leading in hand the riders will be requested to mount, check the girths and adjust stirrups.

Mounting and Dismounting from the Ground

A horse is normally mounted and dismounted on the left or nearside, a tradition dating from the days when swords were worn as part of everyday dress. With the sword on the left side of the body, mounting and dismounting on the nearside prevented the sword from becoming tangled up with the rider's legs.

Mounting

Check the girth first and tighten if necessary. Pull the stirrup irons down the leathers gently; snapping the irons down can not only startle the horse but will weaken the leathers by stretching them and stripping the surface. The stirrups can be checked for approximate length by placing one hand at the top of the leather on the stirrup bar. The stirrup is held up against this stretched arm; the iron should just reach the armpit.

Taking both reins and the whip in the left hand, hold these on top of the horse's neck just in front of the withers. The reins should be sufficiently short to prevent the horse from moving off. The right rein should be a little shorter so that if the horse does move whilst the rider has one foot in the stirrup, the horse's body will swing towards the rider and not away leaving the rider frantically hopping to catch up.

Facing the horse's hindquarters twist the stirrup iron clockwise and place the left foot in the stirrup with the toe pointing down. Turn on the right foot to face the saddle and place the right hand over in front of the cantle.

The cantle should not be pulled on to mount as this will drag it across the horse's spine. Hop on the right leg and push up lifting the leg well over the horse's hindquarters. The seat is lowered gently and quietly into the saddle.

If the horse has behaved and stayed still he will deserve a pat. It is easy to forget that this living animal has just stood and allowed a rider to mount on his back. A reward will encourage him to stand correctly in future.

Checking and altering stirrups when mounted

Once mounted the rider can check the length of stirrup by removing both feet from the irons. The legs should be allowed to hang freely by the horse's sides. The bottom of the stirrup should just reach the ankle bone. In the Stage I it is a common mistake for riders to try and ride with their stirrups too long, believing that this will automatically deepen the seat. At this level it is more likely to weaken it as the rider will try and reach for the irons and become insecure in the saddle. It is wiser to begin with the stirrups a little shorter and to lengthen them later.

When altering the stirrups the feet are put back into the irons and remain there whilst the length is changed. When the length is correct the end of the leather can be placed in the surcingle loop of the saddle if there is one. The position of the foot in the stirrup can also be checked and corrected if necessary. The widest part of the foot should rest on the bar of the stirrup with the iron at right angles to the foot.

Checking and adjusting girths

The girth should always be checked again after a few minutes of riding when it is likely to need adjusting. The girth can be tightened at walk. If the horse is touchy about his girth area or the girth is difficult to alter, the rider should come into the centre of the school and halt to make adjustments. The girth is sufficiently tight when there is just enough room for the flat of the hand to slide between the girth and the horse's side.

Riding without stirrups at walk and trot

When everyone is ready the instructor will ask the ride to walk to the track. The riders must act as a ride with the leader keeping an eye on those behind and everyone maintaining their correct distances - one horse's length between each horse. It is quite in order for a rider to turn across a corner to catch the ride up if this is necessary.

At some point the riders will be asked to halt, quit, cross the stirrups and to ride at walk and trot without stirrups.

When quitting and crossing the stirrups, pull the buckle down well clear of the stirrup bar, twist the leather so that the buckle is underneath and place the stirrup and leather over in front of the saddle. The right stirrup is crossed over first so that if the rider has to dismount the left stirrup, placed on top, can easily be let down for the rider to mount.

The Stage I rider should be capable of riding correctly and comfortably without stirrups for at least 15 to 20 minutes.

The riders will then be asked to take back their stirrups, halt on the centre line, dismount and change horses.

Dismounting

The reins and whip are held in the left hand and the right hand placed on the pommel. Both feet are removed from the stirrups. The rider leans forward and the right leg is lifted well over the horse's hindquarters. The rider lands gently on both feet beside the horse's shoulder.

Riders will now be asked give another rider a leg up or assist from a mounting block.

The Leg Up

This needs practising before the exam with riders of varying heights and weights, using horses of different sizes.

The rider and person assisting should agree first on the timing. Some riders prefer to mount on the count of three whilst others prefer a count of three and then 'up'. It is extremely difficult trying to lift a rider who is not ready!

One important point of which to be aware, is the whip. This should be held in the left hand on the OFFSIDE shoulder of the horse. If held on the nearside it has a tendency to rise up and hit the person assisting in the face. It should also be kept still so that it does not hit the horse.

The rider holds the reins sufficiently short so that the horse does not move forwards (but not so tight that the horse moves backwards). The *right* rein is held a little shorter as in mounting.

The rider's left leg is bent and the assistant, keeping a straight back, holds this leg in both hands. The rider hops whilst counting and pushes up at the agreed moment. At precisely that moment the assistant lifts. The rider should land on the saddle *quietly and gently*, not with a great thump.

Mounting from a block

If the rider is to mount from the ground or a mounting block, the person assisting should stand on the offside of the horse. The assistant holds the reins near the horse's mouth in the right hand, whilst holding the stirrup steady with the left.

This time the rider should hold the whip in the left hand on the *nearside* of the horse. (A whip should never be held in the right hand when mounting from the left, as it will end up being sat on!). Always thank the assistant when finished.

Figure 8: The Leg Up.

Equitation

Each rider will ride two or, at the discretion of the Chief Examiner, three different horses. Part of the session will be performed as a 'ride' and part in 'open order' with riders working individually. Riders will be requested to perform simple school figures at walk, trot (rising and sitting) and canter on both reins; to quit and cross the stirrups and to ride without stirrups at walk and trot. The Examiners are looking for a **firm, secure seat** that does not interfere with the horse.

School Figures

School figures are the manoeuvres performed within the school such as turns, circles and changes of rein. To help the rider practise and prepare for the Stage I, examples are given for school figures and exercises that may be requested during the examination.

Figure 9: Plan of a School.

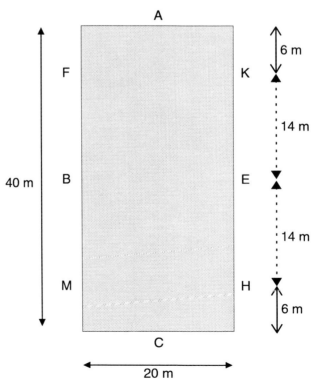

School figures that may be required during the Exam

1.   Twenty metre circles at walk, trot and canter.

2.   Fifteen metre circles at trot.

Figure 10: Circles - showing ten, fifteen and twenty metre circles at B and at A.

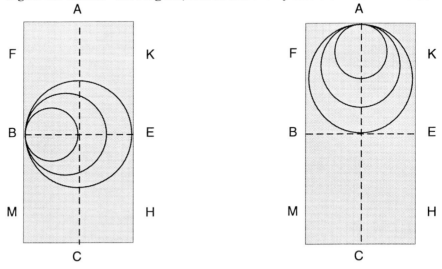

3.   Ten metre circles at trot.

4.   Half twenty metre circles across the school at canter.

Figure 11: A 3 loop serpentine from A on the left rein, each loop going to the wall.

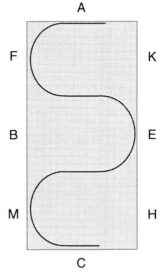

5.   Three loop serpentines in trot.

6. Turns to the left and right.

Figure 12: Changing rein on short diagonal.

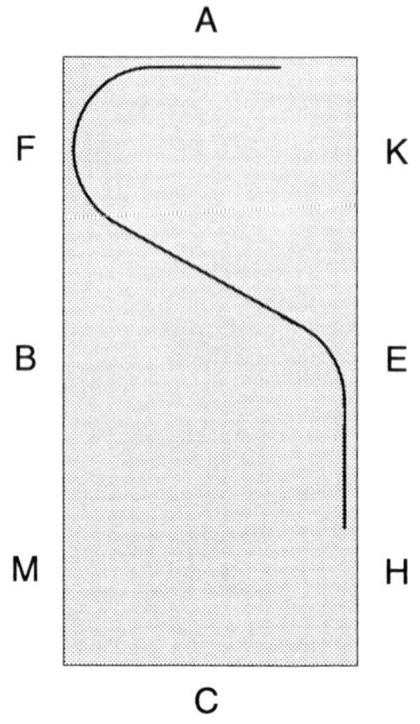

Figure 13: Changing rein from B to E or vice versa.

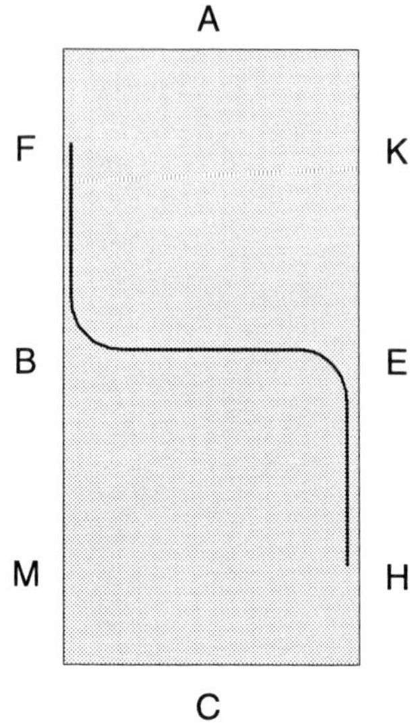

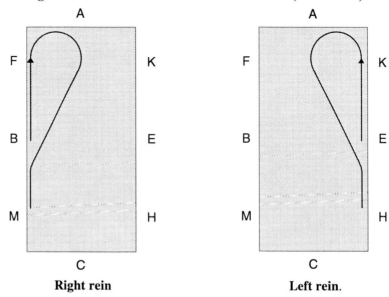

7. Halting and keeping the halt position.

8. Changing the rein across a long diagonal, across a short diagonal, up the centre line, by a half circle incline back to the track, across the school from E to B.

Figure 14: Half circle and incline back to track (Demi-Volte).

Right rein

Left rein.

Figure 15: Change of rein by two half twenty metre circles.

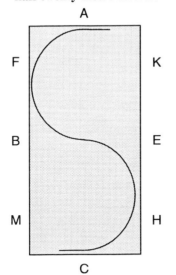

Figure 16: Change of rein by two half ten metre circles.

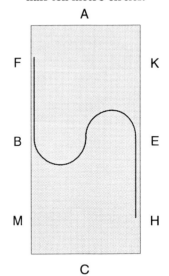

Example of school exercises

These are examples of the type of instructions that will be given to the ride, either by an Examiner or the Instructor in charge.

- Whole ride go forward to walk and track left or right when reaching the track.

- Whole ride prepare to trot and go forward to working trot rising. Trot a twenty metre circle and go large after the exercise.

- In trot, with the whole ride following, leading file turn at A or C markers down the centre line. Change the rein and go large after the exercise.

- Leading files in succession take canter at A or C. At the E or B marker canter a half twenty metre circle before joining the rear of the ride.

- With the rest of the ride in walk, leading file only at A or C, proceed to trot and ride a three loop serpentine. Each loop must reach the wall of the school. Join the rear of the ride.

- With the whole ride in walk, the rear file only halt at A or C and stay in halt for 6 seconds. Proceed to walk and when ready go forward to trot. Pass the whole of the ride in trot and take the leading file. When safe go to walk.

- With the rest of the ride in walk, leading file only go forward to trot and when ready canter. Canter a twenty metre circle away from the ride. Go large and make the transitions from canter to trot and trot to walk before joining the rear of the ride. Each leading file to do this movement in succession.

- With ride in trot the leading file will choose a change of rein, whole ride to follow. Leading file only circle and join the rear of the ride. Each leading file in succession to follow this exercise with a different change of rein.

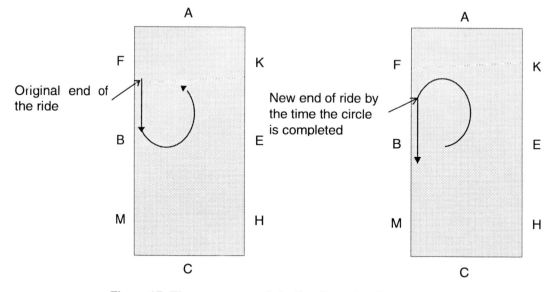

Figure 17: The manoeuvre of circling from the front to the rear of the ride.

- Whole ride in trot leading file only turn inwards and halt on the centre line. As the ride passes go forward to trot and join the ride at the rear.

- Whole ride turn inwards and halt on the centre line.

Examiners may often make up their own exercises even sometimes requesting that certain candidates work as individuals, separate from the whole ride.

School commands

There are certain commands that the rider needs to recognise when in the school or menage.

As a ride   All the commands given apply to all the riders in the school.

Leading file   The rider and horse at the front of the ride.

Rear of ride or *rear file*

         The rider and horse at the back

Open Order   Each rider is equally spaced out around the outer track.

Going large   Riding round the school on the outside track.

Inside or *inner track*

         Riding around the school at about 3 feet inside the outside track.

School Rules

For safety reasons there are also rules for riding in a school with others;

- *Before entering the school knock and wait for permission to enter.*
  Do not open the door just as a horse is passing or try to lead or ride a horse in the school into the path of another.

- *Mount and dismount in a safe place.*
  This is usually in the centre of the school.

- *Correct or safe distance.*
  When riding behind another horse leave a space equivalent to one horse's length.

- *Left to Left.*
  Riders on different reins pass left hand to left hand.

- *Faster paces are given priority.*
  When the ride is in open order and riding at different paces, those riding at a faster pace are given the outside track. The rider in walk should come onto an inner track.

- *Look up around and be aware.*
  Be conscious of the other riders and prepared to avoid a collision.

- *Before leaving the school ask permission of those still inside.*
  If the door is opened and horses leave, this may cause problems for those riding around the school.

After the flatwork the riders will be requested to shorten their stirrups so that they can show work in walk, trot and canter with the shorter length and in the light seat.

The Light Seat

The aim of the light seat is to maintain the balance of both horse and rider whilst the rider, working with shortened stirrups, is poised, keeping the weight off the horse's back. This allows the horse to use his frame and back with complete freedom of movement.

The light seat is often referred to as the forward seat, the forward position or the poised position.

Reasons for the Light Seat

In jumping, the light seat is adopted by the rider when guiding the horse around the track between fences. Because this seat allows the rider increased mobility of the upper body, the rider can then either take a more upright seat, for instance, on the approach to jumps to control the horse, or the fold position when the horse is in flight over the fence.

Shortened stirrups

Riding with shortened stirrups increases the rider's stability and security whilst allowing this flexibility of movement.

The shortened stirrup length closes or decreases the angles at the hip, knee and ankle joints, so that these joints, through their suppleness and spring, can absorb the horse's motion.

Decreasing the angles of the knee and ankle joints also allows the rider's weight to be pressed down into the heel for more security.

With this stability and security the rider can increase and decrease the angle of the hip joint altering the upper body position when required.

The rider shortens the stirrups normally by two holes, but this can vary depending on the flatwork length. **When shortening the stirrups, riders should keep both feet in the stirrup irons and alter the length accordingly**. To take the feet out, or more importantly to take one foot out, whilst altering that length, puts the rider at risk should the horse move suddenly.

The Rider's Position

The rider folds from the hips bringing the seat slightly further back and away from the saddle. The shoulders are brought slightly forward into a position in line with the knee joint and the ball of the foot.

The rider's back remains straight. The rider's head needs to be up looking and well forward. This will maintain the straightness of the rider's back.

The decreased angles of the hip, knee and ankle joints bring the thighs and knees further to the front of the saddle. The heels are pressed down and the toes raised. The toes may be *slightly* turned out to distribute some of the rider's weight down onto the inside of the stirrup. The rider however should not force the toe out or the ankle joint will become fixed and rigid.

The hands are positioned either side of the horse's neck, but not resting on the horse. The rider should keep the 'line' from the elbow, the lower arms, hands and reins to the bit. The shoulders and elbows should remain relaxed and supple.

The rider maintains the light seat through the security of the lower leg. This is the foundation of this position. By keeping the weight down the calf of the leg into the heel, foot and stirrup, and through the suppleness of the hip, knee and ankle joints, the rider maintains the stability and balance.

Exam Format

The ride will be asked to work in open order keeping two to three horses' length between each horse. Then working as a ride the group will go large around the school in walk and rising trot. On the instructor's command the riders will go into the light seat.

Alternatively the riders will be requested to rise to the trot on the short sides of the school taking up the light seat down the long sides. In the light seat the rider should be poised above the saddle, not rising, but absorbing the movement through the ankle joints.

Working as a ride, each leading file in turn will be asked to trot and then to canter to the rear of the ride, taking up the light seat. This will be repeated on the other rein. This exercise will be performed either before or after working over the ground poles.

Polework

After working on the flat in the light seat, the ride will begin to work in open order over ground poles. A single pole will be placed on the three-quarter line either at E or B. The ride will work over this pole in walk and then in rising trot a couple of times.

More poles will be used making sets of three. These will be placed either on a diagonal, or along the long sides of the school.

The whole ride in open order and taking up the light seat will trot over the poles. Where the poles are placed on the diagonal the ride will then change the rein and work over the other set of poles. As an alternative two sets of poles with 36 ft. (approximately 11 metres) between, will be placed along one side of the school.

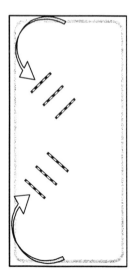 

Working over poles

When working over poles the rider should maintain the light seat, not coming any more forward. The rider may have to give a little with the hands particularly at first if the horse stretches forward over the pole. The aim is to maintain the light seat, the balance and security and, at the same time, have the freedom to allow with the hands. The key to this is the secure lower leg and supple ankle. This gives the remainder of the body stability, which allows the freedom of the hands.

Ride towards the centre of each pole and keep the horse as straight as possible so that he does not swerve and take the poles at an angle. This means judging the turn before the poles, from the short side of the school onto the three-quarter line or across the diagonal. Some horses need more room to turn, others can turn on the proverbial sixpence.

Keep the horse actively going forward. It is easier to maintain a straight line if the horse is active. A horse who is sluggish on the approach can waver and drift; this will make riding over the centre of the poles much more difficult.

Exam Tips

The most important point to remember throughout the riding session is to *try and relax*. This may prove difficult even if you have trained three of four times a week in this particular school and know the horses well. The minute you enter the door you will be aware of a totally alien atmosphere. There will be two or three examiners sitting in the corner, making notes. The horses may be plaited up waiting in anticipation. There will be other nervous candidates as smartly dressed as you. It all adds to the tension.

Now is the time to take deep breaths, breathing in slowly through the nose and releasing the air from the mouth. Once mounted, release the tension by stretching the legs. Do this quietly whilst altering the stirrups. Let your eyes go 'soft' by relaxing the focus. Shrug your shoulders a few times and gently stretch your neck.

Some fortunate candidates excel in these situations whilst others just tense and become rigid. It can help if you have had the experience of going to shows and competing in dressage tests. It is a very similar situation. If however, this is not possible, train for a few weeks before in the clothes you will wear for the exam. Become used to wearing a shirt, tie and jacket.

Many of the exercises requested in the Stage I need careful timing. When working with four or five other riders, these school figures are not as easy as they appear. It is important that you become used to working in a ride, performing exercises that demand good timing and have the ability to work safely and confidently with others. Particular notice should be taken of the figure circling from the front to the back of the ride. This needs good judgment to enable you to arrive back at the track and rejoin the ride as near as possible at the correct distance behind the last horse. Ideally, too, the trot should be kept at the same pace throughout this manoeuvre. Misjudgment will result in rushing after the ride or slowing the horse down to a walk or even a halt. You need to practise within a school or menage and with a different number of riders as this affects the size of the circle.

Be positive in your thinking, concentrate on what you should do rather than what you should not do. Mistakes can happen but this is not necessarily an automatic failure. If for instance you should discreetly check and discover that you are riding on the wrong diagonal at trot, simply change this in the normal manner by sitting for two beats. For canter on the wrong leg come quietly back to trot; wait until a corner and make the transition to canter again. If the horse continues to lead with the wrong leg, it may be that he has a problem and is a little one-sided. No need to panic, the examiners will realize there is a problem. You may afterwards be asked specifically about the canter aids.

When working over the poles in the light seat, remember to keep your head up, looking over beyond the poles. Keep the legs in contact with the horse's sides ready to ask for more forward movement, should he begin to slow down. When working on the long side of the school before the poles, concentrate here on encouraging the horse to be actively going forward.

Practise riding with shorter stirrups and in the light seat well before the Exam so that your position is established, supple and secure. Then begin to practise over poles, so that you are prepared for the change in the horse's pace and elevation.

Occasionally at the end of the riding session the Examiner may question candidates about certain points, for instance the aids, their use and application for specific movements. Candidates may have to describe the aids for transitions, turns and circles. It is worth practising this before the exam with your instructor so that you are able to give comprehensive yet clear and concise explanations.

Actions to avoid

Some situations must be avoided and, without dwelling on these, it is wise to be aware of them. Avoid at all costs riding too close to another horse or of cutting up other riders, that is, riding directly across their path. Whilst in open order, do not make a downward transition on the outside track, unless you are requested to do so. Ride onto an inner track or to the centre of the school and make the transition.

Do not ride constantly on the wrong diagonal or in canter on the wrong leading leg. Always check discreetly. Do not let the horse hare round at a pace that suits him so that it appears you have no control.

Though these problems may seem too obvious, it is amazing how even the best riders make mistakes on an exam day. Remember, the Examiners do understand about nerves and will always try to give each candidate the benefit of the doubt.

C H A P T E R   3
Horse Management

For the Horse Knowledge and Care sections the Stage I student requires an elementary knowledge of horsemastership that, whilst not in any great depth, must be wide and varied. It includes handling the horse in the stable and field and basic practical stable management. The BHS system encourages experience and understanding about the normal daily jobs, the study of theoretical subjects and, most importantly, safety in all aspects of horse care.

The Theory session normally takes place in a separate room. The format will be a mixture of individual questioning and general group discussion on such subjects as psychology, watering and feeding. During the Practical session, candidates are requested to do tasks as individuals such as tacking a horse up and grooming. These are then checked by an examiner. The Practical Oral includes such subjects as points of the horse, colours and markings. This can take the form of individual questioning or a group discussion.

General Principles of Horse Management

Good manners, Communication and Discipline

The principles of good manners, communication and discipline are as important when working with people as they are when handling horses. In the Stage I the examiners will not only be assessing candidates on their knowledge and practical experience but also on how candidates react to each other, and to their fellow workers. They are looking for those who are co-operative, helpful and pleasant. Whilst candidates need to be quietly confident, they must also be willing to listen and learn.

Good manners

Just as people react to the way they are treated so horses reflect the way in which they are handled. Horses are not only totally dependent on their handlers, they are also susceptible to their handler's moods and behaviour.

For instance a bad tempered owner or handler will raise a bad tempered horse that could turn vicious, gain a reputation and be treated accordingly.

The horse, too, must learn good manners and for that he needs to be taught how to act correctly. Simple lessons such as; standing still whilst being groomed, picking up his feet for cleaning without fuss and learning to wait until the rider is properly mounted before walking off. All who work with horses must learn to teach a horse good behaviour.

Communication

Handlers also need to learn to be positive and consistent in their teaching. A horse quickly becomes confused if the handler is changeable or unclear in his demands. Therefore, it is necessary to know what to teach and how to teach it and this comes from knowing the correct ways for working with horses and being confident to do so.

Discipline and reward

Discipline is essential when dealing with horses. If corrected when doing wrong and rewarded when right, the horse will soon learn what actions please and will continue to do these. This will lead to a well mannered animal that will be a pleasure to own. Consequently the horse will have a better life.

Horses need disciplining by firm and confident yet kind and sympathetic handling. They are wild animals that, despite having been domesticated and trained for millennia, still possess their basic instincts. Not only can horses be frightened or angry they can also be mischievous and downright wicked! Many dangerous traits are taught by bad handling, incorrect training or lack of discipline. The horse should never be allowed to persist with bad behaviour or he will quickly learn to act in this manner permanently and it will become a habit.

If the horse misbehaves, he should be reprimanded in a firm, slightly raised voice. This usually stops the misconduct. A firm word or sentence with inflection should be enough.

Constant shouting will make the horse irritable and the handler appear bad-tempered or silly. Eventually the reprimand will be ineffective. The horse will become familiar to the raised voice and ignore it.

If a firm vocal correction is not enough the horse may need contact with a sharp tap of the hand on the neck, hindquarters or, if he bites, on the muzzle. This must be given immediately so that the horse understands why he is being corrected.

Once the horse has learnt his lesson and acts in the right way, he should be rewarded by a pat, a kind voice or occasionally a titbit. He will then associate the good behaviour with a pleasant treat. The ideal is to discipline the horse by correction and reward, **correcting bad behaviour, rewarding good.**

All horses are born relatively innocent, for the most part it is the way in which they are handled which encourages good or bad habits and manners. They are friendly, gentle creatures especially towards human beings and with correct care they gain confidence and trust, develop good habits and become very loving.

Handling The Horse

As previously mentioned, the BHS are concerned principally with safety but into this sphere and connected with it, is the manner and method of handling, working with and treating horses.

The horse is a living animal possessing instincts and characteristics that determine the way he reacts. Horses do not logically work things out; they do not think as humans do. In many ways their senses are far more developed and finely tuned, a result of being a victim rather than a predator.

The horse still retains most of its instinctive defensive mechanisms. These are often used to an advantage in handling. Even so, when dealing with horses, it must be remembered that this animal does frequently react in an unpredictable manner causing injury and even death. Awareness is essential at all times, even with familiar and trusted horses or ponies.

Careful, considerate and correct handling is so important for the development of a horse's character. For instance, if a horse's girth is done up quickly pinching his skin or causing pain, he cannot turn round and say 'Excuse me that hurt.' He can only complain by showing his teeth or lifting a leg. His method of communication is limited to facial expression and posture. If the painful action is constantly repeated, the horse becomes desperate and uses his strength to warn and hopefully prevent it.

Approaching a horse in a stable

Relatively speaking a stabled horse is a trapped horse and though most are not affected by this environmental state, it is possible that a nervous, vicious or highly strung animal can react to this situation. Even the most even-tempered horse may resent his privacy being disturbed, especially when eating.

Approach the horse in his box by walking quietly from the front in plain sight. Shouting, running and bouncing up suddenly at the door will only alarm him. Speak softly, perhaps calling the horse's name.

In the case of a strange horse beware of him lunging over the door. Thankfully not many do this but, with an unfamiliar animal, it is better to be safe than sorry.

Sticking a hand or arm over the box to stroke or pat the horse may surprise him. He may, in reaction, lunge at the door or run to the back of the box.

Look to see where the horse is in the box. Keep talking; this not only puts the horse at ease but informs him of your whereabouts. Most horses will turn and come to the doorway, which is the desired result.

If the horse has his hindquarters facing the door do not enter the box, this action may startle him and he may kick. Encourage the horse's head around so that he is able to see you and be aware of your presence.

When the horse is facing the door, undo the bolt and kick bolt quietly. Open the door just wide enough to enter. Some horses if they see an open door do try and rush through it. Move the horse back quietly if necessary, then close the door and fasten the top bolt. If the stable has a chain or pole, fasten this first before opening the door fully.

Once inside the box approach the horse by walking towards his shoulder and neck. Gain control as soon as possible by putting on his headcollar. Continue to talk to him quietly; this will assure him that you are there as a friend and will put him at ease.

How to work around a horse

When working with horses on a daily basis it is easy to become inattentive, particularly if the horse in question is well-mannered. Even the quietest horse may react in an unusual, maybe violent way, at some time and for some reason.

It is safer to work in the box whilst the horse is out, either being exercised, at pasture or tied up outside. This may not always be possible and there are occasions when the horse must stay in the box.

Always restrain the horse with a headcollar and lead rope whilst working with or around him in the stable.

Never try and work in a confined space between the horse and the stable wall. Manoeuvre him with a gentle push on the hindquarters whilst at the same time telling him to move.

Most importantly do not become pinned into a corner. The situation where a horse is threatening and there is no escape is very dangerous and nerve wracking.

Work slowly and quietly around the horse. Avoid any loud noises or sudden movements.

Be aware all the time of the body language of the horse. Ears flat back does not always mean that he will bite or kick but it is a warning and it does certainly show that the horse is not happy.

General Principles of Yard Work

Physical Fitness

Stable work is strenuous, mucking out, grooming, carrying heavy buckets, bales or feed bags. All these jobs need physical fitness, particularly in the area of the back. In the examination one of the group will be asked to describe the method of lifting a straw bale or feed bag. The examiner may even request that candidates do this then and there. A bale of straw, hay or a feed bag will be made available.

Method

Keeping the back straight, bend the knees and go down to the bale. Then lift it up by straightening the legs; this takes quite a bit of thigh strength. Gently swing the bag or bale over the shoulder and carry on the back.

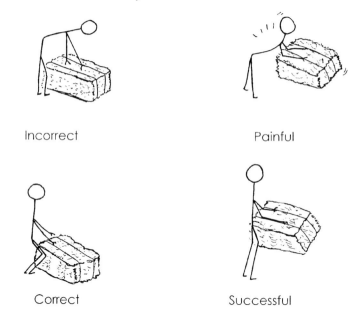

Incorrect

Painful

Correct

Successful

It is safer and easier to carry a heavy weight by wheelbarrow or with the assistance of another person.

When carrying water by bucket always have two buckets, one in each hand for balance. One bucket carried on its own will cause an overload on one side and twist the body. Any damage to muscles or bones will not only affect your work but also your riding.

Back ache, slipped discs, pulled or strained muscles are a constant hazard in stable work. It may seem unimportant to lift heavy weights correctly but it can save days, weeks or months of damage and pain to the back.

Clothing

Wearing the right clothes for the job is essential for safety. Strong footwear for stable work; boots or muckers that can withstand wet, muddy conditions and will protect the feet and toes from crushing or blows. Depending on the weather, shirts, jumpers or jackets properly fastened and trousers or jodhpurs that will not interfere with work or become entangled with stable tools and equipment. Long hair should be tied back away from the face. Scarves or caps are suitable as long as they are not likely to flap around or fly off at an inconvenient moment. Ideally jewellery should not be worn at all; even rings can catch up in tack or clothing causing injuries. Most people would wish to retain their wedding ring and providing this fits well and is not loose there is a minimum risk of injury. Large earrings should never be worn. These can easily become entangled and ripped off, causing damage to the ear and face.

Hats and gloves should be worn at specific times; when dealing with vicious, nervous and young horses or when leading. Though gloves should not be worn when grooming; the handler needs to be able to feel for any injuries, heat or swellings on the horse.

Although it is almost impossible to keep squeaky clean whilst doing stable work, smartness in an owner/rider or handler creates a good impression and it generally follows that a smart person means a smart and well-cared for horse.

Stable Equipment

It is essential that all stable tools are cared for, cleaned and stored correctly. Stable equipment includes shaving forks, pitch forks, brooms, skips, wheel barrows, water buckets, feed buckets, haynets, mucking out sacks, shovels or spades, mangers and feed trolleys.

Working around horses is dangerous enough without the added problem of misuse and neglect of stable equipment. Keeping equipment clean and in good order is essential. It will last longer, be easier to use and save time. Cleanliness and hygiene will also minimize the risk of infection or disease being transmitted around the yard.

Everything should be tidied away after use. This is not merely for the tidiness of the yard or because equipment is expensive, but also to avoid injury to both workers and horses. Many injuries caused by carelessness result in stitches, broken bones or worse. A rusty or dirty pitchfork, for instance, left lying around may result in a puncture wound which can cause tetanus (lock jaw).

Care must be taken with regard to electrical equipment such as clippers or grooming machines. These must always be used by a competent person, in a safe manner, cleaned and stored properly after use.

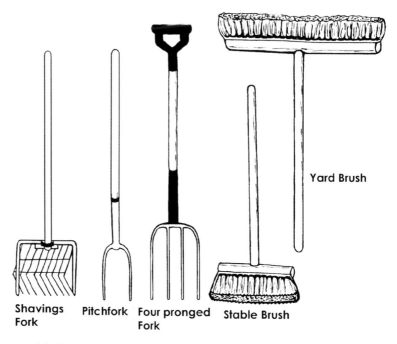

Shavings Fork   Pitchfork   Four pronged Fork   Stable Brush   Yard Brush

It is essential that everyone involved in horse care is taught to use all stable equipment carefully and correctly.

Exam Tips

During the practical session the examiners will not only be assessing the tasks performed by the candidates, but will also observe each individual's behaviour around the horses.

They will be watching how you approach a strange animal, how you enter a box, pick up a horse's foot, treat the horse whilst tacking up or grooming.

Always make sure that the horse is properly secured before handling him. Talk to him. It is all too easy to focus all the attention on the examiner or the job in hand and totally ignore the horse. Providing you do not interrupt the examiner or appear inattentive it is a good idea, especially when holding the horse, to give him an occasional pat or talk to him.

There may be a skip, a fork and a shovel placed outside each exam box. These are there for the purpose of removing any droppings that the horse may pass during the session. If there is time at the end of a discussion or question period, the droppings may be removed. If you do wish to do this, make sure that the horse is adequately restrained first.

C H A P T E R   4
Psychology

Those herds of horses as portrayed in Westerns roaming the plains and occasionally stampeding off into the distance, may seem far removed from the docile animal living its life in a box, whose day consists of eating, working and occasionally grazing in the paddock. Despite how domesticated the horse may now seem, it is still an animal whose behaviour and actions are based on instincts inherited from untamed ancestors.

When working with horses it is necessary to understand their psychology, to know the reactions caused by certain stimuli, to be aware of body language and warning sounds. The most important reason is safety, to avoid danger or injury. This is also essential for the mental and physical health of the horse, to know when the horse is unhappy or ill and to discover the reason for this.

Natural Lifestyle

There are very few herds of wild horses or ponies living free these days and those that do survive, are mostly in remote regions of the world. In their natural habitat horses roam the grasslands, pastures, hills and moorlands in search of food and water. They live in herds for safety and are protected by the dominant stallion who warns the herd of approaching danger.

In the wild a horse's reflexes need to be sharp and quick to survive. A young foal must have the ability to move soon after birth, staying with the herd if it stampedes from danger. Only when cornered will a horse fight and defend itself by kicking, rearing or biting. Sharp hearing, good peripheral vision and speed are necessary for survival in the wild.

Many of the characteristics and instincts derived from the wild are still prevalent in the domesticated animal today. We need to know what these are if we are to understand why the horse reacts the way he does.

Characteristics

The horse has certain qualities or traits that are part of its nature. It behaves and lives in a specific way which makes it different from many other animals.

Herd animal

The horse needs the company of its own kind or in some cases the presence of another animal.

The herd lifestyle is a protective device derived from prehistoric times when horses were hunted and killed by other animals. There is safety in numbers; a chance of escaping attack by predators. The odds are greater for survival in a crowd.

At times horses seem to be constantly fighting, bickering, squealing and kicking each other but they are gregarious and become fretful if left alone. This is often apparent in the field when the horse will show stress by running along a fence, whinnying or even jumping the obstacle to be near the others. Some horses are quite content to be with other animals such as sheep or cows, but few are happy on their own.

This herd characteristic can also cause problems for novice riders and those on young and poorly trained horses. The horse may be reluctant, or the rider not competent enough, to make the horse leave the group or stable yard. This is commonly called 'napping'.

On the other hand this characteristic can be used to a rider's advantage; an older, more experienced horse may lead a younger, reluctant novice over a jump.

Nomadic

In the natural state the herd wanders in search of food, grazing constantly on vegetation and moving from pasture to pasture. Most horses are now enclosed within fields but even here the nomadic instinct is still apparent. The horses will move forwards slowly eating the grass and at times move off to another patch. Interestingly though, horses have a homing instinct that is strong in the modern, domesticated animal. Often a horse which is bolting with or without its rider will make for home or, if the rider is lost, the horse will find its way back to the stable. They all tend to increase their pace towards the direction of home.

Grazing

The horse is a vegetarian eating grass, herbs, shrubs and leaves. He eats small amounts constantly, grazing for 16-20 hours per day and resting only for short periods. This is called 'trickle feeding'. The domesticated horse, therefore, has a totally alien lifestyle being fed unnatural foods at specified times.

Defensive Mechanisms

Most of their reactions reflect the fact that horses are the victims of predators. Their defence is based on either **flight or fight**. The first reaction is to flee, however if cornered, a horse will fight either by biting, kicking, bucking, barging or rearing ~ a foreleg can kick just as well as a hind.

Curiosity

The horse has a tremendous amount of curiosity; often wandering over to investigate something unusual. This trait can be used to catch an awkward horse in the field. My horse, if he is playing hard to get, cannot bear me standing a little way from him fiddling with something, especially if I turn my back to him. Then he will generally walk right up to me and put his head over my shoulder.

Dominant Animal

The horse is certainly not a democrat. But then, in the wild, deciding to escape from a pack of wolves does not allow much time for discussion! Much more practical to have one dominant male, a stallion, and follow his lead. He cares for the herd sensing danger and giving warning, searching out food and drink. In many ways the human has taken over this role for the domesticated animal.

In the domestic herd there is one dominant male or female and a pecking order for the rest. The pecking order of seniority depends on assertiveness and strength.

Imitators

Horses tend to imitate others and it is possible that they pick up bad habits this way, such as weaving or crib-biting.

Good memory

A horse has an excellent memory particularly for pain. If he has been badly treated at some point in his life then, in a similar situation, he will tend to be awkward in future. It is therefore important that the horse is handled correctly from an early age.

As an aid to memory and recall, keywords have been included in the text to make learning easier.

Key Words to Characteristics

- ❖ Herd
- ❖ Nomadic
- ❖ Flight or fight
- ❖ Grazers
- ❖ Curiosity
- ❖ Pecking order
- ❖ Imitators
- ❖ Memory

Instincts

Horses have very strong instinctive behaviour. Instincts are present in an animal from birth; they are emotional responses to situations or influences. In a horse these emotions are shown by physical indications such as body language and noises.

Fear

A horse that is frightened in the open will generally bolt. He may spin round quickly then flee. Sometimes in a field the horse will run from the object of fear but then turn to face the potential enemy. If the threat is no longer apparent, the horse may tentatively approach the object, head lowered, sniffing or blowing but still tensed and ready to run.

On a ride a sudden movement or noise may make the horse jump quickly to the side away from the threat. If the danger persists he may turn quickly and bolt.

In a stable he will retreat to the farthest point away from the object of fear. His head will be held high facing towards the danger, eyes wide and staring, nostrils dilated and blowing, ears pricked and mobile to pick up sound. The body will be side on to the threat, held taut, rise and grow in height, muscles tight and tense.

Nervousness

The head will be held high with eyes wide and alert, nostrils flared, blowing or snorting, ears mobile, pricked and listening. The body will rise and tense, preparing for flight. The horse may quiver, shake or start to sweat. His rate of breathing may increase. He may pass droppings frequently.

Anger

An angry horse holds his head slightly lowered, ears back, laid flat on the neck, eyes mean looking and narrowed, lips curled, teeth bared. He will show an aggressive posture and hindquarters may swing round. He may try to bite or kick.

Pain

The horse will run from external pain, bolting. When cornered his head may be raised and eyes narrowed, he will rear, kick or bite. The important aspect of pain is that the horse remembers it for a long time.

If the rider is causing the pain the horse will not only bolt but try and throw the rider off either by rearing or bucking. Bucking, in some cases, is a defence against a threat from the rear. This would originally have been an attack by wolves or other predators jumping on the horse's back. Bucking can also be a sign of enjoyment and excitement.

Contentment

The horse will appear relaxed and calm, his body soft, his coat shining. His ears will be mobile moving gently to sound.

Unhappiness

He will appear introspective, dull, lifeless, lethargic, angry or antagonistic. His head will be held down, eyes dull, ears floppy, body drooping and tired looking, the coat rough. Sometimes horses develop bad habits such as aggressive behaviour or stable vices.

Interest

The neck will be arched, nostrils sniffing, ears mobile, body alert but relaxed. The eyes are bright and the muzzle pointed forward, searching.

Excitement

Here the head is held high, nostrils flared and sniffing, breathing possibly quickened, ears pricked and eyes bright. The horse will be prancing around possibly bucking; body alert, tail held erect. He may sweat.

Naughty

The ears will be held back but not flat. The eyes will look shifty and narrowed, watching and mean. The nostrils will contract and tighten. The horse may try to cow kick, or lift a back leg.

Playful

The horse may paw the ground with a front foot. He will move quickly, running with short steps then turning and bucking. Play is seen mostly in foals but all horses play sometimes.

Attentive

The ears are pricked and mobile, eyes bright and alert. The body is relaxed but held ready.

Fighting for Dominance

The head may either be held down with neck outstretched or held up with neck arched. The teeth may be bared, lips curled; ears laid flat back; the eyes small and mean. The body is stretched out and menacing. Sometimes the horse will paw the ground with a foreleg, or swing round the hindquarters ready for kicking.

Verbal Sounds

The verbal sounds a horse makes can be a clear indication of emotion or of an impending action.

Neigh	Normally a call to other horses or a method of attracting attention. Often heard when a mare is separated from her foal.
Whinny	A high pitched sound associated with excitement and tension.
Nicker	A non-aggressive call to a nearby horse, recognition of a person or anticipation of pleasure (usually food).
Snort	Indicates excitement, playfulness or annoyance. It can also be used as one of the first signs of fear or for expelling dust from the nostrils.
Scream	Expresses intense anger, aggression, fear and pain.
Blow	Used when scenting territory or smelling horse dung
Bellow	A sound of authority, often used by stallions when challenged.
Squeal	Comes from a mare in season or excited foals at play. A mare may use it to scold a foal
Sigh	Can mean contentment or boredom.

When working or training with horses for a length of time, grooms, riders and handlers become aware of the sounds that horses make, often relating to it as a language. For instance hearing a squeal from within a field, the handler will be almost certain there is a fight going on.

One of the most rewarding sounds is to hear my horse nicker to me first thing in the morning. I always imagine he is saying 'Hello Mum', though in reality he is probably anticipating his breakfast!

Exam Tips

The Stage I examination covers a great deal of horse psychology with examiners asking about equine behaviour, body language, characteristics and instincts. You may be asked to explain the horse's natural lifestyle and the differences apparent in the domesticated animal. You may have to describe the horse's reaction in certain situations; when he is frightened in the stable or on a ride, how a new horse to the yard would show that he is nervous. Practise explaining how a horse shows anger, pain or aggression.

The examiners may ask you to explain why some horses and ponies become difficult to catch, how an awkward horse might be caught and how his behaviour could be improved in future. You will need to know how a horse reacts when turned out in a field with other strange horses, how the herd sorts out the pecking order and how you could recognize the 'boss'. You may have to describe how horses act in a field normally and what you would expect from a pony being turned out to grass for the first time in weeks. The chapter on Grassland Management gives more information on the behaviour of horses and ponies in the field.

Each group of candidates may be requested to list some of the instincts of the horse and to explain what emotions can be detected from the position of the horse's ears or tail. You will need to observe the horse in all situations in the stable and in the field. Watch the horse's body language and how he reacts to other horses within the yard.

Working with horses develops an awareness of their body language and reactions, so that you almost instinctively know how they will act in certain situations. However being able to describe this to an examiner who throws a situation at you can be very difficult. You will need to practise imagining situations and describing how the horse will react and the signals given by his body language.

C H A P T E R   5
Physiology

This section deals with the physical aspect of the horse, the main external areas, points, colours and markings. It is in itself a fascinating subject but it also develops understanding of how the horse's system functions.

External Areas

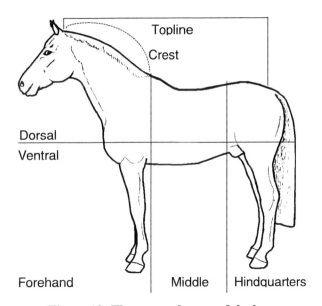

Figure 18: The external areas of the horse.

Forehand	From head to withers including the forelegs.
Middle	The barrel of the horse including the back and belly.
Hindquarters	From the loins including hind legs and tail.
Topline	The top area from the poll to the dock including the crest.
Crest	Top portion of the neck from the poll to the withers.
Dorsal section	The upper half of the body from just above the legs.
Ventral section	The lower half of the horse.

Points   When referred to with regard to colouring are; the tips of the ears, mane, tail and the legs from the hoof to just above the knees and hocks. e.g. a bay is brown with black points.

(These should not be confused with Points of the Horse.)

Figure 19: Pony with Black Points.

Points   When referring to external areas are the names given to specific locations on the horse's body. These are often used to judge the quality or standard of a horse.

Points of a Horse

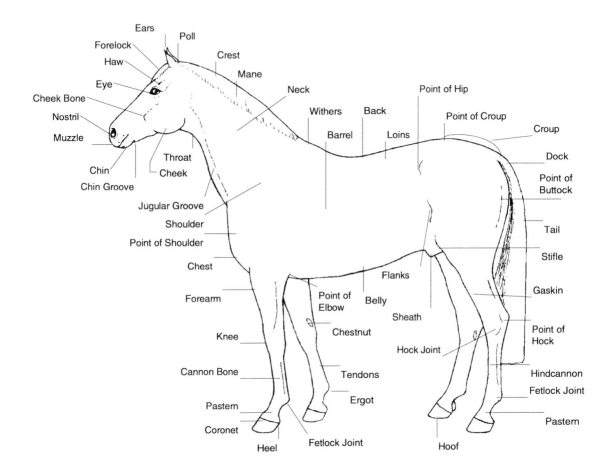

The points of the horse are not only a convenient method of distinguishing external areas, they are also necessary for the further study of the internal anatomy.

Classification

Difference between a horse and a pony

A horse or pony is basically determined by size, though build and movement can also be taken into consideration. Generally speaking any animal 14.2 hands and under is classed as a pony, above 14.2 hands may be described as a horse.

A horse or pony is measured with a measuring stick. The animal must be stood on level ground and the measurement is then taken to the highest point of the wither. The size is calculated in hands, one hand equals 4 inches. Shoes can account for approximately a quarter of an inch.

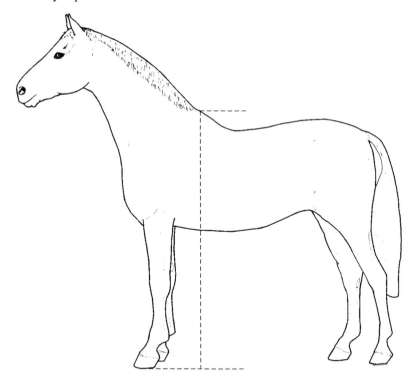

Figure 20: Measuring the height of a horse.

Accurate measurement of height is important when selling or buying a horse, for competitions or showing classes which are restricted to height and for a guide when buying tack or clothing.

Gender

A female horse or pony is a **filly** up to the age of four when she becomes a **mare.**

A **colt** is a male horse or pony under the age of four.

A **gelding** is a castrated male horse or pony. Castration is usually performed when the horse or pony is around a year old. Some heavy breeds are often left until three or four.

If the horse remains **'entire'**, that is, not castrated, the colt becomes a **stallion.** Most male horses if not used for breeding are gelded.

Age

Age, unless specifically known, is determined mainly by the teeth. Other signs of age are the haw, the hollow above the eye which tends to deepen with age, and the general angularity of the shape of the horse or pony. The bony areas appear more prominent with age.

Breeds

Many horses and ponies are descended from pure strains or breeds. For an animal to be classed as a breed its ancestry must be pure, e.g. Welsh Mountain, New Forest, Arab. Most pure bred horses and ponies are registered and have papers as proof of their ancestry. Most breeds have distinguishing features in height, colour, markings and temperament.

Horses or ponies of mixed blood are generally classed in 'types'. Their ancestry may not be known or proved but they exhibit the characteristics of a breed or type; for example, a middleweight hunter, a New Forest type.

Many horses are referred to as hot, warm or cold-blooded, although literally speaking all are warm-blooded mammals. Hot-bloods are usually breeds originating in the East such as Arabs or Barbs. Cold-bloodeds include heavy work horses such as Clydesdales. Warm-bloods are a mixture of the two and include Danish and Dutch Warm-bloods.

Hot-blooded horses are usually more highly strung and may be temperamental whereas cold-blooded horses are generally quieter and steadier.

Native Breeds

There are nine Mountain and Moorland breeds which originate naturally within the United Kingdom and Eire. All nine breeds however are extremely hardy having survived centuries of an environment that can be severe, especially in winter.

The nine native breeds indigenous to the British Isles are:

* Shetland

* Highland

* Fell

* Dale

* Welsh

* New Forest

* Exmoor

* Dartmoor

* Connemara

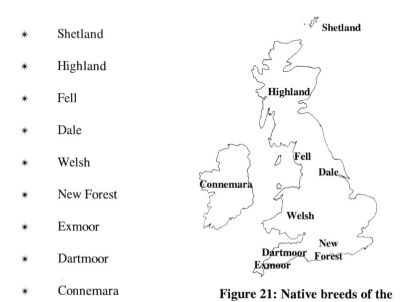

Figure 21: Native breeds of the British Isles.

Other British breeds include the Thoroughbred, (descended from three Arab stallions brought to Britain during the 17th/18th centuries), the Anglo-Arab and the British Warm-blood which is a relatively new strain. There is also the Shire, Clydesdale, Suffolk Punch, Cleveland Bay, Irish Draught and the Hackney.

Colours

The colour of a horse is created by skin pigment, hair colour and markings on the body. Most breeds have distinguishing colours derived from their environment or selective breeding. In some cases in the Show world a horse of a particular breed must have the 'correct' colour. Colours and markings are also an important part of the identification process, when it is imperative that they are described accurately. These are used on the horse's passport or identity card.

Colour is an important consideration when buying a horse as it often indicates temperament and possible future care needed. A good strong colour often signifies hardiness. White markings can mean that the skin in those areas is sensitive, for instance horses with white markings around the heels may be more prone to mud fever. Chestnut mares are often expected to have a fiery or awkward nature. Pure greys can be difficult to keep clean and are more prone to skin cancer in old age.

Black   True black is very rare. An apparent black horse may be very dark brown or bay. To check this look at the flank or under the belly for any slight variation in shading.

Brown   This colour must cover most of the body and there should be no black points.

Bay   Brown with black points - mane, tips of ears, tail and legs are black. Bays can vary from a bright bay, light in colour to a dark, mahogany bay.

Chestnut   A reddish colour that can vary from a bright 'tomato soup' shade to a dark 'liver' chestnut. A chestnut can also have a **flaxen** mane and tail - the mane and tail are light coloured, either silver or cream.

Grey   Often mistakenly called white, **pure greys** usually have a mixture of white hairs on a dark skin. A close look by ruffling the hair will show the colour of the skin underneath.

                 A **dappled grey** has circles of darker hair.

                 The unfortunately named **flea-bitten grey** has little tufts of dark hair, usually brown, all over the body.

                 An **iron grey** is very dark, sometimes almost black in appearance.

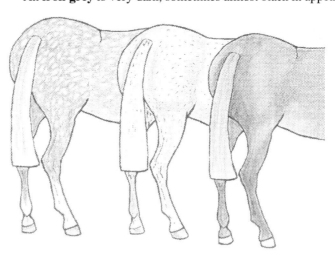

Figure 22: Dapple, Flea-bitten & Iron grey.

Albino   This is rare and occurs where the skin has no pigmentation. The appearance is pinkish-white all over with pink eyes and muzzle. This colouring produces the only true 'white' horses or ponies.

Palomino   This is a golden colour varying from very light to a rich, dark shade with white mane and tail.

Cream   A pale, cream colour on a pink skin. The mane and tail are often silver. Sometimes creams have blue or 'wall' eyes.

Piebald   A horse with two colours, black and white in irregular patches.

Skewbald   Similar to the piebald except the patches are brown and white.

Odd-colour Consists of more than two colours, usually black, brown and white.

Spotted   Horses classed as spotted have a colour that consists of patterns of spots usually on roan or white. The most famous spotted horse of all, the **Appaloosa,** is a breed that originated in North America, though not all spotted horses are appaloosas.

There are five basic patterns:

Leopard-spotted has spots of any colour on a light coat.

Blanket-spotted has spots on the back and hind-quarters only.

'Snowflake' and **'Frosted'** have white spots on a dark coat.

Marble is a mottled colour.

Figure 23: Leopard, Blanket, Snowflake, Frosted & Marble Spotted.

Roan   There are three main types of roan.

A **blue roan** has a mixture of black-brown and white hair that produces a bluish appearance, a black mane, tail and legs.

A **strawberry roan** is a mixture of chestnut and white hair.

A **bay roan** is brown hair with white.

Dun   A **dark or mouse dun** is, as the name suggests, the colour of a mouse.

A **silver dun** appears silvery.

A **yellow dun** is a light lemon colour.

A **golden dun** is a rich gold.

Duns do vary from very light to dark but most have **black points**, a **list** or **dorsal stripe** and **zebra markings** on the legs. Native and ancient breeds usually have a dun colour, such as the Highland.

Eye Colouring

Most horse's eyes are brown but occasionally there will be different colours such as yellow or blue. These are usually associated with colouring or face markings.

Wall Eye is where one or both eyes are either completely blue or bluish.

Markings

All horses have markings whether caused by a different colour, for instance on the legs and face, or by the hair lying in a different direction from the rest of the coat. These are important as they identify the horse by being individual distinguishing marks and may sometimes indicate the nature of a horse or give clues to any weaknesses that may occur. They can also be evidence of previous treatment, for instance white markings on the saddle area or on the legs can indicate past injuries.

White Marks

Natural white markings usually occur on the head or limbs. A horse that has no white markings at all is called whole-coloured.

Head Markings

Feint

A small touch of white usually in the middle of the forehead.

Star

A larger white mark on the forehead.

Stripe

A narrow strip of white down the face usually starting from the forehead and finishing around the nostrils.

Blaze

A broad strip extending usually from the forehead to the nostrils.

White face

A white marking that covers most of the face, forehead, nostrils and mouth.

Snip

A small white marking between the nostrils.

White muzzle

White on the mouth and around nostrils.

White lip

White around the mouth, either upper or lower lip or both.

Leg markings

Areas of white hair on the legs, from the fetlock down, are named after the portions covered;

*   A white **coronet, heel, pastern** and **fetlock.**

Areas of white above the fetlock are described as follows:

*   A **sock** is a white marking from hoof to just above the fetlock.

*   A **stocking** is white from the hoof to below the hock or knee.

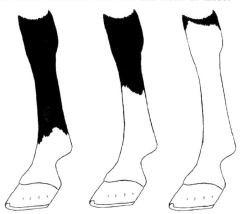

*   A **white leg** is white beyond the knee or hock.

Ermine marks

These occur in areas of white hair and appear as black spots on the white rather like the pattern of an ermine fur. Usually evident on the legs around the coronet or pastern. Can be very small, not always clearly visible.

Further Markings

As well as the normal markings on legs and head, there are other variations of colour or lie of coat which every horse and pony exhibits. Some are so small or hidden that a close inspection is required to find them.

Zebra markings

As the name suggests these are markings arranged in a pattern of black zebra stripes. They occur usually on the back of both fore and hind legs and are a characteristic of some breeds such as the Highland. On light coloured horses and ponies these markings are quite distinctive whereas on a naturally darker animal the stripes are more difficult to see.

List or dorsal line

This is a black stripe stretching from the base of the mane to the top of the tail all along the back bone. Again this is a characteristic of certain breeds, as in the Highland and Norwegian Fjord.

Mixed or bordered

On coloured horses, piebald, skewbald or odd-coloured the patches of darker colour can sometimes have a border of a different colour.

Flecked and ticked markings

On darker coloured animals flecked markings are apparent as white patches of hair, ticked markings show up as small, thin stripes. These can either be all over the animal or cover barrel, belly and flank only.

Liver and strawberry mark

These show up as dark patches on a lighter coat. Liver marks usually occur on chestnuts and strawberry marks on greys.

Toad Eye

This appears as a lighter shading surrounding the eyes.

Mealy Muzzle

Where the shading of the muzzle is lighter or cream in colour. The mealy muzzle and toad eye are characteristics of certain breeds such as the Exmoor pony.

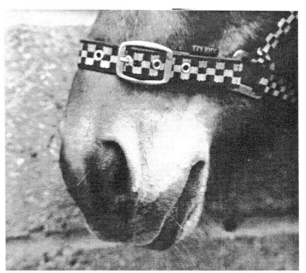

Figure 24: A mealy muzzle.

Flesh marks

These are normally found on light coloured horses or those with a white face or light coloured muzzle. Around the muzzle the skin is pink where the pigment is absent. Darker areas of skin show up in patches.

Hair Markings

Whorl

The hair lies in a different direction to the coat usually occurring on the forehead, neck, chest and flanks. Whorls can vary in size and are usually arranged in circles or lines. They are individual to each horse and are an excellent means of identification.

Injury marks

These are apparent particularly on darker coloured horses where the hair has grown white over an old injury. They are particularly evident around the saddle and girth areas or on the legs around the site of wounds or damage.

Prophet, miller's or devil's thumbprint

Small thumb sized indentations in the muscles, usually on the neck and shoulder areas.

Horn

Chestnuts

The horny growths, one on the inside of all four legs, have characteristics which are unique to each horse. They are reputed to be as individual as fingerprints and are used as a form of identification. On the foreleg chestnuts are just above the knee and on the hind legs just below the hock.

Hoof colours

Again markings on the hooves are supposed to be unique to each horse and many owners take photographs of their horse's hooves for identification. Hooves are usually dark, markings here include white stripes or patches, normally associated with white leg markings. Occasionally horses have a white hoof.

Artificial Marks

Many owners wish to identify their animals more positively and have various markings put on parts of the body.

Freeze marking

A method of identification marking. A listed number is applied by extreme cold turning the hair white. In the case of greys the marking turns pink. This remains on the horse as a permanent feature for life. A national register is kept of all freeze-marked horses and this acts as a deterrent to thieves.

Figure 25: Freeze Mark.

Note: Injury marks on withers caused by an ill fitting saddle in the past.

A Brand

This is a scar on the skin made by a hot iron. Many countries practise this method and it is also used specifically for various breeds of horse.

Lip and Ear Tattoo

As the name implies numbers are tattooed into the skin usually on the ear or under the top lip.

Hoof brand

The farrier brands letters or numbers, sometimes a postcode, onto the hoof wall. This has the disadvantage of eventually growing out.

Tail trims

A section of the horse's tail is cut. Used particularly to identify native wild breeds. Again, this type of identification will eventually grow out.

Exam Tips

For the session on anatomy each candidate will be required to name several points of the horse usually showing their relative position. As this is a group session you could be asked to start from anywhere on the horse. For instance, if you are fourth or fifth in the group you may be required to name the points on the hindquarters or legs. When studying for the exam, try repeating the points starting from different areas of the horse's body.

During this session also candidates will be asked to examine a horse briefly and describe its colour and markings. A general discussion will follow about further colours, natural or artificial markings and distinguishing features. Practise looking at horses closely and identifying colours and markings.

C H A P T E R 6
Health

For all horse owners, or those who have horses in their charge, it is essential to be able to recognize when a horse is suffering from ill health. Often the signs are not glaringly evident and may simply be a slight change in behaviour. Recognition is vital if diagnosis and treatment are to be effective.

The first duty in the daily routine is to check that the horse is in good health. For a stabled horse a quick observation will usually be sufficient to notice if anything is radically wrong. In the case of field kept animals a check can be made either from the gate or from within the field if the horses are out of sight.

Closer inspections must be done later in the day. Horses and ponies in whatever environment must be thoroughly checked at least once a day. This is particularly essential for those living out at grass permanently.

Good Health

The basic sign that the horse is in good health is that he is **behaving normally**, acting in his usual manner. If he has his head out over the door first thing in the morning, nickering and holding his head high, this is a good sign that he is well.

He may, on the other hand, be the sort of horse who normally stands in the box looking dozy and quiet, perhaps with one hind leg resting. In this case if he became restless in the box looking agitated then it would be obvious that something was wrong.

It is therefore, important to **'know your horse'**, be aware of his normal mannerisms and be alert for anything that is unusual in his behaviour. 'Know your horse' is an excellent cliché to remember. (The horse world is full of clichés which, being generally founded on centuries of experience and knowledge, are a good guideline to Horse Care.)

Initial Signs

In the Stable

- The horse is **bright** and **alert** with **ears pricked, moving to sound**.

- He is **interested** in his surroundings. Even if he is standing at the back of his box he should look round and come over to the door should his handler call.

- His **coat** is **dry** and **glossy, lying smoothly** over the **bones** and **muscles**.

- His **eyes** and **nostrils** should be **clean**.

- He is **breathing regularly**.

- He is **standing square** on **all four legs**. (A hind leg is often rested. However, should the horse always rest the same hind and not wish to use it properly when exercising; it would be a warning note.)

The Bed

- Should be fairly **neat**.

- The **number of dung piles is correct** and of the **right consistency** for his diet. (Horses can pass about eight to ten piles of dung a day. Usually in the morning there will be about four to five piles.)

His Food

- Should **certainly be eaten** and though some can be fussy eaters, a horse should never miss more than one feed. He should also have **drunk some water**.

All this can be noticed from the first check in the morning or when the horse is being watered and fed.

In the field.

The normal behaviour of the horse or pony kept permanently at pasture depends on the **time of the year**.

During the spring, summer and early autumn:

- The horse should be **with the herd** or a little way apart.

- He should be **grazing** or standing near the others perhaps **nuzzling necks or flicking each other with tails**.

- Some may lie down for a while near the herd but all should look **relaxed** and **at ease**.

On winter mornings:

- The **herd** will be gathered by the gate, or wherever the food is brought in to the field.
- They may **stand close together** for warmth, or be **tentatively grazing** at patches of grass.
- All should look **bright** and **alert, anticipating food.**

Thorough Check

A good time to do this is when grooming or brushing down before exercise.

- The coat should feel soft, shiny and smooth.
- The limbs should be cool and free of swellings, lumps, wounds and sores. This check is made by running the hand down each leg.
- When the feet are cleaned they can be checked. The hooves should be cool, and the foot underneath free of any bruising, discoloration of sole or horn, wounds or stones.
- The horse should be a normal warm temperature, not sweating unduly, shivering or trembling. Feeling the base of the ears is a good way of determining temperature. They should be warm, not hot or cold.
- The horse's eyes should be clear, free of discharge.
- His nostrils should be clean and dry.
- The membranes of the eyes, gums and nostrils can also be inspected; these should be salmon pink in colour. If they are white, red, bluish or purple, this can be a sign of trouble.
- The horse's general demeanour should be alert but relaxed, interested but not agitated.
- He should stand on all four feet evenly when asked to do so.

Basic Rules to Keep a Horse Healthy:

- ★ Visit the horse every day checking for good health.
- ★ Make sure that all necessary inoculations are given on time.
- ★ Worm regularly.
- ★ Feed correctly.
- ★ Make sure that clean water is available constantly.
- ★ Maintain hygiene and cleanliness in the stable and with clothing.
- ★ Groom daily.
- ★ Maintain shoeing correctly and regularly.

★ Make sure the horse is warm enough and well rugged up in winter.

★ Check all fields and pasture daily.

★ Avoid contact with horses that have infectious or contagious diseases.

★ Exercise horse properly.

Ill Health

In many cases it is obvious that the horse is ill but just as frequently the signs are extremely small and subtle. **Any deviation from normal behaviour must be closely monitored**. This may not signify physical ill health but generally if a horse behaves abnormally then something is wrong.

Initial Signs

❖ If the horse is standing at the back of the box looking **lethargic and droopy,** this could signify that he is not in good health especially if he will not turn round when called.

❖ He may be **sweating or show visible dried sweat marks.**

❖ He may be **trembling** or **shivering.**

❖ His whole body may be **'tucked up'** with his back rounded and his **tail held tight** against his hindquarters.

❖ He may be **kicking at his flank** or trying to **bite his sides.**

❖ His **feed or hay may remain uneaten** or **water untouched.**

❖ If he is wearing a **rug** this may be **torn or askew.**

On a Closer Inspection

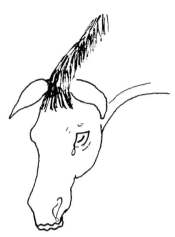

❖ His **eyes** may be **dull.**

❖ **Ears immobile** and **drooping.**

❖ There may be **discharge** from **eyes** and **nostrils** or evidence of such on the floor or door.

❖ His **coat** may be **dull and 'stary'**, that is instead of lying flat the hair sticks out from the body.

❖ His **breathing** could be **irregular** or he

may be **wheezing**, **coughing** or **sneezing**.

❖ It may be obvious that he has had a **disturbed night**; the **bedding** may be **tossed** around or heaped in the middle of the box. There may be signs that the **walls**, **floor** or **door** have been **kicked**.

❖ There may be **no dung** or what there is may be **too soft or too hard**. There could be signs of **diarrhoea** down his hind legs (known as **scouring**).

❖ He may be **pointing a foot**; only the toe of the foreleg touches the ground and the heel is raised.

❖ His **legs** may look **swollen and painful**.

❖ His **hooves** may feel **hot** to touch.

Figure 26: Pointing a Foot.

In the Field

❖ Here the horse may be standing at the gate looking **sorry for himself**.

❖ He may stand **apart from the herd** looking **droopy** and **dishevelled**.

❖ He would appear **uninterested in food**.

❖ He may be **lying down** for long periods, have difficulty rising or be **rolling** constantly.

❖ He may be **pointing or keeping the weight off the fore feet**, leaning back on his hind legs.

❖ He may be **shivering and trembling**.

❖ He may even be **lame**, so it is important to see the horse move, if only in walk.

Report

When any sign of ill health appears it is vital that a report is made to senior staff or someone in control. It is far better to be safe than sorry, that care is taken immediately before the horse becomes seriously ill. Even a matter of an hour or so could make a difference.

Also, it is the groom's responsibility that the horse is properly cared for and monitored. Any delay in reporting abnormal or worrying behaviour, which then leads to ill health, will reflect back on the groom.

Daily Routines

A routine is a regular method of procedure. There are two main reasons why such a method is important for Horse Care; the welfare of the horse and the efficient running of the yard.

1. **'Horses thrive on routine'** another equestrian cliché that is completely true. For physical and mental reasons horses need a routine.

    Physically   The horse needs to be fed little and often. Having a small stomach, (roughly the size of a rugby ball with a capacity of 4 - 6 lb.), he cannot eat large amounts at one meal. Food can also take 2 to 4 hours to pass through the stomach leaving a horse feeling hungry about 5 hours after being fed. To follow as closely as possible his natural feeding habits and to keep his digestive system working properly, the horse must be fed small amounts at regular intervals.

    Mentally   Horses become nervy and apprehensive when faced with constant change. Just the simple act of always picking out the feet in a routine way helps to keep the horse in a happy frame of mind. Horses seem to have an in-built clock, especially for feed times, and will soon become used to a routine of feeding, grooming, exercising and pasture time. If for any reason these times are changed they can become excited or anxious.

2. The efficient running of a yard and the organisation of horse care depends on a routine of work. Jobs organised for the same time every day are easier to complete. The human mind works better if programmed to a routine timetable.

Daily routines will necessarily be different for each stable and depend upon several factors:

*   Type of yard and therefore the work the horses are doing.
*   Time of year.
*   Availability of workers.
*   Number of horses.
*   Visits by Vets or Farrier.

The only variables should be in cases of competitions, shows, outings and different types of work to avoid the horse becoming stale.

The basic elements of a routine are; that the horses are **watered** and **fed regularly**, **exercised**, **groomed**, **mucked out** and allowed **rest** or **pasture time**, that **tack is cleaned** and the **stable yard tidied**.

To create a practical timetable for a yard, a chart is worked out for the necessary jobs, those that must be accomplished at certain times of the day. Other tasks can be fitted in when convenient.

A sample routine

07.30	Check horse. Clean out water bucket and refill. Give hay net and morning feed. **Have breakfast.**
09.00	Tie horse up safely preferably with a haynet. Muck out stable. Clean yard around stable. Give horse a brush down and pick out his feet.
10.00	Tack up and exercise.
11.30	Untack after exercise and groom thoroughly. Rug up if necessary.
12.30	Refill water bucket. Give a small feed.
13.00	Put on New Zealand if necessary and turn horse out into field. Skip out stable. **Lunch.**
14.30	Clean and check tack, once a week thoroughly. Wash numnah and boots for next day. Dry in airing cupboard.
16.00	Bring horse in from grass. Give small haynet. Brush down and pick out feet.
17.00	Tea.
18.00	Skip out and put down night bed. Refill water. Put up haynets.
20.00	Night feed. Refill water. Set Fair for night.

This routine applies to one horse - in a busy yard where there are a number of working pupils and the horses are worked regularly during the day, the routine will vary.

Exam Tips

For the session on health, individuals within the group will be asked to describe the signs of good and ill health and why an immediate report is vital. At this stage candidates do not need to know the causes or treatment of illnesses but simply how to recognize when a horse or pony, in the stable or field, is unwell.

CHAPTER 7
Headcollars

The horse should always be correctly restrained when anyone is caring or working around him. Grooming, tacking up, putting a rug on, are all safer with the horse tied up with a headcollar and lead rope. There is much less risk of injury.

Types of Headcollars

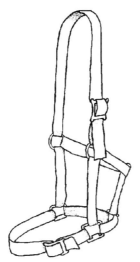

There are varying designs of headcollar but most are made up of a headpiece, a noseband and a throatlash section. Often the noseband and throatlash are connected by a strap.

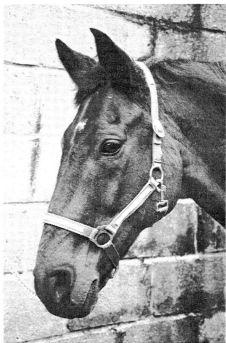

Figure 27: Headcollar.

Headcollars are usually made from nylon or leather. Nylon is less expensive to buy, available in a variety of colours and easily cleaned by washing in soapy water. Leather is expensive but much smarter in appearance.

Figure 28: Clip on the throatlash.

The fastenings vary too. Most usual is the headcollar that has one fastening on the headpiece, but there are those that also have a clip on the throatlash.

The most useful type is one that features a second clip or buckle on the noseband. This can then be unfastened, when putting the bridle on, and the headcollar placed around the horse's neck easily, without undoing the headpiece buckle.

Figure 29: Buckle on noseband.

Sizes

There are different sizes of headcollar ~ **Pony, Cob, or Full.** The cob size will fit a large pony or even a horse with a small, fine head. However, though headcollars are fairly easy to alter in size, it is not possible for a pony headcollar to fit a heavy hunter!

Halters

The halter is similar to a headcollar but without the throatlash. It is usually made from one piece of rope or webbing. Being less secure than the headcollar, the halter cannot be left on if the horse is untied in the stable nor whilst he is out in the field.

Figure 30: Halter.

Putting on a Headcollar

Approach the horse quietly from the side, walking towards his neck and shoulder. If the horse is likely to be awkward, raising his head or moving around the box, placing the lead rope quietly around his neck first will prevent his misbehaviour.

To prepare the headcollar the buckle on the headpiece should be unfastened. The lead rope may be clipped onto the ring of the headcollar; this prevents fiddling about later and allows a firmer hold when the horse is caught.

Gently slip the nose band on, place the head piece carefully over the head behind the ears and fasten the buckle.

The lead rope is clipped onto the ring underneath the horse's chin. The opening of the clip should face away from the head so that it will not catch the horse's jaw bone.

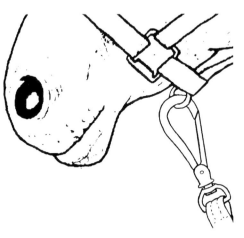

Figure 31: Clip should face away from head.

Fitting

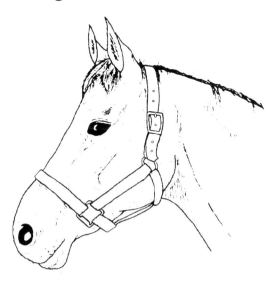

Once the headcollar has been fastened the fit is checked. The noseband should lie approximately two to three fingers width below the horse's projecting cheek bone. There should be one to two fingers space between it and the horse's face.

The headcollar should fit firmly enough so that it does not slip off should the horse pull back but not so tight as to cause rubbing or pain.

Figure 32: Correctly fitted headcollar.

Problems of ill-fitting or dirty headcollars

The fit is important especially if the horse or pony must wear the headcollar in the field. Too loose and the headcollar could become caught up in fences or bushes. Too tight and the result will be a horse with bare patches, which may become sore and infected. Ideally a horse or pony should not need to wear a headcollar when at grass, but there are times when this is unavoidable.

An incorrectly fitted headcollar can cause physical injury and long lasting mental problems. If the headcollar is wrongly fitted or uncomfortable, the horse may try to escape by pulling back. This can cause considerable pain around the poll area, resulting in a horse that is 'head shy' for many years to come.

As with all equipment, clean headcollars and halters are essential to prevent sores, diseases and infections. Most headcollars and lead ropes can be washed either by hand or in the washing machine with unscented soap or non-biological washing powder. Leather headcollars are cleaned in the same way as bridles and saddles, with a sponge, saddle soap and a regular oiling.

Tying Up a Horse

A horse should never be tied directly to a fixed object; a fence, gate, tree, metal ring or trailer. A horse pulling back in a headcollar can panic and injure himself.

The lead rope should always be tied to a piece of string which is attached to the fixed object. Then should the horse pull back, the string breaks under the strain, releasing the pressure on the headcollar and the horse. Many stables use baling twine for this purpose but this is really too strong and does not break easily. String is better or, alternatively, baling twine that has been untwisted.

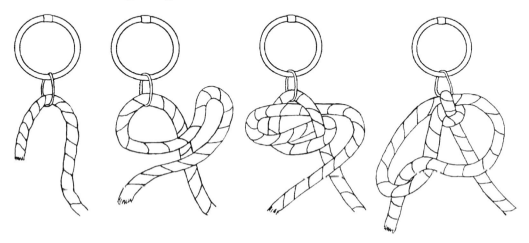

Figure 33: How to tie a quick release knot.

The lead rope is tied to the string with a quick release knot, so that when necessary the horse can be untied quickly.

If dealing with an awkward horse or performing some task on a horse that may make him nervous, the lead rope can be passed through the string without being tied. The end of the rope is held by the handler or an assistant. In the event of the horse pulling back the leadrope can be released easily.

A horse should never be left in a headcollar with the lead rope dangling to the floor. Horses often tread on the rope and pull back immediately, causing damage to themselves and the headcollar.

Tying Up in the Stable

In the stable there are usually metal securing rings to which a loop of string should be attached. There are self releasing rings on the market now which, it is claimed, come out of the wall if the horse pulls back.

The rings should be situated on the side walls of the stable. The horse should never be tied up at the back of the box with his hindquarters facing the door. This is obviously dangerous for anyone entering the box.

Tying Up Outside

When the horse is tied up outside, the surrounding area must be safe.

- The ground must be firm so that the horse is not likely to slip or fall.

- There should be no other horses nearby in case of biting and kicking.

- The horse should not be tied up where vehicles are likely to pass or in a situation where anything else may startle him.

- The horse should be tied where there is sufficient room for him. In a confined space where he cannot move around, the horse may panic and hurt himself.

- He should never be stood near electric cables, hose pipes, taps, sharp objects, water troughs, tree stumps or under low branches.

- The horse should not be left unattended or out of sight for any length of time.

- The leadrope should not be tied too short to restrict the horse's movement, nor too long allowing him to get his leg caught.

How to Stand Horse Up

Holding in a Headcollar

The handler stands on the nearside of the horse facing the front, with the right shoulder by the horse's left shoulder. The lead rope is held near the horse's chin in the right hand; the remainder being held in the left to keep it from trailing on the floor.

For more control the right hand can be reversed so that instead of the fingers uppermost the back of the hand is uppermost and the fingers below. This gives a firmer hold and should the horse try to move off or attempt to barge forwards, he can be restrained by pressing gently with the elbow on the side of his neck. Whips or crops should be held in the left hand.

For Treatment or Inspection

To hold a horse for clipping, the farrier, the vet, or for a prospective buyer, the handler turns around to face the horse, with the left shoulder by the horse's head. The lead rope is now held by the horse's chin in the left hand; the excess and crop being held in the right. In some cases, where a stronger restraint is necessary, the bridle can be used instead of a headcollar.

When holding the horse for treatment or inspection the handler stands on the same side as the inspection is taking place. For instance if the Vet is examining the offside, the handler should also stand to the offside, with the right shoulder next to the horse. The leadrope is held in the right hand near the horse's chin. The handler can now see what the person dealing with the horse is doing and be warned of any action that may startle the horse, ready to calm and control him.

To Stand a Horse Up Correctly

The horse should stand with all four feet level on the ground, the fore feet together and the hind feet together. The horse's head should be raised so that he appears alert. The horse does not look so good with his head drooping. In show circles or for inspection by a prospective buyer, usually the fore feet are together but the near hind foot is farther back than the off hind.

Leading in a Head collar

When leading a horse the handler should always wear gloves and suitable footwear, boots or strong shoes that will not slip. A riding hat is also essential if leading on the public highway or when dealing with a young horse. (In these cases a bridle should replace the headcollar for further security.)

As a rule horses are led from the left or near side, but they should be accustomed to being led from either side.

- Hold the lead rope near the horse's chin in the right hand and the other end in the left. Do not allow the rope to drag on the ground.

- *The lead rope should never be wrapped around the hand.* This is extremely dangerous. In the event of the horse racing off the groom may be dragged along or, at least, end up with considerable physical damage to the hand.

- Facing to the front, stand by the horse's neck just in front of his left shoulder and ask him in a firm voice to 'Walk on'. Taking a small step forwards, encourage the horse to move off and walk beside him so that effectively he is leading.

- *Never get in front of the horse and never, never pull him.* This usually makes him stop, raise his head and in some cases pull back and escape.

- Instead should he stop or refuse to move; he may be tapped on his side either with a crop or with the end of the lead rope and told once more firmly to 'walk on.'

- The whip should be used *immediately* the horse shows any resistance. He should not be allowed to have a 'tug of war' as this teaches him bad habits. A firm response to his misbehaviour is essential for future discipline.

- The horse must walk forward actively. If he plods or ambles along, immediately encourage him to walk forward energetically by telling him again in a firm voice to 'Walk On' and by taking quicker, more determined steps beside him.

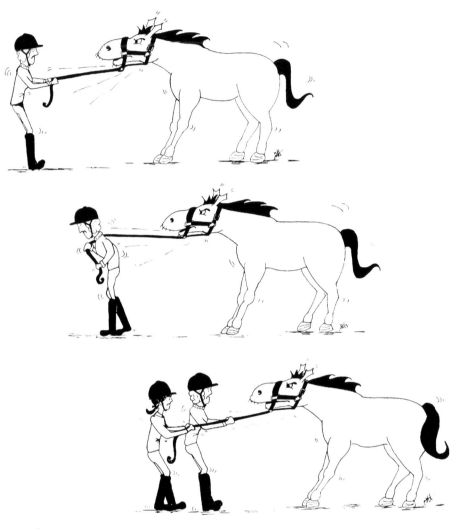

Trotting in Hand

To trot in hand the horse must first be *walking actively*. Then, taking quicker steps beside him, give the firm instruction to 'Trot on'. Again the whip must be used if the horse does not go forward willingly.

Turning in Hand

This must be performed at the walk. The turn must be made with the handler on the *outside* of the horse

Figure 34: On the nearside turn to the right.

Figure 35: On the offside turn to the left.

This helps the horse to balance himself correctly and prevents him from swinging his hindquarters out, possibly slipping. It also minimizes the risk of him treading on the handler's feet.

Exam Tips

At some point in the practical section, one candidate in the group will be requested to put a headcollar on a horse in the stable and to comment on the fit. Another candidate will tie the horse up with a quick release knot. If there is no string attached to the ring the candidate may point this out to the examiner.

After this the examiner will usually ask one person within the group to lead the horse out of the stable and stand him up correctly for inspection. You may be requested to lead the horse in hand at walk, possibly trot and to execute a turn.

In preparation for the exam practise leading a horse, turning correctly and making him walk and trot *actively*.

CHAPTER 8
Grooming

Grooming is part of the daily routine of a stabled horse. In a field-kept horse this is slightly different to suit the environment, weather, time of year and workload.

Reasons for Grooming

Good health Grooming is a necessary part of the horse's welfare. Removing waste products, such as sweat, grease, dust, dead skin and hair, it helps to keep the pores open and clean whilst encouraging good blood circulation.

Prevent disease
It helps to prevent many skin diseases and infections caused by dust and dirt. It also discourages parasites as they feed on dead hair and skin

Condition It is a form of massage which improves muscle and skin tone.

Appearance Grooming helps to keep the horse clean, healthy and well toned.

Cleanliness It also helps to keep the tack and clothing clean, preventing sores and infections.

Contact The daily grooming session develops a rapport between handler and horse.

Soundness The handler has time and opportunity to inspect the horse closely and thoroughly.

Grooming Equipment

All who work with or own horses should have their own grooming kit. This is much more efficient than constantly asking to borrow someone else's. It is also more hygienic as other people's grooming equipment may be dirty or spread infection and disease.

A grooming box or container

This needs to be fairly sturdy, spacious, easily cleaned and portable. Grooming boxes can be expensive but there are a variety on the market. Some are strong enough to stand on; handy when plaiting the mane. Alternatives, such as a nappy container or baby utility box, are just as suitable. It must be kept clean, well maintained, organised and out of harm's way, especially when grooming the horse.

Hoof pick

These include the folding type, the pick and brush or ordinary pick. The point of the pick should be blunt to prevent damaging the foot. Hoof picks are made of metal or plastic. Some have brightly coloured handles that are easily seen if dropped in the bedding. For a dark coloured pick a good tip is to tie some colourful string to the handle or paint it a bright colour.

Figure 36: Ordinary Pick and Pick & Brush.

Dandy brush

This is used on the coat of an unclipped or coarse-coated horse to remove mud and sweat. The dandy brush is too harsh for a thin-coated or sensitive horse. The dandy should not be used on non-muscular, bony parts of the horse, or on the tail.

Figure 37: Dandy Brush.

Body brush

This is the brush used most often when grooming the horse. Due to its close, fine fibres it cleans deep down to the skin. Types vary from brushes with stiffer bristles for horses with thick, coarse coats to softer brushes for horses with fine hair and sensitive skins.

Figure 38: Body Brush.

Water brush

Similar to a dandy but with softer bristles, the water brush is used either for damping down and laying the mane and tail or for scrubbing off the horse's hooves. This brush can also be useful for removing mud from the sensitive parts of the body such as the hocks.

Figure 39: Water Brush.

Rubber curry comb

This can be used in two ways; in conjunction with the body brush, (although less effective than the metal curry comb), or directly on the horse's body.

The body brush is used on the horse and afterwards swept over the curry comb to remove dirt and grease from the bristles. The dirt on the curry comb should then be removed by banging the comb on the floor of the stable.

Figure 40: Rubber Curry Comb.

On the horse's body the curry comb is used in a circular movement removing mud or sweat and bringing scurf to the surface. Excellent for removing loose hair when the coat is changing. It also encourages circulation by its massaging action.

Curry combs can also be made of plastic, in which case the comb has many small spikes. This type should only be used on heavy coated or thick skinned horses and ponies.

Metal curry comb

In conjunction with the body brush this is used in the same way as the rubber curry comb; the brush being wiped across it between strokes. To use this curry comb efficiently; hold the handle in the palm of the hand with the body of the comb laid back along the wrist. The brush can then be rhythmically stroked across the comb with no possibility of skinning the knuckles. *The metal curry comb should never be used on the horse.*

Figure 41: Metal Curry Comb.

Mane and tail comb

There are two sizes of comb; a large one for combing, and a smaller, thinner type used for pulling the mane and tail or as an aid in plaiting. Combs can either be made from metal or plastic.

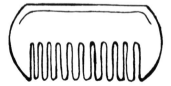 

When cleaning out the tail it is preferable to use a body brush as the comb will split or break the hair.

Sponges

These are essential for cleaning the eyes, nostrils, dock area, sheaths or udders. Sponges can also be used to wash off mud or for wiping the saddle and girth area if sweaty. For hygiene, different sponges should be kept, one for the eyes and nostrils and another for the dock area. To avoid getting these mixed up, use different coloured sponges.

Hoof oil or ointment

The thick, black hoof oil is not so popular now as it may prevent the natural osmotic action of the horn - the free exchange of moisture to and from the hoof. There are many ointments on the market or a simple vegetable oil, such as Soya, Linseed or Olive is just as effective. An old, clean paint brush is ideal for use with hoof ointment.

Scissors

Blunt, curved scissors are used for trimming the bottom of the tail and the whiskers. The mane should never be cut or trimmed with scissors as the growth will become too thick and the mane stand on end. The method of pulling the mane to shorten it also thins it, encouraging it to lie on one side.

Hay wisp or leather massage pad

Traditionally a wisp was made out of hay or straw but now massage pads or gloves are available. These tone up the horse's muscles and improve the circulation. They are used by banging down on the muscular parts of the neck, shoulder and hindquarters. Learning to wisp correctly is important; misuse can cause irritation or actual physical injury to the horse.

Stable rubber

A soft cloth or old clean tea towel wiped over the horse after grooming gives a final polish to the coat and removes any remaining dust.

Sweat scraper

Normally used to remove surplus water from the horse after washing off or bathing, the sweat scraper can also be used for a horse that is sweaty.

Towels

Clean towels are useful for drying off the horse either after bathing or if the legs are wet.

Grooming Machines

Some Yards have grooming machines, of which there are various types on the market. Though these save time and labour, they can be expensive to purchase. A grooming machine should not be used daily but every four to seven days.

Tail bandage

This bandage is applied after grooming to help shape and tidy the horse's tail. Tail bandages are usually made of an elasticated material and can be bought in almost any colour.

Tail bandages, as well as being used during grooming are also useful on other occasions:

- Protection when travelling.

- Shaping the tail after being dampened or washed.

- Keeping the tail out of wet, muddy conditions during activities such as polo or eventing.

- In the case of a reflective tail bandage, as a warning to motorists when riding in dark conditions.

Other Items

Other items useful in a grooming kit are Vaseline and fly repellent. Good quality fly repellent is preferable as cheap ones do not work as well.

Care of Kit

The grooming kit should always be kept clean and in good repair. A dirty kit will not clean the horse efficiently, will deteriorate quickly and may spread disease, infections or cause skin problems. The brushes should be washed regularly in warm water and a mild unscented soap. All metal parts must be kept clean and dry. Bandages must be washed, dried and rolled ready for use. All sponges need cleaning thoroughly in a mild antiseptic solution.

Tail Bandages

Putting On

Check first that the bandage is rolled up correctly with the tapes on the inside. Tie the horse up with a head collar and lead rope. If dealing with a strange or awkward horse, ask an assistant to help.

Pat the horse on the shoulder and continue to stroke and talk to him whilst approaching his hindquarters. If the horse's tail is suddenly grabbed from behind, he could kick.

Damp down the top of the tail with a moistened water brush to make the bandaging easier.

Standing square at the back of the horse, place about four to six inches of the bandage above the tail on horse's hindquarters. The roll of the bandage should be on top. If the roll is underneath it is much more difficult to wind around the tail.

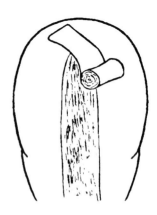

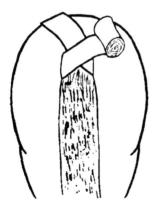

Lift up the tail with the left hand if starting to the right, vice versa if rolling to the left is easier, and roll the bandage under the dock as far up as possible. This is the difficult part, keeping the bandage high enough without it slipping. Practice does help.

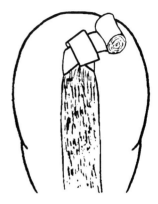

Roll the bandage around the dock twice, firmly. Turn the flap down and roll the bandage over the flap.

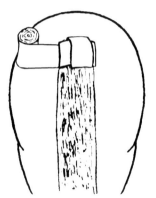

Gradually roll the bandage downwards around the tail, overlapping to approximately half a width, until just above the end of the dock bones. These can easily be felt.

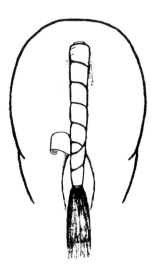

The bandage now travels up the tail until the tapes are reached. Wrap the tapes around the tail and tie them on the outside. Twist the end of the tapes into the bandage to keep them safe, out of the way and tidy. Get hold of the tail and slightly bend it into the shape of horse's rump.

When travelling the tapes can be tied to one side of the tail in case the horse rubs on the back of the trailer and manages to unfasten the tapes.

Ideally a well-bandaged tail should have *no hair sticking out of the top*, *look tidy* and have an *even tension*. The tension of the bandage should be tight enough to prevent slipping.

The tapes should never be tighter than the tail bandage. As this will damage one particular area causing a pressure point.

The tail bandage should not be left on for too long a period and should certainly **not** remain on all night. It should never be applied when wet, because when it dries it will contract and tighten.

In the above two cases the blood supply to the dock bones will be impaired; the horse will either end up with white hairs in his tail or he could lose his tail altogether.

The tail bandage can be left on for up to four hours. After this it should be removed and the tail massaged to restore the circulation. When travelling long distances a tail guard is a good substitute for the bandage.

Removing the bandage.

To remove; simply undo the tapes, hold the top of the tail bandage and slide it down the tail until it comes away. The bandage should be washed, thoroughly dried and rolled up ready to be used again.

Exam Tips

Each candidate should be familiar with the grooming kit. During the Stage I you will be given one piece from the kit; asked to name it and describe its use.

At some point during the session on grooming you will have to put on a tail bandage. Tail bandaging does need practice. In an exam situation fingers seem to turn into thumbs and the bandage takes on a life of its own, springing away at the slightest chance and rolling around in the bedding! Try practising with curtains at home, if there is no handy horse tail available.

C H A P T E R 9
Grooming Techniques

There are three types of grooming; '**Strapping**', '**Quartering**', and '**Brushing Off**'. 'Strapping' is the thorough grooming given daily, usually after the horse has worked. The skin is warm and, because the pores are still open, dirt and grease are easier to remove. 'Quartering' is the quick clean given first thing in the morning before exercise and 'brushing off' is the final grooming of the day. This chapter also covers bathing the horse, washing the mane and tail and cleaning the sheath.

Strapping

Strapping can take from twenty minutes up to one hour depending on the speed, efficiency and thoroughness of the groom. Fitter horses are easier to keep clean because they sweat less.

Method

Prepare the grooming kit and tie up the horse. If the horse is wearing a rug, this can be removed unless the weather is very cold.

The sequence for strapping is:

- Picking out and cleaning the feet.

- Brushing the body.

- Brushing the mane and tail.

- Cleaning the head.

- Sponging the eyes, nostrils, dock, sheath or udders.

- Wisping.

- Oiling the hooves.

- Finishing off.

Picking out the feet

The feet should be cleaned in the same rotation each time to teach the horse a routine. The sequence usually starts with the near fore and the near hind, then the off fore and off hind. Most horses do learn to pick up each foot in readiness. When changing sides, walk around the front of the horse

Method

Tie the horse up safely.

A small skip or bucket is placed behind each foot in turn so that the dirt falls into it and is easily cleared away. This keeps the bedding clean or, if picking out the feet in the yard, saves having to sweep the dirt up afterwards.

Starting with the near fore leg; hold the hoofpick in the right hand, stroke the horse's shoulder with the left and continue down the back of the leg to the fetlock. The horse should pick up his foot automatically. If he does not, squeeze the fetlock gently and tell him to pick up his foot. If he still refuses, lean against his shoulder until he complies. Hold the underneath of the hoof in the left hand and use the pick in the right.

The action of the hoof pick should be in the direction of heel to toe. Bringing the pick upwards towards the heel can prick and damage the frog.

Use the pick down each side of the frog and round the inside of the hoof wall. Clean the central and lateral clefts of the frog carefully. The lateral clefts are the two grooves each side of the frog.

As much dirt as possible should be removed from under the shoe. If the hoof pick has a brush this can be used to clear away remaining dirt.

If necessary, the foot can now be scrubbed with a wet water brush. Keeping the hollow between the heels dry by protecting it with the thumb; scrub the sole and frog gently.

To clean the hind leg, begin by patting the horse on the shoulder and continue to run a hand down the horse's body to the hindquarters. This will give the horse ample warning and prevent him from being startled and perhaps kicking. Continue stroking down the hind leg to the fetlock. Now *pass the hand in front of the leg and hold the hoof from the inside*. This will prevent an injured or broken arm if the horse kicks.

Whilst picking out, carefully inspect each foot for injuries and diseases such as thrush. Thrush is an infection in the foot that can detected by a foul smell and a moist, black discharge around the frog.

Check also that the shoes are secure.

When placing the horse's foot down, control it so that the horse does not drop it with a bang or hit his other leg.

Allow time for the feet to dry before applying any hoof ointment.

When picking out the horse's feet, the handler's back should be kept as straight as possible. This prevents strain or injury should the horse snatch his foot away quickly.

Brushing

The horse is now prepared for brushing.

Caked mud or dried sweat marks can be removed with the dandy brush unless the horse is thin skinned or clipped. Wet mud or sweat must never be brushed as this causes skin problems such as mud fever. Wash the mud off or wait until it dries and brush clean. The rubber curry comb used in a circular motion removes dried mud efficiently and is a good alternative to the Dandy.

The dandy brush is stroked very carefully over the sensitive parts; the belly, loins and lower legs. It is never used on the horse's head.

Body brushing always starts on the nearside of the horse. If the horse's mane falls to the left, lay it over to the other side. Begin at the poll and with the brush in the *left hand* (in order to put body weight into the strokes) and the curry comb in the *right*, clean down the neck. The body brush is used with short strokes in the same direction as the lay of the coat.

Keeping the arm fairly stiff but with the elbow slightly bent, *thoroughly* brush the neck, crest and shoulder area. Use the brush gently when reaching bony or ticklish spots such as knees, hocks and the girth area.

The horse can be brushed in the following sequence:

1. Poll to withers to include shoulders and chest.

2. Barrel, back and loins.

3. Hindquarters.

4. Girth area and belly.

5. Foreleg.

6. Hind leg.

The body brush should be frequently cleaned by sweeping it across the rubber or metal curry comb. This is done after every four or five strokes. If the brush is cleaned after every stroke, not only is it strenuous and time-consuming, but the brush deteriorates and wears out more quickly. Tap the comb on the floor to remove the dirt.

On the offside repeat the procedure with the brush in the *right hand* and the curry comb in the *left*.

Mane

Starting at the withers and working up towards the poll, brush the mane a few locks at a time. If possible encourage the lay of the mane to the *right hand* side of the neck by using a dampened water brush. There is often confusion as to which is the correct side to lay the mane. Traditionally the mane should lie to the right but with some horses the mane falls naturally to the left.

Tail

Holding the tail in one hand and working a few strands at a time, very gently brush out bedding and tangles with a soft body brush.

Thin or fine tails can be cleaned by finger combing when the bedding is removed by running the fingers through the hair rather than the brush.

To tease out really stubborn knots use a mane and tail comb gently. Never pull the comb through as this will break the hair and the horse will end up with a thin tail. A body brush is used on the bony part of the tail to remove scurf.

Tail Bandage

With a wet water brush dampen the tail slightly and put on the tail bandage.

Cleaning the head

This should be done very gently. Undo the headcollar and fasten it around the horse's neck, leaving the head free. *Unfasten the quick release knot and leave the leadrope hanging through the string. This prevents the headcollar from damaging the horse's neck should he pull back suddenly.* Using a hand to steady the head, very gently brush around the face, avoiding the eyes or nostrils.

With a head shy or nervous horse it may be safer to leave the headcollar on with the leadrope untied and left through the string as described.

Sponging

Using a damp sponge, gently wipe the eyes and nose. With a different sponge clean the dock, sheath or udder. Dry off these areas in winter with a towel to prevent chapping.

Gently clean the eyes, nostrils, dock, sheath or udders with a sponge and tepid water. An application of Vaseline to the dock or udders helps to keep these areas soft and pliable.

Wisping

This part of strapping is rarely done in busy yards as it is time consuming. There are also those who believe that wisping may damage the muscle fibres. Others consider it is beneficial to the horse to be given a weekly wisping, as a form of massage, developing and hardening the muscles. It produces a beautiful shine on the coat by drawing oil from the glands and stimulates the skin by increasing the blood circulation. Traditionally wisps are made from hay, but leather massage pads or gloves are now available and can be used instead.

Wisping is performed quite vigorously so it is wise to find out first whether or not the horse will accept this action.

If made of hay, damp down the wisp slightly, and use it by slapping it on the muscular part of the horse's body. Bang it strongly in the direction of the coat about a dozen times. Do not wisp the horse's head, any bony parts or the tender loin region.

Oiling the Hooves

The dry hooves can now be oiled. There are hoof oils and ointment on the market that can be used for weak or split hooves. The sole and frog can be oiled as well.

Finishing off

Finally, wipe over the horse with a stable rubber. This gives a final polish removing any remaining dust. The stable rubber can be damped down if required.

Quartering

This term traditionally refers to the method of grooming given to horses when wearing a rug. The front buckles are unfastened and the rug pulled back from the withers onto the hindquarters. The two front 'quarters', left and right, are groomed. The rug is then replaced onto the forehand and the back part of the rug folded over onto the front; the two hind 'quarters' are cleaned. This type of grooming can therefore be achieved without removing the roller or surcingles.

Quartering now refers to the grooming performed in the morning usually before work. This is a condensed form of strapping and usually takes about ten to twenty minutes.

The procedure for quartering is as follows:

- Pick out the feet.
- Brush the body.
- Clean the Mane and Tail.
- Sponge eyes, nostrils and dock.

The purpose of quartering is to remove the dirt accumulated overnight and to clean the horse ready for exercise. Bedding, straw or shavings are brushed off the body and out of the mane and tail. Stable stains need to be cleaned, particularly on grey horses and ponies. Unless the weather is freezing a damp brush can be used or, for really stubborn stains, a damp sponge,

Brushing Off

The horse is given a quick clean and brush down before he retires for the night.

The feet are picked out; the horse given a quick brushing over and the eyes, nostrils and dock sponged. In winter the rugs should not be removed completely except if changing to a night rug.

Grooming the Grass Kept Horse or Pony

For the horse or pony permanently at grass, the amount and frequency of grooming is different. Whilst daily attention is necessary, particularly with regard to the feet, full grooming depends on the time of year, the weather conditions and the need for insulation.

Daily Care

The feet need picking out every day. Hoof oil or ointment can also be applied.

Grooming can be done daily during spring, summer and early autumn. This grooming resembles Quartering or Brushing Off more than Strapping because the horse needs to keep a certain amount of oil, grease and even dust in the coat to endure wet, windy or cold weather. After brushing, a coating with a fly repellent is an excellent idea. The eyes, nose, dock, sheath or udder should be cleaned regularly.

Winter Care

In the winter months insulation is vital. Though the feet need picking out daily; during this time a quick brush down before exercise is all that is needed. The mane and tail can be brushed. Sponging is not advisable during very cold or freezing weather. Horses and ponies at grass still need to be kept relatively clean and examined every day for injuries, cuts, bruises, swellings, sores or thorns.

After exercise care

After exercise any dirty areas on the horse or pony should be cleaned. If the horse or pony is very sweaty this can either be cleaned by hosing in summer or with a sponge in winter. *All wet areas should be dried scrupulously with a towel before the horse or pony is put back into the field*

With grass kept horses and ponies, it is essential to keep a balance between cleanliness and the need for insulation. It is important to keep the feet in good condition, to examine for any problems and to allow time for contact with humans, so vital for the horse and pony permanently out at pasture.

Safety Points Whilst Grooming

1. Never stand directly behind the horse.
2. Never sit or kneel beside the horse when grooming the lower parts. Always bend or squat.
3. Never place hands on the floor, the horse may tread on them.
4. Never crawl under the horse's belly to reach the other side, no matter how well you know the horse!
5. Never lean in front of the hind leg when brushing the sheath or udder area. Horses can be very ticklish here and may kick.

When not to groom

As mentioned above horses and ponies out at grass, particularly during the winter, should not be given a thorough daily groom.

In addition ill or invalid horses are not usually given a strapping, particularly if very ill, as they need peace and quiet. A very light brushing or even just wiping the eyes, nose and dock area with a warm, damp sponge will suffice.

Bathing the horse

Horses are occasionally given a bath; in spring to remove any remaining winter coat or in the summer to improve the appearance before a Show. They may also be bathed for medical reasons; to help skin problems heal properly.

Horses however should not be bathed too frequently as this will remove vital oils and grease, making the coat and skin dry and scaly. A horse should not be given a bath on a cold day, even on a warm or hot day bathing should be completed as early as possible to prevent the horse getting a chill.

Bathe with warm water if possible or, if the horse will accept it, cold water from a hose pipe. A horse shampoo or baby shampoo is suitable as long as it is unscented.

When using warm water, begin at the poll and wet the neck. With a hose pipe start at the feet and gradually move up the legs and body, allowing the horse to become accustomed to the cold water. If the horse hollows his back when the cold water is applied, stop and use a sponge.

Continue down the length of the body and apply the shampoo. (The horse can be washed in sections rather than all the body at once.) Build up a good lather by rubbing with the hands or a rubber mitt. The mane can also be washed at this time.

Rinse off thoroughly. It is important that all the shampoo is washed out completely or it may cause irritation to the skin. Start at the top of the horse's body and rinse down towards the legs. Repeat the process on the opposite side.

Using the sweat scraper in long sweeps, remove excess water from the horse's body. Dry the lower legs with towels and, if possible, put a sweat rug on the horse and walk him until dry.

The head is washed using clear water only, *no soap*. Remove the headcollar and fasten it around the horse's neck. Wet the head gently with a sponge taking care that no water gets inside the ears.

Washing the Mane

As well as being washed with the rest of the body the mane is often washed on its own.

Tie up the horse correctly with headcollar and lead rope. Prepare warm water, horse shampoo, a large sponge, towels and a sweat scraper.

Starting at the forelock, avoiding the eyes and ears, wet the mane with the sponge and thoroughly rub in the shampoo. Rinse with warm water making sure that all the soap is removed. Sweep away any surplus water with the sweat scraper. Dry with a towel and brush out the mane with a clean brush.

Washing the Tail

Soak the tail by immersing as much of it as possible into a bucket of water. Take care when the water reaches the dock area, particularly if the water is cold!

Wet the top part of the tail with a sponge. Apply the shampoo and rub in thoroughly. Wash around the dock area to remove scurf. Rinse the soap out completely.

Dry the tail by holding it half way up and, standing to one side, swish the lower part of the tail around in a circle. Some horses do object to this action so be prepared to stop immediately should the horse become upset.

Dry the dock area with a towel.

Brush out the tail gently with a clean brush and apply a tail bandage.

Washing the Sheath

The sheath should be washed regularly; if neglected it becomes infected, sore and the horse may experience difficulty in passing water. Dirt in the sheath can also cause a noise when the horse is moving, (though this is also due to trapped air in the sheath, an indication that the horse is tense).

An assistant may be necessary to hold the horse.

Prepare a bucket of warm water, a mild, non-scented soap or sheath wash and a rubber glove. Instead of soap, some water with a small amount of antiseptic can be used.

Approach the horse correctly from the neck and shoulder and stroke him along the back to his hindquarters. Place the glove on one hand and immerse this hand into the bucket of water. Apply the soap to the glove. Gently insert the gloved hand into the sheath and wash, carefully picking off bits of dirt and grit. If preferred, a sponge can be used in the same way. Thoroughly clean the glove or sponge afterwards.

Exam Tips

During the grooming session the group will be divided, into individuals or pairs. Each will be given one grooming kit and instructed to groom a stabled horse, put on a tail bandage, pick out and inspect the horse's feet. Before starting to groom, restrain the horse correctly first. Do not groom with gloves on as you need to feel and inspect the horse's body for injuries, wounds or swellings.

The examiner may ask questions about grooming procedures, the different types of grooming methods, the time each takes and when each is performed. The Examiner may also ask about grooming grass-kept horses and ponies and when not to groom.

CHAPTER 10

Bedding

For stabled horses or for those spending short periods in a box or stall, bedding is put down on the floor and used for several reasons;

1. To prevent the **jarring** effect on the feet and legs of a horse standing for hours on a hard surface.

2. To provide **insulation, warmth** and **protection** from draughts.

3. To encourage the horse to **stale.**

4. To allow the horse to **roll and rest** in comfort.

5. To prevent the horse from **slipping and falling**.

Types of Bedding

Straw

This is the traditional type of bedding. It has a number of advantages and disadvantages:

✓ Easy to obtain.	✗ Labour intensive. There are no short cuts with a straw bed, it must be mucked out thoroughly each day.
✓ Economical to buy.	
✓ The bales are convenient to store	✗ Straw may be eaten by the horse.
✓ Permits free drainage, as long as the stable floor has drainage outlets.	✗ Can be dusty or contain fungal spores causing respiratory problems.
✓ Makes a bright, comfortable, warm bed.	✗ May be difficult to obtain good straw constantly. There is no guarantee of good quality so the buyer must always be more observant to avoid bad straw.

Figure 42: Straw Bed.

There are three types of straw.

1. **Wheat** is the best type and the one most commonly in use.
2. **Oat** is very palatable and likely to be eaten by the horse. It is also quite porous and tends to become saturated and heavy.
3. **Barley** straw is palatable and, though modern farming methods are making this less likely, it may contain sharp ears or awns irritating to the horse's skin.

Figure 43: Woodchip & Straw Bales.

Woodshavings or Wood chip

As the name implies this is chippings or shavings of wood packed into plastic bags, sometimes called bales. There are several varieties to choose from including large wood chip or softer, finer shavings. The bales are also available in different sizes, from the smaller bale of 20 to 25 kgs, extending to the larger bales of 30 to 35 kgs.

✓ Economical.	✗ A bed of shavings needs to be kept very clean as it is quite porous. It quickly becomes soggy and dark in colour. Droppings and soiled patches need to be removed frequently.
✓ Easy to obtain	
✓ Makes a bright, comfortable bed.	
✓ Labour and time saving if kept clean and droppings removed frequently.	
	✗ Cannot be disposed of easily.
✓ Will not be eaten by the horse.	✗ Not quite as comfortable as straw unless a very thick bed is laid.
✓ Good for horses with respiratory problems.	✗ Not as warm as straw because there is no trapped air.

Peat moss

This can provide a comfortable bed but needs cleaning frequently.

✓ This bedding is not palatable.	✗ Expensive to buy.
✓ There are no dust or spores.	✗ Becomes very soggy and heavy.
✓ It does not burst into flame so is particularly useful where there is a risk of fire.	✗ Tends to be very dark in appearance.
	✗ Can be difficult to dispose of even though it is an excellent garden manure when rotted.

Shredded Paper

This bedding consists of paper pieces.

✓ It is dust free, beneficial for horses affected by stable dust. ✓ Inexpensive to buy.	✗ Being absorbent, paper becomes very heavy when saturated which makes it difficult to muck out. ✗ When dry the paper can blow about the yard in windy conditions. ✗ Shredded paper is often made from old printed newspaper which may leave stains on the horse, particularly a grey.

Rubber matting

Common in trailers and horse boxes, rubber matting is being used more often as a stable bedding. It can either be used on its own or with other bedding material on top.

✓ When used on its own it is obviously dust free. ✓ Is very easy to muck out as the dung is removed and urine cleaned by hose pipe. ✓ After the initial outlay there is no other bedding to buy, so upkeep can be cheap.	✗ It does not allow the horse to lie or roll in comfort, if at all. ✗ It can appear revolting when not cleaned properly and the dung is trampled around by the horse. ✗ There is often a smell from the ammonia fumes. ✗ Urine often streams out into the yard. ✗ The stable needs good drainage to allow the urine to drain away. ✗ It can offer little warmth. ✗ There are no banks for insulation, to protect from draughts or to prevent the horse from becoming cast.

Deep Litter

This is not a type of bedding but a method of keeping a bed, usually with straw or shavings. Initially the bed is made very deep and only mucked out completely every three to six months. Soiled or damp patches and dung are taken out regularly and clean bedding placed on top.

This method is labour saving initially and provides a deep, warm bed. When the full mucking out has to be done though, it takes a long time and is very heavy work. The box then needs to be dried out thoroughly.

The deep litter method is rapidly declining in popularity. It is now thought that problems are caused by the fungal spores which thrive in the constantly warm, damp conditions.

New ideas for bedding occasionally appear on the market but the above are the most usual types. The decision about the type of bedding to use depends on several factors. The first consideration is the horse, whether he is likely to eat the bedding or if he suffers from respiratory problems. Other factors include cost, convenience of storage, disposal, management of the yard and personal preference. Straw is the most popular but is unsuitable for some horses, in which case shavings or shredded paper are better.

Keeping the Bed Clean

A stabled horse may be standing for long periods on the bedding, sometimes as long as twenty-three hours a day. In this time he will pass droppings, urinate, lie down, roll and sometimes eat the bedding. For hygiene and his physical well-being, the bed must be regularly cleared of wet, soiled patches and dung.

A dirty neglected bed can cause serious problems. The horse may eat the soiled bedding and suffer from colic. There is a greater likelihood of worm infestation from the dung. Vermin and insects will thrive in warm damp conditions. The box will certainly smell offensive and if the walls of the box are wooden they will rot. The horse may suffer skin irritations; any scratches, grazes or wounds on his body will become dirty and infected. It will definitely be more difficult to keep the horse clean.

Bedding is cleaned by 'Skipping Out', 'Mucking Out' and 'Bedding Down'.

Skipping Out

At frequent intervals during the day, dung is removed from the bed using a fork and skip. Ideally it should be done every time a horse passes droppings, but at least three times a day. This not only keeps the bed clean but also makes mucking out easier.

Mucking Out

Performed once a day, usually in the morning, this involves the complete removal of dung and soiled bedding.

All the necessary tools are prepared; a fork (pitchfork, four or five-pronged fork or shavings fork depending on the bedding) skip, mucking out sheet, bucket or wheel barrow, brush and shovel. The horse should be restrained with a head collar and lead rope either in the box or ideally outside.

All dung is removed together with the heavily soiled patches. Dried bedding is separated from the remaining wet areas and tossed to the side of the box. Straw needs to be shaken with the fork to reveal the dirty bedding. With shavings, wet patches can be distinguished by colour and weight - these are either a deep golden or a dark brown colour, very heavy and may be stuck together.

The clean bedding and banks at the sides of the box are sifted through with the fork to remove any remaining droppings. The floor is brushed clean. On warm days bedding can be piled against the walls of the box to allow the stable floor to dry.

To lay the bed, the old bedding is put down and new bedding, thoroughly shaken out, placed on top. The banks around the sides of the box are built up high and wide, then levelled by skimming the fork across the top. The bed is also flattened down by skimming the fork across it. This is particularly necessary for shavings in order to create a level bed. The edges of the bed by the door and any other clear areas are tidied with the brush. All muck is removed by wheel barrow or muck sheet to the muck heap and the tools put away properly.

At regular intervals, every four to six weeks, the floor can be treated with a disinfectant. Both floor and walls need regular treatment to kill off any disease or infection and to remove offensive odours. Some products are available which, when sprinkled on the floor, get rid of all offensive smells. These are effective but can be expensive.

Bedding Down

In the evening the bed needs to be cleaned and tidied once more.

Dung and soiled patches are removed. More bedding is laid down as a night bed. There are two types of bed, the day and the night bed. The day bed should be deep enough to be comfortable. The night bed is deeper as the horse will be standing on this for some 8 - 12 hours.

To test the depth of the night bed gently let the fork drop, points first, into the bed. These should not hit the floor. If the fork can be heard hitting the ground then the bed is not deep enough.

Setting Fair.

Another term used with regard to the stable area is 'setting fair'. This means cleaning the area within and around the box. Brushing and clearing away all dust and bedding in the yard area, and generally tidying away tools and equipment.

Banks.

Wide, high banks are laid against the walls, usually the two side walls and the back wall. The banks should be one to two feet in height above the bed, of an even thickness and level along the top. Droppings and soiled bedding should always be cleaned out and never left in the banks.

Figure 44: Banks in a Woodchip Bed.

Banks are important with all types of bedding:

1.   To prevent the horse becoming cast.

     Sometimes when a horse rolls or lies down, his legs become trapped against the wall. In this situation he cannot either roll over or push himself up, he is 'cast'. The horse may then panic, go into shock or injure himself. Banks help to prevent this predicament; they stop the horse from getting too close to the walls and give his legs some leverage should he lie down or roll.

2.   To provide insulation against cold and draughts.

A correctly laid bed will be clean, warm, soft and free from sharp objects, with the banks tidy and level. The whole box will provide the horse with a comfortable, safe and warm environment in which to live.

Muck Heaps

Another important part of yard management is the keeping of the muck heaps. A yard can be judged by its muck heaps. If this area is well managed, kept clean, tidy and hygienically controlled; then the rest of the establishment should be efficiently run.

Ideally there should be three muck heaps;

1. One that is well rotted and ready to take away.
2. One in the process of rotting.
3. One in use.

Daily care is needed to keep the muck heap correctly. The new muck should be put on the appropriate heap and forked into shape. Various yards have different methods of building the heap. Some prefer heaps built in steps; others prefer squares with vertical sides. Whichever method is used the correct stacking of muck is essential for tidiness, hygiene and to allow the manure to rot properly. There should be no muck left lying around or blowing about the yard; the whole area should be frequently cleaned, brushed and set fair.

It is ideal to have the heap in an enclosed area such as a square, walled on three sides, perhaps with a ramp for wheelbarrows and the open side a convenient access for lorries.

Site of the Heap

The position of the muck heap in relation to the yard is vital. This should be at a convenient distance for the stable hands carrying or wheeling muck; yet not too close constituting a health threat or a possible fire hazard should the heap overheat or be burnt deliberately. If laid against wooden buildings or boxes, the damp muck will rot the walls.

Heaps should be situated down wind from the yard to minimize any unpleasant smells and, if possible, kept out of sight. A muck heap by the side of the driveway into the stables is not a pretty sight, particularly if it is not kept well!

If the yard is situated in hilly country, ideally the muck heap should be positioned down hill. The workers will not then have to haul the muck uphill. All heaps should have an access that is easy and dry, even better if the access is made of concrete. There is nothing worse than trying to push a loaded wheelbarrow up a steep, muddy track to the heap in cold, wet weather!

Disposing of muck these days is not easy. Many farmers do not require shavings and even disposing of straw may be difficult, though gardeners still like to use horse manure (especially for roses)!

It is definitely not a good idea to spread muck over fields to be grazed by horses. This does not encourage the growth of the right type of grasses and there is also the danger of spreading worms and their larvae.

A well-managed yard will have efficiently run Muck Heaps.

Stable Construction

This subject is not included in the syllabus for Stage I, but occasionally Examiners will ask basic questions about stables or boxes; size, construction, materials, fixtures and fittings.

Size

'I still say she needs glasses!'

The box must be large enough to accommodate the horse or pony, allowing him to turn around, feed, lie down or roll in comfort. A box size of 12 feet by 14 feet will accommodate the largest horse; 12' by 12' for horses around 16 hands; 10' by 10' for around 15 hands and 8' x 8' for small ponies. Checking the size of a box is done by striding the area. There should be approximately three feet to one stride. A dark box will look smaller.

Height

The box must be of a sufficient height for the horse so that he does not hit his head. The ceiling or roof needs to be from 12 to 15 foot high.

Door

The door should be high and wide enough for the horse to enter and exit without hitting his hips or banging his head. This means a minimum of 4 feet wide and, depending on the size of horse, a height of 10 feet approximately. Doors on pony boxes are often smaller in size. Most stable doors are split to allow the upper portion to be opened for ventilation.

Condition and Ventilation

The box must be waterproof, dry and warm, but without being stuffy. Good ventilation is essential. Horses and ponies do need a good supply of fresh air but there must be no draughts. For this reason the door and window should be on the same side of the box to prevent air streaming through from one side to another. There should be kicking boards all round.

Floor

The floor should allow drainage towards the back of the box. A horse should never have to stand in a pool of water and urine stagnating at the doorway. The floor needs to be strong enough to withstand wear and tear from four shod hooves. It should not be slippery.

Fixtures and Fittings

These should be kept to an *absolute minimum*. If there is anything on which the horse can catch himself, hurt, injure or wound himself then that is precisely what he will do (usually the night before a major competition or outing)!

Essential fittings are; two securing rings on which to tie the horse and haynet; a device for water, either an automatic water bowl or water bucket and some extremely safe lighting.

The securing rings should have string attached to which the horse can be tied. If water is given in a bucket it must be set in a safe, static position or placed within a rubber tyre.

If the horse is fed from a feed bucket, this must be removed from the stable immediately after use. If it cannot be removed quickly then it must be made safe by being placed in a rubber tyre. There are alternatives such as the bucket designed to fit over the door or the soft rubber feed skip which will not injure the horse if it is tossed around. A bucket hung from a clip is often used but again it adds another fixture within the stable which may provide a hazard.

Light must be available in the box. It is extremely dangerous not to have light within a stable if the horse is being dealt with after dark. There should be no exposed light bulbs or wiring; these must be adequately protected. All electrical wires must be properly insulated. All electrical components must be completely safe, regularly checked and out of the horse's reach.

Ideally there should be no clips or hooks, projecting nails or screws, no light switches, exposed cables, splintered or rotting wood, glass - anything on which the horse could injure himself.

Fixtures and fittings should be kept to a minimum in the box!

Exam Tips

Before the exam day, take a look at various types of bedding; ask working pupils or owners which type of bedding they prefer and why. Practise describing the various methods of mucking out and laying the bed. Even if this is a daily task it is not always easy to explain in a clear and concise way. The next time you muck out, talk yourself through the various stages; from tying the horse up outside with a haynet, preparing the wheelbarrow and shavings fork to laying the bed down neatly. Often in exams the important point is not how much knowledge you have but how you communicate this to the examiner.

For stable construction practise estimating size, observe the construction and fittings; start assessing boxes critically. Consider possible improvements for safer, more efficient fittings and attachments if any.

Light must be available in the box. It is extremely dangerous not to have light within a stable if the horse is being dealt with after dark. There should be no exposed light bulbs or wiring; these must be adequately protected. All electrical wires must be properly insulated. All electrical components must be completely safe, regularly checked and out of the horse's reach.

Ideally there should be no clips or hooks, projecting nails or screws, no light switches, exposed cables, splintered or rotting wood, glass - anything on which the horse could injure himself.

Fixtures and fittings should be kept to a minimum in the box!

Exam Tips

Before the exam day, take a look at various types of bedding; ask working pupils or owners which type of bedding they prefer and why. Practise describing the various methods of mucking out and laying the bed. Even if this is a daily task it is not always easy to explain in a clear and concise way. The next time you muck out, talk yourself through the various stages; from tying the horse up outside with a haynet, preparing the wheelbarrow and shavings fork to laying the bed down neatly. Often in exams the important point is not how much knowledge you have but how you communicate this to the examiner.

For stable construction practise estimating size, observe the construction and fittings; start assessing boxes critically. Consider possible improvements for safer, more efficient fittings and attachments if any.

C H A P T E R   11
Watering

Horses require both food and water to survive. However, of the two water is more vital. A horse can survive some time without food but will dehydrate and die within days if deprived of water. It is essential for life; all bodily functions need water to work efficiently and chemical reactions within the body take place in a water solution.

A horse's body comprises of approximately 70% water and this is needed for;

- **Digestion**   Lack of water can cause colic particularly if the horse is fed dry foods.

- **Temperature Regulation**   As in sweating where evaporation of moisture from the skin has a cooling effect.

- **Lubrication**   In areas such as joints and eyes.

- **Metabolism**   For the proper working of the chemical reactions in the body.

- **Waste disposal**   As in urine, droppings and sweat.

Water must be available to the horse constantly and it must be clean, free of dirt or pollution. Horses can drink an average of 8 gallons a day, sometimes up to 15 gallons in hot weather. They can be fussy drinkers, refusing tainted water.

The amount of water necessary depends on certain factors;

- **Temperature**   In hot weather the horse will sweat, losing fluids from the body.

- **Work**   Heavy or fast work will also result in sweating and again loss of bodily fluids.

- **Diet**   If the horse is fed dry food and hay he will drink more water.

- **Milk production**   Brood mares need more water to produce the milk for their foals.

- **Faecal and urinary loss**   Diarrhoea results in an abnormal loss of fluids.

Rules of Watering

1. A horse must have a constant supply of clean water.

2. Water utensils and containers must be kept clean.

3. Water before feeding.

4. Do not water when the horse is hot after work.

5. Do not work the horse hard immediately after a deep draught of water.

6. Containers should be large and deep enough to allow a good deep drink.

7. Containers should be safe and sturdy.

When NOT to Water

A horse should NOT be given water:

After a feed

This flushes undigested food out of the stomach. (Though in most cases where the horse has a constant access to water this is not a drastic problem.)

After very hard work when the horse is hot.

Cold water given to a hot horse will cause a shock to the system. Slightly warmer water only should be given until the horse has cooled down sufficiently. The warmer water can be made up by adding some hot water to a bucket of cold water, until the temperature is lukewarm.

Hot or exhausted horses should be given about a quarter of a bucket at a time, approximately every twenty minutes.

Before hard, fast work

The liquid will bloat the stomach and may restrict breathing.

Stagnant, stale, polluted or dirty

Usually horses are fussy and will not drink tainted water. If there is no clean water available though and the horse is thirsty enough, he may drink unsuitable water.

Water in the Stable

There are two main ways in which to water horses in the stable - by bucket or by automatic drinking bowls.

Buckets

The water bucket must be heavy enough so as not to tip over and large enough to allow a deep drink. It should be of strong rubber or plastic; metal is not really suitable. Ideally it should be light enough to be carried even when almost full of water.

A bucket can be secured by a clip on the wall.

A better method is to place the bucket in a rubber tyre on the floor; the horse cannot injure himself or tip the bucket over and decide to play football with it!

✓ Easily cleaned.	✗ Buckets can be extremely heavy and cumbersome to carry around the yard. Not a pleasant job in mid-winter when it is cold and the ground is slippery.
✓ Intake can be monitored.	
✓ Intake can be regulated. The water can be taken away from the horse at times when he should not drink.	
	✗ Hazardous in the stable if not properly secured.
✓ In winter ice can be removed and the bucket refilled with fresh water.	✗ Labour-intensive and time-consuming; filling, cleaning and refilling.

Automatic Drinking Bowls

This is the most popular method of providing water for the stabled horse. The bowls are usually of metal or fibreglass. They are connected to the water supply and operated by a ball cock method. Horses soon learn to operate them.

Advantages:

✓ Provides a constant supply of clean water.	✗ Can be hard to keep clean unless religiously done every day.
✓ Labour and time saving - can be significant in a large, busy yard.	✗ Metal bowls may rust.
	✗ Some bowls are quite small and do not allow the horse a deep drink.
	✗ Water cannot be regulated.
	✗ Water cannot be monitored.
	✗ Can have a tendency to freeze over in winter, or the pipes may become frozen

Despite the fact that the disadvantages seemingly outweigh the advantages, if properly maintained automatic drinking bowls do work extremely well.

Water in the Field

Water can be provided in three ways within the field; naturally by stream or river, by a trough, or by buckets.

Rivers and Streams

Nowadays it is a sad fact that many rivers and streams are polluted. Even at best there is always a doubt that the water is clean and pure.

The river or stream must have a gravel bed. A sandy bed can cause sand colic as the horse ingests sand in the water. The approach to the drinking area must be kept safe and clean or it can quickly become 'poached', that is churned up by the horses' hooves, muddy, slippery and dangerous.

Any polluted water, dangerous rivers, stagnant pools or ponds, bogs or swamps, poached or dangerous banks must be fenced off and the horse kept away. All these areas are life threatening to the horse.

Troughs

This is a popular method of watering in the field. The most efficient type is the self-filling trough that is connected to the mains water pipe and controlled by a ball cock. The animals can take water whenever they need it. The only problem with this type of trough is that unless the pipes are properly insulated, they can become frozen in winter.

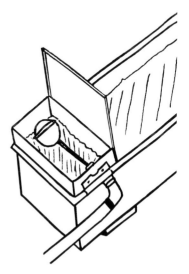

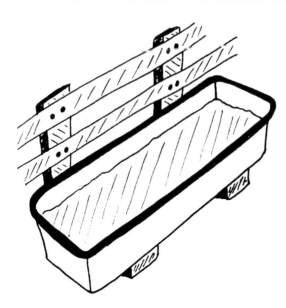

Another container used frequently is the 'bath' trough filled either by buckets or by a hosepipe. Old baths are good water containers if made safe first. All sharp corners must be smoothed and the taps removed altogether. The bath must be kept sufficiently filled with water particularly during hot weather.

The trough should have a good water supply either by a mains pipe, a hosepipe or be at a convenient distance for workers carrying refill buckets.

In winter the water needs to be kept clear of ice. In a trough this can be achieved either by daily breaking the ice or by placing a large rubber ball in the water. The ball floats around preventing the ice forming. (In severe weather daily inspections will be necessary as the water may still freeze over.)

As with all types of water container, the trough must be kept clean. This necessitates regular and frequent emptying, scrubbing and thorough rinsing of the trough.

Site of the trough

The position of a trough is important. It needs to be convenient for the horse without constituting a danger. A trough situated by a fence may either be parallel or at right angles to it. If it is slightly away from a fence, a horse may become stuck behind the trough leaving him vulnerable to bullying from others.

Placed in the middle of the field the trough creates an obstacle that can easily cause injury. A trough should not be placed under deciduous trees; the water will become clogged with leaves, flowers, seeds and twigs.

Approach

The approach to the trough should be kept dry either by laying a concrete or hard-core surround or by covering the ground with straw or shavings. The water trough must be situated well away from gates, muddy areas or hollows, where the ground very quickly becomes poached.

If the trough is regularly and properly maintained it is the most convenient and efficient method of watering in the field.

Buckets

Providing water by buckets in the field can be hard work. It is not a convenient or efficient method, being labour intensive and time consuming. Buckets need to be constantly cleaned and refilled. They can also be kicked over and become a hazard. There are times, however, when buckets must be used in place of other watering systems, which are either inoperative or unavailable.

Exam Tips

In preparation for the exam, inspect various types of watering systems used in stables, farms, yards, fields and boxes. Assess these systems recognizing the positive and negative points.

CHAPTER 12
Feeding

Correct feeding is essential for the health of the horse. A well-balanced diet should provide all the necessary nutrients to maintain the horse in good condition.

Aims of Feeding

A horse needs food for the following reasons:

1. **To maintain body temperature**

   Maintaining body temperature is important particularly for horses living out in winter.

2. **Growth**

   A variety of nutrients are necessary for growth especially in young stock.

3. **Energy**

   Certain foods are needed to create energy so that the horse can perform his work.

4. **To maintain correct weight**

   Keeping his natural body weight is essential; an underweight or thin horse will find it difficult to keep warm or perform work properly.

5. **Breeding in the case of stallions and brood mares**

   For breeding, stallions need energy and condition; mares need to provide food for the foetus and eventually the foal.

At this point it is as well to mention that overfeeding a horse can be disastrous, resulting in illnesses caused either by obesity or hyperactivity. Here comes another cliché **'the eye of the Master maketh the horse fat.'** In other words doting owners tend to overfeed. Starvation is obviously not beneficial but as a rule it is wiser to underfeed a little rather than overfeed. Of course the ultimate aim is to feed the right amount.

Rules of Feeding

A horse's digestive system is quite finely tuned and, if incorrectly fed, a horse can easily develop digestive disorders, which at worse can be fatal. There are certain rules therefore which help to prevent any stress to the system and thus minimise the risk of digestive problems.

The ten rules of feeding are:

1.	**Feed little and often**	The horse's stomach is small in relation to his size, so food must be given in small amounts at frequent intervals. This will also follow, as closely as possible, the horse's natural lifestyle. Ideally a horse should never go for more than 8 hours without food.
2.	**Plenty of bulk**	The horse's digestive system needs to be constantly filled to work efficiently. Bulk foods such as hay and grass achieve this.
3.	**Correct amount and type**	Feeding too much, too little or the wrong type of food can cause physical and mental problems. See Considerations of Feeding.
4.	**Good quality food**	Inferior foods lack nutritional value and may contain dust.
5.	**Make no sudden change to the diet**	All alterations to diet must be gradual to avoid digestive problems.
6.	**Do not feed directly before exercise**	This can cause colic and breathing problems. A horse must be allowed at least one hour after a feed before he is worked.
7.	**Routine**	Horses are creatures of habit and need to be fed as near as possible at the same time each day.
8.	**Cleanliness**	All utensils must be kept scrupulously clean.
9.	**A succulent each day**	Foods such as apples, carrots or swedes add variety to the diet and provide some essential vitamins. Particularly important if the horse is not at grass frequently.
10.	**Water before feeding**	To prevent undigested food from being washed out of the stomach if the horse drinks after the feed.

Considerations of Feeding

There are three basic elements to feeding; the first is to calculate the **total daily amount** the horse or pony needs. The second is to divide this amount into **concentrates and roughage**. (Concentrates are 'hard' foods, those that provide energy and stamina. Roughage is bulk food, such as hay and chaff). The third element is the **type of food** to give. All three, that is the **amount, percentages** and **type** depend on certain factors.

These will vary according to:

1. The weight of the horse.
2. The breed.
3. Temperament.
4. Amount and type of work.
5. Type of rider.
6. Whether fully stabled or out at grass.
7. Time of year.
8. Type of pasture.
9. Age of the Horse.

Amount

The total daily amount is calculated from the **weight** of the horse. There are four main methods of working out the weight.

i.   **A weigh bridge.**
The horse is weighed on a special bridge.

ii.   **A Weigh Tape.**
The horse is measured around the barrel, just behind the withers in the girth area.

iii.   **A Weight Table.**
This gives height, build and approximate body weight in kilos and pounds.

iv.   **Estimation by height.**
In practice, the last method is the simplest and easiest to use, unless for specific reasons the horse's diet must be absolutely precise. In the examination, candidates should be able to work out an approximate daily amount from the height.

17 hands = 34 lbs.
16 hands = 30 lbs.
15 hands = 26 lbs.
14 hands = 22 lbs.
13 hands = 18 lbs.
12 hands = 14 lbs.

For those horses and ponies who are half a hand or 2 inches higher, an extra 2 lbs. is added. For example a 13.2 hand pony will need 20 lbs.

Estimation of Weight from Height

Here are some simple calculations that may help to remember the above numbers.

Example 1

Multiply height x 2 and deduct 2,4,6,8 or 10.

16 hands x 2 - 2 = 30 lbs. (16 x 2 = 32 - 2 = 30)
15 hands x 2 - 4 = 26 lbs. (15 x 2 - 4)
14 hands x 2 - 6 = 22 lbs. (14 x 2 - 6)
13 hands x 2 - 8 = 18 lbs. (13 x 2 - 8)

Example 2

Height - 10 x 4 + 6

For a 15 hand horse:

15 - 10   = 5
5 x 4   = 20
20 + 6   = 26

Example 3

Remember that 12 hands = 14 lbs. and add 4 lbs. for every additional hand.

Each student and candidate will need to discover which calculation is the easiest to remember. Some will find one way simpler than another, depending on whether they have a good memory or a mathematical brain! Alternatively candidates may choose their own method of working out the amounts.

Variables

Once the total daily amount is worked out there are two points to take into consideration which will affect this amount.

1. The horse's build.
2. If he is kept at grass.

Build

Horses of the same height can vary in build. This often depends on breeding and ancestry. For instance a Thoroughbred will have a tendency to be fine or small boned and will consequently weigh less than a heavy hunter of the same height. The estimate, based on a medium build, can be modified to cover this variable.

A fine boned horse can be given 2 lbs. less than the total calculated and a heavy horse will need 2 lbs. more. For example a 16 hand thoroughbred will need 28 lbs. and a heavy hunter type of the same height, 32 lbs.

Grass Kept Horses and Ponies

The amounts as calculated are for fully stabled horses and ponies and for those allowed very little pasture time. Horses and ponies living out at grass during the winter will also need the *same amount of food as a stabled horse*. They need this to maintain their health and condition during wet or cold weather.

For horses and ponies kept at grass from early spring right through to autumn before the weather becomes cold and the grass loses its goodness, the amount of supplementary foods can be reduced. Native ponies living at grass during the warmer months with a light or medium workload will need very little extra food.

At Stage I level candidates are not expected to know the variations for feeding animals kept at grass, it is sufficient to understand that the amount of supplementary foods needed will vary during the seasons.

Percentages

The next element is the percentage of concentrates to roughage that the horse will need. This depends on the amount and type of work that the horse is expected to perform. A horse in light work certainly does not need a lot of energy giving food. This would 'heat him up' and make him unmanageable. Conversely a horse in hard work needs the extra 'hard' or concentrated food to enable him to perform safely, satisfactorily and to keep him healthy.

The amount of concentrates and roughage is calculated basically from the hours of work.

Level of Work	Hours of work	Type of work	Percentages
Light Work	Approximately 4 - 6 hours a week.	Hacking, light schooling, some riding school horses and most ponies.	30% concentrates to 70% bulk.
Medium Work	Approximately 6 to 10 hours a week.	Schooling up to 2 hours a day, dressage, show jumping and hacking.	50% concentrates to 50% bulk.
Hard work	10 hours and over or hard, fast work.	Eventing, hunting, point to point, racing, endurance riding.	70% concentrates to 30% bulk.

For Example: a 16 hand Irish Draught/Thoroughbred, medium build, doing 10 hours schooling and hacking a week will need a total daily amount of 30 lbs. This will be split 50/50 with 15 lbs. of concentrate and 15 lbs. of roughage.

There is one important point that must be considered; *all horses are individuals*. The calculated amount, whilst being a good basic beginning, may need varying if necessary.

The horse should be monitored over a period of time to see that the amount suits him. If he puts on weight or becomes a little 'hot', the concentrates ration may be reduced and the roughage increased. If he loses weight or condition then his feed may need altering as necessary.

Having calculated a daily amount, this is then split into three or four feeds a day. The concentrate ration is given as one in the morning, one in the evening and one or two during the day depending on the horse's timetable. Keeping in mind that no one feed should be more than 5 or 6 lbs. the largest feed can be given at night and at breakfast, providing the horse is not being worked too early. For example our horse is fed 15 lbs. of hard feed he can have; 4 lbs. in the morning, 3 lbs. at midday, 3 lbs. for tea and 5 lbs. at night. The hay ration can be divided in the same way; the largest portion given with the last feed at night.

Exam Tips

For the examination you will need to learn thoroughly the aims, rules and considerations of feeding. You must also try to *understand* them and the reasons why they are important. You should be able to calculate the daily amount of food by height and the percentage of hard and bulk foods from the amount of work the horse is doing.

Feeding is the 'pet' subject of quite a few examiners who may probe deeply into this aspect of horse care. You are not expected to be an expert on feeding or able to conjure the accurate amounts out of your head immediately. Do not be confused if the examiner suddenly throws a question at you as follows:

How much hard food would a 15 hand Welsh cob/Thoroughbred need per day doing about 10 hours a week at a riding school?

Take one step at a time:

1. **Height**   ⇨   **amount**
    Work out how much food in total from height = 26 lbs.

2. **Build**   ⇨   **amount**
    Consider build, cob/thoroughbred should be medium = 26 lbs.

3. **Work**   ⇨   **percentages**
    Decide what type of work = medium
    What percentage of hard food is needed = 50%.
    50% of 26 lbs. is 13 lbs. of hard food per day.

Always state that this is the initial amount to feed this horse but *he should be monitored for a few weeks or months to see if this suits him.*

Feeding horses is a complex, complicated and often confusing subject, particularly as it depends on so many variables, traditions and personal preferences. Learning the basics step by step; understanding the reasons, rules and considerations will certainly help to illuminate the mystique of feeding.

C H A P T E R   13
Types of Feed

Grass is the natural diet of the horse and the *right pasture* at *certain seasons* of the year, provides all the nutrients in the right quantities for his maintenance. *Maintenance is defined as that level at which a horse can be kept in good condition without doing any work, or in some cases performing light work.* Once the horse is asked to work longer hours or more strenuous exercise he will need extra foods and different types to maintain his condition.

Basically, food is divided into two categories:

1. Concentrates

These provide the horse with energy and maintain his condition; grains and cereals such as oats, barley and maize. This also covers foods that are added to provide extra nutrients and to make the feed more tasty; such as molasses and linseed. (These are termed 'openers' or 'mixers'.)

Into this category as well fit the specifically manufactured 'Compound' feeds. These are made up by Feed Companies and sold as hard cubes, nuts and wafers or as a mix.

2. Roughage

This adds bulk to the diet and slows down the rate at which the concentrates pass through the digestive system giving time for the nutrients to be absorbed; foods such as hay and chaff (chopped hay or straw). Some traditional foods, such as Bran, and openers such as Sugar Beet, are also used for their bulk content to add roughage to the diet.

Traditional Feeds

Because the domesticated horse has an artificial lifestyle, he needs extra foods to make up for the lack of pasture and to provide the extra energy needed for the work performed. Over the centuries various foodstuffs have been used for equine nutrition and these have become known as Traditional feeds.

Oats

❖ This grain is considered the best as it is the closest nutritionally to the horse's needs.

❖ It is high in energy yet does not make the horse fat.

❖ Good quality oats are hard, clean, plump, heavy, golden and sweet smelling.

❖ Oats are best fed either bruised, rolled, crushed or crimped.

   ▲ Oats lack certain minerals and should be fed with the addition of other foods.

   ▲ Oats should never be fed in excess as this can make the horse 'hot' and uncontrollable.

   ▲ Bad quality oats are thin, dark in colour and smell sour and should not be used for feed.

   ▲ Once the husk has been broken open, the oats start to lose their value and should not be kept longer than 3 weeks.

   ▲ Whilst whole oats are often fed quite successfully, some horses may have difficulty digesting them.

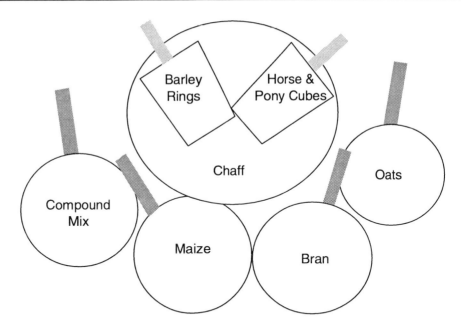

Barley

❖ Barley has almost the same nutritional value and can be fed as a substitute for oats.

❖ It is slightly less heating but more fattening, therefore good for a horse who needs to put on weight.

❖ Barley can be fed flaked, rolled, crushed, boiled, or micronised.

   ▲ This cereal needs to be fed with other food because of the low fibre content and lack of certain minerals.

   ▲ It is low in fibre.

   ▲ The grains are small, hard, difficult to chew and therefore must not be fed whole unless cooked.

Maize

❖ Maize provides extra energy and is beneficial for horses in hard work.

❖ The high starch content puts weight on a thin animal.

❖ Maize is normally fed flaked or micronised, is yellow and similar in appearance to corn flakes.

   ▲ The protein content is of low quality.

   ▲ Fibre content too is very low.

   ▲ Maize is very heating and should be fed in small amounts of no more than 25% (one quarter) of the total grain fed.

Bran

Bran is made from the husks of wheat grain separated from the flour. It is a roughage food, with the appearance of fine brown bread crumbs.

❖ Bran adds extra bulk to the diet.

❖ A bran mash can be fed to a horse who is off work and box resting, as a laxative.

❖ A bran mash is also beneficial for a tired horse after long, hard work or as a feed on the night before the horse's rest day.

❖ Bran helps to alleviate minor bowel conditions. For instance dry bran can be given to a horse with loose droppings, (diarrhoea). As a laxative to help in cases of mild constipation, bran can be fed wet as in a mash.

❖ Bran can be useful as a medium for administering medicines.

Though bran used to be considered an essential part of the horse's diet, it is unpopular nowadays for two reasons.

1. With the efficiency of the milling process of flour it is difficult to purchase good quality bran.

2. It is considered to be nutritionally incorrect. Amongst the elements contained within Bran are the two minerals Calcium and Phosphorus. These need to be present in the diet at the correct ratio; approximately two parts calcium to one part phosphorus. However, bran contains a high level of phosphorus and a low level of calcium, which, if fed exclusively and excessively, creates an imbalance in the diet. Calcium is essential for bone development and a deficiency of this mineral can cause bone deformities and weaknesses. This is particularly so in young animals who can developed rickets.

For these reasons many establishments will not feed bran at all. Some yards and stables feed bran with the addition of limestone flour to make up for the deficiency of calcium.

Linseed

Linseed is the seed of the flax plant. In appearance the uncooked seeds are small, oval, shiny and brown.

❖ Linseed is high in protein, fats and oils.

❖ It is traditionally fed to horses in winter or in poor condition as a pick-me-up.

❖ It improves the condition of the horse's coat giving it a shine and gloss.

❖ It can also improve hoof condition.

❖ Depending on the amount of water Linseed can either be fed as a jelly or a tea.

❖ Linseed oil can be purchased in bottles similar to normal vegetable oil. This, of course, saves a lot of time.

▲ It is **very poisonous** if not prepared properly.

▲ Linseed should always be fed sparingly, no more than 3 to 4 ozs of dried seed three times a week.

Peas/Beans

❖ Peas/Beans are rich in protein.

❖ They are fed split or crushed to horses in hard work.

❖ These legumes provide energy and help to maintain weight.

  ▲ Fed in excess peas and beans are heating and fattening, no more than about 1 lb. should be added to any one feed.

Molasses

Molasses is a by-product from the production of sugar; in appearance a dark, sticky syrup that looks like black treacle.

❖ It supplies energy and improves the condition of the coat.

❖ Small quantities only are needed and one teaspoon in warm water poured over the food is sufficient.

❖ Most commercial compound feeds include molasses in their ingredients.

❖ It has a very sweet taste, which tempts poor feeders or fussy eaters.

  ▲ Its palatability should not be used to encourage a horse to eat poor quality or stale food.

Sugar Beet

❖ Sugar Beet is a good source of energy and roughage.

❖ It is beneficial to horses doing longer, slower work as in riding schools or hacking.

❖ Sugar beet maintains weight and also, being a roughage food, adds bulk to the diet.

  ▲ Because it is relatively slow to digest, the bulk in the gut makes it an unsuitable food for horses doing fast work.

  ▲ Sugar beet comes in the form of shreds or cubes, both of which must be soaked thoroughly before being fed. If eaten dry, sugar beet will swell in the horse's stomach causing severe colic or even death. Sugar beet shreds are soaked in a double amount of water for 12 hours. The cubes need soaking in a triple amount of water for 24 hours.

  ▲ Cold water must always be used for the soaking. Though the beet does ferment even in cold water, hot water will make it ferment much more quickly.

  ▲ The pulp must also be kept cool, particularly on hot days, and fed within a few hours.

  ▲ Sugar beet needs feeding in small amounts, no more than 3 lbs soaked weight each day.

  ▲ It does have a laxative effect on some horses.

    Sugar beet cubes look very similar to horse and pony cubes. When stored they must be clearly labelled so that they are not fed by mistake. This could be fatal to a horse or pony.

Soyabean Meal

❖ Soyabean meal is extremely high in protein.

❖ An excellent addition to the feed for horses in hard work.

    ▲ It should be fed sparingly, no more than 1 lb. per day, as an excessive amount of protein can cause digestive problems.

Salt

❖ Salt is an essential part of the horse's diet. The chemical reactions that take place within the body actually occur in a salt solution.

❖ This mineral is provided as a salt lick or as rock salt in the manager.

❖ Blocks can be bought either unflavoured or with the addition of minerals or mint.

❖ Another method is to add one to four ounces to the feed each day.

❖ Salt is particularly important in the summer when horses are working hard. Water and salts are lost through sweating.

Compound Feeds

Over the past decade or so Feed Merchants have found equine nutrition commercially viable. Many manufacturers now employ professional nutritionists who research into a variety of foodstuffs for horses. The trend now is towards a food that is a complete and balanced mix of all the nutrients necessary to the horse. The great advantage of Compound food is that they are very simple to use. Instead of having to weigh and mix a variety of traditional feeds there is just one food to give very easily and quickly.

These 'compound foods' are split into two types-

1. **Nuts, cubes or wafers** - the ingredients are ground up, steamed and pelleted.

2. **'Coarse mix' - appears more as a traditional feed.**

There are various types of compound food. These are made up for horses and ponies of all ages, in all types of work and environment, even those who are ill and resting. For example; there are Competition Cubes or Performances Mixes for those horses in hard work and competing. Stud Cubes or Yearling Cubes are available for brood mares and foals. Convalescence Mixes or Cereal Meals are specifically for invalid horses out of work. Leaflets listing all the different types are available from local Feed Merchants.

Manufacturers use many different names for similar foods but there is no difference between one type of cube and its corresponding mix. For instance; a competition cube will have just the same nutritional value as a competition mix. The choice is based on the preference of the horse or owner.

Advantages of compound foods:

- ❖ Provides a constant, balanced diet.
- ❖ Easy to feed, especially when different members of staff make up the feeds.
- ❖ Easy to store, one bag of compound food instead of three or so bags of traditional foods.
- ❖ Easy to transport.
- ❖ Labour saving.
- ❖ Clean.
- ❖ Dust free.
- ❖ Palatable. Most of the compound foods include molasses.
- ❖ Always of good quality. Manufacturers keen to keep their good reputation make sure they buy the best foodstuffs, so the quality is guaranteed.
- ❖ Time saving, no mixing or weighing three of four different foods.
- ❖ Take away the 'guesswork' by providing one food for any type of horse.

Disadvantages of compound foods:

- ▲ Expensive unless ordered in bulk.
- ▲ The cubes or nuts, unless moistened or dampened, can be dry - risk of choking.
- ▲ Not easy to adjust. With a traditional food, such as oats, it is simple to increase the amount in the feed. With compound foods, (though it is possible to mix one sort of compound feed with another), a whole new bag would have to be bought to give the horse a different balance. This is awkward for large establishments that buy in bulk.
- ▲ They may be boring as a diet. This relates to the cubes or nuts; the mix certainly seems appetising. In any case it is hard to believe that an animal whose natural food is grass could find compound foods boring. Some horses may refuse to eat cubes or nuts but this is generally due to some ingredient in the cube.
- ▲ This food deteriorates when stored. This is true but so does all other foods when kept for any length of time.

Chaff, Mollichop (chaff with molasses) and sugar beet are often mixed in with a compound food but, according to the Manufacturers, it is inadvisable to add anything else such as oats or barley. This will cause an nutritional imbalance. All compound foods, except for those produced as mixers or supplements, are designed to be a complete meal including all the nutrients necessary.

Compound foods are extremely popular; most owners, grooms and stables feed these nowadays. They are a simple, balanced, complete diet that eliminates the labour-intensive and time-consuming part of making up traditional foods.

Cooked Foods

Some foods such as linseed must be cooked. For oats and barley steaming or boiling softens the grain and makes them easier to digest. Steaming is preferable; during boiling some nutrients are dissolved in the water and lost from the food.

Aged horses who have trouble chewing and digesting, invalid horses, tired or overworked horses or shy eaters can all be fed cooked foods. As can those who get little or no time at grass, in which case cooking their food can help to prevent constipation.

Oats

Ingredients.

- ♦   2 to 4 lbs. oats or quantity as required.

- ♦   Water: at a ratio of one part oats - two parts water.

- ♦   A teaspoonful of salt.

Method.

Boiled: Place the oats and water in a pan and bring to the boil. Continue boiling until the oats are soft. The mixture must be watched carefully in case it starts to burn. Add salt and leave until cool enough to eat.

(When boiled oats tend to absorb a lot of water. This can give the horse a fat, soft condition.)

Steamed: Put the oats into a large sieve and place this over the water in a pan. Cover the pan and boil the water gently until the oats are soft.

Cooked oats can be mixed with boiled barley, bran mash or other cooked foods.

Barley

Ingredients

- 2 to 3 lbs. of Barley or amount required.
- Water; ratio of one part barley and two parts water.
- A teaspoonful of salt.

Method

Boiled   Whole barley is boiled in a similar fashion to oats then allowed to simmer for 4 to 6 hours until the grains split and soften.

Mash   To make a mash use flaked barley. Place the barley into a bucket and pour on boiling water. Cover and leave until cool then add the salt. A barley mash can be fed to a horse after hard exercise, to fussy eaters and those that are underweight.

Cooked barley may also be mixed with cooked bran or oats.

Bran mash

Ingredients

- 2 to 4 lbs. bran or 2/3 of a bucket.
- Up to 1/3 of a bucket of boiling water.
- 2 ozs. limestone flour.

Method

Pour some of the boiling water onto the bran in the bucket. Stir and add more water if required. The bran should be damp and crumbly but *not too wet*. Cover and leave until cool enough to eat. To test for the right consistency, take a handful of bran when cool enough and squeeze it into a ball. This should hold its shape. Add limestone flour and linseed jelly, oats or boiled barley and salt if required.

Linseed Jelly

Ingredients

- 2 to 3 ozs. dried seed.
- 4 pints of water.

Method.

Cover the linseed with water and soak overnight. Then add the rest of the water to the linseed mixture and bring to the boil. Watch the linseed carefully as it can burn or boil over, if necessary add more water. Simmer for six hours and allow to cool. This will solidify into a jelly. Add linseed jelly to bran mash or other foods. To make linseed tea, simply add more water. Linseed must be properly cooked otherwise it is *very poisonous*. It can be cooked with other foods such as oats or barley, as long as the seeds are cooked thoroughly enough.

Oatmeal Gruel

Ingredients

- 2 handfuls of oatmeal.
- Boiling water.

Method

Place the oatmeal into a bucket and pour on boiling water until the mixture is the right consistency; either crumbly or wet enough to drink. Stir well and allow to cool. This gruel is particularly beneficial for an ill horse or one that has difficulty eating.

Some cooked foods can take quite a long time to prepare. Stables or yards who frequently feed cooked foods purchase slow cookers or Oat Boilers.

Exam Tips

During the session on feeding you will be handed, or asked to choose, a sample of food. You will then be questioned about the sample; asked to name it, describe it, to give its properties, advantages and disadvantages. You will also be asked to assess the quality. The examiner may probe further and ask when each type of food should be fed to a horse and in what quantity. There may be a general group discussion about the advantages of feeding traditional or compound feed and the reasons for these preferences.

Before the exam you will need to familiarise yourself with different foodstuffs and compare good and bad quality feed. Take particular notice of sugar beet cubes, make sure you know the difference between these and pony cubes.

A visit to the local feed merchant is useful; to look at the different feeds available. There are usually leaflets and booklets that you can take home and study at your leisure.

Do not, however, overload yourself with too much information. There is a bewildering selection of feeds and supplements, which can be confusing. Learning about the basic feeds and their properties as well as having an awareness of the varieties available is quite sufficient for the Stage I.

C H A P T E R   14

Hay and Haynets

Roughage is a vital part of the diet and should make up *at least 30% of the total daily food intake.* Hay, which is basically dried, cut grass, is mostly composed of fibre and provides the majority of roughage in the diet for stabled horses. It is the essential foundation of a good diet for horses living in all year round and for grass kept horses during autumn, winter and early spring. All hay should be of good quality; inferior hay should never be fed to horses or ponies.

Types of Hay

There are two types of hay, Seed hay and Meadow hay.

1. **Seed hay**
   - The grasses for this type of hay are sown as an annual crop and contain top quality plants such as rye grass.
   - Seed hay is nutritious, suitable for horses in hard work.
   - This hay is usually free of weeds and poisonous plants.
   - It is tougher than meadow hay and more difficult to digest.
   - It is more expensive than meadow hay.
   - It should be stored for at least six months to one year before use. New hay can cause digestive problems such as diarrhoea.

2. **Meadow hay**
   - This type of hay is cut from natural pasture.
   - The grasses are allowed to grow naturally, which means meadow hay usually contains a greater variety of plants.
   - It may also contain some inferior grasses.
   - The grass is allowed to go to seed before cutting. This gives a softer and sweeter hay, considered by some to be more palatable for the horse.
   - This hay is suitable for all horses.
   - It is less expensive than seed hay.
   - It should be stored for about six months before being fed.
   - Meadow hay is often greener than seed hay.

Hay Quality

All hay should be of good quality and it is important to be able to recognise good hay and to distinguish it from inferior grades.

	Good quality hay	Inferior Hay.
Smell	Clean, sweet, pleasant smell.	Sour, tangy, musty, damp and mouldy.
Colour	Varying from green-brown to golden-brown.	Colourless or dark brown to black. Watch out for hay that has white areas and black areas. This is 'mow-burnt' hay that has overheated in the rick; caused by baling before the stems are dry. Very green - the hay is too new to feed, and will cause digestive problems.
Feel	Dry and crisp.	Wet, damp, slimy, dusty.
Dust	It will be as free of dust as possible.	Dusty and powdery.
Content	Good quality grasses with no poisonous plants.	Inferior grasses, quantities of weeds and poisonous plants.
Taste (try the other tests first!)	Sweet and chewy.	Sour, musty and bitter.

To test the quality of hay; check the bale for colour, particularly at the edges where it may be mouldy, wet or black. Take some hay and smell it, check for texture and look for any poisonous plants or weeds.

The quality of hay depends on many variables such as; the **types of grasses** from which it is made, the **land and soil** on which it is grown, the farmer and his **standard of grassland management**, the **time of year** it is cut, **weather conditions** and how it is **stored**. Hay quality can vary from year to year depending on the weather.

Other Types of Forage

There are other methods of conserving grass which to some extent limit these variables. Their differences are dependent on the moisture quantity and the method of packaging.

Moisture content of different hay types

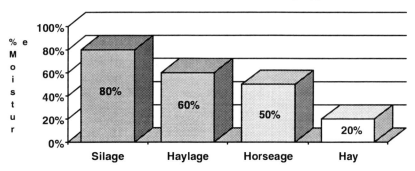

Vacuum-Packed Forage (usually known as HorseHage*)

HorseHage* is hay in a different form. (There are several different spellings of this name but they all refer to the same vacuum-packed semi-wilted grass.)

It is produced to combat the respiratory problems in horses caused by dust and fungal spores. It is completely dust free.

HorseHage is made up of the best quality grasses, usually ryegrass or alfalfa mixtures. It is always of a good quality unlike normal hay that can vary.

The grass is cut and baled within a matter of days so that it only partially dries. In comparison to hay, which is 80% dry, HorseHage is around 50% dry. The bales are compressed to half their size, then vacuum-packed and sealed to exclude air.

Fermentation takes place within the bale. This preserves the nutrient levels within the grass. It also gives HorseHage its rich golden colour, sweet smell and taste. Most horses love it.

HorseHage can either be fed straight away or, because it is vacuum-packed, kept up to a year or more. Once a bale is opened however, (even if accidentally torn), the HorseHage will deteriorate if not used within 5 days.

Though HorseHage provides the bulk in the diet, it is far more nutritious than normal hay and therefore is fed in smaller quantities. Even the concentrate quota may be reduced slightly except for horses in really hard work.

---

* HorseHage is the registered name of Marksway HorseHage.

It is excellent for fussy eaters, those doing faster work and, because it is dust free, for those with respiratory problems.

It is however more expensive than ordinary hay, usually about twice the price.

There are approximately five types of HorseHage on the market at present, but the two main ones are the Ryegrass or high protein HorseHage and low protein/high fibre HorseHage.

Haylage

This is often confused with HorseHage, but it is different. Haylage is very similar to Silage but with a lower moisture content; being approximately 40% dry. Sometimes haylage is fed to horses but it is not as popular as HorseHage. It usually comes in big bales that are not very easy to store, handle or transport.

Silage

This is not a popular feed for horses as deaths from Botulism after eating silage have been recorded, some very recently. However, a few establishments are experimenting with types of silage and may be feeding it with some success.

Silage is wilted grass, 25% dry, treated and sealed in large, airtight bags. Some silage includes additives that may not be suitable for horses.

How to Feed Hay

Hay can either be fed dry, moistened or wet. Whilst in most cases good quality hay may be fed dry quite satisfactorily, there are a number of horses and ponies who develop problems when given dry hay. Hay contains fungal spores which, when inhaled through the nostrils, can cause an allergic reaction. This may develop into ailments ranging from a simple cough with a discharge from the nostrils, to respiratory problems and damage to the lungs. In this case the hay should be dampened; some yards prefer to damp down all the hay.

When the hay is moistened, by soaking in water or steaming, the fungal spores swell so that they become too large to pass into the lungs. Also when wet, the spores tend to stick to the stems in the hay instead of being inhaled.

Soaking

Hay can be soaked for several hours or even overnight. However, some of the water-soluble nutrients are washed out of the hay and drain away with the excess water. Also, if left submerged for a long time, hay begins to smell sour and some horses refuse to eat it.

It is now considered that 20 minutes is sufficient. Tests have shown that this is ample time for soaking and fewer of the nutrients are lost.

Method

The hay is put into a haynet, placed into a container such as a plastic dustbin and water is poured over it from a hosepipe. Some yards have water tanks into which the whole bale is immersed.

Steaming

This is preferable as the nutrient loss is minimised. The haynet is placed in a rubber or plastic dustbin or tank, and boiling water is poured over it. The container is covered and the hay left to cool.

Haynets

There are different ways in which hay can be fed to horses in the stable or out in the field. Certainly in the box the most economical, convenient and hygienic method is from a haynet.

Haynets are available in a variety of sizes, colours and materials; from plain brown rope nets to brightly coloured nylon, with large or small holes. The decision as to which type to purchase, depends on the type of hay fed and the personal preference of the owner. Nets with smaller holes can be used to feed HorseHage as this makes the smaller proportions last longer.

Feeding hay in a net does have certain advantages over other methods:

* It is easier to weigh the hay, giving a more accurate calculation of feed.

* It is less wasteful than feeding hay off the floor and though the horse does drop some hay onto the ground this tends to stay clean and can be put back into the net.

* Haynets are easier to carry.

* It is convenient when travelling. Haynets can be used in trailers, horse boxes, or outside on a fence.

* The haynet can be used at varying heights to suit a horse or a pony.

* It is more hygienic, as it keeps hay off the floor yet does not allow spores or dust into the horse's eyes.

* Birds and vermin cannot live in it.

* Damping down or steaming hay is much more efficiently done in a haynet.

Haynets do have some disadvantages:

- The net can be heavy when the hay is wet. (Though wet hay is heavy whatever method is used.)

- If not correctly tied up, the net may become tangled around the horse's legs causing injury.

- Haynets can be damaged and need repairing or replacing.

How To Fill, Weigh And Tie Up

To fill a haynet

Gently shake and loosen a wedge or two of hay. Hold the net by the top and open the neck as wide as possible. If convenient, ask someone to hold the neck open while the hay is placed inside. Once the correct amount has been placed in the net, tighten the string.

Weighing

Weighing the haynet is relatively easy with the use of hanging scales. The scales are suspended from a nail or hook in a convenient spot and the haynet placed on the weighing hook.

Tying up a Haynet

The important point about tying up a haynet is to raise it *high enough, so that when empty the net does not hang too low.* If the empty net drops low enough there is a risk that the horse will trap a leg in the net either when rolling or pawing the stable wall.

The securing ring onto which the haynet is tied, should be about five feet above the level of the bed.

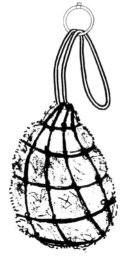

Pull the drawstring through the ring as far as possible.

Keep the net steady, by holding it with a hand or placing a knee beneath it, and place the end of the string through the lower part of the net.

Pull the string and draw the net up as high as possible, securing it with a quick release knot.

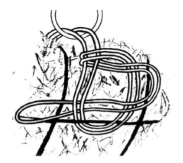

Twist the net around so that the knot is against the wall, preventing the horse from pulling the knot too tight or releasing the net.

The net must always be tied with a quick release knot then, if the horse does manage to become caught up, it can be unfastened quickly.

In the field a haynet must always be tied up safely; at a correct height with a quick release knot for exactly the same reason as in the stable.

Other Feeding Methods

There are other ways in which to feed hay to a horse and briefly these are:

Hayracks

In the box

A hayrack, usually made of metal bars placed high in a corner of the box, saves time as the hay can simply be placed into the rack. Racks are not used as much these days as there are certain disadvantages:

•   They tend to be positioned rather high up, making it quite difficult to put the hay in.

•   It is unnatural for a horse to feed in this position.

•   The height allows dust and spores to fall into the horse's eyes and nostrils when eating.

•   Old hay often gets left inside and goes mouldy.

•   Birds and vermin often use this as a nest.

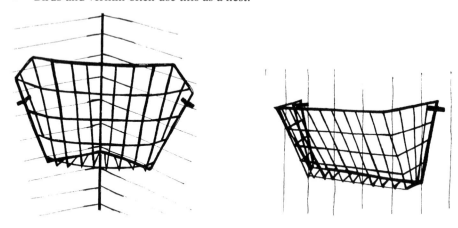

In the field

Here the hayrack is the most economical and efficient method of feeding hay. There are no problems providing the rack is **appropriately situated** in the field so that the **ground does not become poached.** It must also be a **horse feeding rack;** not a cow rack.

- The only disadvantage is that if one of the horses in the herd is a bully, he may prevent other horses feeding from the rack.

The Floor

In the box

Some yards prefer this method as it is **convenient, labour saving** and **more natural for the horse** to eat from the ground. It does have certain disadvantages:

- It causes a **lot of waste**. The horse mixes the hay up with the bedding and can stale on it.
- It may **encourage bed eating.**
- There is an increased possibility of **infestation by worms** as larvae from droppings can migrate to the food on the floor and be ingested.

In the field

This is certainly safer than haynets or hayracks, with the horses and ponies eating the hay quite simply off the ground. It can help to minimise fighting and bullying; several piles of hay can be placed separately from each other, allowing those horses further down the pecking order a chance of getting enough fodder.

- This method is wasteful, as the hay is kicked around the field, trampled on and left uneaten.

Exam Tips

In this section you may be asked to name the different types of hay and to recognise good and bad quality. You will also be asked to describe the various methods of feeding hay and how to fill and tie up a haynet. If there is a net available, one of the candidates will be asked to tie this up.

As part of the preparation for the exam, take a look at some hay, test its quality by appearance, feel and smell; compare this with HorseHage. Practise filling and tying up a haynet correctly, so that you gain practical experience and will not be worried if asked to do this in the exam.

C H A P T E R   15
Snaffle Bridle

A bridle is used to control the horse's pace, speed and direction. There are several different designs of bridles and bits that assist in achieving this control, such as the snaffle, pelham, kimblewick, the gag, the double and the bitless bridle. For the Stage I candidates need to know about the snaffle bridle; the various bits in the snaffle group and the different nosebands used in conjunction with this bridle.

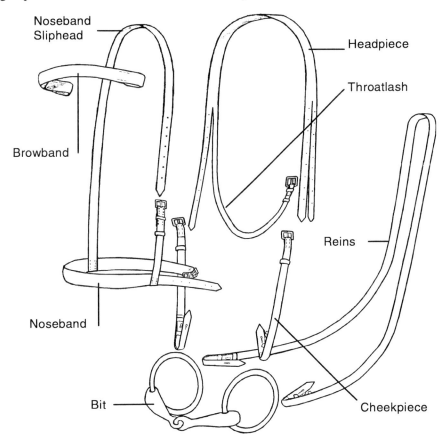

Figure 45: Points of the Snaffle Bridle.

Parts of the Bridle

A snaffle bridle consists of the bit, cheekpieces, headpiece, noseband and sliphead, throatlash, reins and browband.

Reins

The longest reins measure 5 feet, used mainly for show jumping or eventing. Normally reins measure 4 feet 6 inches with pony reins measuring 4 feet 3 inches. It is important that reins are of the **correct length**.

Reins that are too short will encourage the rider to lean forward in an incorrect position. Long reins are dangerous as they can become caught around the rider's foot and stirrup. This is particularly so for children on ponies

Reins are made from different materials depending on use or personal preference. Leather is the most popular and is available in plain, plaited or laced designs. Leather reins can also be covered with rubber. Other materials include webbing, nylon and linen.

Reins of plaited leather or those covered with rubber are more practical, particularly for jumping, eventing or in wet weather. These provide a firmer hold and help to prevent the reins from slipping through the fingers.

Browband

The browband is the part that fits around the front of the head, just below the ears. It is connected by loops to the headpiece and prevents the bridle from slipping backwards down the horse's neck.

Browbands are available either as plain leather or decorated with brass studs or fancy stitching. They can also be purchased wrapped in velvet ribbon in a variety of colours.

If the browband is too small it will cause discomfort and rubbing around the ears. Too large and it will flap or allow the bridle to slip backwards.

Headpiece

The headpiece, which fits over the head behind the ears, includes the throatlash and the straps to which the cheekpieces fasten.

When the cheekpieces are connected to the straps of the headpiece, the buckles should lie above the horse's eyes under the browband. Any lower would indicate that the bridle is too large or the cheekpieces too small. The buckles might also catch and damage the eye. The cheekpieces on both sides should also be of equal length so that the bit is level in the mouth.

Throatlash

The throatlash or throatlatch fits under the cheek and around the throat of the horse. This prevents the bridle coming off if, for some reason, it is pulled forwards.

Correct fitting should allow the horse to flex his neck without any restriction to his breathing. The handler should be able to get the *width of a hand* between the cheekbone and the throatlash.

The throatlash is fastened on the nearside of the horse's head.

The Bit

The bit is connected to the cheekpieces. If the cheekpieces are correctly fitted to the headpiece then the bit should be level in the mouth.

Mouthpieces are made from a variety of materials; stainless steel, chromium plated steel, pure nickel, copper, vulcanite, nylon, rubber and the more recent Nathe bit. This has a metal strip covered with a pale yellow, rubbery plastic.

Stainless steel is the strongest and the best.

Nickel	Recognised by its yellow appearance, Nickel is not used extensively because it is weak and tends to snap.
Vulcanite	Is rubber made stronger by heat treatment.
Rubber	Is kind to the horse's mouth but, because of its softness, can be bitten through.

Types of Snaffle Mouthpiece

There are three main types of snaffle mouthpiece:

Single Jointed

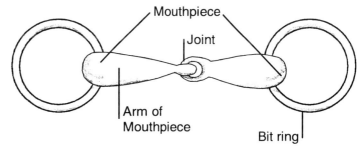

This bit has a single joint in centre of the mouthpiece. Bits with thick arms are generally milder than thin-armed bits though it can depend on the size of the horse's mouth. A horse with a small mouth can find a thick bit uncomfortable. *The single jointed snaffle has a 'nutcracker' action.*

Double Jointed

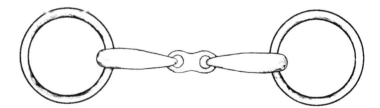

These bits have a link in the centre of the bit. The **French Link** is considered by some to be milder than the single jointed snaffle as it has no nutcracker action. The link lies flat on the tongue. The **Dr. Bristol**, on the other hand, is a very severe bit because of the angle of the link, which puts more pressure on the tongue.

Straight Bar and Mullen Mouth

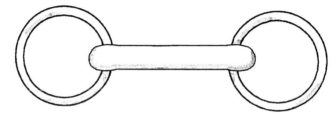

These have no joints and are the mildest form of bit. The **Mullen Mouth** has a slight half moon shape allowing more room for the tongue. These bits are often made from Vulcanite, or metal covered with rubber.

Ring Types

There are also a variety of rings that connect the bit to the bridle. The most popular are:

Loose Ring

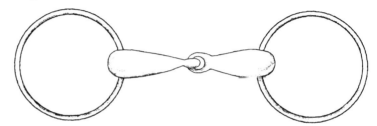

The loose ring snaffle has large rings that pass through holes at the end of the mouthpiece.

★ Because the bit moves more easily on the rings, it allows the smallest movement of the hands to be transmitted to the horse's mouth.

★ The loose ring allows the horse to 'mouth' or play with the bit without interference from the rider's hands.

★ A Loose or wire ring is useful on a young horse because it is more difficult for these rings to be pulled through an open mouth.

▲ Where the ring passes through the mouthpiece the metal can wear thin and become very sharp, sometimes cutting the horse's lips.

Eggbutt

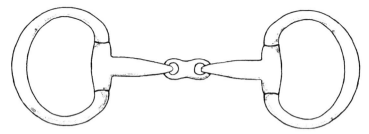

The mouthpiece is rounded and tapered onto the rings in the shape of a 'T'.

★ This type of ring, because of its shape, does not wear thin and eliminates the problem of cutting and pinching at the corner of the mouth.

▲ The eggbut is much less mobile and not suitable for a horse with a dry mouth or a fixed jaw.

▲ Because this design does not allow any movement between the ring and the mouthpiece, the bit itself can become more 'fixed' within the mouth, particularly if the rider is a novice or has strong hands.

D Ring

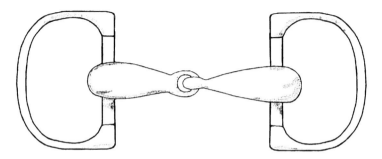

Named because the ring looks like a D.

★ Prevents the ring from being pulled through the mouth.

Bit Variations

The following are variations of the bit itself rather than the ring:

Loose Ringed Fulmer

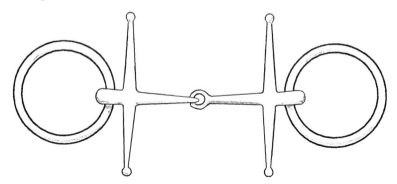

This bit has long cheekpieces. It is usually known as the 'Fulmer' or the 'Australian Loose ringed snaffle'. The cheekpieces should be fitted into keepers attached to the bridle to hold the bit in place.

★   Good for young horses or those who open the mouth as the cheekpieces prevent the bit from being pulled through.

★   The 'cheeks' help to steer the horse by pressing on the opposite side of the mouth.

★   This is considered to be suitable for riding school horses as it lessens the effect of novice hands on the horse's mouth.

▲   Some horses learn to evade this bit by 'leaning' on the long cheek pieces.

Full Cheek Snaffle

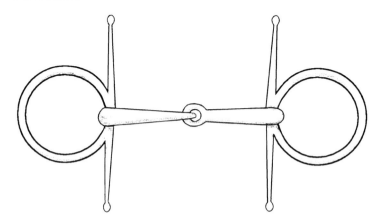

This is similar to the Loose Ringed Fulmer except the cheekpieces are part of the ring.

★   Good for young horses as in the Fulmer.

▲   This bit can tend to have a more fixed and less mobile action.

There are other sorts of snaffle that have cheek pieces but the above two are the most popular.

Nosebands

There are types of noseband which, being fitted at varying heights on the horse's face, have different functions. The sliphead is the slim strap placed under the headpiece and through the loops of the browband to connect the noseband to the bridle.

Cavesson Noseband

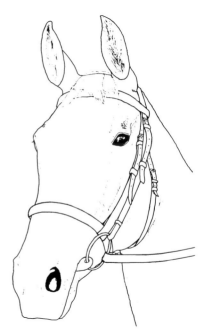

This is the commonest type in use and consists of a plain noseband and sliphead. Usually made of leather, it fits around the horse's face below the cheekbones.

Its use is mainly cosmetic, giving the horse's face a better appearance by foreshortening the length. It is also used in conjunction with the standing martingale, almost the only noseband to do so apart from the Flash.

Fit

When fitted correctly the noseband should lie *two fingers width* below the projecting cheek bone and have *two fingers width* between it and the horse's face. This is checked by placing two fingers between the nose band and the horse's nasal bone on the front of his face.

Figure 46: Cavesson Noseband.

Flash

This is a cavesson noseband with a loop attached at the centre through which a thin strap is passed - *the flash strap*. This strap goes *below* the bit, round into the chin groove. Both the cavesson part and the flash strap are fastened firmly. This is to prevent the horse evading the bit by crossing its jaw or opening its mouth.

The flash was originally designed to combine the properties of the cavesson and drop noseband. A standing martingale could theoretically be attached to the top portion.

Fit

The cavesson part is placed in the same position as the normal cavesson but fastened slightly tighter. The flash strap must be four fingers width above the nostril to prevent restricting the horse's breathing. The tightness of the flash must allow room for one finger to fit underneath. Its purpose is to prevent the horse from opening his mouth. The buckle should **not** be fastened in the chin groove or around the lips in case it injures the horse.

Figure 47: Flash Noseband.

Drop noseband

The front portion, between the sliphead straps, is similar to a narrow cavesson and fits over the front of the nose. The lower straps, those to the back, are connected by rings to the sliphead, pass below the bit and into the chin groove.

Fit

The frontal strap should not be fastened too low. There should be *four fingers width* above the nostrils.

The Drop straps should be fastened *tightly enough* to prevent evasion, but not so tightly as to clamp the mouth shut or impede breathing. There should be enough room for one finger's width between the drop strap and the horse's face. The buckle ideally should not be fastened in the chin groove or interfere with the lips.

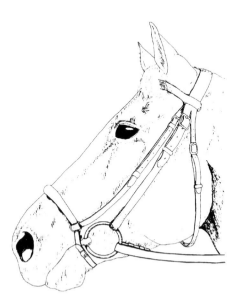

Figure 48: Drop Noseband.

Grakle

This consists of two straps of leather crossing over the front of the nose. There should be a small leather pad lined with sheepskin where the straps cross to prevent chafing on the horse's face.

The Grakle prevents the horse opening his mouth or crossing the jaw but, in acting over a larger area of the head and the pressure point on the nose, it has a stronger effect.

Fit

The top straps are connected to the sliphead and fasten behind the jaw. The position of these straps is slightly higher than a cavesson, just below the protruding cheek bone. The lower straps fit below the bit and in the chin groove, similar to the flash.

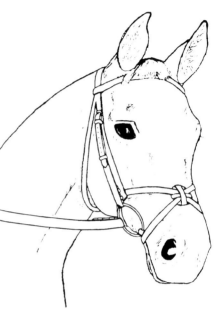

Figure 49: Grakle Noseband.

Sheepskin Noseband

This covers a cavesson and its purpose is to keep the horse's attention from straying by focusing it forward. This is used mainly for racehorses.

These are the nosebands in normal use. A snaffle bridle can be used without a noseband but this tends to make the horse's face look long.

Putting on and Fitting the Bridle

If the bridle is not the horse's own, then a quick assessment of fit is made first before the bridle is put on.

1. The horse should first be tied up in a head collar and lead rope.

2. With the headpiece held in the right hand and the bit in the left, the bridle is held against the side of the horse's face in approximately the position it would be when put on. This is a quick guide. If the bridle is either too long or too short, it can easily be altered by changing the length of the cheek pieces.

3. When the bridle appears to be the right size, prepare it by removing all the straps from the runners and keepers. These are the loops in which the straps are held, the keepers are the static loops, the runners those that move. This makes any alterations much easier once the bridle is on the horse.

4. The reins are placed over the horse's head. The headcollar is undone and refastened around the horse's neck. **At this point the lead rope should be unfastened and left hanging through the string to prevent injury should the horse pull back.**

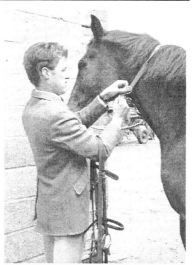

Figure 50: Headcollar is undone and refastened.

5. With the bridle in the left hand, the right arm passes under the horse's head, round to the offside and is positioned about half way down the front of the horse's face.

6. The bridle is now passed to the right hand and held a little below the browband. Some horses have a tendency to raise their heads, evading the bridle and bit, if so press heavily with the right hand on the horse's nose and speak to him firmly.

Figure 51: Bridle in the left hand, the right arm passes under the horse's head.

7. Cradling the bit in the left hand, between the thumb and the second two fingers to hold it apart, place it on the horse's lips. He should open his mouth. If he does not, place the left thumb in the side of the horse's mouth. The horse has a space between the incisor (front teeth) and the molars (back teeth) where the bit normally lies. If the horse still refuses to open his mouth, wiggle the thumb, touch the top palate or depress the tongue.

8. Once his mouth is open, gently slide the bit in, at the same time raising the bridle with the right hand. Holding the bridle steady, gently fold the ears under the headpiece and tease the forelock forward.

9. The throatlash can be fastened and the fit checked by placing a hand widthways between it and the horse's cheek.

10. A cavesson noseband can be fastened and checked for fit. Other nosebands remain unfastened until the bit has been checked.

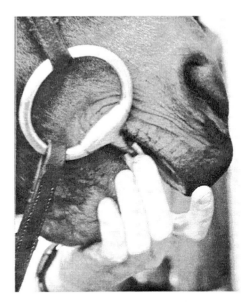

Figure 52: Gently slide the bit in.

The Bit

Position

When the bit is in the correct position, it should just cause a wrinkle at the corners of the mouth; as though the horse is grinning. If it is too low it will bang on his incisor teeth. Too high and it will be uncomfortable, causing damage to the lips or coming into contact with the molar teeth.

The cheekpieces must be fastened equally on both sides, buckles in the same number holes of the headpiece, so that one side of the bit is not higher than the other.

Size

The width of the bit can be assessed by straightening it within the horse's mouth and placing the tip of each thumb on either side by the horse's lips. There should just be the width of the thumb tip between the lips and the bit rings, approximately a quarter of an inch either side of the mouth. If the bit is too narrow it will pinch the lips or the ring itself will be pulled through the mouth. Too wide and the bit will be uncomfortable, the action within the mouth incorrect.

Once the bit has been checked and fitted, the noseband can be fastened.

Any alterations to the bridle whilst it is on the horse should be done gently and quietly. Once the fit is correct all the straps can be replaced into the runners and keepers.

If the horse is not be used immediately, the bridle is made safe by twisting the reins around each other several times and then by fastening one rein up inside the throatlash. This prevents the horse from getting a leg caught through the loose reins. The headcollar can be replaced and fastened over the bridle and the leadrope fastened with a quick release knot.

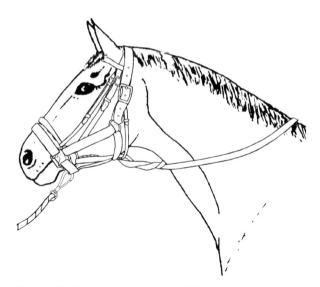

Figure 53: Headcollar over bridle and reins twisted.

Removing the Bridle

Place the headpiece of the headcollar around the horse's neck and fasten the buckle. The leadrope hangs loose through the string on the securing ring.

Unfasten the noseband and throatlash first. Take the reins in the right hand and bring them to the headpiece by the horse's poll. Then, standing in front of the horse, with both hands hold the headpiece and reins either side of the horse's head adjacent to the browband. Gently ease the bridle over the ears.

Slowly lower the bridle. The horse should open his mouth and let the bit slip out. The bridle should never be pulled off roughly or too quickly, as the bit will bang the horse's teeth. Replace the headcollar and tie the leadrope up with a quick release knot.

Note. When tacking a horse up, the bridle should be put on first and then the saddle. When untacking, the saddle is removed first and then the bridle.

Running Martingale

The running martingale is used to prevent the horse from raising or tossing his head beyond the point of control and evading the bit.

Description

This is a 'Y' shaped leather strap with a loop at one end which attaches to the girth. Each of the two thinner straps has a metal ring through which the reins pass. A neck strap, connected via a rubber ring, keeps the martingale in place.

Functions

1. Prevents the horse from raising his head above the level of control.

2. Prevents the horse from tossing his head from side to side.

3. Lessens the involuntary movements from a novice rider's hands.

4. Useful in the training of some young horses.

5. Keeps the reins in place and allows some control in difficult circumstances.

Putting on

Hold the martingale with the buckle of the neck strap on the left hand side, the two straps in front of the rubber ring and the girth loop behind. Now place the neck strap over the horse's head onto the neck. Undo the reins at the buckle and thread each rein through the appropriate ring. Check that there are no twists in the reins and refasten. Each rein must have a rubber stop positioned in front of the martingale ring, to prevent the ring from slipping forward and interfering with the bit. Before fastening the saddle girth, pass the girth loop between the horse's fore legs and pull the girth through the loop.

Fitting

There should be one hand's width between the neck strap and the horse. If the neck strap is too tight it will restrict breathing. Too loose and it will allow the martingale to hang down; it is possible the horse may catch a front leg in the straps.

The girth loop should be central under the horse's belly and flat against the skin; if it is twisted and bent it may rub or pinch.

Check the fitting of the two straps before the reins are passed through the rings. Holding the straps either side of the horse, the rings should just reach the level of the withers. Alternatively, measure the straps by taking them towards the angle of the horse's jaw. With the horse's head in its normal position, the rings should just reach the throat.

If the straps are too short the resulting downwards pull will interfere with the action of the reins. The constant pressure on the bit could also damage the horse's jaw. The two straps may, on occasion, be fitted a little shorter but never more than one hand's width below the withers. The martingale should come into effect only when the horse lifts his head above the angle of control. *It must never restrict the horse's normal action.* If the straps are too long, the martingale will have little effect.

Cleaning the Tack

It is imperative that all tack is clean. Dirty tack causes endless problems for the horse and rider. As well as being uncomfortable and distressing to the horse, dirty tack can cause sores, galls, open wounds, infections, blood poisoning or tetanus. The horse may even end up 'tack shy'. Dirty tack deteriorates, quickly becoming worn and unsafe. All tack should be cleaned after use and have a complete strip down about once a week.

Cleaning is divided into two categories - the 'after exercise' or quick clean and the weekly thorough clean.

After Exercise Clean

The 'after exercise clean' removes dirt, grease, dust, mud and sweat from the surface of the leather. The equipment needed is saddle soap in a bar or tin, a sponge or soft cloth and warm water.

Bridle

It is easier if the bridle is suspended from a cleaning hook. Remove all the straps from the keepers and runners. Wipe the leather thoroughly with a *damp* sponge so that all the dirt is removed. Now wipe the slightly damp sponge over the saddle soap. Avoid creating a lather as this will stain the leather. Rub the sponge over the bridle, pushing the saddle soap into the grain.

The bit is washed in clean water, including particularly the areas around the rings and the joints. Saddle soap should not be used on the bit.

Saddle

The saddle is cleaned after use with the saddle soap and sponge. The numnah is removed and all areas, under the flaps, girth straps and linings given a quick clean. The stirrups can be wiped over and any mud removed.

This type of cleaning should be done every time the bridle and saddle are used but at least once a day.

Girths

A dirty girth causes sores, infections and girth galls. Grit and mud are kicked up from the horse's hooves onto the girth area, so it is particularly important to clean this part of the tack every time it is used.

Girths can be cleaned either by wiping over with a damp cloth or, for leather girths, with a little saddle soap. Most synthetic girths can be washed in the washing machine. All types of girth must be completely dry before use.

Thorough Clean

Once a week the tack should be thoroughly cleaned. This involves stripping it down completely and systematically washing and cleaning all the leather and metal work.

Bridles are taken apart, each piece cleaned separately and the bit washed in clean water. The bridle is reassembled with all the buckles replaced into the correct holes.

Saddles should have their girths, stirrups and stirrup leathers removed, together with the buckle guards. Every part is thoroughly cleaned, including the underneath parts of the skirt, flap, girth straps and linings.

Girths and numnahs should be washed and thoroughly dried.

All metal work, apart from the bit, can be cleaned with a metal fluid.

Once every six to eight weeks the leather will need to be oiled or worked over with a leather dressing. A new bridle may need two or three dressings of oil to make it soft and pliable.

The tack is inspected for any rotten stitching, splitting leather, holes, thin metal work and wear to the bit.

Care of Tack

Bridle

The bridle should always be stored on its bridle holder.

To hang it neatly, pass the throatlash round the front of the bridle, through the reins and around the front again, fastening it to its corresponding strap. This will prevent the reins dragging on the floor and getting dirty. Fasten the noseband around the whole of the bridle to keep everything in place.

Bridles may be carried by placing the headpiece and reins over one shoulder.

Saddle

The saddle should always be handled carefully. When not in use the saddle should be placed on a saddle rack in a cool, well ventilated, dry position. When carrying a saddle, it is easier to carry it on the forearm with the pommel at the elbow. The saddle should never be placed flat on the floor or left lying in damp areas, near extreme heat or in the reach of horses.

Exam Tips

For the examination you should know the parts of the bridle and have a basic understanding of their function. You should be able to recognise and name different snaffle bits. If by some chance in the exam you are questioned about a bit that is unknown to you, do not panic. Instead describe the type of mouthpiece, the thickness of the bit and severity, ring attachments if any and presence or absence of cheeks. You should be familiar with each type of noseband and be able to fit them correctly.

You must be capable of putting on and taking off a bridle and of assessing the fit of the bridle, bit and appropriate noseband. Before the exam inspect both good and ill fitting tack so that you learn the points that need to be noticed. Do this several times until you are confident with all types of tack and its relevant fitting. The examiners may also question you about cleaning, care and storage of bridles and bits.

C H A P T E R   16
Saddlery

Saddles

There are various designs of saddle used for different purposes, such as the showing saddle, child's saddle, side saddle, the long distance, western and racing saddle. These have special features according to their use. However for Stage I, candidates need only refer to the three main types.

The 'General Purpose saddle', as the name implies is used for all types of activities, dressage, show jumping or cross country. The other two are specialist saddles, namely the 'Dressage' and the 'Jumping' Saddle.

General Purpose Saddle.

This is the most popular type of saddle for work where there is a combination of disciplines, such as schooling and hacking, when jumping may be included. It is also very useful for riding schools where a variety of work is performed.

The general purpose saddle has a medium cut flap, that is the flap is cut neither too straight nor too forward, allowing the rider to take up a position for flat work or jumping.

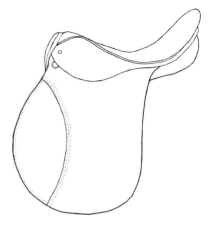

Figure 54: General Purpose Saddle.

Dressage Saddle

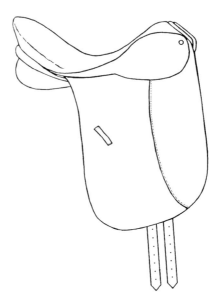

Figure 55: Dressage Saddle.

The Dressage saddle is used solely for flatwork. It features a straight cut flap encouraging the correct position of the leg and allowing a closer contact with the horse's side. In some dressage saddles this is further enhanced by having long girth straps which fasten to a short girth. This girth, called a Lonsdale, fastens on each side of the horse's belly, not under the saddle. The Dressage saddle usually features a deeper seat.

Figure 56: Leg Position ~ Dressage.

Jumping saddle

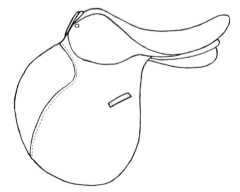

Figure 57: Jumping Saddle.

The flaps for this saddle are more forward-cut, allowing the rider's knee to be bent. There are usually knee and thigh rolls that help to keep the leg in place. The seat is flatter allowing the rider's body to move into the fold position.

Figure 58: Leg Position ~ Jumping.

Structure of Saddle and Material Used

The saddle is based on the **'tree'** usually made of **laminated beech plywood** but it can be constructed of other materials such as **plastic or fibreglass**. Bands of **webbing** are stretched along the tree and onto this framework is placed the **stuffing** and the **leather seat**. The stuffing can be made of **wool, felt, foam rubber** or other similar material. The **stirrup bars** are then attached to the tree.

Saddles are usually made of leather, which has many excellent qualities. It is hard wearing, durable, strong and easily cleaned. The new synthetic saddle is gaining in popularity being lightweight, comfortable to ride on, easy to clean and relatively inexpensive to buy.

Points of a Saddle

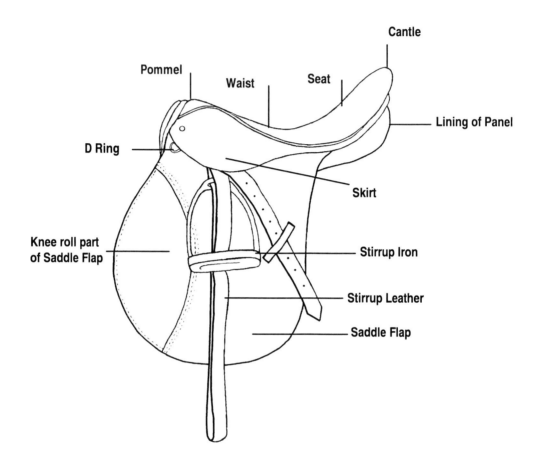

Cantle

Pommel

Waist

Seat

Lining of Panel

D Ring

Skirt

Knee roll part
of Saddle Flap

Stirrup Iron

Stirrup Leather

Saddle Flap

Figure 59: (a) Points of the Saddle.

The **pommel** is the front of the saddle, above the withers.

The **seat** is the part on which the rider sits.

The **waist** is the narrowest part of the seat.

The **cantle** is the rear part of the seat.

The **skirt** is the flap that covers the stirrup bar.

The **stirrup bars** are pieces of metal, one each side of the saddle, from which the stirrups are suspended. These can either be **open ended or have a latch**. This latch, in normal circumstances, remains open allowing the stirrup leather to slip off. This is designed to prevent a fallen rider from being dragged if his foot is caught in a stirrup.

At other times the latch can be turned up, to keep the stirrup and strap in place. This is necessary when the horse is not being ridden - for instance in lungeing or with the led horse in Ride and Lead. *The latch must never be turned up when the horse is being ridden.*

The **saddle flaps** cover the side panels and girth straps. These flaps should be large enough for the rider's legs and the correct shape for the type of saddle.

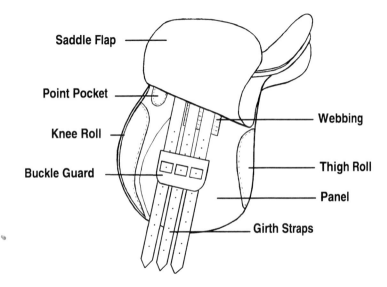

Saddle Flap

Point Pocket

Knee Roll

Buckle Guard

Webbing

Thigh Roll

Panel

Girth Straps

Figure 60: (b) Points of the Saddle.

The **panels** are the bearing surface on the horse's back and sides. The panels in contact with the horse's back are usually stuffed with wool or felt. The panels on the sides are normally thin so that the rider's legs can come into closer contact with the horse. A portion at the front can be stuffed to provide a **knee roll** and at the back, a **thigh roll.** Some side panels are cut short and fully stuffed. This **'half panel'** design is usually used for pony saddles.

There is sometimes a **sweat flap** between the side panel and the **girth straps**.

The **girth straps** are connected to the saddle by webbing strips. Most saddles have three straps, but on some dressage saddles there are only two.

There should be a **buckle guard** which fits onto the girth straps, protecting the saddle flap from marking or damage caused by the girth buckles.

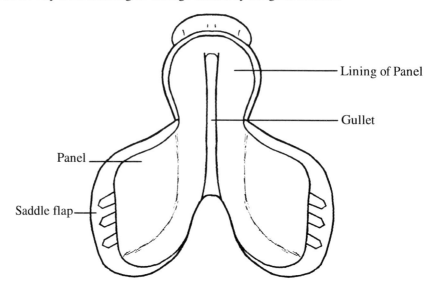

Lining of Panel

Gullet

Panel

Saddle flap

Figure 61: (c) Points of the Saddle.

The **Lining** is the underneath covering of the panels. This is usually made of leather, which is easy to clean and durable if kept correctly. Other materials can be used such as linen or serge, and whilst these are soft and comfortable for the horse they are not as hard wearing or as easy to clean as leather.

Assessing the Condition of a Saddle

The saddle should be regularly checked for condition. This can be done once a week when it is thoroughly cleaned.

The saddle should be inspected for any holes, cracked or split leather. This is particularly important in areas that are potentially vunerable, such as the girth straps and the webbing to which the straps are connected. If the girth straps are worn or split, or have become insecure around the webbing area, the saddle should not be used. Make sure that both sides of the saddle are checked; the nearside and the offside.

The underneath panels should be checked for any lumps or hard areas that may cause the horse discomfort. The side panels are inspected for any holes, split leather or cracks.

The girth is checked for frayed areas, splits, holes or broken buckles. If there is any problem that could make the girth unsafe then it should not be used.

Checking for a broken tree

Occasionally saddles are accidentally dropped or trodden on, which may result in a broken tree. The tree is checked by holding the pommel against the stomach and pulling the cantle forwards towards the pommel with both hands. The movement felt in the saddle should be slight. If there is excessive movement or any noise, the tree is broken. The saddle should not be used.

The Pommel

To test the pommel, rest this part of the saddle on the knee and holding both sides flex the pommel inwards and outwards. Any movement, creaking or clicking noises would indicate that the front arch is broken.

Putting on a Saddle

The bridle is put on first and the headcollar over the top. The horse is then restrained with the headcollar and lead rope.

First check that the stirrups are run up the leathers correctly and secured; the stirrups must not slip down and bang the horse.

The girth can be removed and placed on the handler's shoulder for convenience. This is safer for a Lonsdale or short girth that tends to flap around and hit the horse's side when the saddle is placed on top. Most girths can be left fastened to the offside straps and laid over the top of the saddle, as long as they are secure and will not slip.

Pat the horse on the neck and continue to stroke along his back. This smoothes down the hair and prepares the horse for the saddle. There is nothing more off-putting for a horse than to have a heavy saddle dumped on his spine without warning.

Place the saddle gently on the withers and slide it backwards until it lies in the correct position, with the pommel just behind the withers. Again sliding the saddle back encourages the hair to lie in the direction of the coat. Do not allow the saddle to slip too far back into the delicate loin area.

If the girth is completely detached from the saddle, walk around the front of the horse to the offside and fasten the girth onto the straps. Check that the panel and buckle guard are lying flat. Gently place the girth so that it is hanging down by the horse's side.

Return to the nearside, via the *front* of the horse, pat his shoulder and crouch down to reach the girth. Gently fasten the girth onto the straps on the nearside. Watch for any reaction from the horse; some can be quite sensitive. Check that no part of the saddle is bent under or twisted.

The girth should be fastened to the same two straps on each side. These should either be the first and second girth strap or the first and third, *never the second and third*. These straps are attached to the saddle by the same webbing and, should this be damaged or come away from the saddle, then the girth will give way.

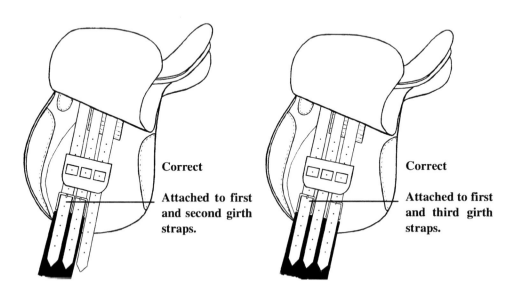

Correct

Attached to first and second girth straps.

Correct

Attached to first and third girth straps.

Figure 62: Correctly Fastened Girth.

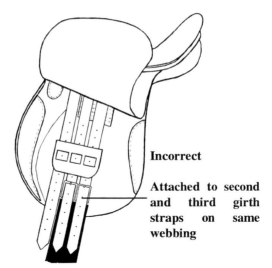

Incorrect

Attached to second and third girth straps on same webbing

Figure 63: Incorrectly Fastened Girth.

The girth is tightened gently. This is normally done on the nearside but to prevent the girth being higher on one side than another; it can be tightened on the offside. Ideally the buckles should be on the same number hole on each side and, when the girth is tight, should reach halfway up the straps.

The girth is sufficiently tight when the rider can *just* fit the flat of the hand between the girth and the horse. The girth must always be rechecked five to ten minutes after starting the ride. Some horses are masters at expanding their girth area and it is amazing how much tighter the girth can be fastened.

If the girth is on the very top holes before work commences then the girth is too long and MUST NOT BE USED.

If the girth only just reaches the lowest holes on either side then it is too short. It will be difficult trying to tighten the girth later and if the leather around the hole splits the saddle will no longer be secure.

Checking the Fit of a Saddle

When checking the fit of a saddle, a numnah should NEVER be used.

Size

Check the **size** first. Ask someone to hold the horse; stand back from the nearside and take a general look at the saddle. It should be immediately obvious if the saddle is **too small** or **too big** for the horse.

Too long a saddle will stretch back over the loin area and possibly damage the kidneys.

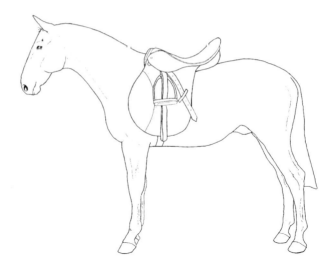

Figure 64: Saddle too large.

Too large and the saddle flaps and the panels underneath will encroach forward onto the shoulder area restricting the horse's movement. The horse will not have the freedom to move his shoulder properly.

Too short and the rider's weight will not be distributed evenly over the horse's back but concentrated in one area. This may lead to the development of sore pressure points. The saddle flaps will also be *too small for the size of the rider.*

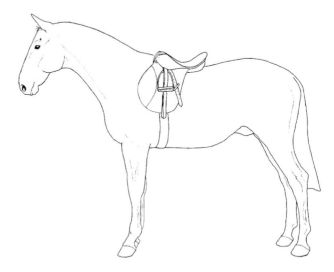

Figure 65: Saddle too small.

The cantle should be slightly higher than the pommel, (but only slightly or the rider will be tipped forwards into an incorrect position). If it is lower, the saddle is too flat for the horse's shape in which case the gullet will not have enough clearance from the backbone. This will encourage the rider to sit too far back, placing her in an incorrect position and possibly bruising the horse. The saddle may simply just not fit or may need re-stuffing. A professional saddler or tack shop would be able to tell if the saddle needs re-stuffing.

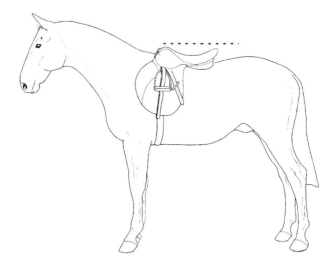

Figure 66: Cantle too flat.

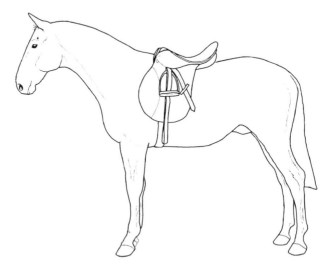

Figure 67: Correctly fitted saddle.

The Fit

Now an assessment of the saddle is made in specific areas.

The most important point to check is the space between the saddle and the horse's spine. There are two areas to look at,

1.   The front at the withers.

1.   From behind the horse along the gullet of the saddle.

The Withers

The pommel of the saddle should be **four fingers width** above the withers with *a rider mounted.*   If, therefore, the pommel does not have *at least* four fingers' clearance above the withers, without the rider on top, then it certainly will not fit.

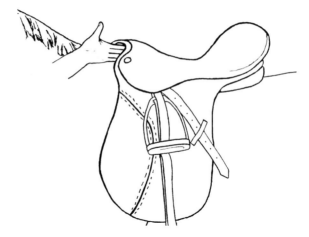

Figure 68: Checking Pommel Clearance.

Check this by inserting the fingers under the pommel between it and the horse's backbone. If there is less than the width of four fingers, the saddle will certainly come into contact with the horse's spine when a rider mounts and flattens it. Pay particular attention to that part of the gullet just behind the pommel. This area sometimes dips and comes into close contact with the horse's spine.

Now check for pinching either side of the withers around the shoulder area. Feel with the tips of the fingers between the panels and the top of the horse's shoulders. The saddle should fit snugly but smoothly. If it is tight and pinching the horse's skin, the saddle is too narrow. If it is too wide, almost certainly the saddle will be too low on the horse's back.

Finally, check for movement of the saddle. Holding the cantle, lift it gently up and down. If the girth is tightened sufficiently there should only be a slight movement. If the saddle can be raised to a large degree it is too wide. This will allow excessive movement when the horse is ridden, making the saddle bang down on the horse's back, particularly with rising trot.

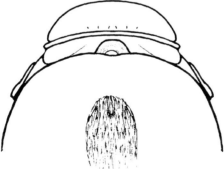

Now move to the back of the horse carefully, to avoid being kicked, and from the hindquarters look along the gullet of the saddle. There should be a clear space all along.

If the saddle comes into contact with the horse's spine at any point it will cause damage and result in pressure points. These are areas of rubbing and bruising causing lumps, soreness and possible ulceration.

Check also from the hindquarters that the saddle is sitting straight on the back. It should not slant or tilt to one side. More pressure will be applied on this side and the rider will be forced to sit incorrectly.

In Use

If everything is satisfactory, it is correct to ask that someone rides the horse. Once the rider is mounted assess again the space between pommel, gullet and the horse's spine.

The saddle should now be checked from all angles whilst the horse is in movement, to see that it stays quite secure. Particular notice should be taken from the back with the rider in rising trot; the saddle should not swing from side to side or bounce up and down. There must be no excessive movement on the horse's back, as this will cause chafing and bruising.

Incorrectly Fitting Saddles

The perils of an ill fitting saddle are numerous and can be long lasting. Because the saddle is in close proximity to the spine, a very vulnerable part, any discrepancy in the fit could result in problems. These can range from bruising around the spinal area, sores, galls, misalignment of the spine and a 'cold back' that can last a lifetime.

A horse that has a 'cold back' is one who has probably suffered pain from an ill fitting saddle in the past. He may be extremely difficult to tack up, suffer discomfort and become awkward when mounting.

Correct fitting is essential for the mental and physical health of the horse, his freedom of movement, the comfort and correct positioning of the rider. The last point is relevant because any constant incorrect position of the rider can give the horse a sore back and pressure points.

Numnahs and Saddle cloths

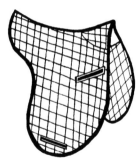

Figure 69: Numnah.

Figure 70: Saddle Cloth.

In theory a numnah or saddle cloth is unnecessary with a well-fitted saddle but most riders prefer to use one, believing that they are kinder and more comfortable on a horse's back. They also help to keep the saddle clean.

There are however, a variety of circumstances in which they are useful;

- If the horse's back is 'soft'. This is usually after a period off work when the saddle has not be used for some time.

- If the horse's shape has changed. This again may be after a period off work and is a temporary measure until the horse regains his normal muscular physique.

- If the saddle does not fit correctly, for example when it needs re-stuffing. (This must be corrected as quickly as possible.)

- If using another saddle for a short period. This situation must also be amended as quickly as possible. A numnah should not be used to ease the problems of an ill-fitting saddle.

- If the rider is a learner or novice and does not sit quietly in the saddle.

- In long distance, endurance riding or when the horse is ridden for any length of time.

- With a deep seated saddle that concentrates the rider's weight in a small area.

- With a 'cold-backed horse' to help lessen his fear and to provide a warm, comfortable covering under the saddle.

Putting on the Numnah or Saddle Cloth

The numnah or saddle cloth can either be put on the horse's back separately before the saddle or attached to the saddle first.

If separate, place the numnah on the withers and gently slide it backwards to lay the hair. Place the saddle on top and pull the front of the numnah or cloth well up into the pommel of the saddle. Take the numnah loop under the first girth strap and fasten it around the second strap. This keeps the numnah in place.

Then, picking up both numnah and saddle again, place them forward on the horse's withers and slide back into the correct position. *Make absolutely sure that the numnah stays well up into the gullet of the saddle.* If there is another loop at the bottom of the numnah, pull the girth through or, in the case of a dressage saddle, pull the long girth straps through.

If the numnah is already attached to the saddle, check that the fastenings are correct and secure. Then holding the numnah well up into the gullet, place both the saddle and the numnah onto the horse's withers and slide backwards into position. Once the saddle and numnah are in the correct position, it is now time to check the fit.

A numnah is cut closely following the shape of a saddle. When it is the correct size it will be approximately an inch larger than the size of the saddle all round.

A saddle cloth is usually a square or oblong shape and should be larger than the saddle. It should not be so large as to interfere with the rider when he tries to use his legs or whip.

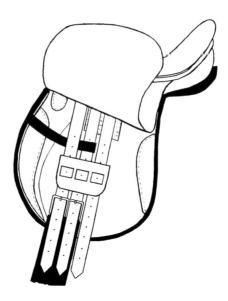

Figure 71: Numnah attached to Saddle.

Untacking the Saddle

Secure the stirrups by pulling the leathers through the irons. Restrain the horse with a headcollar and lead rope.

Unfasten any attachments such as a breastplate. Unbuckle the girth gently on the nearside and allow it to hang down. The girth should not be dropped or it may hit the horse's leg. Any martingale loop should now be slipped off the girth.

Walk around the front of the horse to the right side and fold the girth over the seat of the saddle, otherwise the girth will scrape across the back when the saddle is removed.

Return to the nearside and take hold of the pommel in the left hand, the cantle in the right. Slide the saddle backwards slightly to lay the hair. Then raise the saddle cleanly above and off the horse's back. *It should never be dragged across the spine.* Pat the horse's back to help restore circulation.

The saddle must be placed in a safe spot where it will not be damaged, preferably stored away on a saddle rack. If placed onto the floor for a short while, it is laid gently down pommel first with the girth underneath, and the cantle resting against a wall. If the saddle is incorrectly placed or stored it will become damaged.

Exam Tips

Candidates will be requested to put a saddle on a horse and to comment on the fit. You may be asked to do this individually or in pairs. You should be able to show how to check the fit and to explain your assessment.

When approaching the horse to check the saddle, remember to do this correctly. It is so easy in an exam to become pinpointed on the task in hand and forget the basic rules. The examiners will understand but it will create a good impression if you treat the horse as you would normally.

Whilst checking the fit of the saddle, if at any point you feel that the saddle does not fit the horse, this must be pointed out. Do not be afraid to say what you think but at the same time do not criticize for the sake of it. If it is possible, and there is time, make a quick check of the saddle before it is put on. Look underneath at the condition of the panels and linings.

In the examination, after the check has been made on the horse, you may state that the saddle should now be assessed with a rider on top. This will probably not be possible in the exam but you may be asked to describe what you would look for whilst the horse is being ridden.

In preparation for the exam, look at as many saddles as possible assessing good fit, bad fit and condition. This will increase your confidence and knowledge, which will certainly help in the exam situation.

C H A P T E R   17
Clothing

There are different rugs and blankets for various occasions but the two principal types, the stable rug and the New Zealand, are used in the colder months to keep the clipped horse warm and dry.

During the autumn the horse grows a thick winter coat which, together with the grease and oils that the horse's skin produces, insulates the animal against the extremes of cold, wet and windy conditions. Though many native ponies live out through the autumn and winter months without the protection of rugs, most horses and ponies in work are clipped either completely or partially.

The main reason for clipping is to prevent the horse in work from sweating. This can cause discomfort, distress and ill health. Once the natural coat is clipped the horse or pony needs another form of insulation and protection.

Traditionally Jute Rugs with Under Blankets were used, but the new synthetic rugs are now becoming very popular, being warm, lightweight and easy to clean. The New Zealand rug is worn as a protection for a horse spending time at grass.

Other types of rug include the summer sheet, the woollen day rug and the anti-sweat or cooler rug. New designs and materials are being marketed all the time.

Rug fastenings

There are several different types of straps and fastenings used to keep the rug secure on the horse.

Rollers

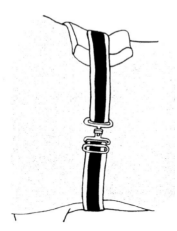

Figure 72: Elasticated Roller.

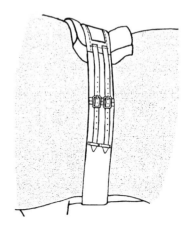

Figure 73: Leather Roller.

A roller is a single strap made from webbing, jute, leather or an elasticated material.

Fitting over the back of the horse behind the withers; a roller is fastened either by buckles or a clip on the nearside.

A roller should always have some kind of padding between it and the horse's back to protect the spine. This Wither Pad can consist of one piece of sponge, a thick layer of sheepskin or of two cushioned pads fitting either side of the backbone.

The **Anti-cast roller** has an additional purpose, namely to prevent the horse from rolling over in the box or stable and becoming cast. There is a metal hoop or arch attached to the top part of the roller where it fits on the horse's back. This type of roller can be heavy but for a horse who consistently becomes cast it is a good deterrent.

Fit

To fit a roller, lay it over the horse's back with the longer part to the offside, making sure that the pad is in the correct position. Buckle up on the nearside. The roller should be *almost* as tight as a girth, if fastened too tightly, it can damage the horse's spine.

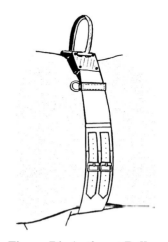

Figure 74: Anti-cast Roller.

Surcingles

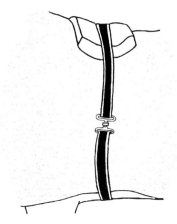
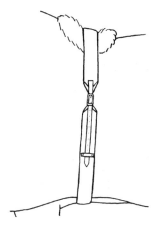

Figure 75: Elasticated single surcingle.   **Figure 76: Leather or webbing single surcingle.**

Surcingles can either be a single strap or two straps that cross over each other.

Cross-over surcingles are sewn onto the rug, cross under the horse's belly and fasten on the nearside with buckles or clips.

When fastened the surcingles should be tight enough to prevent the rug from slipping off but not so tight as to prevent movement or cause discomfort.

Fillet String

This fits at the back of a rug and is slipped under the tail as extra security.

Normally used on summer sheets or light rugs to prevent the wind from blowing the rug up over the horse's back.

Fillet strings are usually made from plaited cotton.

Figure 77: Fillet String.

Leg Straps

These are fastenings normally attached to a New Zealand rug and worn around the hind legs of the horse. There are two straps, one each side, attached on the inside of the rug at the back. Each strap wraps around a hind leg and is looped through the other strap.

Care in fitting is necessary; too tight and the straps will rub and cause sores. Too loose and the horse may catch a leg in the straps.

When removing a rug a frequent mistake is to forget to undo the leg straps. It is always wise to check, whatever the type of rug. When unfastened, the straps should be clipped to the rings on the same side to keep them safe and tidy.

Figure 78: Leg Straps.

Front fastenings

These can vary quite considerably from buckles, plastic clips, thread-through fasteners or twist clips.

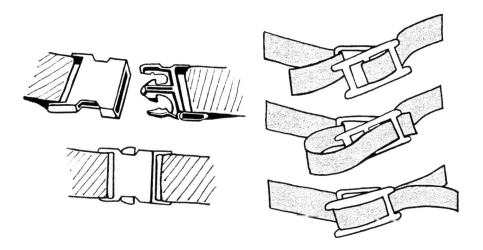

Figure 79: Clip fastener   **Figure 80: Thread through Fasteners.**

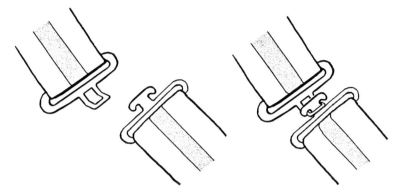

Figure 81: Twist Clip.

Types of Rugs

Jute Rug

This is a traditional rug made of natural jute fibre, either fully or half lined with wool or cotton. Special rot proof Jutes are now available.

The Jute is often worn with a roller, but cross-over surcingles can be sewn on if preferred.

Though traditionally used with an under-blanket, a Jute is quite warm enough on its own.

Jutes are made from natural materials, are hard wearing and warm. They are however, difficult to clean because they shrink.

Under Blanket or Witney Blanket*

This blanket is made from wool and is usually a yellow or red colour with stripes.

It is normally used under a Jute rug for extra warmth, though this combination can be quite heavy on the horse.

---

* Witney is a registered trade name.

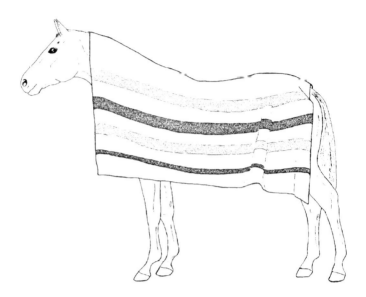

Figure 82: Place blanket high up.

The blanket itself can be a little awkward to fit. To put on; the front of the blanket is placed high up on the horse's neck and folded back, then when the Jute is laid on top, the blanket can be taken back over the front of the Jute.

Figure 83: Fold back.

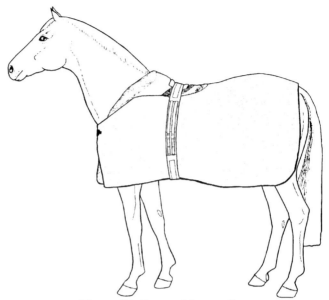

Figure 84: Secured by a roller.

This type of blanket is becoming less popular. There are now fitted under blankets on the market, many of which are made from synthetic material that is easier to maintain.

Stable Rug

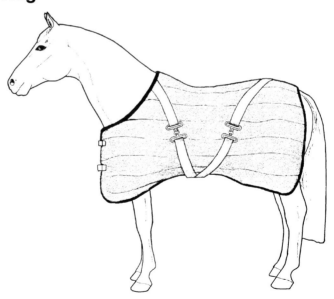

Figure 85: Stable Rug with cross-over surcingles.

An extremely popular rug, the stable rug, night rug or Polywarm* acts like a duvet which is used in the stable during the autumn, winter and spring.

Usually made with an outer covering of nylon, a cotton lining and a fleecy filling, the stable rug is available with varying thicknesses and warmth factors.

The fastenings are normally cross-over surcingle straps around the body, two buckles at the front and sometimes a fillet string.

- A lightweight rug.
- Convenient to use.
- Hard wearing.
- Durable.
- Very easy to clean; it can be washed in a washing machine.

Stable rugs are easily purchased and available in a variety of colours. There are rugs on the market now which claim to take the place of several blankets. These have the appearance of a thick duvet and some include a covering that reaches up the neck of the horse.

Woollen Day Rug

As its name implies, this rug is made out of wool.

During autumn and spring, because it is not as warm as a stable rug or a Jute, the horse can wear this rug on milder days.

The woollen day rug is also used as a smart rug at shows and is often specially made in the owner's colours with a contrasting binding and matching surcingle.

Anti-Sweat Rug

This is a specialised rug used when the horse has become wet either through sweating, in the rain or after a bath. It has the appearance of a large string vest.

Its purpose is to regulate heat loss. The air under the rug is warmed by the horse's body temperature. Whilst a certain amount of this air escapes through the holes, cooling the horse down; some of the air remains trapped under the strands of material, preventing the heat from escaping too rapidly.

It is normally used with another rug on top or with thatching - straw is placed underneath the rug and the circulating air dries the horse.

The Anti-sweat rug can also be used under another rug when travelling.

---

* Polywarm is a registered trade name.

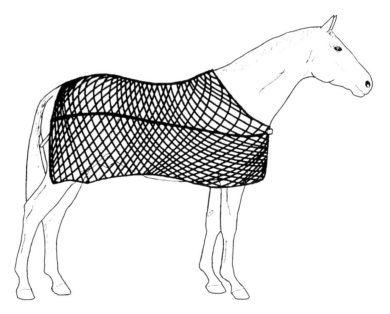

Figure 86: Anti-Sweat Rug.

The Anti-sweat rug, (or Sweat rug as it is more commonly though incorrectly called), is normally fastened at the front with a strap and at the back with a fillet string.

As alternatives there are several new 'cooler' rugs on the market. These have a closer mesh slowing down the rate of heat loss.

Summer Sheet

A thin, cotton sheet worn on cool, summer evenings.

Also used to protect the horse from flies or, when travelling to a show, to keep the horse clean.

The Summer Sheet is fastened by a front buckle and a rear fillet string. Sometimes a light roller strap is used for more security.

New Zealand

This rug is mainly worn by horses out at pasture during the autumn, winter and spring. Occasionally it is worn by horses at grass on wet summer days to keep them dry. A horse should never be tacked up or ridden when wet.

New Zealand rugs come in all shapes and sizes; new designs are introduced onto the market frequently. Some are plain, straight rugs; others have tail flaps to protect the back of the horse from wind and cold. Some include a covering for the horse's neck.

Figure 87: New Zealand.

Made of a waterproof material, usually canvas, and lined with wool, cotton or fleece. The New Zealand needs to be tough, strong and of good quality to survive bad weather and rough usage.

Normally fastened by one or two front buckles, cross over surcingles and leg straps at the rear.

The fit must be correct for the horse to obtain the full benefit of this rug.

Some types are **self-righting** and should remain in place even when the horse rolls.

The New Zealand rug does need special cleaning if the waterproofing is not to be affected. Occasionally the rug will need re-waterproofing which can either be done professionally, or at home with a waterproofing spray.

Often in very windy, wet weather, when the rain gets underneath, the New Zealand can become damp. It is wise to have two New Zealands so that one rug can be dried whilst the other is in use.

Rugs for a Stabled Horse

All the rugs mentioned are the most popular for normal use. A fully stabled horse will need:

1. A Stable Rug for winter, providing it is warm enough to protect against the coldest nights. Alternatives are the Jute rug with or without an Under-blanket.

1. A New Zealand, ideally two.

1. A Summer sheet for the warmer months.

1. An Anti-Sweat Sheet.

Most new horse owners start with the minimum and gradually buy other rugs to add to their stock.

Measuring and Fitting a Rug

Rugs are available in many sizes ranging from those for the smallest pony to the largest horse. It is important to obtain the right size.

A rug that is too small will be uncomfortable for the horse and cause rubbing and sores. A rug that is too large may become tangled in the horse's legs.

Normally rug sizes are available in measurements rising by 3 inches, for example 5 foot 9 inches - 6 foot - 6 foot 3 inches.

To measure a horse for a rug;

a) Use a tape measure or a piece of string.

a) Measure from the middle of the chest right round the side of the horse to a point corresponding to the top of the tail.

a) If this does not fit exactly to a length available in the shop, it is better to obtain a size larger rather than smaller. Experience has shown that rugs do sometimes shrink a little when cleaned and it is no great problem if the rug overhangs the tail slightly.

When the overall length is known, the rug should be checked on the horse for correct fitting.

There should be enough depth of rug to cover the horse's body. Some rugs are the correct length but are too short around the belly. This leaves part of the horse's body exposed and vunerable to the weather.

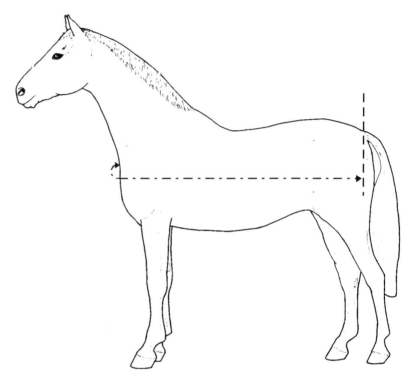

Figure 88: Measuring a horse's length.

It is important that the rug fits around the shoulder, wither and chest area. Check this by placing a hand under the rug at the withers and sliding it right down to the front strap. This area should give the horse plenty of room. There should be no tightness here or there will certainly be rubbing. If the rug is too tight in this area it will be extremely uncomfortable, restrict the horse's movement and result in bare patches and sores around the shoulder. It will be necessary either to get a bigger rug or another design with a different style and cut.

Horses wear rugs for many hours during the winter months and it is essential that a rug fits well.

Putting on a Rug

The rug should be placed on carefully and gently; some horses do object to having a rug thrown on roughly. The safest method especially with an unknown horse or one that is rug-shy is as follows:

The horse should be restrained by a head collar and lead rope. The surcingle straps of the rug should be tied up so that when rug is put on these do not swing around and hit the horse in his ribs or belly.

Figure 89: Tie Surcingle Straps.

Hold the front of the rug in the right hand and the rear in the left.

Figure 90: Fold Front to Back.

Fold the front end over the top of the rug so that it meets the back. Straighten the rug and place it over the left arm, front uppermost near the elbow.

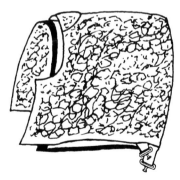

Figure 91: Until the front meets the back.

Approach the horse from the nearside shoulder, talking to him quietly. Gently place the quarter of the rug nearest to the horse on to his neck and shoulder, a little higher up the neck than the rug will normally lie. With the right hand take the portion of the rug lying over the left arm and fold it over the withers and the neck so that it hangs down on the offside of the horse.

Figure 92: Place rug on neck and shoulders.

Taking the top half of the rug in the right hand, lay it gently over the back of the horse towards the tail.

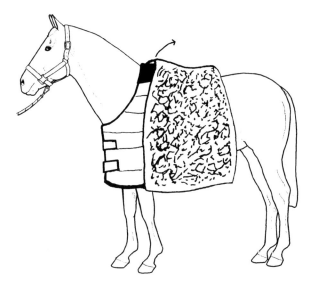

Figure 93: Lay gently over the horse's back.

The front buckles are now fastened.

Slide the rug back; so that the lie of the hair is correct. The rug should never be pulled forward as the hair will bend in the wrong direction. When the rug is in the correct position the front will be just above the withers with the rear reaching the top of tail.

Fasten the surcingles. The straps should be tight enough to prevent the rug from slipping or the horse from getting his legs entangled. But not too tight to restrict movement or cause sores.

If there is a fillet string, gently pull the tail through. Back straps go around the inside of the legs and link through one another to prevent them rubbing and chafing the inside of the thigh.

Check from both sides for folds or crumpled areas.

There is a debate as to which should be fastened first on a rug; the front buckles or the surcingles/roller.

- When the front straps are fastened first the rug can be pulled back on the horse to the correct position before the surcingles are buckled up. If the surcingles are fastened first and the rug is not in the correct position or it shifts slightly, the rug will have to be removed and put on again.

- On the other hand fastening the surcingles first prevents the rug from being blown about on a windy day or from being dislodged should the horse move quickly.

Neither method is wrong but, in practice, the front straps are usually fastened first. The method used depends on practicality and the temperament of the horse.

Removing a Rug

- Unfasten the front straps.
- Undo the straps between the hind legs and clip them onto the corresponding rings.
- Unfasten the centre straps or surcingles.
- Taking the front of the rug, fold it over the horse's back to the tail section.
- Now holding the rug with the front half in the left hand and the back in the right, slide it off the horse's back completely in the direction of the tail.
- The rug can be folded into quarters as mentioned above so that it is ready to put on next time.

Rugs should be hung over a bar or beam or put away in a rug room. Rugs should not be left on the floor or allowed to fall onto the bedding; this is untidy, dirty, and may result in damage to the rug.

Care of the Rug

If a rug is treated and stored properly it will last a long time. All rugs, rollers and accessories should be kept clean and dry, otherwise they can cause skin conditions, infections, rubbing and sores.

Rugs can either be washed in the washing machine and dried outside or taken to the Launderette. Some Tack Shops will clean them professionally.

Great care should be taken with the type of cleaning fluid or washing powder used to clean rugs in case the horse's skin suffers from an adverse reaction.

Rugs should be stored in a dry, cool, well-ventilated area to prevent contamination with mould or fungus.

A horse should never have to wear a dirty, ill fitting, wet or damp rug.

Exam Tips

In the examination there will either be a variety of rugs made available or, during the colder months, a horse wearing a rug. You may be asked to identify certain rugs, to describe them, the materials used and to give the function, advantages and disadvantages. You may then have to put a rug on a horse, show how to measure the fit and remove it afterwards.

C H A P T E R   18
Shoeing

A horse's feet are constantly growing. In the natural state this growth is worn away at approximately the same rate by the action of the hoof across the ground. In an artificial environment, with the pressures of work and stress on hard surfaces, the hoof wears away too quickly. It is essential that the feet are protected.

Whilst the shoe protects the horse's foot, it also prevents the natural wearing down of the hoof. The hoof then grows too long causing other problems such as injury, lameness and incorrect action. *All horses regularly need their feet attending to every four to six weeks.*

Here comes another cliché ~ **'no foot, no horse'**. A tremendous amount of weight and stress is placed on the foot. A horse with weak feet is vulnerable to all kinds of problems including intermittent or even permanent lameness.

Foot Structure

To understand shoeing, it is necessary to know the basic structure of the horse's foot.

1. **Horn or Wall**

   This grows down from the coronet at the top of the hoof, just under the hair. The average monthly growth is about a quarter to three eight's of an inch. It can take 9 to 12 months for a whole new wall to grow. The horn should be healthy and shiny in appearance, with no cracks.

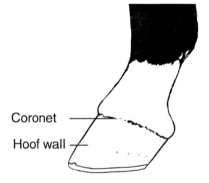

Coronet

Hoof wall

2. **Frog**

This is the soft, rubbery portion on the underside of the foot. It is larger at the heel decreasing to a point, roughly triangular in shape. It has an indentation down its centre, *the cleft*, and two hollows either side, *the lateral clefts*. The rubbery texture of the frog helps to absorb concussion; its shape and clefts help to provide grip.

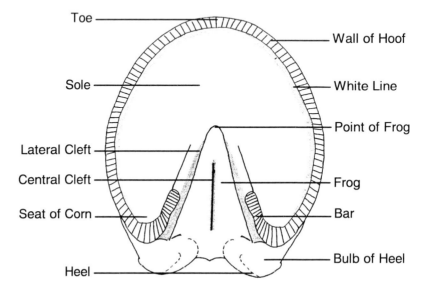

Figure 94: Points of the Foot.

3. **Sole**

This is the area of the foot between the frog and the wall. The shape of the sole is important; it should be *slightly concave*. Too flat a sole increases the possibility of bruising, injury and concussion. Too concave a sole and the frog may not come into contact with the ground.

4. **White Line**

This is a thin waxy strip on the inside of the wall that separates the sensitive from the insensitive parts of the foot. The farrier uses this as a guide for positioning the nails that secure the shoe.

5. **Bars**

These are a continuation of the wall turning inwards at the heel for a short length, parallel with the frog. They help to provide grip.

Shoeing

Shoeing is necessary for a number of reasons;

1. To **protect** the foot from damage.

2. To **reduce concussion** to the foot and leg.

3. To help **correct defects** in **conformation or action**.

4. As part of **veterinary treatment**.

The horse's feet should be cared for by the farrier at least every four to six weeks, even when the horse is unshod and at grass. If left for a longer period, problems will arise with the shoes and the feet.

Indications that shoeing is necessary;

*   The shoe has been **cast;** it has come off completely.

*   The shoe is **loose.**

*   The shoe is **sprung**; barely hanging on by a nail.

*   The shoe has **worn thin** at any part.

*   The **clenches have risen** and stand out from the wall. A clench is formed at the point where the farrier's nail emerges from the hoof. These should be flush with the wall of the foot.

*   The foot is **overlong and out of shape**. A foot is overlong when the wall starts to grow over the shoe. Initially this will begin at the toe.

Many of these defects are apparent just by looking at the foot. When the clenches have risen they will clearly stand out from the wall. It is also quite possible to feel prominent clenches when picking out the foot.

An 'overgrown foot' is apparent when the wall grows over the shoe. In the hind feet the farrier will occasionally shoe this way, setting the shoe back a little. This is to minimize the damage of over-reaching, if the horse has a tendency to do this. Over-reaching occurs when the horse hits his front leg with the toe of the hind.

A sprung shoe may be hanging off the foot. A loose shoe can be heard when the horse moves on hard ground, particularly a road. A worn shoe may be seen when the foot is on the ground but is more usually spotted when the foot is picked up and cleaned. It will appear thin or even cracked in one area. It is easy to check the foot and shoe when daily picking out the feet and this should be done as a routine.

Even if the shoes do not need renewing, the horse will still need its foot trimming. The farrier can remove the shoe, trim the foot and replace the old shoe. This is known as a **'remove'** or a **'refit'**. Some horses need their feet trimming every four weeks, but for most six weeks is sufficient. Horses and ponies at grass may need their feet trimming more often during spring and early summer when the grass is rich and the hoof grows more quickly. If the feet are cared for regularly and the work is carried out by a good farrier, the horse is less likely to suffer problems with its feet or shoes.

The Shoe

Horse shoes, in one form or another, have been used for centuries and today, with new technology, different designs are still being created.

Concave Fullered shoe - (Hunter Shoe)

The most common type of shoe is the 'concave fullered', so called because of its shape and groove.

The inner side of the shoe from the ground surface to the bearing surface, (the part that touches the horse's foot) is slightly *concave*. This imitates the natural shape of the wall and provides extra grip. It also helps to prevent suction from the ground particularly when the conditions are wet.

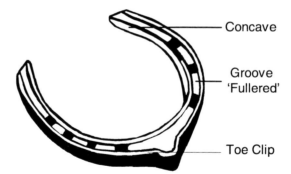

Figure 95: Front shoe; ground surface uppermost.

The description 'fullered' refers to the groove that is cut from heel to heel on the ground surface of the shoe. This groove not only makes the shoe lighter but also provides grip, particularly on slippery ground.

There are usually seven nail holes, four on the outside and three inside. This number can vary depending on the condition of the foot, the type of shoe, the farrier and the work the horse performs.

There is normally one *toe clip* on each front shoe. The hind shoes have two *quarter clips* leaving the toe free. This is to minimize any injuries caused by over-reaching; to prevent the horse hitting himself with a metal toe clip.

Quarter clips

Figure 96: Hind shoe bearing surface uppermost.

Exam Tips

In the examination you may be requested to inspect a horse's foot and shoe and to describe the condition of both. You may be asked to estimate when the horse was last shod.

Check the shoe first whilst the horse's foot is on the ground. If the foot has recently been shod, the wall will be flush with the shoe and the clenches flat. If the wall projects over the shoe, the clenches stand out or the hoof is cracked and split, the farrier is probably due for a visit.

Pick up the foot and look at the frog, sole and shoe. Feel with your fingers around the hoof for risen clenches, overgrown horn and for wear on the toe or branches of the shoe. This will also indicate approximately when the horse was last shod or if he is due for shoeing.

To prepare for the exam, practise as much as you can by inspecting horses' feet and shoes and, if possible, watching the farrier at work. Most farriers are very helpful and will gladly give valuable information if approached politely and bribed with numerous cups of tea or coffee!

C H A P T E R   19

Grassland Management

All horses and ponies should spend time at pasture. Apart from grass being the horse's natural food, time spent in a field will encourage relaxation. Some horses live out permanently while others are given an annual holiday which may extend to weeks or months. Stabled horses in full work usually spend their days off in the field. Whatever length of time the horse spends out, it is important to ensure that all fields provide a safe environment.

What to look for in a field

There are certain aspects of a field that must be assessed before being used for horses:

Fencing

There are two considerations with fencing, the possibility of injury or escape. Fencing that is not properly maintained may pose a hazard and cause injury. Any insecure fencing will allow the horse to escape either by pulling it down, pushing through it or jumping over it.

Post and Rail

This is the most efficient and safest artificial boundary, but probably the most expensive. Wooden posts support two or three wooden rails one above the other. This fencing must be kept well maintained, any rotted posts or broken rails replaced immediately. The wood should also be treated with creosote as a protection against weather conditions and to discourage horses from chewing the fence.

Post and Wire

Less expensive than post and rail. Wooden posts will either support a rail on top and wire underneath or four to five strands of wire. The wire needs to be taut and securely fastened to the posts. The lowest strand of wire should be approximately one and a half feet from the ground to prevent a horse putting a leg through and becoming caught. If the lowest strand is too high the horse may put his head underneath it.

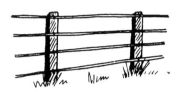

Electric fencing

Generally used to divide fields rather than as a permanent boundary, electric fencing is efficient as long as the horse has knowledge of its position. There is a possible danger to humans, particularly children. One good idea is to cut strips from plastic bin liners and tie these along the wire so that it can be easily seen.

Other Boundaries

Hedges

A natural boundary that must be dense enough to prevent escape, well maintained so it does not become a hazard and free of poisonous shrubs or plants. Hedges can also act as shelter.

Walls

These should be high enough to prevent horses from jumping over and sturdy enough to withstand being knocked down.

Unsuitable Fencing

Some types of fencing should ideally never be used;

Pig or Sheep Netting

This netting is produced by strands of wire that cross vertically and horizontally, creating squares. This can be dangerous as horses tend to put their feet through and become caught.

Sheep posts or stakes

These are made from thin stakes of wood with sharp pointed ends. The sharp points of these posts can cause injuries.

Barbed wire

This type of fencing is used quite extensively around fields where horses are kept and can be a sufficiently good boundary. However sometimes horses do rub themselves on the wire and can sustain quite nasty cuts and scratches. The wire also needs to be checked regularly and kept in good condition. *It must be kept taut.* Horses have ended up with horrific injuries when loose barbed wire has become wrapped around a leg. The horse panics, thrashes about causing the wire to tighten and cut deeply into the flesh.

Checking outside the boundaries is also important as horses can often reach poisonous plants or trees over the fence line. Any defect with fencing or boundaries needs to be dealt with immediately.

The Gate

The gate must be wide enough for animals and machinery to pass through and kept in good condition, so that it can be used efficiently. People should be discouraged from climbing on or over it. This can result in a gate that drops and is difficult to use. All gates should be fastened with a sturdy padlock and a thick chain, preferably at both ends to prevent the gate being taken off its hinges. Horse thefts are on the increase and any weakness around the gate will be exploited.

The position of the access is important. A gate situated on a busy main road is not ideally suitable. It will be dangerous leading horses on the road and it may make horse theft easier. The access needs to be convenient, efficient and safe.

Water

A supply of clean water must be constantly available. This may be naturally by river or stream or artificially by trough or buckets. See the Chapter on Water.

Shelter

Horses at grass must be provided with shelter of some kind, either naturally with trees, a good thick hedge or more ideally with a Field Shelter. This protects them from wind and rain in winter and from heat and flies in summer.

A Field Shelter needs to be large enough to accommodate a number of horses and ponies with ease. It should have a wide entrance to prevent a horse from being boxed in and bullied. There should be a solid approach which will not become poached and slippery. The Shelter needs checking regularly for any defects or damage.

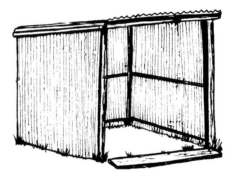

Figure 97: This type of shelter is unsuitable as it does not provide room for a number of horses or ponies.

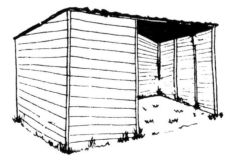

Figure 98: The opening is too small; if a horse or pony becomes trapped inside there could be bullying.

Figure 99: This shelter is large enough to accommodate a number of horses and is open to allow escape from bullying. It also includes a hayrack.

Size of field

The field needs to be large enough to accommodate the number of horses and ponies grazing on it. Too small a field will become overgrazed and horse-sick. When living out and relying mainly on pasture for food, each **horse** needs **one and a half to two acres**, each **pony** needs **one acre.**

Quality of Grazing

A field that has little or no grass on it will not offer the horse any food. He may start eating unsuitable and even poisonous plants, or become thin and ill.

On the other hand grass that is too rich can be just as harmful causing obesity and ill health. Horses do not need lush, rich grass. They need a variety of grasses and a little clover.

Type of Land

The geography of the land is important. Flat land that is liable to flooding is not suitable. The wrong types of grasses will grow in a waterlogged environment and the horse, if stood in wet muddy conditions, may suffer from skin problems such as mud fever or thrush. Undulating land is best, with gentle hills and slopes. This allows free drainage as well as giving the horse some exercise whilst he is grazing.

Hazards

All fields before being used for horses, must be checked closely for possible dangers or hazards. Anything that may constitute a danger must either be removed from the field or fenced off safely to keep the horses and ponies away.

Such hazards include low overhanging branches, rabbit holes, pits, ditches, slippery areas, swamps, bogs, stagnant pools, stakes, sharp implements, rubbish tips with cans or broken glass.

Poisonous plants

There are various plants which, if eaten, are poisonous and can be fatal to the horse. The more common plants are Ragwort, Buttercup, Foxglove, Horsetail, Deadly Nightshade, Hemlock, Purple Milk Vetch, St. John's Wort and Yellow Star Thistle.

Some bushes, shrubs and trees can also be poisonous. These include Privet, Laburnum, Buckthorn, Rhododendron, Yew, Laurel and the acorns from Oak trees.

Any poisonous plants, shrubs or trees should either be removed immediately from the field or fenced off well out of reach of the horses and ponies. If the plants have been pulled out of the ground, they must be removed from the field immediately. Withered, poisonous plants must never be left in the field as they are often more palatable to horses than the live plant.

Grass cuttings should never be fed to horses, eating these can and often does result in colic. Unfortunately many people do dump their grass cuttings in the fields in the mistaken belief that these are good for horses.

Keywords

❖ Fencing

❖ Gates and access

❖ Water supply

❖ Shelter

❖ Size of field

❖ Quality of pasture

❖ Geography of land

❖ Hazards.

Field Maintenance

Daily Inspections

It is important that all pasture is inspected daily, if at all possible, to ensure the safety of the horses and ponies grazing or living in the fields. Fencing should be checked for fallen or rotted posts, damaged railings or broken wire. Natural hedgerow needs frequent inspecting for poisonous plants.

The water supply should be checked daily for cleanliness, the efficient working of the system and the amount of water available. In hot weather horses drink large quantities of water.

The field needs to be inspected for any hazards; fallen trees after a gale, new rabbit holes, boggy or swampy areas after wet weather or rubbish dumped in the field.

Droppings

Ideally all dung should be collected and removed as often as possible. This is to control worm infestation. All horses have worms but with the removal of droppings, together with a regular and correct worming programme, the worm infestation is kept to a minimum. Worm eggs are passed out of the horse in the dung. The eggs hatch and the larvae migrate to the pasture where they are ingested by the horse and the cycle begins again.

In large fields where collection of dung is not practical, the droppings can be harrowed. The harrowing should be done during hot, dry periods in order to kill off the larvae. As larvae thrive in warm, wet conditions, spreading the droppings during these periods will simply increase the worm population.

Worming

All horses and ponies should be wormed regularly at least every six weeks. This is an important aspect of horse care and is closely linked with good Grassland Management. Failure to worm correctly can lead to infestation of the pasture, ill health for the horse and in extreme circumstances even death.

The Horse sick field

Basically a horse-sick field is the result of the owner's negligence. It is bad Grassland Management. Horses are destructive grazers and, if left in a field for too long a period, will quickly spoil the pasture. If the area is overstocked, that is too many horses grazing on it, then the field will quickly deteriorate.

Recognizing a field in such a state is not difficult:

- Bare, overgrazed areas where the horses have stripped the land of nutritious grass.
- Rough spots, usually covered with droppings, where the unpalatable grasses, poisonous plants and weeds grow.
- 'Poached' areas - muddy spots ground up by the horses' hooves, usually around the gate and water trough.
- Trees may often be stripped bare of leaves or bark.
- Fences in bad condition, broken or trampled down by horses trying to feed from the other side of the boundary.

- Water fouled, dirty and green with algae.

- Horses and ponies on the field will look thin, 'ribby', lethargic and ill. They may stand in groups by the gate or fence and be desperately nibbling at the bare ground.

Keywords

❖ Overgrazed

❖ Excess droppings

❖ Weeds

❖ Poached

❖ Poor fencing

❖ Fouled water

Maintaining good pasture

Ideally all fields should be given a period free of horses and allowed to go fallow or be grazed by other stock. Cows and sheep eat different grasses and will crop the rough, unpalatable areas. In addition they digest and kill off some of the worm larva originating from the horses' droppings.

Rotation

This is the method by which the sequence of grazing and 'resting' pasture is alternated over periods of time. For example a large field can be split into three portions, one being grazed by horses, one left fallow or resting and the third being stocked with other animals. These can then be 'rotated' so that each portion has a period of rest, a period being grazed by horses or other livestock. The pasture will then provide good grazing for horses.

Turning the horse out into a field

There is a procedure for turning a horse out which ensures maximum safety. Horses can become quite excitable when being turned out and cause problems for both horse and handler.

The horse should be wearing either a headcollar and leadrope or a bridle. If the field is close to the stables or farm, a headcollar will be adequate for a quiet horse. A bridle is necessary if the field has to be reached by road.

- Walk the horse to the gate quietly. Open the gate wide enough so that the horse does not catch himself. Lead the horse in from the near or offside, whichever is convenient, and shut the gate immediately.

- Take the horse a little way into the field and turn him so that he is facing the gate. Some horses do become excited at this point. *The handler must never be positioned between the horse and the field.* The horse may barge through or inadvertently knock the handler down.

- Standing by the horse's head, quietly slip the restraint off and step backwards. Avoid standing too close to the horse and never slap him on his side or hindquarters, this will encourage him to gallop off and he may buck and kick out.

- Watch the horse for a while until he settles. Fasten the gate properly and check that it is secure.

If two or more horses are being turned out together, they should all be faced towards the gate and released at the same time. If one horse dashes off the others may become excited causing problems for the handlers.

If the horse has not been out for some time, he may want to 'party'! In this case the handler must be prepared and treat the horse with care, avoiding any situation that may lead to injury.

Bringing the horse in

This can again be a difficult time, particularly if the horse is hard to catch or if there are a large number of horses and ponies in the field.

- Prepare the headcollar and leadrope, straightening them out so that there is no fiddling with them whilst trying to catch the horse. If necessary take some pony nuts or a carrot hidden in a pocket. Once in the field the headcollar and leadrope can be hidden behind the back out of view in case the horse feels like playing games!

- Always approach the horse from the front, preferably towards his nearside neck and shoulder. A horse in a field should **NEVER** be approached from behind; he could easily be startled and kick out.

- Holding the noseband, quietly slip the headcollar on and fasten the head piece. If the horse is a little head shy, hold the noseband near his nostrils and allow him to put his nose into the headcollar first.

- If the horse is likely to walk away or mess about whilst his headcollar is being put on, the leadrope can be passed around his neck first. This does seem to quieten down some horses as if they believe the leadrope is a firm restraint. Should the horse jump or move away quickly, release the leadrope immediately.

- If the horse is reluctant to come near, attempt to entice him with the titbits. Alternatively the titbits can be given after the headcollar is on, as a reward. Lead the horse quietly to the gate.

- If possible prevent the other horses from following. When there are a number of horses milling around the gate waiting to push through, it is not only dangerous but frightening. Encourage the other horses to move off, alternatively use another gate or get someone else to help.

Whenever food is taken into a field where there are a number of horses, handlers must be aware of the possible danger. Unless it is absolutely safe or necessary, a bucket of food must not be used to entice a horse. This will definitely cause trouble! The situation can quickly become dangerous, particularly if all the horses gather round and start to fight. It is a terrifying experience being surrounded by a number of horses and ponies who are lunging at each other or kicking.

Some horses can be trained to come to a call. To encourage this, make a noise or call the horse's name whilst he is in the yard and then feed a treat immediately. Eventually the horse will associate the call with a reward and, with any luck, calling him from the gate of the field will be sufficient.

Difficult horses

For the horse who is very reluctant to be caught bringing him in at the same time each day as a part of his routine, can improve the situation.

Alternatively bring him in solely for a treat or feed so that he does not associate coming in with work only.

If the horse is really awkward to catch and tends to run off, great patience is required. Occasionally walking after him (not running or this will become a great game), will eventually convince him that the handler really means business. Take care not to get near his hindquarters in case he kicks.

Some horses are really difficult in which case bringing all the other horses and ponies in from the field may succeed. Horses generally do not like being left alone and, to avoid being separated, the horse may come in with the others.

It may help to turn the horse out in a headcollar. This should only be a temporary measure though as the headcollar can become caught up in fencing or trees. It also makes it easier for the horse thief. As an extra measure a short length of rope (4 to 6 inches) can be attached to the headcollar.

Whatever the circumstances, *safety is of the paramount importance*. A situation where a horse can kick or cause injury must be prevented at all costs. Catching a really difficult horse requires patience and determination but the horse must never win. He should be caught eventually or he will learn to evade and become undisciplined.

Safety in the field and paddock

Regular checks and maintenance within the pasture and boundaries saves a lot of problems later. Handling horses correctly when feeding, taking in or bringing up from the field correctly and knowing how to deal with awkward animals helps to prevent accidents and injuries.

Feed times

During the colder months horses and ponies living out permanently need to be given extra food. The herd tends to crowd around the gate or wherever the food is put into the field. There may be barging, kicking, squealing and fighting. To minimize the risks to horses and handlers there are safety measures that can be followed.

- Always put out as many feed buckets as there are horses, one extra if possible. This helps to prevent bullying.

- Space feed buckets out so that the horses have adequate distance between each other.

- Place hay piles a good distance from each other.

- Place a couple of extra piles of hay than the number horses.

- If feeding one or two horses in a herd, it is safer to take them out of the field and feed them somewhere else.

- Never take a bucket of food into the middle of the herd.

With good grassland management, handling and care the field should provide a safe, healthy and peaceful environment where horses can relax and graze.

Exam Tips

Observation is important for assessing Grassland Management. Visit various fields and make notes of the relevant points - fencing, gates, poached areas, water systems. List the good and bad points; learn to be critical. Look for the poisonous plants and shrubs; most of these are quite common and will be easily identifiable.

Turning out and bringing horses in from the field is a daily event for some owners and riders but if you do not have the opportunity, then practise doing this correctly.

Safety in the field and paddock

Regular checks and maintenance within the pasture and boundaries saves a lot of problems later. Handling horses correctly when feeding, taking in or bringing up from the field correctly and knowing how to deal with awkward animals helps to prevent accidents and injuries.

Feed times

During the colder months horses and ponies living out permanently need to be given extra food. The herd tends to crowd around the gate or wherever the food is put into the field. There may be barging, kicking, squealing and fighting. To minimize the risks to horses and handlers there are safety measures that can be followed.

- Always put out as many feed buckets as there are horses, one extra if possible. This helps to prevent bullying.

- Space feed buckets out so that the horses have adequate distance between each other.

- Place hay piles a good distance from each other.

- Place a couple of extra piles of hay than the number horses.

- If feeding one or two horses in a herd, it is safer to take them out of the field and feed them somewhere else.

- Never take a bucket of food into the middle of the herd.

With good grassland management, handling and care the field should provide a safe, healthy and peaceful environment where horses can relax and graze.

Exam Tips

Observation is important for assessing Grassland Management. Visit various fields and make notes of the relevant points - fencing, gates, poached areas, water systems. List the good and bad points; learn to be critical. Look for the poisonous plants and shrubs; most of these are quite common and will be easily identifiable.

Turning out and bringing horses in from the field is a daily event for some owners and riders but if you do not have the opportunity, then practise doing this correctly.

CHAPTER   20
Safety and Accident Procedures

Accidents do happen in any sphere of life and working around horses is potentially a dangerous occupation. The BHS emphasises safety in every aspect of Horse Management. In Stage I a specific amount of time is devoted to this subject when candidates are questioned about safety in the yard, when on a hack or riding on the public highway. Candidates will also be expected to know about fire precautions and accident procedures.

The first part of this chapter will deal with safety precautions in the yard, in the stable and around horses. The second part deals with accident procedures and the actions to take in the event of an accident.

Safety Precautions

The yard can be a dangerous place. For humans because horses are large, strong animals that can cause injury if not handled properly; for horses because they can react suddenly to situations and may injure themselves or others. All persons working with and around horses, all those learning to ride and indeed everyone, whether partaking in some capacity or merely watching, must be made aware of the possible dangers.

Many establishments have a list of safety precautions in the yard. Making people aware and teaching them the correct method of handling horses minimizes the risk of accidents.

Safety in the Yard

Clothing   Suitable clothing and footwear should be worn at all times and jewellery kept to a minimum.

All tack and horses' clothing should be checked regularly and properly maintained.

Equipment   All personnel must be instructed on how to lift weights correctly and to use equipment and machinery safely.

All stable equipment must be kept clean and in good working order.

Equipment and machinery must be cleared away after use. It should never be left lying around the yard or in the horse's box.

Handling   All horses should be approached and handled correctly at all times.

Personnel must be taught never to walk around the back of a horse or at least to allow plenty of room.

Handlers should never kneel or sit on the ground when working around horses, nor place their hands on the floor near the horse.

Horses should always be enclosed or restrained correctly.

Fire   There must be **NO SMOKING** on or near the yard.

Fire fighting equipment must be easily accessible and in working order.

All staff must be instructed regularly on the use of fire fighting equipment.

All electrical wires must be kept out of the horses' reach and correctly insulated.

Rubbish and litter must never be left on the yard but removed immediately.

The Yard   All buildings, loose boxes, tack rooms, feed stores and all surrounding areas must be kept clean and free of obstructions

Noise and activity must be kept to a minimum on the yard.

Emergencies All personnel must be given instruction on dealing with emergencies.

The telephone numbers for the Vet, doctors and hospitals should be easily accessible.

Safety in the Box or Stable

All new staff must be shown how to work around horses safely. This subject was covered under the section concerned with handling horses but here are a few of the more important points to remember.

❖ Always tie the horse up when working around him or with him.

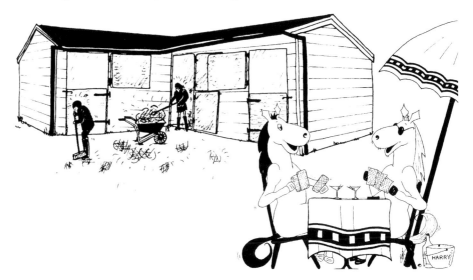

❖ Work in the box, muck out, skip out and set fair beds whilst the horse is out if possible.

❖ Always tether the horse to a piece of string which is tied to a solid object (e.g. a ring), never tether a horse directly to a solid object.

❖ Always be attentive and aware when working with horses, avoid dangerous situations.

Safety when Hacking

It is always safer to hack with someone else, but this is not always possible.

If hacking out alone:

❖ Always let someone at the stables know your approximate route.

❖ Take some form of identification, preferably in the pocket of a jacket. It is usual to have your name and address inside your hat, but in the case of an accident the hat should never be removed unless it is absolutely necessary.

❖ The horse should also have some form of identification on him; the name and address of the stables in case he is found on his own. This could be a card inside a plastic luggage label fastened to the saddle or bridle.

❖ Take some form of first aid kit if possible. Carry a **clean handkerchief**; a piece of **string or twine**, a **lead rope** and a **folding hoof pick**. A spare stirrup leather is also an excellent idea.

❖ Take some **money,** or a **phone card** for the telephone. If you are fortunate to own one, a **portable phone** properly secured in a pocket is very useful when out alone.

If in charge of a hack:

❖ Check all the tack on the horses and ponies in the ride. If someone else has tacked up, never assume that this is correct. Make sure everyone's girth is tight enough and stirrups are the correct length. The girth and stirrups should be checked again about five minutes after the start of the ride.

❖ Inform the person in charge at the stable, or another responsible person, the route the hack will be taking, and the approximate return time.

❖ Take two lead ropes, a clean handkerchief, hoof pick and some money for the telephone, or a portable phone if possible.

❖ Always carry a whip.

❖ Never try to do anything that may be risky or potentially dangerous. *The standard of the hack should be that of the least experienced rider on it.*

Safety for Children

Children have little perception of danger. Also many of them tend to look upon a horse or pony as a pet and are astonished when this 'pet' acts, whether aggressively or not, in a manner that causes the child harm. Children often take little notice of adult warnings and have to learn from their own experiences. It cannot be stressed too strongly that any horse or pony has the capacity to hurt and injure a child severely. Warnings must be given constantly and firmly.

As well as the basic rules for working around and handling horses, children should be taught;

❖ Never to walk around the back of a horse or pony. This may seem elementary to an adult but frequently children do not know this basic golden rule.

❖ To wear correct clothing at all times and preferably a body protector when riding.

❖ To be quiet and calm around horses. Never to run, shout or act in a loud and aggressive manner.

❖ To avoid feeding titbits. If it is necessary to give a treat, the child should be taught to do so with the hand flattened out to prevent the horse from biting a finger.

❖ Never to get in-between two or more horses.

Fire Precautions and Regulations

Stables are particularly vulnerable to fire because the materials used are very flammable. For the same reason if a fire starts, it usually spreads very quickly and needs prompt, competent action to control it. *It is vital that in any establishment there are regular, frequent fire drills for staff and customers.*

1. Instructions for the fire drill should be clearly visible.

2. Fire fighting equipment, extinguishers, fire hoses, fire buckets filled with sand or water, should be placed around the yard in easily accessible positions.

3. All staff should know where the extinguishers are and how to use them.

4. The whole yard should be kept scrupulously clean and free of litter and rubbish.

5. All entrances and exits should be marked, clear and free of obstructions.

6. There should be NO SMOKING anywhere near the stables or yard, around hay or straw.

7. 'NO SMOKING' signs should be displayed clearly around the yard and strictly enforced.

8. All electric cables, wires, insulation, switches and lights should be frequently checked and well maintained.

9. All doors, particularly of stables, should be in proper working order and if necessary oiled so that they work efficiently.

10. Any bonfires should be kept well away from the stables, under control and supervised until extinguished. A spark carried by a high wind can set alight a bale of hay or straw.

11. Hay and straw should never be kept in the stable block or near stables or loose boxes.

12. All staff should be taught to telephone the Fire Brigade quickly and efficiently giving all the correct relevant information. A display card by the phone giving all the necessary information is extremely useful.

Fire can cause panic; but with frequent practice of the fire drill, correct action will be automatic.

The Public Highway

Safety on the road is absolutely necessary. So many horrific accidents could be prevented if safety rules and regulations were strictly followed.

Leading a horse on the road

❖ If the horse is wearing **tack**, this must be in a **good condition** and **fitted correctly**.

❖ If the horse is untacked then he **must** be led in a **bridle.**

❖ The horse's shoes must be in good condition and secure.

❖ All handlers must wear a **hard riding hat, boots and gloves**.

❖ Horses must be led on the offside so that the handler is between the horse and the traffic.

❖ Considerate **drivers** must always be **thanked.**

Riding on the Road

❖ Never ride on the public highway if the horse is likely to misbehave. All roads, and certainly main or busy roads, must be avoided if the horse is nervous or traffic-shy. If the horse is temperamental ride on the road in the company of another; on the inside of a quieter, more experienced horse and rider.

❖ All tack should be well maintained and fitted correctly. The horse's shoes must be in good condition.

❖ The riders should wear the correct clothing, riding hat, boots and gloves. If the weather is cold and a jacket is worn, this must be fastened properly. It is also wise to wear a body protector. A whip should be carried in the right hand; on the offside.

❖ The pace must be kept steady. Roads can be slippery especially in certain weather conditions. Keep the pace to a walk around corners and roundabouts.

❖ Be attentive and aware of surroundings. Keep a sharp lookout not only on the road but also in surrounding areas, hedges, gardens and behind fences.

❖ Thank all considerate drivers. There are plenty of inconsiderate drivers on the road; those that wait, slow down and give a wide berth deserve thanking.

❖ Groups should keep together and avoid becoming strung out or separated. It is possible to split large groups into two rides. With any number there should be a competent rider and horse at the front and the back of the ride. Novices should be kept in the middle.

❖ Riders and horses need to be clearly seen. This is particularly important in murky weather or at dawn, dusk and essentially at night.

❖ The ride should never be more than two abreast and on narrow roads should be kept to single file.

❖ All riders on the public highway should know the highway code and obey traffic signals and the police.

The Country Code

All land these days belongs to someone, farmers, landowners, County Councils, Forestry Commissions and other authorities. To prevent horses from being prohibited from country areas all riders must avoid damaging property, destroying vegetation and areas of natural beauty, causing injury or loss to livestock and from hurting or frightening pedestrians. Through consideration and courtesy from all riders, authorities may be encouraged to introduce and maintain bridleways, offering riders a greater freedom within the countryside.

Where there are designated bridleways riders should stay on these and not stray into footpaths or restricted areas. Horses churn up the ground, particularly in wet conditions, destroying plant life and causing problems for pedestrians.

Rules of the Country code:

❖ Riders should leave all gates as they found them; if a gate was shut then the rider must shut it after passing through.

❖ Riders must keep to bridle ways through fields or ride around the edge. Horses must never be ridden over crops.

❖ Livestock must not be disturbed.

❖ Fence, hedges, walls and gates must never be damaged.

❖ Litter must never be dropped and left lying around.

❖ All risks of fire must be avoided.

❖ Dogs must be kept under control. It is not a good idea to exercise a dog whilst riding as the dog cannot be kept under strict control from horse back.

Most safety precautions are just common sense but it is easy to become complacent in familiar surroundings with a horse who is usually well behaved and docile. Accidents do occur causing injuries which at best are mild and at worst can be fatal to both horse and handler. Safety procedures and precautions should be a matter of habit; they should be strictly enforced from the start with children and new staff, then safety will become a way of life not a chore.

Accident Procedures

When an accident does occur there are proper procedures to follow which will minimize the effect of the accidents, prevent further injuries and keep panic down to a minimum.

In any kind of accident there are four priorities to follow:

1. **Assess the situation.**
2. **Prevent any further accidents.**
3. **Assess the casualty.**
4. **Send for Help.**

Situation   In the first few seconds after an incident it is vital to try and ascertain exactly what has happened. Look around for a few seconds take in all the information available.

Accidents   Assess the surrounding area to discover if there are other problems that may arise. The other riders and horses may be nervous. The ride may need to dismount or you may need to ask someone capable to go for the loose horse. There may be pedestrians close by who can offer aid. If riding on the road you may need to stop the traffic and ask for help. The first few seconds are vital if you are to prevent a catastrophe, it will also give you time to calm yourself and others around you.

Casualty   When the whole situation has been taken under control you must now assess the casualty. Fortunately in most cases the casualty is not badly injured. The fallen rider may have got up by now, no worse than bruised or shaken. Assess the injured party by asking how they feel and then make the decision as to what to do next.

Help   You must never try and deal with a situation that is beyond your capabilities. It is not your job to give medical treatment or advice. If there is the slightest doubt, even if the injured person seems perfectly healthy, it is wise to have them medically examined sometime in the future, or at least advice them to do so. In cases where medical help is needed immediately, send for help and wait until a professional medical practitioner arrives.

In any incident keeping the four priorities in mind, follow the BHS Accident procedures.

If there is an accident whilst hacking

1. Keep calm. Evaluate the situation and use your common sense.
2. Dismount and hand your horse to someone capable.
3. Dismount the rest of the ride if necessary and safe.
4. Go quietly and calmly to the casualty.
5. Get someone competent to catch the loose horse.
6. If necessary send for help.

Whilst on the Highway

1. If it is necessary to stop the traffic, send one capable rider up the road and another down the road to halt vehicles.
2. Keep the rest of the ride calm and safe.
3. Assess the injured rider and if necessary dismount and go to the casualty. If the rider is uninjured and able to remount, take the ride home quietly.
4. If the casualty is injured, call for help immediately. The police may have to be informed.
5. If there is a loose horse on the road inform the police.
6. If the horse is injured, call the Vet.

Injuries

Occasionally injuries are inflicted which need medical treatment. *Under no circumstances, unless you are a qualified First Aider or a medical practitioner, should you give medical treatment of any kind.*

Remember the priorities

Assess the situation   there may be a qualified First Aider around, a
                                  pedestrian, motorist or one of the ride. If so let them
                                  look after the casualty.

Prevent further Accidents   Keep the people around you safe and calm.

The Casualty

If there is no-one qualified around then you may have to look after the casualty, until
some one more qualified arrives. In certain circumstances it may be imperative that
you give simple First Aid though it must be stressed that this must only be in life
threatening situations. However, an elementary knowledge of the basic steps for
profuse bleeding or unconsciousness can not only save a life but can give you
confidence when dealing with such a situation.

If the rider is injured but conscious:

❖   Keep the casualty calm and comfortable.

❖   Talk to the casualty, ask if there is pain and where. Obtain as much
     information as possible as to how the casualty is feeling. Be observant look
     for obvious signs such as broken bones or bleeding.

❖   It may be necessary to stem any serious bleeding.

❖   Keep the casualty warm by using a jacket or coat as cover. The casualty may
     be in pain and suffering from shock.

❖   **GET HELP!**

To Stem Bleeding

Apply direct pressure to the wound using a clean handkerchief or other material.
Elevate the wounded limb if at all possible.

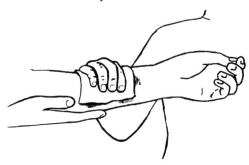

NOTE: DO NOT use a tourniquet. If applied and maintained incorrectly the
tourniquet can make the injury worse, it can make the bleeding heavier or damage
bodily tissues, possibly even cause gangrene.

Injured Horse

If a horse is injured, assess the injury if possible. Stemming serious bleeding is basically the same as human first aid. Lead the horse home or to safety if he is able to walk without worsening the injury. Seek more experienced advice as soon as possible.

If the Casualty is Unconscious

1. **SEND FOR HELP IMMEDIATELY**.

2. Go to the casualty and check the RESPONSE. Call the casualty's name and gently shake the shoulders. There are many states of unconsciousness; it may be possible that the casualty revives. If this is the case, keep the casualty still, warm and calm until help arrives.

3. If the injured person remains unconscious, OPEN THE AIRWAY. An unconscious person is at risk especially if lying face-up, because they cannot cough or regurgitate to clear the airway. They lose control over the muscles that keep the airway open; the tongue can slip back and block the throat.

4. Check the casualty's breathing by watching the rib cage and feeling for breath by placing your cheek near the casualty's mouth.

5. Stem any serious bleeding.

6. Put casualty into the recovery position.

To Open the Airway

1. Clear the airway of any obstruction. Look into the casualty's mouth to see if there is a blockage and remove anything obvious.

2. To open the airway; put two fingers under the chin and one hand on the casualty's forehead and tilt the head back gently.

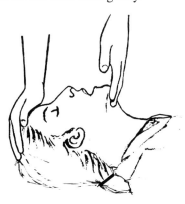

Recovery Position

1. Make absolutely sure that the airway is open. Straighten out the casualty's legs.

2. Kneel beside the casualty and take hold of the nearest arm. Bring it out at right angles to the body and bend the elbow.

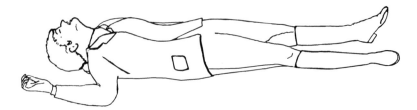

3. Take the other arm and bring it across the chest. Lay the hand, palm outwards, against the cheek nearest to you.

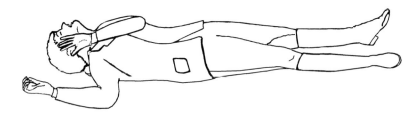

4. Gently take hold of the farthest leg just above the knee and bend it.

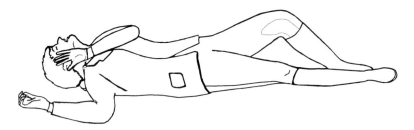

5. Now holding onto the leg and keeping the casualty's hand against the face, gently roll the casualty over towards you. Keep the bent leg at right angles to the body so that the casualty cannot roll too far.

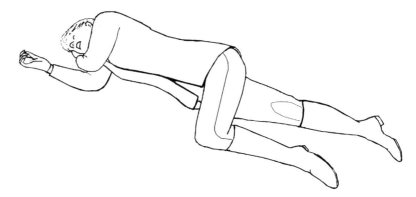

6. Check that the casualty's head is tilted back and the airway open.

7. Cover the casualty with a coat or jacket.

The recovery position is vital if, for any reason, the casualty must be left alone whilst you get help. Any unconscious person should not ideally be left but there may be circumstances when this is unavoidable.

Fire

If there is a fire in the stable or yard DO NOT attempt to put it out unless you are sure you can do so correctly and completely. Never put yourself at risk. A small fire may be put out with an extinguisher but, **if there is any doubt**, get everyone to safety first and call the Fire Brigade.

A fire in a yard with horses is a horrendous experience. Get help immediately. Open all the doors of the stables to let the horses out. It may be necessary to close the yard gates to prevent the horses from rushing onto the road. If possible get them into a field or a safe place where there is air and they will not suffer from smoke or fumes.

If it is absolutely necessary to go into the stable to get a horse out; take a headcollar and a jacket to place over the horse's head in order to lead him quietly out of the stable. If, however, this action puts human lives at risk **then it must not be attempted.**

A fire in a yard can spread more quickly than may seem possible. The emergency services must be brought in as a priority.

Sending for Help

Whenever professional help is needed the person telephoning should state:

* The telephone number.
* Exact location of the accident.
* The type and seriousness of the accident.
* The number of casualties involved.

❖   As much information as possible about the injured, their possible ages, sex and any medical knowledge that is available.

❖   Details of any dangers or obstacles within the area.

If you have sent someone to telephone for help, ask them to return and confirm that help is on its way.

Accident Report Book

Any incident, no matter how trivial, must be recorded within the Accident Report Book. All establishments must have an Accident Report Book and BHS Accident Report Forms for accidents occurring on the public highway.

The incident must be recorded as follows:

- Date and time that the incident occurred.
- Name of the casualty if any or of any person involved.
- Name of the horse involved.
- Name of any witnesses, their address and signature if possible.
- Details of the accident, giving the facts only, not impressions or accusations of blame.
- Injures if any sustained.
- Action that was taken at the time and by whom.
- Results - whether the casualty was taken to hospital or was given treatment and if the casualty accepted treatment.
- Name of the person in charge of the lesson or hack and their signature.

Later on more information can be added such as a stay in hospital and the length of time it took the casualty to recover.

If it is necessary to complete a BHS Accident Report form, this should be sent to the BHS Road Safety Officer when completed.

Exam Tips

This may seem to be a large amount of information for Stage I, but the BHS are rightly concerned about safety and procedures in cases of accidents. Candidates will be asked about safety rules and accident procedures and may be given an hypothetical situation such as; if you were riding out with a friend who falls off their horse, hits the head and is lying unconscious what would you do? Would you remain with the injured party or leave?

Although it is not necessary to take a First Aid course for the Stage I, learning about the basic first aid procedures benefits everyone, in whatever walk of life. For information on courses contact your local British Red Cross, St. John's Ambulance or St. Andrew's Ambulance Association.

C H A P T E R   21
Exam Information

For many, the BHS Stage I is the first experience of this type of examination. Almost everyone takes exams at some time, but the BHS Stages are different. The various sections, riding, practical/oral and theory, are performed in small groups of four or five candidates in front of examiners. For some it is a daunting experience but with study, practice and correct examination technique it can be less arduous. With good preparation, these examinations can often be an enjoyable event!

Prior to the Examination

Prospective students can obtain directly from the British Horse Society some useful publications to help them in their training and study. The 'Where to Train Directory' lists approved training establishments and the Examination Starter Pack includes the syllabus, application form and the current fees. A list of Exam centres and dates for Exams may also be useful. Students, if they are not already a member, will need to apply for British Horse Society membership; an application form can be obtained from the BHS.

The address is:

> British Horse Society,
> British Equestrian Centre,
> Training and Education Dept.,
> Stoneleigh Deer Park,
> Kenilworth,
> Warwickshire CV8 2XZ
> Telephone 01926 707700

Applying for the Stage I

Before the application is made, the student should be assessed by a BHS qualified instructor who will check if the standard, especially in riding, has been attained. This will allow time for training and improvement before the examination. Ideally on the day the student should be above the grade required as 'exam nerves' can have quite an effect on ability!

The application for the Stage I must be completed in plenty of time as test centres book up quickly. The date and venue of the examination should be decided and the application forwarded at least three months in advance. Candidates can telephone the BHS before sending the application form to check if the chosen centre has places available. Other centres and dates can be given as alternatives on the application form.

The BHS will forward a confirmation letter once the application has been accepted. The notes accompanying this confirmation should be read carefully.

Preparation for the Exam

The essential point is to choose a good training establishment with BHS qualified instructors. If at all possible, the candidate should have a few lessons at the chosen Exam Centre where the instructors will know the exam format and the points that the examiners will be assessing. At least then on the 'big day', the centre will not be totally new and unknown!

Clothing

Candidates need to make sure that they have the correct clothing and equipment. All clothes worn on the day need to be smart and clean. For riding this should be a hacking jacket, shirt with a collar, tie, beige jodhpurs, long boots or jodhpur boots. For Stage I a sweatshirt or a v-necked jumper on top of a collar and tie is permitted as are different coloured jodhpurs, providing they are not too gaudy! A secure BSI approved hat and a pair of gloves are compulsory. Whips must be no more than 30 inches in length. Hair should be neatly tied back or contained within a hair net.

Riding Hats

The new standard riding hat, the PAS (Product Approval Specification) 015, (EN 1384) is now compulsory at all BHS Examinations. There are a variety of designs incorporating this standard of hat, skull caps worn with a silk, or designs similar to the traditional type of riding hat. The hat should also fit correctly.

During the Care Section a waterproof jacket may be worn but this must be properly fastened. Long hair must be tied back away from the face.

The only jewellery allowed to be worn is a wedding ring. Earrings or studs in pierced ears are not permitted.

The Day of the Examination

All candidates need to arrive at the Test Centre in plenty of time. Ideally this should be at least 30 minutes before the start of the exam. Being late creates stress and gives the examiners a bad impression.

If the Centre is unfamiliar, it is helpful to plan the route beforehand, if possible by visiting the venue before the exam day. Candidates do occasionally turn up late after losing their way, a mishap that does not offer an auspicious start! Candidates who are particularly late, may even be barred from taking the exam.

Some candidates have found it helpful to book a lunge lesson, an hour or so before the commencement of the exam. This can help to supple and loosen tight muscles and calm the nerves. Enquire at the chosen Centre about this soon after the BHS have confirmed the date and venue.

Format

When everyone is present each candidate is given a number and a name badge for identification. Candidates may be nervous, but be assured the examiners will be encouraging and give every assistance possible.

The Stage I examination normally begins at 08.30 a.m., and continues until 12.30 - 1.00 p.m. Groups are formed of four or five persons who take the appropriate sections together. The results are given about 15 minutes after the end of the examination.

A timetable on display at the centre will show the order and timings for each section.

BRITISH HORSE SOCIETY STAGE I EXAMINATION		
Timetable		
09.00	Candidates 1- 6	Ride
	Candidates 13 -18	Practical
	Candidates 7-12	Practical/Oral/Theory
10.00	Candidates 7-12	Ride
	Candidates 1- 6	Practical
	Candidates 13-18	Practical/Oral/Theory
11.00	Candidates 13-18	Ride
	Candidates 7-12	Practical
	Candidates 1 - 6	Practical/Oral/Theory
12.00	Finish. Examiners confer	
12.30	Results	

Figure 100: Example of an Examination Timetable.

When everyone is ready, each examiner will take a group to a specific part of the centre where each session begins.

The British Horse Society

The British Horse Society, a registered animal welfare charity formed in 1947, is internationally recognized as the premier Equestrian organization in the United Kingdom. The BHS incorporates the Pony Club.

The BHS is involved in animal welfare, safety, training, rights of way and all aspects of horse care.

Aims

The BHS aims to improve the quality of life for all horses and ponies, preventing cruelty and neglect by;

- Systematic training and education in all aspects of riding and horse management.

- Offering guidance and help throughout with breeding and training of horses and ponies.

- Encouraging the protection of all horses and ponies.

Training and Education

The BHS training and education system is one of the best in the world. It offers training to a very high standard of proficiency and provides recognized qualifications for the industry. It also ensures that approved riding schools and establishments maintain a good standard.

Benefits for Members

Members have a governing body which helps and advises them and through which they can communicate to the higher authorities, for example the Government and the EEC.

Members are entitled to a free Personal Liability and Accident Insurance and access to a legal and tax helpline which gives advice. They are also entitled to take examinations and to enter certain BHS approved competitions. Special facilities and enclosures are available to members at various events around the country.

For further information about the various departments of the BHS, their aims and the benefits for the member, consult the BHS Yearbook.

Exam Tips

The day before the examination, make sure that all riding, stable clothes and equipment are prepared. Above all relax; if possible have a hot bath in the evening and try to get a good night's sleep. Last minute revising can often cause confusion and sheer panic!

On the day, arrive at the Centre a little early if possible; there is nothing worse than being flustered and agitated through rushing or arriving late.

During the Horse Knowledge sessions take a little time over doing the practical tasks. Not too much or you will appear slow, but do not rush; yielding to the temptation to get the job over and done with quickly. It is all too easy to make silly mistakes. Be confident and sure - but not over-confident.

If, at any time, the examiner offers you advice or a different point of view, do not collapse thinking this is an automatic failure - be attentive and listen. Some emphasis is placed on the attitude of the candidate, whether or not they are willing to learn.

Remember the examiners want you to pass, they will assist and help as much as they can.

A P P E N D I X
Recommended Series of Lectures/Practical Sessions

This recommended series of lectures and practical stable management sessions reinforce the information already given. Whilst much can be learnt from a book there really is no viable alternative to practical experience in horsemastership, no substitute for the 'hands on' method.

1 Psychology

- Psychology

  Discuss the horse's natural lifestyle, his instincts and characteristics. Discover how these are adapted and used to encourage the horse to conform to the handler's needs and requirements. Discuss the horse's body language and observe horses in the field and stable.

- Handling horses.

  Discuss working around horses correctly and safely in stable and field, the lifting of weights and performing simple stable tasks.

2 Physiology & Health

- Physiology.

  Name the points of the horse. Observe the colours and markings on several horses and ponies.

- Health.

  Discuss the signs of good and ill health. Observe some horses and assess their condition. Talk about the importance of when and why a report should be made when a horse is ill.

3   Routines

- Routines

  Discuss the importance of routines for stabled horses and those at pasture.

- Stable Equipment.

  Discuss the purpose and care of stable equipment.

- Grooming.

  Talk about methods and reasons for grooming. Study each item in a grooming kit and discuss its correct use, cleaning and storage. Groom a horse.

4   Headcollars

- Headcollars

  Discuss headcollars, halters, lead ropes, where and how to tie up a horse in the stable, yard and field. Put on a headcollar and lead rope, discuss the fit. Stand a horse up correctly and hold for treatment by the Vet or Blacksmith.

- Leading In Hand.

  Lead and turn a horse correctly at walk and trot in hand. Put on tack and practise leading a horse with and without a martingale.

- Turning the Horse Out To Grass.

  Lead a horse correctly to the field and turn him out. Catch a horse or pony in the field and bring him in.

5   Hay

- Hay

  Discuss the different methods of feeding hay, their advantages and disadvantages. Fill, weigh and tie up a haynet correctly. Discuss the different types of hay.

- Bedding.

  Discuss the principles, types, advantages and disadvantages of bedding; the methods and reasons for laying down a day and night bed. Learn to muck out, skip out, set fair a stable and yard.

- Muck Heaps.

  Discuss the principles of muck heaps; their situation in relation to the stables; their maintenance and disposal.

| 6 | **Watering and Feeding** |

- Watering

  Discuss the importance of water, the principles and rules of watering. Assess different types of watering systems in the stable and at grass, discussing their advantages and disadvantages.

- Feeding.

  Study some food samples, observing the different types and their quality. Discuss the basic properties of each food type and under what circumstances these would be fed. Discuss the principles and rules of feeding and the amounts of feed an average horse in light and medium work would need.

| 7 | **Saddlery** |

- Snaffle Bridle.

  Learn the points of the bridle. Strip a bridle, clean and reassemble. Know the different types of snaffle bits. Put a bridle on a horse and fit correctly.

- Saddle.

  Learn the points of a saddle. Put on a saddle and discuss the fitting and condition. Know the differences between a General Purpose, Dressage and a Jumping saddle. Put on and fit a numnah/saddle cloth and discuss the advantages and disadvantages of both. Discuss the care, cleaning, and storage of saddlery. Recognise worn and ill fitting tack.

| 8 | **Clothing** |

Discuss the different types of rugs, uses, fitting, cleaning and storage. Put on and remove a variety of rugs with and without a roller and assess the fit.

Roll up and put on a tail bandage. Talk about its uses and care.

| 9 | **Shoeing** |

Study the basic structure of a horse's foot. Discuss the reasons for shoeing and the points to look for in a newly shod foot. Make a practical study from a variety of horses' feet, discussing the state of the shoes and recognising whether or not a horse needs shoeing. Inspect some common shoe types. Talk to the Farrier.

10   Grassland Management

Assess some fields, discussing quality of pasture, size, watering systems, types of fencing, gates, shelter, danger areas, poisonous plants. Discuss the daily inspection of pasture and how to recognise a 'horse-sick' field.

11   Safety and Fire Precautions

Talk about safety in the yard, in the stable, in the fields, out on hacks and on the public highway. Discuss fire precautions, types and localities of extinguishers and procedures in case of fire. Discuss the procedures for accidents in the yard, when hacking or whilst riding on the roads, basic first aid and how and where to get help. Talk about the country code.

12   General

Discuss the aims of the British Horse Society. Revise any sections necessary. Discuss examination techniques, clothing and other requirements.

During these sessions or in a 'mock' exam, practise having questions fired at you so that you learn to answer quickly and clearly.

To help with the studying, design your own timetable that suits your lifestyle. Perhaps taking in a chapter per week divided into theory and practical sessions.

Index